ROMANCE LOVERS ARE FALLING FOR THE SONS OF DESTINY

"The magical land Johnson creates is a whimsical treat, and the brothers are a joy to behold. Readers will look forward to more in the Sons of Destiny series." —*Booklist*

"Cursed brothers, fated mates, prophecies, yum! A fresh new voice in fantasy romance, Jean Johnson spins an intriguing tale of destiny and magic." —Robin D. Owens, RITA Award–winning author of *Heart Quest*

"What a debut! I have to say it is a must-read for those who enjoy fantasy and romance. I so thoroughly enjoyed [*The Sword*] and eagerly look forward to each of the other brothers' stories. Jean Johnson can't write them fast enough for me!" —*The Best Reviews*

"Enchantments, amusement, eight hunks, and one bewitching woman make for a fun romantic fantasy . . . humorous and magical. A delightful charmer." —*Midwest Book Review*

"I love this world and the heroes and heroines who reside there . . . a lively, wonderful, and oh-so-satisfying book. It is long, beautifully written, and entertaining. Light and dark magic are everywhere . . . fantasy romance at its best." —*Romance Reviews Today*

"A fun story. I look forward to seeing how these alpha males find their soul mates in the remaining books." —*The Eternal Night*

continued . . .

"An intriguing world . . . an enjoyable hero . . . an enjoyable showcase for an inventive new author. Jean Johnson brings a welcome voice to the romance genre, and she's assured of a warm welcome."
—*The Romance Reader*

"An intriguing and entertaining tale of another dimension . . . quite entertaining. It will be fun to see how the prophecy turns out for the rest of the brothers."
—*Fresh Fiction*

"A paranormal adventure series that will appeal to fantasy and historical fans, plus time-travel lovers as well. Jean Johnson has created a mystical world of lessons taught, very much like the great folktales we love to hear over and over. It's like *Alice in Wonderland* meets the *Knights of the Round Table* and you're never quite sure what's going to happen next. Delightful entertainment . . . An enchanting tale with old-world charm, *The Sword* will leave you dreaming of a sexy mage for yourself."
—*Romance Junkies*

"An intriguing new fantasy romance series . . . a welcome addition to the genre. *The Sword* is a unique combination of magic, time travel, and fantasy that will have readers looking toward the next book. Think *Seven Brides for Seven Brothers* but add one more and give them magic, with curses and fantasy thrown in for fun. Cunning . . . creative . . . lovers of magic and fantasy will enjoy this fun, fresh, and very romantic offering."
—*Time Travel Romance Writers*

The CAT

JEAN JOHNSON

BERKLEY SENSATION, NEW YORK

THE BERKLEY PUBLISHING GROUP
Published by the Penguin Group
Penguin Group (USA) Inc.
375 Hudson Street, New York, New York 10014, USA
Penguin Group (Canada), 90 Eglinton Avenue East, Suite 700, Toronto, Ontario M4P 2Y3, Canada
(a division of Pearson Penguin Canada Inc.)
Penguin Books Ltd., 80 Strand, London WC2R 0RL, England
Penguin Group Ireland, 25 St. Stephen's Green, Dublin 2, Ireland (a division of Penguin Books Ltd.)
Penguin Group (Australia), 250 Camberwell Road, Camberwell, Victoria 3124, Australia
(a division of Pearson Australia Group Pty. Ltd.)
Penguin Books India Pvt. Ltd., 11 Community Centre, Panchsheel Park, New Delhi—110 017, India
Penguin Group (NZ), 67 Apollo Drive, Rosedale, North Shore 0632, New Zealand
(a division of Pearson New Zealand Ltd.)
Penguin Books (South Africa) (Pty.) Ltd., 24 Sturdee Avenue, Rosebank, Johannesburg 2196,
South Africa

Penguin Books Ltd., Registered Offices: 80 Strand, London WC2R 0RL, England

This book is an original publication of The Berkley Publishing Group.

First edition: June 2008

Library of Congress Cataloging-in-Publication-Data

Johnson, Jean, 1972–
    The Cat / Jean Johnson.— 1st ed.
      p. cm.
    ISBN 978-0-425-22149-5 (trade pbk.)
    I. Title.
    PS3610.O355C38 2008
    813'.6—dc22   2008003963

10 9 8 7 6 5 4 3 2 1

AUTHOR'S NOTE

This book, and the one following it, The Storm, have been written from two separate sets of perspective. They cover two different stories, with two different plots, but they also cover many of the same incidents, as the two stories take place more or less simultaneously. There will be certain differences because of these separate viewpoints in those parts where the two tales coincide, in dialogue as well as other areas.

Ask two people who have just had a conversation to recite exactly what was said on both sides during that conversation . . . and you'll get two slightly different answers, because of those differences. Ask two witnesses to a car accident exactly what happened, and you'll get two similar but still somewhat different accounts of what took place. This will usually be determined by what each person was focused on at the time and how much each one could personally see from their individual vantage points.

Hopefully, you'll enjoy these two stories, both for their similarities and for their differences.

Thanks go to my beta-editing team, NotSoSaintly, Alienor, Alexandra, and Stormi, and special thanks to SoulBound, who cold read these two books.

As always, come visit me at www.jeanjohnson.net.

Thank you for reading,

~JEAN

ONE

The Fifth Son shall seek the sign:
Prowl the woods and through the trees
Before you in the woods she flees
Catch her quick and hold her fast
The Cat will find his Home at last

Amara was so very tired. Tired to the point of feeling cranky, in fact. Tired of swimming. Tired of pulling. Tired of running . . . but there wasn't anything else either of them could do, anymore. Resentful, too—and why shouldn't she be? Born to be a queen, but forced to be a refugee. Who wouldn't resent such a reversal of fortune? Oh, yes, she resented her situation and was very, very tired of it.

But did she resent her sister? No . . . and yes. If it weren't for Arora, neither of them would be in this situation. Yet Amara didn't wish her sister to the bottom of the ocean; that fate, she reserved for their pursuers, who were responsible for this mess. If they hadn't been so determined to capture her twin, Amara wouldn't be so tired, and not just physically. Tired of being strong, tired of putting someone else's needs before her own, tired of those needs stripped from both of them, demanded of them, denied to each of them . . .

She was tired of swimming, tired of drinking seawater and eating raw fish, tired of being stuck in this sea-creature shape. Modified, of course; this kind of creature didn't naturally have a spiraling horn, but it was a necessary adaptation. The makeshift raft her sister rested upon was nothing more than several planks, part of a barrel, and a spar lashed together with a bit of sail-rope. That rope had a loop at one end, and into that loop Amara's horn went, allowing her to pull the raft forward. Southward, in the direction her sister insisted they go.

It wasn't as if she had a better idea of where to go. Except for north; Amara didn't dare let either of them return that way. Just because they had lost their most recent set of pursuers didn't mean others weren't still looking for them back on the continent. That left east, west, south . . . and Arora said south. Originally, their intent had been to try and reach Fortuna; surely the oldest Empire in the whole of the world had some sort of solution to Arora's problem. But Fate, Fortuna's Threefold God, had intervened by dashing their ship against the shallow coral reefs of the Sun's Belt.

So south it was. But how much farther? It felt like Amara never stopped swimming, save for a rare moment of rest. Even when she had to catch fish for the two of them, she *still* had to swim.

Amara blamed the storm for part of their predicament. It had swept up over them, driving their ship much farther south than intended, into the treacherous, reef-filled waters of the Sun's Belt region. The other part of the problem existed simply because of what her sister was, an anomaly that—in the wrong hands—could cause an incredible amount of damage to their world.

Arora had learned through trial and error how to hide her uniqueness from mage sight; only a direct touch from a mage could reveal what she was. Which meant avoiding mages and avoiding crowds. They hadn't been able to find a ship without a mage, but they had picked a vessel with a relatively weak mage and had done their best to avoid the other woman until other ships had appeared on the horizon, pursuing them into the teeth of a storm too powerful for their onboard mage to avert.

Sheer luck had allowed the two of them to survive, where so many others on board had perished under the pounding power of the storm-whipped surf. Luck, and Amara's abilities. Few others of her kind could have managed to shift into a sea-adapted creature, coming from a landlocked kingdom as they did, never mind one capable of swimming her sister free of the disintegrating wreckage. But she couldn't swim and support her sister above the waves all of the time.

Providence had brought them close to a drifting scrap of hull and a floating chunk of barrel still bound by iron at one end. A spar torn from one of the masts had enough rope still clinging to it to allow Arora to bind everything together, giving herself a place to rest. When Amara needed to rest, she joined her twin on the planks in her smaller, human form, but that ran the risk of putting them at the mercy of the great oceanic currents, utterly unknown on this side of the Sun's Belt.

But that had been too many days ago, at least two weeks' worth. Tired and miserable, Amara now found herself having to dodge to the right around annoying patches of seaweed, something she hadn't seen since they had left the shallow waters of the Sun's Belt reefs . . . shallow waters . . . *shallow waters*!

That woke up her tired mind. Seaweed forests meant shallow waters and—she dodged to the left, avoiding an outcrop of rock that loomed unexpectedly through the darkness. Now she had to swim through the kelp-bed while trying not to deviate so much that she tangled the fronds in her towline from course corrections. It also meant a potential coastline, which her sister had been promising lay ahead of them, but it was difficult for Amara to gauge just how close they were to an actual shore. Her eyes in this form were positioned for a broad field of view to either side, sacrificing most of her depth perception. Not all, but most of it.

She could also hear the faint rush of surf somewhere up ahead, the lapping of waves against rocks and other things. Surfacing, Amara twisted her body, peering into the fog that had risen while she was busy swimming underwater. Her sister called out to her, encouragement in her tone.

"I *knew* there was land in this direction. Keep swimming! Ahead and just to your right, if you can. I think I can see trees in that direction."

"I zzzee it!" The lips and tongue of this style of creature weren't designed for speaking clearly, but at least she didn't have the beak of a bird; the big tongue she currently had was bad enough, making her sound slow and stupid, but a bird's beak was even worse. "I sshall aim vor it!"

Ducking underwater again, Amara swam forward, surfacing from time to time to check her progress both below and above the surface. Her eyes were shaped for light enhancement, making the most of the thin light from Sister Moon, a barely visible sliver rising on the horizon off to her left, to the east. Brother Moon was just now setting to her right, a larger, somewhat fatter crescent curled the opposite way, as He raced ahead of His Sister at roughly three times Her stately pace through the sky.

Amara was tired of the ocean, tired of water all around her. She was a worshipper of Mother Earth and Father Sky, not a follower of any water-based Gods. She wanted dry earth beneath her legs—for that matter, she wanted *legs*, rather than flippers, flukes, or fins. And fruit rather than fish, though it was doubtful any existed this far south. From the chill of the water, the rumor that the southern hemisphere had its winter opposite Aiar's summer was regrettably true. If it was indeed the start of winter down here, then fruit would be scarce, but Amara was so *tired* of catching and eating nothing but raw fish. She might be in the shape of a sea-swimmer, capable of digesting the necessary sea-based diet, but her taste buds were still quite human at the end of the day . . . and her sister was entirely human. Raw fish was taking its toll on Arora, too.

Putting more energy into her swimming, Amara thought long-ingly of sand between her restored toes, or maybe the lumpy clutter of a pebble beach, each rock rounded by centuries' worth of pum-meling from the churning surf. She spotted sand down below, inter-spersed with clumps of seaweed, rock, anemones, crabs—shore-dwelling creatures. Not far, now.

Not far at all; within minutes, the surface came so close, she had no choice but to shift her form, rising above the water with a gulp of air that was half salt water. She spat it out of a blowhole, shifting from gills to lungs, then shifted the rest of her body. Legs were more useful than fins and flukes. And if she shifted legs, then she shifted some arms, too. Grabbing the rope as she did so, she let the horn phase back into her flesh. She didn't discard the scales or the thick layer of body fat, though; the air was just as cold and damp as the water, and her sister was wearing both sets of their clothes. Amara needed the extra insulation for the time being.

Literally, all the two women possessed was the raft, the broken half-barrel, the clothes on Arora's back, and the few things that had been on their belts. Well, that and the pair of boots laced to the half-barrel. Arora could only wear one set of footgear at a time. But both belts and their nearly empty money pouches were slung around her waist. They only had one knife between the two of them, but that was alright; Amara had not needed a knife since she had gained control of her powers.

Increasing her size, she hauled the raft well past the watermark. That half-barrel was important; it held their only freshwater supply, at least until they could find more. So were the planks, in their own way. Propped up by a tree limb or a rock, they could form a lean-to shelter. And one side was slathered in tar; if nothing else, once the boards dried out, they could be used to start a fire. If the sisters could *get* a fire going.

But being on land after the weightlessness of the sea was exhausting. Tugging the makeshift raft all the way to the tree line, Amara pulled it into a grassy patch between trunks and bushes, and collapsed onto the boards next to her sister.

"No farther," Amara panted, glad to have her own lips and tongue back in their normal working order. "I can't go any farther . . ."

Her twin planted a hand on her shoulder, shoving on it heavily in order to gain her own feet. "Rest. I'll look for something edible, *without* any fins."

"Mother Bless your quest," Amara groaned, leaning back on her elbows. She sat up a little, worrying as she watched Arora stagger into the darkness. For more than a year, she had guarded her sister. Exhaustion was no excuse to let down her guard. "Hey, don't go far—we don't know if this place is inhabited!"

A backward wave was all she got from her sister. Too tired to argue the matter, no matter how much her paranoid nature demanded it, Amara lay back on the planks and rested. She wasn't concerned about her twin's ability to see in the dark. It wasn't the same as actually shifting the shape of her eyes, but Arora said she could *think* about seeing things in a different way, blink twice, and that was all she needed to do to *see* things in a different way.

What she saw, Arora couldn't always articulate. Amara didn't understand her sister's vague talk about "auras" and "half-images," whatever those might be. No, regular eyes were just fine, whether they were the eyes of a hawk or the eyes of a human. Right now, she was enjoying the enhanced vision of a cat, sacrificing color in the quest to intensify overall perception, even if half-forms were considered sloppy shapeshifting.

Her sea-creature shape had been useful, but cobbled together. As was her current form, plump and covered in scales, since scales were the easiest kind of hide to dry. Had she been back among her own people, Amara would have needed to don her own clothes at this point. A shifter could cobble together a covering of fur, scales, or feathers for casual use, but pure forms were what everyone strove to achieve. Modified forms were looked down on as halfhearted, even undisciplined. Beneath someone of her status and ability.

There was a perfectionist side drummed into her that was irked by the whole being-chased ordeal they had undergone. Being chased required being stealthy and creative, which was good, yes . . . but it was a creativity fashioned of half-forms and pseudo-ness, and of running instead of standing and fighting like a proper Shifterai.

That was another resentment to try to shove aside. Once her twin's specialness had been grasped and understood, Amara had been given the task of protecting and guarding Arora, a task that had forced Amara to set aside her own ambitions. Here she lay, the best shifter in the two hundred years of her people's history . . . exiled by annoying circumstance from her rightful chance at the throne of her people.

She heard Arora coming back and sat up. It wasn't her *sister* that annoyed her, but their circumstances. From the bulge swinging in her sister's gathered sleeve, it was apparent Arora had met with success on her foraging quest. By Auora's shiver, Amara could tell her twin was also chilled to the bone. Amara sighed under her breath and held out an arm. She was dry enough now to switch from scales to fur without the risk of trapping moisture beneath the guard-hair layer.

"Here, sit by me; I'll wrap myself in fur and warm both of us up."

Sighing with relief, Arora did as she was bid, curling up next to her sister. Amara extended pseudo-wings of furred flesh, wrapping them around her sister like a living cloak. The fur helped insulate her own flesh. Once she was settled, she let her twin feed her, since her arms were wrapped around Arora's body.

"I should give back your clothes," Arora offered quietly after a few moments.

"Keep them for the moment. At least until we can find a stream or something to wash them in and a way of creating a fire to dry them out," Amara returned pragmatically. "Not to mention a fire to keep you warm."

Arora nodded, accepting her sister's offer, her green eyes drooping sleepily.

Summer-weight linens and leathers weren't enough to keep a person warm in this cold, damp place, not with just one layer. Two was barely sufficient. True, they were now south of Sun's Belt, but that meant going south was like going north; the farther away they went from the midline of their world, the colder the climate became.

If Amara's twin had been born a mage instead of . . . whatever she was . . . it wouldn't have been a problem. Even the weakest of mages could cast a simple cantrip-spell to keep themselves warm, or so she had heard. But her sister was something else, and the Gods hadn't exactly included a letter of instruction with Arora when she was born.

Whatever might happen to them, Amara couldn't stay awake much longer. It was with relief that Arora shifted in her reshaped arms, wanting to stretch out on the slowly drying planks. Settling down with her, Amara smothered a yawn. She thickened her fur, wanting both of them to stay warm against the damp pre-morning fog, and shaped her ears a little bigger, capable of swiveling and pricking up at any noise that sounded potentially dangerous. Tired or not, it was her responsibility to protect her twin.

Whether or not she wanted that particular responsibility.

Mara, her mother, Ziella, had once said when Amara was very young, *you have a great destiny ahead of you. You will be a princess of our people, once you learn to control your powers. You will probably even become our queen, one day . . . but being a queen carries with it many responsibilities, and if you want to be the queen, you must prepare yourself in more ways than just shifting your shape . . .*

But when those outlander mages had first taken note of Arora, after literally bumping into her during a trading foray into an outlying kingdom, her parents' words had changed.

Mara, her father, Fennon, had warned her, *you must protect your sister against outsiders. The lust for magical power is what shattered Aiar, hundreds of years ago. We of the Shifting Plains cannot use this power, so it is not a temptation for us . . . but others can, and they will use your sister if you do not protect her. They have proven they will harm anyone who gets in their way. You are the most powerful Shifterai that I have seen; you were also born as Rora's twin. It is clear the Gods wanted you to have the power to protect your twin, thus it is your responsibility, now.*

Responsibility. Responsibility. Responsibility. Amara was tired of this responsibility, which had driven her far from her home, far from her people, far from her rightful place in the universe. Not her sister, who was already asleep, judging from the limp weight of her body and the soft steadiness of her breathing, but the responsibility of keeping her safe in a world that wanted to use and harm her.

They would be able to stay here for a while, as they had stayed in other places for a while, but eventually something would happen to drive them forth from this land. Someone would uncover what Arora was, or take too close an interest in what *she* was. This far from the

Shifting Plains, a Shifterai was bound to be an attention-drawing novelty. But she would be better able to face that attention if she first got some real sleep, rather than the few hours snatched here and there, resting on the raft next to her sister while the southern ocean currents had swept them who-knew-where.

Wakened by distant wardings, Morganen cleared most of the sleep from his mind with a deep inhale that ended in a stretch meant to tap some light into the room via the lightglobe attached to the corner post of his bed. Since breaking off officially from the Empire of Katan, he had started keeping a scrying mirror in his bedchamber. The Katani were *supposed* to leave the Isle of Nightfall alone, giving the residents of Nightfall time to turn their incipient kingdom into a real one, but he didn't trust them to play entirely by the rules. Nor their other potential enemy, the Mandarites.

These were not the wardings tied into the recently erected crystal towers spread across the island. The alarm chiming in his mind was for ones set farther out. And something to the north, he realized, sinking onto the padded bench placed in front of the small table in the corner of his bedchamber. It looked like a vanity table, since it did have a mirror propped up against the back wall, but the rectangular surface wasn't meant to show his own face for long.

A mutter linked the ward-alert to the silvered glass. Like most of the mirrors in the palace, it was warded to prevent an outsider from tapping into it and scrying into the room, but that didn't prevent him from using it to scry outward. There were very few mirrors on Nightfall that weren't warded against outside scryings; two of them were in his workroom in another section of the compound, but then he wasn't being summoned to be engaged in a conversation.

The reflection of his own face, lean with almond-shaped aquamarine eyes, a straight nose, and plain, light brown hair mussed from sleep, faded like patchy fog. It was replaced with actual fog, dark from the fact that it was still night. But the nature of the warding spell highlighted the figures approaching the island, limning them and their makeshift vessel with a faint blue halo. Not that *they* could see the glow; it was just an enhancement of the spell, designed for his own viewing needs.

Squinting, still a little tired, Morganen eyed the figure on the raft. Female, shivering, clinging to a scrap of hull. She looked young, but an adult. A bit plain, though; if Trevan was the next of his brothers to fall in love, as Seer Draganna's Prophecy proclaimed each of them would, the lady on the raft would need to be something special on the inside to make up for her average outside. That wasn't to say his fifthborn brother had only ever courted the prettiest of maidens back before their exile . . . but surely after knowing so many women, it would take someone extraordinary to capture Trev's elusive heart. Since it was Morg's job to ensure his brothers *did* meet their matches, he would have to study the approaching woman.

The . . . creature . . . towing the raft was his next target of interest. It was unlike anything Morganen had seen before. Something like a dolphin, something like a smallish whale, and something like a *yaskinna*, save that it only had the one extra-long spiral horn on its snout, not the three shorter ones he would expect. Tapping the edge of the mirror frame so that it centered itself on the beast, Morg traced a rune directly on the glass. He would have to polish it later to remove the smudges, but it was important to know *what* the swimming creature was.

It took a moment for the rune to sink through the scrying mirror and touch the nature of the beast with such a curious shape. For a moment, the image of the sea-swimmer glowed green. Katani letters swirled out of the glow, forming a brief, astonishing description in only five words, fading in and out as each gave way in succession to the next.

Human. Adult. Female. Aian. Shapeshifter.

Blinking, Morganen considered the second . . . female. If that creature was a shapeshifter, she was indeed extraordinary. Of course, there was no guarantee she was meant for Trevan; if there were two females coming to the Isle, not just one, then one of them would no doubt be meant for Rydan . . .

Rydan. Wincing, Morganen quickly reviewed in his mind the command spells for the crystal towers. Any minute now, the pair on the raft would breach the range of the crystal towers, which had their own approach-sensitive wards. It was nighttime, which meant Rydan was awake and aware. Whatever it was that he did at night—not even Morg was completely sure—one of the sixthborn brother's tasks was to keep an eye on the island to protect it, including the newly enchanted towers and their scrying wards.

Rydan, unlike Trevan, didn't relish the thought of having a woman in his life, extraordinary *or* plain. He would object most strenuously to the presence of a second unattached female. He also controlled a Fountain, a wellspring of pure magical energy, through which he could toss said female to some other Fountain in some other, far-distant corner of their world, should any woman get close enough to bother him. There had to be a way to stop him from doing that. Prophecy was Prophecy, and Rydan's foretold Destiny had to be fulfilled, the same as the rest of them.

Serina's spell-equations finally came back to Morg; the Arithmancer had been quite thorough in her mathemagical calculations when creating the island's new communication system. There was a way to quell the wardings for a brief stretch of time. Stretching, he grabbed his cryslet from the nightstand behind him and flipped open the clasped lid of the communication bracelet. The spell-word to muffle the wardings, keeping them from alerting anyone for a short period of time, was *Pillulla-noh.*

That was it. The translucent, faceted, white cabochon mounted on the back of the lid glowed violet for a moment, then shifted to translucent, faceted cream. Hopefully his elder brother wouldn't have seen the brief alteration. Morganen's Destiny was to match-make his brothers, to help ensure each ended up happily married. Whether or not they *wanted* to be happily married.

It was the only way *he* would get to have his own happily married Destiny, after all.

Thankfully, it wasn't necessary to hold the wardings in abeyance for long. Turning his attention back to the mirror, Morganen watched as the pair of females managed to reach one of the northernmost beaches. The shapeshifter altered her swimming shape into something more humanoid; she pulled the raft up onto the shore, then the human-looking female went out foraging. They shared the small bounty that was available, and the shapeshifter grew fur, sheltering the two of them against the chilly winter air.

The worst they would have to deal with was a bit of cold, damp fog. The island wasn't positioned far enough to the south to risk frost; not down on the beach, and not on a mild winter's day like today promised to be. The two women would be safe enough, sleeping among the trees; there weren't any predators on the island large enough to risk disturbing humans. Releasing the abeyance-charm on the cryslet, Morganen stifled a second yawn. Now that the outer wards had been passed, he could go back to sleep.

But not for too long. Morg had to come up with a way to get the fifth of his seven brothers to notice at least one of their visitors, and think up some way for the sixth of his seven brothers to *not* notice the other woman. At least, not until it was too late.

Glancing around his bedroom, sleepy from having been awakened early, Morganen eyed the stacks of books on his dresser and nightstands. One of them caught his eye, the title embossed in gilt-leaf on the spine. *Dreaming of Love.*

He had found the original among the books in the library archives at Koral-tai, in Natallia. The opportunity had come while he was distance-scrying his thirdborn brother's adventures on the other continent and had spotted the intriguing title on the archive shelves. A couple of spells, a blank book, and a keg of ink, and he had copied it for his personal collection a couple months ago, just as he had copied many other volumes through the years.

Getting up, he crossed to the dresser, extracted the copy from the others in the stack, and retired to his bed. A harder rap of his knuckle against the glowing, translucent sphere brightened the lightglobe's illumination. Propping up his pillows, Morg started idly flicking through the index, reviewing the spells, charms, amulets, and potions contained in the tome. It wasn't a weighty text by any means; most of these were simple enchantments, low-powered, low-key, and mostly designed to help encourage the divining and encountering of one's true love.

Since the Gods had wisely increased the odds of finding a true love by ensuring there was more than one person running around the world who might qualify, with even more who lurked unsuspectingly in other universes—ones who would qualify under the right circumstances, that was—such spells rarely showed the inquiring person who, exactly, their true love might be. But they often showed where to look, or under what circumstances they'd be most likely to meet, that sort of thing. Some even put the target into a more receptive frame of mind, which could be a useful thing for a mother suffering from a son or daughter reluctant to wed and provide her with grandchildren to spoil. Or so the compiler of the spells suggested in the side notes.

One of the potion titles caught his eye. Flipping through the book to the listed pages, Morganen read the description of its effects. As he did so, the last vestiges of sleepiness faded. This was interesting—this was *very* interesting . . . If he could administer *this* particular combination of herbs and energies, and did it *before* Rydan met one of those two women . . .

It didn't matter which one was the intended Destined bride; the Gods would provide the correct woman. It was They who had prompted Their greatest Seer to speak the verses of her Curse a thousand years ago. Marking the page with a bit of ribbon, Morg abandoned his bed in favor of getting himself dressed and out to his workroom; he didn't have much time before breakfast.

The knock on his bedchamber door disturbed the tail end of another restless night's sleep. Scowling, Trevan sat up, shoved the covers aside, and padded across the scattered carpets lining the floor. His feet might have been protected from the temperature of the floor, but it was chilly in the room. At least it was helping to soothe his rampant, sleep-depriving problem.

It occurred to him at the second round of knocking, just before he reached the door, that it could be one of the island's four women on the other side of the wooden rectangle—one of the four *married* women. They probably wouldn't approve of such an unobstructed view of his current condition. Grunting under his breath, he padded over to his wardrobe, opened one of the doors, rummaged inside, and pulled out a plain green dressing robe. Magic could have fetched the robe, but he was too tired to try at the moment.

Whoever it was knocked again, then spoke as well, impatient at the delay. "Trev? Are you awake yet? We really need to talk."

The voice was Koranen's, second-youngest of his siblings. Sighing roughly, guessing what it was about, Trevan shrugged into the robe, loosely tied it shut, and headed back to the door. Opening the door, he eyed his younger brother. Kor was like a leaner, darker-haired version of himself. They were both redheads, but his own chest-length tresses were more coppery-blond in hue, while Koranen boasted a rich auburn mane.

Kor's shadow-rimmed hazel eyes were just as bleary and blood-shot as his green ones felt. It wasn't likely one of their sisters-in-law would just barge in here without asking for permission, and Kor had shut the outer door of his suite before knocking on the inner one, but Trevan felt the urge to tighten the sash on his robe all the same. Mainly because he was just as uncomfortable about what he knew his younger sibling had come here to discuss. He waited for Kor to speak, giving him a sympathetic, tired look.

"It's not working, is it?" Koranen finally muttered, defeat slumping his normally straight shoulders. "I don't know what's wrong; we've tried everything we could think of over the last few weeks, but . . . it's just not *right*. At least the real ones giggled and squirmed and . . . and *participated*—that's the word for it, isn't it? They're not *participating*."

"Going through some of the motions, maybe." Running one hand through his locks, Kor gestured with the other, grimacing. "Jinga's Tits, the courtiers we made to impress the Mandarites were more realistic, and *they* were only designed for light conversation!"

Frustrated, Kor rumpled his dark red hair under both of his hands. Heat radiated from his half-naked body, clad as it was in light blue trousers stitched with anti-conflagration runes. Trevan absently basked in that heat, even though it made him sleepy. As a Pyromancer, Koranen was much more popular to be around in the winter than in the summer. Frustration only lent itself even more to the younger man's radiant urges, and Kor was very frustrated by now.

Their mutual problem had begun with the somewhat recent visit of half the Council of Katan to Nightfall Isle, where the most powerful mages in the Empire had exiled the eight brothers over three and a half years ago. The brothers had activated the illusionary courtiers to fill out their ranks and make an impressive showing, since they were seceding from the mainland that had neglected them for so long. One of the Councilors had quipped that the brothers must be using the illusionary women as substitutes for real ones, since they had been exiled to the Isle without any female companionship.

If they hadn't been in desperate need of a show of imperturbable strength, Trevan would've whacked his head against the nearest wall at that comment. They *did* have enough magic to create tangible females, which meant they *could* have been interacting with said illusionary ladies for the last three and a half years, in the most tangible, interactive way a male and a female could interact . . . but which they stupidly hadn't thought up on their own. For all three-plus years, until now.

As soon as the Council had left, Koranen and Trevan had put their reddish heads together. Of the four remaining, unattached brothers, they were the two most desperate for female companionship. Trevan's younger twin, Rydan, loathed his Prophesied Destiny, while Koranen's younger twin, Morganen, was already enamored of an outworlder woman. The four older brothers had already snared their own Destined brides, so it was up to Trev and Kor alone to collaborate on creating adequate substitutes for feminine companionship.

Trevan didn't know what was wrong with their enchantments, but something *was* wrong. He *knew* how women responded; of the eight Corvis brothers, Trev had been the most licentious in their pre-exile days. Koranen was the one who had the least experience when it came to physical relationships; he literally burned with his passions, which was hazardous to any young lady wishing to dare the darker redhead's charms. Ironically, it was Koranen who had the most experience in creating illusionary people from enchanted glass beads.

Together, theirs was a case of the debauched and the desperate struggling to find a source of relief.

Koranen stared at him now, frustration giving his hazel eyes a plaintive glint. "*What* are we doing wrong, Trev? We can make a courtier who can bow or curtsy, who can laugh at a joke and carry on a reasonable length of conversation just like a real person . . . but *we*"—and he gestured between them to emphasize that Trevan was equally, if inexplicably, at fault—"cannot make a woman who responds appropriately to her lover! Kata's Sweet Sacred Ass—I can make an illusionary *man* who responds in all the right ways under my touch, but why not a woman?"

That quirked Trevan's brow and made him blink. While it wasn't forbidden, it wasn't exactly encouraged, either, in the Katani culture of their youth. "You made a *man* and tested it sexually?"

Blushing, Kor gestured in an awkward, explanatory way. "Well, as an experiment, and I only just, you know . . . what *we* do to ourselves. *Touched* him, a bit. It didn't really do anything for me—but at least *he* responded the right way! Why can't I make a *woman* who responds like that? For that matter, why can't *you* make a woman who responds like that? You know everything about what it's like to have a woman exploding in ecstasy in your arms, or . . . or whatever it is they do!"

Brain cells underneath his coppery locks finally woke up. Trevan blinked twice then rubbed at his face, groaning. "Oh . . . it *can't* be that simple."

"*What* can't be so simple?" his younger brother demanded. "Brother, if you're holding out on me—"

Dragging both palms down, Trevan sighed wearily. The first few months of sexually frustrated exile had been bad, but he had eventually gotten used to being on his own when it came to those urges. Having the *hope* of feminine companionship—even if it was literally an illusion—had reawakened not only his sexual desires, but his sexual frustrations. But hope alone couldn't give them what they wanted.

"Kor, you managed to make a sexually responsive male, because you *know* what it's like to be a sexually responsive male. We made interactive, joke-laughing, conversation-holding courtiers, because *we* know how to interact by laughing at jokes and joining conversations. We can even curtsy like a woman, because it's something both men and women can do . . . but sex . . .

"Sex is *different*, between the genders. Women just don't respond at all like men do. We literally don't know enough reference points to *create* a truly, accurately, interactively functional female." This time it was *his* hand that flicked between the two of them. "*We're* not female! Even the few times I've tried enchanting myself into a female didn't help me simulate the right responses for a properly responsive female, and the Gods know I've tried."

It was Koranen's turn to groan in frustration and hide his face in his hands. More heat washed outward from his half-naked flesh, warming Trevan's equally half-clad skin . . . then it faded and died. Trevan wrapped the folds of his dressing robe tighter around his body, in the hopes of trapping the lingering heat from his brother against his skin, warding off the morning chill. Kor mumbled something, but his voice was muffled by his palms.

"What was that?" Trev prodded his sibling.

Kor lowered his hands, looking tired and drawn. "I said, I don't know if the others can help us. Kelly has no magic whatsoever. Alys does, but doesn't have much. I think Serina is still suffering bouts of morning sickness, and Mariel is just too . . . *nice*. If I asked her to let me record her sexual responses—even if it was indirectly, without actually being there at the time—she'd probably faint from the shock of it."

"Or Evanor would kill us," Trevan agreed wryly. The fourth-born of their siblings was the nicest and most polite of all the brothers, but when riled, Evanor could be just as formidable as any of them. Niceness didn't necessarily mean Ev would be willing to share, not even through something as indirect as remotely enchanting an illusion. "Serina *might* be willing to help us, since I've noticed she's rather open about those sorts of things, but Dominor wouldn't like it, and he is more powerful than either of us."

"Wolfer would rather beat the manure out of us than even suggest it around *his* precious, delicate Alys," Koranen agreed dryly. "Who would be even more likely to faint from the shock of it than Mariel . . . and Saber would castrate us both if we looked sideways at Kelly. Or Kelly herself might do it."

Trevan laughed briefly. "Though she's weird enough, she might actually say yes to having her physical responses remotely recorded."

"Maybe . . . maybe, if we explained to *all* of them that we're not looking for *their* exact responses, but rather a general feminine-style physical response . . . maybe appealed to their sense of pity and compassion?" Koranen asked his elder brother, his tenor voice almost cracking, caught somewhere between wistfulness and burgeoning desperation. The vague gesture of his hands shifted once more into a rumpling of his auburn hair. "If I don't get some relief *soon*, I'm going to be seriously eyeing that male illusion I created, and I'm *not* actually interested in men!"

"*You're* desperate enough to look at men?" Trevan shot back. He bit back the rest of his retort. At least *he* had known the pleasures of bedding a willing maid. Koranen hadn't ever gone past fondling. By himself, Kor could find relief in the usual solitary way, but with a female, he literally scorched the poor woman with his touch. "Alright . . . we'll raise the subject at breakfast."

Koranen's shoulders slumped with relief.

"Don't get your hopes up, Brother," Trevan warned his sibling. "You and I could be eunuchs before this particular conversation is at an end."

"Well, then at least I wouldn't have to *suffer* anymore," Kor muttered wryly, rubbing at his tired eyes with the heels of his hands.

"True. Go on and get dressed," Trev instructed his younger brother. "I'll meet you there. I get to help my twin make breakfast this morning."

Koranen snorted. "If only I could be more like *him* and not give a damn about women—do you think *he'd* be interested in an illusionary courtesan male?"

"Do you really want to ask him if he's switched his interests?" Trevan retorted dryly. "He *was* woman-oriented in his teens, you know."

"Sweet Kata, no." Koranen shuddered. "Morg may be more powerful, but at least *my* twin has a sense of humor. Rydan doesn't. See you at breakfast."

Nodding, Trevan shut the door between them. Once it was closed, he leaned his forehead against the solid wood. He was tired of being alone, tired of having to go without feminine company and companionship . . . just plain tired.

It wasn't just the lovemaking he missed, though that was definitely part of it. He missed the *love*-making. The little things, like holding hands, prolonged glances, shared laughs, and just holding a woman in his arms . . . the kinds of aches that no amount of self-ministration could alleviate. The things that his elder brothers could now share at will with their delightful, loving wives. Things that made him flinch, because *he* couldn't have it, too. Not until his Destined bride arrived, whenever *that* might be.

Some days, Trevan wished he could just retreat from the others on the island, avoiding them all—save only for the most necessary of contact—like his twin had successfully done.

TWO

·❦·

Since he doubted his younger and rather virginal sibling would be comfortable bringing up the subject, Trevan sighed, cleared his throat with a sip of the milk the ladies had taken to serving with breakfast—it was either milk, fruit juice, or water, now that the days of the eight brothers drinking stout for breakfast seemed to be over, thanks to the nine-year-old in their midst—and addressed the others with as much nonchalance as he could muster. Everyone, including his reticent, black-haired twin, was gathered at the long rectangular table that had been selected to replace the original octagonal one.

"Koranen and I have a . . . problem . . . to resolve," he said, speaking in a break between the conversations around him.

"A problem?" Saber asked, arching one of his honey blond brows. As eldest brother, it had long been his habit to be the first to tackle any problems in their family.

"Yes," Trevan agreed, ignoring Kor's suddenly flushed face. Since the boy, Mikor, was still at the table, he chose his words carefully. "Kor and I have been working on a special project—creating more of the illusionary people we've used for courtiers. But we're aiming for a specific effect . . . and falling short in our goals."

"Falling short? How so?" Dominor inquired. As the most ambitious in the family, the dark-haired mage rarely turned down a challenge.

Again, Trevan selected his words carefully. Mariel's son was only nine, but that was still possibly old enough to understand, if he spoke too bluntly. "We're looking to create realistic reactions in adult females, but as we ourselves are not adult females, our efforts have been falling short of such a deeply *desirable* goal."

Serina got it. She was the first, in fact, and she got it so much that the platinum-haired arithmancer spat her mouthful of milk back into her mug, choking on her realization, then hastily reached for a linen napkin to blow her nose. Mikor laughed, finding it funny that his honorary aunt had just snorted her beverage. The other adults seated around the table flushed with either amusement or embarrassment.

Kelly coughed into her own hand, clearing her throat. Aquamarine eyes bright, she studied Trevan with an amused look. "Yeah . . . well . . . What sort of *feasible* solution did you have in mind?"

"We'd like to record—remotely, of course," Trevan stressed, "and with no direct involvement ourselves—the, ah, appropriate reactions."

"Absolutely not!" Saber asserted, scowling at his redheaded sibling. His twin, Wolfer, growled, but thankfully said nothing. Dominor had a dark, speculative look in his blue eyes that suggested he was reviewing all the castration spells he knew. Evanor, Dom's twin, had flushed almost as red as his sister-in-law, who was still blowing her nose and clearing her throat from her little liquid mishap.

"I must agree with Saber," Ev said sternly. "That is highly inappropriate to suggest, even if it *were* 'remotely recorded'—find your own source for such things!"

"I've been *trying*," Trevan retorted, sitting forward in his earnest frustration. "Do you see one showing up at the castle gates? We're lucky we can get the trader-captains to visit us once a week with smuggled goods, these days! They're still not quite willing to smuggle us more people, let alone more women!"

Morganen spoke before the others could, his light tenor calm yet pointed. "Trevan, have you forgotten your own verse in the Song of the Sons of Destiny? The last few weeks, Brother, you've been hanging around *here* . . . yet your verse clearly states you'll find your woman somewhere out *there*, in the forests of the Isle. Perhaps if you were to go out into the woods to the north—where you *normally* roam—the Gods will surely provide, as Their Seer foretold a thousand years ago?"

"Well, that's fine for *him*," Koranen finally spoke up; he was blushing, though thankfully not radiating at the moment. "But what about *me*? I can't do anything without . . . without . . ." He trailed off, eyeing the curly-haired youth in their midst, then looked at Mikor's mother and newly made next-father.

Mariel quickly got the point. "Mikor, isn't it time for you to start your chores?"

Groaning, knowing when the adults were up to something, but wouldn't let him stay and figure out what it was, the boy slid out of his seat and headed for the door, sighing with youthful frustration. "I *never* get to stay for the *big* discussions."

Kor waited until the door to the dining hall closed, stalling by picking up his water glass. As soon as the boy was gone, he continued in a low but intense tone. "I cannot do anything without risking *burning* a woman, but it's a moot point, since there *aren't* any free women on this island to do anything with! I'm sick and tired of being an object of *pity* for not ever having done anything with a woman, and I *want to get tumbled*!"

His cheeks flushed almost as dark as his auburn hair, but it got his point across. As did the steaming of the water in his glass. Setting it down and smacking his napkin onto the table next to it, Kor shoved to his feet. The scent of heated linen filled the air, as did the palpable wave of warmth emanating from him. Struggling, Koranen controlled his temper, his magic, and his tone with a slow, deep breath.

"I want what everyone else gets to have. Even if it's with a stupid *illusion*. At least with one of those, I wouldn't have to fear *burning* her. But, no, it seems that none of you will help Trev and me." Another rough sigh, and the second-youngest brother ran a hand through his dark red locks. "If you'll excuse me, I don't feel like remaining in your company right now."

Not waiting for permission, he turned and strode out of the room.

"He has a point, you know," Trevan told the others, most of whom looked anywhere but at the remaining male redhead in their midst. "Even if it's just with an illusion, it would be better than nothing. In fact, it was highly stupid of us to not realize in all this time that we *could* have created illusions to help alleviate our needs. And just because most of *you* have women—or hate them"—he added, nodding to his twin, who was slouched in his seat, brooding inscrutably into a cup of fruit juice—"doesn't negate *our* needs.

"And before *you* go on again about the damned Curse, Brother," Trev added to Morganen in specific, "it's not like I'll get all the way to the north end of the Isle and discover my ideal woman lounging right there on the beach, waiting for me with open arms, this very morning. It could be days, weeks, or even *months* before she shows her face—after all, it took Kelly three years and *your* personal intervention for *her* to show up!"

No one had an answer to that. Morg did look like he would reply, but he subsided after a moment, sighing softly. Picking up the pitcher of fruit juice in front of him, the youngest among them filled up his glass, then Rydan's, as if action would fill the awkward silence in the room.

Only Kelly dared to meet Trevan's gaze, but she was married, and she wasn't offering to be a test subject in the face of her husband's open objection. Rising from his chair, Trevan laid his own napkin on the table more gently than his brother had, though with no less frustration. What had started out as a tenuous hope had been crushed under the heels of his family.

"Go ahead. *Refuse* to help us solve our immediate problem," Trevan said with disdain, heading for the doorway. "Who gives a damn if Koranen and I suffer until the end of time itself, waiting for *our* Destinies, so long as *you* can be selfishly happy—with *or* without women in your lives!"

Slamming the door shut behind him—just to make his family jump and feel worse about what they had, or rather, hadn't done— Trevan headed up the corridor. Perhaps he should bury himself in his work, maybe try to turn his frustration into productive energy, but the thought of putting anything in his hands, which were clenching at the moment with rising frustration, suggested that wielding a tool right now might not be a good idea.

So, rather than taking the northeastern path when the main wing split in half like the ends of a *Y*, he took the stairs up to the ramparts. Emerging in the brisk, cold morning air, Trevan slammed that door shut, too, and leaped over the parapets, plummeting toward the ground.

Before he had fallen more than a single floor, the mage shifted his shape into one of his two most comfortable, familiar, soothing forms, that of a broad-winged, reddish gold hawk. Pulling up out of his plummet, he soared across the gardens, beating his wings hard not only to gain altitude again, but to exorcise some of his frustrations. Not the ongoing urges to tumble about with a willing woman, as Koranen had put it, but the urge to smack the happiness off his brothers' faces.

He wasn't normally so volatile, but after having had his spirits lifted with the hope of *maybe* coming up with a suitable enchanted substitute, they had been crushed with the incompletely responsive and thus utterly disappointing results. It just wasn't the same, if the female—illusionary or otherwise—didn't respond. It wasn't *fun*. A man wasn't built to get his physical hopes raised up like that, only to have them thwarted again and again, leaving Trev and his younger brother restless and sleepless and gods-be-damned frustrated!

A piercing cry escaped his shapechanged throat, partly in frustration, partly in challenge to Fate Themselves, the Threefold God of distant Fortuna. He'd fly all over the damned Isle if he had to this morning, to prove to his brothers that there wasn't any such Prophesied woman waiting for him!

Leading the way through a small gap in the bushes, Amara splashed into the waterfall-fed pool sheltered in the midst of the forest greenery. They had slept well, despite the hard raft and chilly morning air. Shortly after waking at some point around noon, she and her sister had found a stream bisecting the shore and had followed it up the gently sloping land. At least there was enough heat in the middle of the day that the water of the pool felt comfortably cool in comparison, even if the nights were chilly in this southern land.

Amara wriggled her toes in the mud covering the bottom of the pool. She had left her boots back at the raft, preferring to remain unencumbered in case they encountered anything dangerous, but she had shifted scales onto her soles to protect them from random rocks and twigs. So far, nothing momentous had happened since waking up, other than a brief argument over whether or not her sister had been right about the relative safety of this place.

Still, she wasn't going to be convinced until she knew a lot more about this land. Such as whether or not the water was drinkable, for a start. Stopping midstream, she lifted a double handful of water to her lips. It was sweeter than she expected, sweeter than the spray-contaminated rainwater they had been drinking. Arora joined her only after unlacing and pulling off her boots, stuffing her socks into the footwear and hanging them around her neck so that she, too, could wade partway into the sandy, silty pool before drinking.

"This place is perfect," Arora stated, moving forward until she was thigh-deep in the water. "Look, edible fruit over there—and I think that one's a relative of soapweed!"

"Be careful, Arora," Amara warned as her twin stooped to get another palmful of the sweet water. Sea creatures might be able to handle the salt of the ocean, but she preferred being a woman of the land. She eyed the pond warily. "There might be leeches, or worse."

Her sister retorted carelessly, "Well, if there are any, just pick them off!"

Does nothing ever get through her damned, obliviously happy facade? Amara wondered a little sourly. Here she was, trying to be *practical* about potential dangers, and her twin just brushed them off! She stayed irritated for a few moments, following her twin to the mossy patch of ground, until she saw Arora gathering up more berries and leaves. Happy or not, at least her sister could tell what was safe to eat in this corner of the world.

Hungry, Amara joined her twin, following her lead and memorizing which sun-dappled plant parts were edible. Arora had long ago told her sister of her ability to "see" edible foods and whether they had to be cooked first, or if they had been tampered with. She still wasn't entirely sure what that meant, but was willing to trust her twin. It had saved them from being drugged during their travels, and now saved them from empty stomachs here in this foreign land.

There wasn't much in the way of variety, just more of the roots, the spinach-like greens, and a few bushes of berries ranging from ripe to overripe, but it was a very welcomed change from fish. They scattered a few birds out of the berry-laden bushes, making Amara long for a bow and a quiver of arrows. Bird meat would taste extra lovely after weeks of subsisting on sea life and would definitely fill up the corners of their stomachs that the plants they gathered couldn't quite touch.

Perhaps, after I've broken my fast and had a bit of a bath, I should shift shape into a hawk and see if I can bring down one of those birds. It had been a while since she had taken to the skies, but flying was something she loved to do. Hunting was fun, too. Once she had begun training for administering the Shifting Plains, she had found less and less time for just taking to the sky, circling on a breeze, and peering about for something worthy of a good, hawkish pouncing. Even a mouse would be better tasting than fish, lots of fish, and just too much fish.

The rounded, sun-drenched tops of a couple of large rocks projecting into the pond would have been a warmer perch for their impromptu picnic than the half-shaded, mossy bank, but Amara wasn't interested in making her backside numb just to be a little warmer. She was concerned for her twin, but Arora looked comfortable.

Arora also finished her meal of roots, leaves, and partially fermented berries with more enthusiasm and speed than her sister did. Dusting off her hands, she swallowed and announced happily, "Time for us to wash our clothes, I think."

Part of Amara wanted to point out that her sister was wearing both sets, while she was stuck in just her shifted skin, and thus Arora should do all of the work, having dirtied all of their clothes over the last two weeks. But some of the garments were hers, too, and if the weather improved now that they were away from the damp chills of the ocean, maybe Arora wouldn't need quite as many garments to stay warm, permitting Amara to resume a semblance of a civilized appearance.

Sighing, she finished her own berries and dusted off her hands. "Fine. Where's that soapweed you thought you saw?"

Turning her head, Arora squinted at the far bank. She blinked a couple of times, then nodded. Amara was never quite sure what, exactly, her twin saw when she did things like that. The shortest, most succinct explanation Arora had ever been able to give her was the one-word answer of *colors*. Which wasn't very informative. The longwinded explanation was, "I look for whatever I think I should see, and if it is there, then I see it. It usually shows up as different colors, with different meanings."

She supposed it made complete sense to her twin, but Amara had to take such unbelievably—in the sense of not quite being able to fully believe—simple explanations on faith, since her sister did seem to be right about many of the "colors" she saw. Amara wasn't an expert on normal magic by any means, but she had learned enough from the old records and from chance comments overheard in their travels to guess that this was not the normal way such things worked. Still, it worked, and that meant it was not for her to argue.

If it pertained to the management of a city, a Family, a Clan, or even the whole of the Shifting Plains, Amara could speak with great confidence, but this was her twin's domain, and she felt as out of water as a real sea creature would have been.

Arora stood up and stripped off the layers of her clothes. "I'll fetch the weeds, if you'll find a good rock to mash them with."

Nodding, Amara stood as well, peering into the foliage lining the pond. It didn't take her long to find what she wanted, a rounded stone that would fit well into a slightly hollow dip on the top of one of those boulders submerged partway into the pond. She bundled up their clothes, the knee-length *chamsa* tunics, the *breika* trousers, undershorts, and doubled pair of socks, which she rescued from her sister's boots. One of the socks had a hole in it; that one was hers. She wasn't sure which of the other three was its mate; they were all fairly identical and visibly worn, but only the one had a thumbnail-sized hole.

A glance up to locate her sister showed Arora floating at about mid-pool, clearly fascinated by the waterfall. Amara thought it was lovely, too, but she had more practical considerations on her mind. She did take a few moments to admire the splashing sheets, though, before picking her way out to her selected, sun-drenched rock. The view reminded her of the time one of her cousins had picked up a bag of winter wheat, a bag with a hole in it, and of how the grains had spewed down to the ground. Of course, that had been a pale, dull yellow, not a glistening white, but it was still mesmerizing.

Tearing her attention away from the water, Amara waded carefully into the pond. Her sister returned her own attention to her task and in a short span of time returned with a fistful of the odd, solid, small leaves. Soapweed—the kind she knew about—was a common herb used to soften and supplement hardsoap, but it was as broad as a palm and scattered with holes.

Thankfully, though the mashed pulp was rather green, it didn't stain their *chamsas*. Arora's was still a light, somewhat faded pink, and hers was still a pale blue when they had been scrubbed, rinsed under the waterfall, and draped over a couple of bushes on the mossy bank side of the pond. Their light brown *breikas* were next, and then their socks, and by then, Arora had to swim back across the pond to fetch more leaves.

Arora laughed as she applied the mashed mess to her light brown hair. "If this turns my head funny colors . . ."

Amara grinned back. "You should've been born with black hair like mine, not that plain, plebian brown."

Her quip earned her a poke of her twin's tongue, but it was with a lighter heart that Amara scrubbed her own hair. There wasn't any real way to comb out their hair, save for their fingers, but the soap-weed relative worked even better than the leafy kind they knew; it was slick and creamy when mashed with some water into a crude paste and worked to detangle Arora's locks. Amara's hair wasn't tangled like her sister's, but then she *was* a shapeshifter. She did shift her nails into dull-tipped claws, using them to rake gently through her sister's hair.

It wasn't Arora's fault that she wasn't a shapeshifter. Forty-nine of fifty men on the Plains were shifters by birth, but only one in fifty women, and that was counting the least-skilled among them as well as the best, the ones who could attain only a single shape after much effort and concentration, as well as the *multerai*, those who could assume ten or more distinct animal forms. Amara had yet to find a shape she couldn't shift into, provided it was at least as big as a robin. But her twin couldn't shift anything, save for some strange way with her eyes that allowed her to see the world differently.

Tired though she still was, Amara didn't feel quite so resentful anymore. They were safely on dry land, they had water and food—of a non-fish sort, if not much of it—and they could build themselves a shelter and a fire with the one knife they had salvaged, their hands, and their knowledge, given time and effort. Of course, it would be nothing as fine as a proper *geome* tent without animal skins to cover it in, nor as formal as an actual building, lacking tools beyond that one knife, the sort of tools that would allow them to cut wood and chisel stone.

Of course, if they had reached an inhabited stretch of land, there would be buildings available to move into, provided they could pay for them somehow. Arora had claimed she was leading them to a safe haven, but whether that meant people who would not actually want her twin for her power if they learned of it—which Amara doubted—or a land that was deserted, the elder of the twins couldn't tell. In the meantime, she would simply have to be vigilant and protective, as was her duty.

When she finished claw-combing her sister's hair, Amara set aside her doubts long enough to scrub her skin with some of the remaining soapweed cousin. Wading deeper into the water, she swam across the pond. Arora followed, angling her green-slimed frame more toward the waterfall. Since the pounding spray would do a better job at removing the mashed lather, Amara veered that way as well.

The water directly under the spray was shallow and filled with age-rounded rocks. As was the deeper water a little farther out, though they were hidden underwater by the rippling, foaming surface. Amara discovered that unfortunate fact with her shins. She also discovered an odd shadow behind the silvery-white cascade, and studied it warily.

Her twin, noticing her interest, tapped her on the shoulder, and shouted in her ear, since the rushing of the water was quite loud, up close. "It's some sort of cave! I want to go exploring it, in a minute!"

Rolling her eyes, Amara wondered about her twin's fascination with a foreign cave. Not that her interest in underground anything was unusual. Arora had often been caught spending time deep in the subterranean vaults that had survived the destruction of the capital of Aiar. This wasn't a bad thing, either; a lot of old records had been stored down there, moldy books, crumbling scrolls, various accounts of what had happened aeons ago in the old Empire. They had lived in the Shifting City—the only permanent city on the Shifting Plains—for several years in a row, which had given both young women plenty of time to learn all sorts of things.

While Amara had undertaken lessons in practical city and country management, her sister had delved into the region's distant past with the fervor of a scholar. She had made herself useful at the meetings of the various princesses, too, since she had a fair and quick hand for scribe work . . . but Arora was no shapeshifter, and scribal work was all she was good for, when it came to sitting on the City, Clan, and Family Councils.

Here, there were no meetings to attend, no decisions or debates to record. Though she did roll her eyes, Amara didn't begrudge her sister her odd spelunking hobby. It wasn't as if Arora would find anything of interest underground this far from any sign of civilization, after all.

"You do that," she returned, projecting her words into her twin's ear. "As soon as I'm rinsed off, I think I'll go back and get my boots and anything else I can scavenge from the raft!"

Nodding, Arora gestured for her to maneuver under the falling spray first. "It's a good place to set up a temporary camp!"

Her sister said more, something about coming back, but Amara couldn't hear all of it through the pounding splatter from the waterfall. Not that she needed to guess hard as to what was running through her twin's mind; this place *would* make a good base camp for exploring the local terrain.

The water stung at her shoulders, flinching her skin instinctively into a tougher surface of scales. Rinsing the pulped leaves from her hair, she finally swam free of the waterfall, letting Arora take her place. The pond had rinsed the rest of the soapweed-like mash from her skin, leaving it soft and scented faintly. Whatever that plant was, it had a slightly spicy aroma when mashed. Climbing up onto one of the clean, dry rocks, she squeezed water out of her hair, letting her naked form dry in the sun, while her sister rinsed under the waterfall.

When Arora came back, she stopped by Amara's boulder, looking up at her elder sister. "Going to fetch your boots, you said?"

Mara nodded. "I'll fly out there, grab them, come back, I think, maybe see if there's anything tasty I can bring down." The thought of fowl rather than fish made her mouth water in anticipation. "We'll have to dig a firepit, but something roasted would be heavenly. Here—dry yourself up here while I'm gone."

Patting the boulder, she shifted shape, launching herself in her smallest form, that of a plain brown sparrow. Flapping hard and fast, she gained altitude until she was level with the tops of the trees, then shifted shape into a larger, safer hawk body. A circle of the little pond showed her sister climbing onto the rock to enjoy the sunshine as she dried. Satisfied, Amara soared to the north, flying toward the coast.

It felt good to stretch her muscles in flight, to shape her skin and bones into feathers and wings. Flapping was hard work, especially after weeks of flexing more of her abdominal and leg muscles than her upper limbs. But it was exhilarating to ride a thermal over a patch of darker, denser forest, to bobble in a wind shear, to dart teasingly after some local, yellow-and-black bird that was too small to be more than a mere mouthful, before veering northward again.

Of course, the drawback to flying was that she couldn't quite match the exact route she and her twin had taken down beneath the trees. Hunting for the mouth of the stream, Amara winged down toward the shore. She finally spotted the winding mouth—and squawked, startled. Diving into the trees, she landed as quickly as she could, peering through the branches with a racing heart. Someone was out there!

Her eyes, as keen as a real raptor's, made out the figure of an adult male, clad in shades of green and tan, with hair that gleamed like tangled copper, fluttering in the steady onshore wind. He turned as she watched, mouthing something, arms spreading wide in some sort of abrupt gesture. She couldn't hear anything—between the surf, the wind, and the fact that birds just didn't have the best hearing—but it looked like he might be upset about something.

Amara had seen that sort of dramatic gesticulation in someone who was holding a passionate argument before, though she couldn't see his audience. Thrusting off her current perch, she flew closer, to the edge of the trees, though still back far enough in the branches to hopefully not be seen. Craning her avian head, she peered up and down the beach; the man was alone. It looked like he was just venting verbal steam, far from anyone who might overhear it.

His clothing was alien, with his tunic and trousers fitted rather than gathered at waist and neckline. But the material was finely woven, edged with ribbon trim in abstract swirls, and his boots, while plain along most of their length, did have a bit of intricate tooling at their tops. He didn't seem to be wearing a weapon that she could see, but there was something silvery on his wrist, silvery and creamy.

Careful observation showed it was some sort of bracelet set with a large oval stone—marble or moonstone, she wasn't sure at this distance. He didn't have a pectoral, of course, but then neither did she, having lost hers when their ship had crashed. Not to mention, this place was well beyond the reach of the Shifting Plains. The odds of finding a fellow shapeshifter here were extremely low, even if she didn't know how heavily populated this land might be.

He was kind of handsome, in an exotic way. Reddish hair was rare on the Plains, but not unheard of; one of her first courters had been a red-haired young man. He had turned out to have no shifting abilities, though, and she had gently discouraged his suit. When the Centarai had come to give the Family Whitetail a shapeshifter born among their own kind, the youth had left with them in kin-exchange.

Amara had been glad to see signs of happiness in the boy—Povan, that was his name—at being kin-gifted to the riders of the Centa Plains, going to a place where he would have a chance at earning status and wealth. But if she were honest, she had been just as glad to see him ride off, rather than endure the uncomfortable, silent censure of a Shifterai princess being courted by an ordinary young man.

Over and over, she had heard the same refrain. Someone of her abilities should have a worthy mate. Povan had been charming and funny, but being shapeless in a culture flooded with male shapechangers had left him with low social status. It was one thing to be female and shapeless, but entirely another to be male and shapeless, among the Shifterai.

Aside from their hair color, this man and Povan had nothing in common. Povan had been short, stocky, and deeply tanned. This fellow was tallish, lean, and lightly tanned. Povan's carroty-red hair had been vigorously curly; this fellow had straight, copper-hued locks. Povan had worn riding leathers dyed in cheerful yellows and reds; this fellow wore soft materials in cooler tones.

As she watched, he kicked at the top of the sandbank lining the stream, then turned and headed eastward along the shore, ambling along in that aimless way of someone deep in unhappy thought. Off to the east was the place she had hauled their makeshift raft, and if he kept walking that way, he would encounter it. Launching herself from the tree, Amara winged up hard into the sky, gaining altitude so that she could soar back toward the hills and the pond where her sister waited.

Her naked sister. Amara could see the cream of her sister's skin basking in the sunshine, the dark thatch of her groin and the long strands of her slowly drying, waist-length hair. Angling down into the clearing, she landed on the rock next to the mashed bits of plant, shifting back into a human crouch. Arora smiled at her, but Amara didn't wait for a greeting.

"I've spotted someone on the beach. He'll probably find the raft in a few moments," Amara told her twin. "Gather up some food and get yourself into the cave. Take your half of the clothes," she added. "I'll take mine, go back to the raft for my boots, and act like I'm the only one here. Until we know what the local people are like and how dangerous they are toward you, it's better if no one knows that you're here."

Arora complied without any fuss, to Amara's relief. The younger, lighter-haired twin slipped into the water, wading for the bushes on the mossy bank where their clothing had been spread. Amara followed her, though she did it the expedient way, shifting shape briefly to that of a sparrow again to keep herself out of the water. Landing by her twin, she donned the blue *chamsa*.

"I don't know how long I'll be gone, making contact with the locals. I don't even know if I'll be able to communicate, since we certainly don't speak the local tongue, and it's doubtful anyone here speaks Aian," Amara added, tying the *breikas* over her freshly scrubbed undershorts, which her sister had also been wearing up until now, layered with her own things.

The fabric was damp, cold, and uncomfortable, but it was better than wandering around in fur, feathers, scales, or bare skin. Among their own people, someone who was naked was presumed to be a shapeshifter, usually someone about to shift into or having just shifted away from a coating of fur or some such. Other cultures weren't quite so relaxed about bared flesh; either it was a shameful thing or an open invitation for activities no Shifterai would engage in without previously arranged permission.

"But I'll do what I can to figure out what's going on. You have enough food around here to keep yourself going until tomorrow, from the looks of things," Amara continued, glancing around the little clearing. "I'll try to come back late tonight, or tomorrow morning, depending on how things go. Keep yourself out of sight, alright? We know nothing about this land or its people. Until I know just how dangerous the locals are, it's better for them to remain completely ignorant, where you're concerned."

She saw the little twitch that said her sister was trying to not roll her eyes. "I'll be fine. I do know how to take care of myself, Mara."

"Just make sure you do. I'll try to get my hands on something better to eat, and bring it back with me," Amara promised her twin.

"Please do," Arora agreed. "Now go. Find this fellow you've seen and try to communicate some *peaceful* intentions, alright?"

"Spoilsport," Amara teased. She hugged her twin, then snagged the socks—the pair with the hole in one foot—and started retracing the route she and her sister had walked earlier. It would be better to hide her shapeshifting abilities from the start, if she could. Arora wasn't the only one with rare magic, though it was considered the more valuable by those who coveted such things. "Remember, stay well out of sight until late tonight!"

Heading for the shore, Amara picked her way through the subtropical foliage. A final glance behind her showed her sister bundling up her things, then the jungle got in the way, screening her twin from view. Facing forward, Amara retraced their journey back down to the shore. She had a redheaded man to find and distract, preferably before he found tracks made by two women headed up to the pond.

THREE

nothing. Absolutely nothing, all the way up the western coves. Some had navigable beaches, others were rocky and inhospitable, but Trevan had searched diligently and thoroughly, even flitting through the forests inland for a ways, in case anyone had come ashore. The mist had hampered his attempts, but he had looked for a new woman on their shores.

Fruitlessly, though. Now he was at the northernmost cove on the island, taking a break before swooping over the sandy sprawl of the eastern beaches on his way back to the palace . . . and there was no one here waiting to greet him. Trevan spent several minutes venting his frustration verbally, though the long bout of flying had helped calm him.

Railing at his youngest sibling had been therapeutic, since no one was around to hear his choice of epithets, but now he was hungry. Abandoning the edge of the stream he had paused by, Trevan headed eastward along the tree line. If he remembered right, there should be a patch of late-ripening *billa* berries up ahead, something to settle his stomach until he could hunt down a rabbit or maybe snatch up a fish. The last time he was all the way up here, it was just past that triple stand of trees . . . which was just past the faint, wind-blown hint of gouged lines in the sand.

Blinking, Trevan stopped, turning to examine the tracks. The steady sea breeze had erased most signs, but he was almost as good as Wolfer, his secondborn brother, at tracking and hunting. Someone had dragged something up the beach, something big and heavy, and then walked next to the tree line, where the dune grass anchored the sand into a semblance of firmness. They had reached the stream in the distance, where he himself had stood only a few minutes before.

Heading the other way, he tracked the marks to the drag lines. It wasn't difficult to find their source. Not when the collection of planks, half of a broken barrel, and a pair of boots slung by their laces still lay in the shadow of the forest not more than a dozen feet from the edge of the beach. The cut of the boots was unfamiliar, and he had seen the styles not only worn in Katan, but Natallia, its arch-rival Mandare, and even the fabled, distant Moonlands, not to mention glimpsed some of the strange versions of footwear found in another universe.

Their size suggested either a smallish man, or an average-sized woman. *I hope it's the latter*, Trevan thought, anxiously scanning the trees for any sign of the owner. Judging from the traces of water in the barrel, the owner of those boots had wandered off in search of a stream to drink from. Which meant he should retrace his steps to that stream, and start looking for the owner there. Undoubtedly the shipwreck survivor—for the planks composing the makeshift raft had the curved look of a section of storm-damaged hull—had headed upstream in search of something salt-free to drink.

Untangling the boots, Trevan whacked them to make sure there were no bugs inside, then draped them over his shoulder. Whoever they belonged to would surely be happy to have them back, and if he lost their trail visually, he could always try enchanting himself into a canine form and sniffing for clues to their whereabouts. Having the boots on hand would be handy for that.

He preferred feline forms when on the ground—they were far more graceful, sensual, elegant, and dignified than dogs or even wolves—but he could shift into one if necessary. Wolfer was the one who preferred a canine form when he shifted his shape. Trevan preferred most of all to take the shape of a cat, followed by a hawk.

Then again, he thought sardonically, *unlike my elder brother, I am not afraid of heights.*

It was tempting to shift shape and take to the air to look for her—or him, he had to concede the possibility that the newcomer to the Isle was a male—but Trevan refrained. According to his verse in the Prophecy, he was to meet and chase his Destined bride through the forest and then catch and hold her. Chasing he could do in a winged form. Holding was another matter.

There was the trail, windswept and thus faint, of tracks leading into the forest. The marks were too muddled to tell how many times the owner of the boots had passed this way; all he could tell was they had moved through the underbrush at least twice, possibly more. The farther into the forest he got, however, the clearer the tracks became, and the odder.

Trevan could now discern two sets of tracks, and only two: One set was made by bare feet, the other by boots. Both headed upstream, interweaving over each other. Literally, for at one point, the boots had trampled over the barefoot marks, and a few yards farther into the jungle, the bare feet had tromped all over the boot marks. Stranger, in the few patches of fine, damp earth found among the forest debris . . . those bare feet had a sort of scale-pattern to them, as if their owner were clad in socks made from a reptile's hide.

Frowning in confusion, Trevan double-checked both trails. One pair of boots had been left behind, its owner choosing to don snakeskin socks, or maybe lizard slippers. Why, he didn't know. The other pair of boots looked more or less normal, if smallish.

Removing the boots from his shoulder, he compared the size of one sole to one of the boot prints. They were, if not identical, at least very close in size, but the one in his hand was slightly wider than the print in the forest soil. The bare footprints seemed more the size that would fit in the boots he carried, because the ball of that foot looked a little wider.

Two people . . . both possibly female . . . Oh, Sweet Kata—two *women on the Isle? My twin is* not *going to like this!*

Crouched next to the tracks, Trevan stared off into the underbrush, torn between wanting to groan and wanting to laugh. *Two* women to choose from, one for himself and one for his next-youngest brother, if the trend continued to hold regarding how his siblings had met their Prophesied mates in birth order . . . Well, except for Alys. They'd known her when they were younger, but she hadn't shown up again in their lives until after Kelly had arrived, and she had done so before Dom had met Serina, and Evanor had met Mariel. Trevan didn't really count his family knowing Alys from their pre-exile days, since that was before they became interested in finding brides.

So, whomever I meet first on this trail is my Destined bride. Or maybe it's the one whose boots I'm holding—*no, Rydan isn't going to like this. He's going to resist it with all his might.*

Tough, Trevan decided. *Women make life worth living. They make life interesting, exciting, and civilized, and I am going to drag my brother out of his brooding little night-loving lifestyle, kicking and screaming if I must.*

Movement at the edge of his vision made him glance up sharply. Someone was picking their way through the forest; he couldn't see the person's head, but he could see a pair of light brown trousers of some sort, gathered just above the slender ankles briefly visible through the underbrush. A flash of more naked skin excited him; that looked like a woman's foot.

So it's the owner of the boots I'm carrying that I'm going to meet. But I don't see the one wearing the boots . . . The trouser legs passed behind a clutch of trees. Standing up, Trevan waited for the owner to come into view again. He caught a glimpse of pale blue, a hint of curves, as the woman hesitated a long moment, then moved forward, bringing her and most of her figure into view.

Bushes obscured her from the waist down, giving only glimpses of her knee-length blouse and trousers, but he could clearly see the rest of her. Her blouse was gathered at neck and wrist, falling in loose, unbelted, damp-looking folds, obscuring the details of her figure. There were enough curves to tell she was a full adult, but no sign of the kind of fitted corset Katani women favored. Nor were her garments the side-slit dresses Mariel liked, nor the odd mix of styles Kelly had come up with. The garment was lightly embroidered around the neck with repeating little animal motifs, but otherwise was unornamented . . . save for a pair of socks slung over her shoulder.

The heart-like shape of her face, with a small chin and broad cheekbones, was different from the oval facial features he was used to seeing. Above those cheekbones were wide, golden eyes not dissimilar from Wolfer's, or all that far from Serina's honey brown eyes. But where his secondborn brother had chest-length, light brown hair and his third sister-in-law had thigh-length hair so creamy pale it looked white, this woman had jet black tresses that fell to her waist. Her brows and lashes were equally black, providing a contrasting, complimentary frame for her gaze.

That gaze searched for him as soon as she came around the clump of trees. She knew he was waiting for her. Wanting to reassure the woman, Trevan offered her a friendly smile and lifted the boots he carried, dangling from his hand by their laces. He didn't know what language she spoke, and until she spoke it, the Ultra Tongue he had drunk wouldn't be capable of translating his words into a format she could understand. But smiles were universal, as was the gesture of offering someone their belongings.

Hesitantly, she approached. Trevan knew that the verse concerning his own fate in the Song of the Sons of Destiny specified that he would end up chasing her through the trees at some point. He *could* do something to precipitate that chase right now, but he carefully refrained. She looked a little too wary. Chasing a woman for mutual fun was one thing, but chasing her when she didn't know what his intentions were wasn't an idea worth pursuing, literally or figuratively. So he just lifted his arm a little higher, offering her the boots he had found.

She cautiously moved forward, gaze darting between the footwear and him, lingering briefly on his green tunic and tan trousers, then on his smile, before finally staring into his green eyes. Glancing down as soon as she emerged from the bushes between them, Trev noted that her feet looked like they just might be wide enough to match the bare prints he had been following. He lifted the boots a little higher and nodded, still smiling, letting her know without words that she was free to take them. Inching forward over the last few feet between them, the woman stretched out and snatched the boots from his fingers. Trevan didn't resist and didn't let his friendly smile slip.

She mumbled something, and his ears twitched. The translation powers of the Ultra Tongue—half potion, half spell—went immediately to work. Within two heartbeats, it translated her mumble in his mind to a soft-spoken, "Thank you."

"You're welcome," Trevan said carefully, doing his best to match the quality of the tones he heard. The potion made it seem as if he were speaking in his own native Katani tongue, but in a distinct, unique accent. What it actually did was trick both of their minds into thinking they heard their own native language. He wasn't the level of mage-scholar that his elder brother Dominor and his youngest brother Morganen were, but Trevan did know that much of how the highly complex potion-spell worked.

Unfortunately, his friendly reply made her golden eyes snap wide with shock, and a touch of fear. "You're—you're *Aian*?"

"What? No!" Trevan quickly said, holding up his hand as she shifted, clearly tensing to flee. He didn't know why she feared the idea, but at least she had paused long enough to listen. "Katani! I'm from Katan, west of here." She didn't bolt, giving him time to be a little more honest with her. "Well, actually, I'm now a citizen of Nightfall, which is this island you're on, but I was born on the mainland, in the Empire of Katan."

She stared at him warily, fingers gripping her boot laces tightly. "And yet you speak Aian. Like a native."

"I only drank a translation potion, nothing more," Trevan reassured her. "All of us living here on Nightfall have done it, so that we can communicate with any visitors, from however far away. Such as yourself." Shifting his gaze from her to the forest around them, he peered through the jungle. "So, what is your name?"

"What is yours?" she countered quickly.

Trevan made an allowance for her wariness; she was alone with a strange man, after all. "Forgive me my poor manners; I should have introduced myself sooner. My name is Trevan. Trevan of Nightfall, of the family Corvis. But you may call me Trev, if you like."

Her chin lifted slightly, her golden eyes glittering. "I am Amara Fen Ziel, of the Shifting Plains."

"And your companion?" he inquired, glancing through the trees around them.

"I have no companion," the woman denied. "I came here alone."

Trevan didn't believe her. He was competent enough as a tracker to know when footprints interwove like that. *So why is she lying? And why is she scared?* She didn't cower with fear, so much as seem wary of a potential predator. Doubly grateful he had chosen to refrain from chasing her this very first time, Trev tried his best to charm her instead. *After all, whatever reasons she has for lying, the truth will come out soon enough.*

"Then judging by the poor condition of that raft, you probably need food, shelter, and so forth, since you've already found water. Luckily for you," he added, tipping his head and giving her a boyish grin that had never failed to melt a few hearts back on the mainland, "my family has all of that and more. And it's not too far away, if we travel by horseback."

"Horseback?" the woman asked, arching one of her black brows skeptically.

"Yes, horseback," he repeated, though he wondered if he could remember the spell his elder brother used. His favorite forms were different from Wolfer's.

It was Amara's turn to gaze around the forest. "I don't see any horses."

"Well, that's because I haven't made one, yet," Trev confessed.

Again, her brow rose. "*Made* one?"

He nodded. "Yes. I'm a shapeshifter."

The other brow rose as well; it seemed he had impressed her. "A shapeshifter? All the way down here?"

"Of course. Mind you, I'm a little rusty at horse forms. My elder brother, Wolfer, does horses far more often than I. And wolves, of course. His name means 'wolf-like' in our Queen's native tongue," Trevan added lightly. "But I think I can remember the spell for it."

The dark-haired woman recoiled, staring at him with wide eyes, her fear and wariness returning threefold. "You're a *mage*?"

Instinct told Trevan he had just undone most of his friendly progress with this woman, if not all of it, though he had no idea why. The thought of her fearing him disappointed him. "Well, yes . . . but . . . Look, what have you got against mages? What have you got against *me*, for that matter? You've only just met me! Give me a chance; I *might* turn out to be nice."

"I don't trust mages," Amara said bluntly, "because they try to take things that aren't theirs, and they bully people, just because they've got magic, and they think that makes them superior."

"No one on this island is a bully, my lady—and even if someone tried, our Queen wouldn't allow it!" Inspiration struck, with that comment. Trev gave Amara the truth. "We're not a magocracy. Mages don't rule the Isle. Only the best person for the job rules, here, and our Queen *isn't* a mage."

Amara frowned at that. "She's not?"

"Nope. She has no magical powers whatsoever," Trevan admitted freely, spreading his hands, "yet she rules us with an iron fist. She insists on civilized behavior, and apparently, it isn't civilized to bully anyone. Or leave one's socks on the floor . . ."

The odd comment made her laugh. It was an involuntary one, but she did chuckle. "How . . . civilized, indeed. But I don't trust mages."

"Well, you're going to have to trust me, if you want to get to a place where there's food and shelter," Trevan told her, gesturing toward the south. "Because the nearest place for that is about twenty-five miles to the south, as the hawk flies. And unless you can turn *yourself* into a hawk, I have to turn myself into a horse to give you a ride. Assuming I can get the spell right. It's not a common form, for me."

"How did you get all the way out here, if it is so far from civilization, if not as a horse?" Amara asked him dubiously.

"As a hawk. It's one of my two favorite forms," he confessed, shrugging.

That made her frown. "Then how did you get your clothes to come with you? Your boots alone would be too heavy to carry that far."

"The spell transforms them along with the rest of me, of course."

A strange look flashed across her face. It was there for only a second or so, but Trevan thought it might be envy. She nibbled on her lip, studying him warily, then sighed. "Fine. If I hand you my clothes, will you promise to carry them in your transformed hawk spell?"

Hand me . . . her . . . ? Trevan felt his face flushing with heat. He didn't know whether to choke or faint. It took him a few moments to manage the complicated process known as speech. "You . . . want . . . naked?"

Her eyes narrowed, turning into little golden dagger-slits. "Get your mind out of the midden heap! I'm a shapeshifter. A *natural* one. I'm not bound by spells, like you are, but only my flesh shifts shape, which means I can't take my clothing with me." Her finger jabbed at him, piercing the air between them. "*You* will be respectful of me, when I do so!"

She definitely has a few attitude issues, Trevan thought, eyeing that finger. "Why don't you tell me why you don't trust mages, so that I know what things to avoid around you? Maybe then you can relax a little."

"That's none of your business," she retorted stiffly.

"Lady, if someone else has wronged you, but you're taking out your anger against them on *me*, that *makes* it my business," Trevan told her. "I have done you no wrong—I even brought you your boots!—and yet you treat me like a criminal. Where is the civilized behavior in that?"

She glanced down and away at that. In the shadows of the forest, Trevan wasn't sure if she flushed or not, though he thought he saw a faint hint of color in her face.

"Look, Nightfall isn't Aiar. We do things differently, here," he stated gently, hoping he was getting through to her. "I don't know what happened to you, or why you ended up on that raft, but when you washed up on this shore, you became our responsibility to welcome to the island. If you need a home, you can find it here. If you need a safe haven from your enemies, you won't be the first one to flee to the Isle, and you'll find we're very friendly and helpful . . . but only to those who are civilized, just to warn you. Queen Kelly has a temper and a decided opinion about uncivilized behavior.

"Now, if you'd prefer to ride to civilization, rather than walk all the way, I can try my horse-shaping spell. Or if you can shift yourself into a horse or whatever, we can travel that way, and I can carry your clothes for you. I'll even turn my back while you change, if you like. Either way, you *are* invited to come visit my family at Nightfall Castle."

"Your mother is the Queen?" she asked, glancing up at him.

"Sister-in-law. She married my eldest brother," Trevan said. He glanced up toward the canopy overhead, gauging the angle of the sun. "If we ride, I think we can make it back in plenty of time for supper."

"And if we fly?" she asked.

He glanced down at her. "You can shift into a bird form?"

She snorted, looking as if the question was never in doubt. "I am Amara of the Shifterai. Of course I can."

"Well, then . . . why don't we shift shape and fly together? Here, I'll turn my back," Trev offered politely, suiting action to words. "Chirp when you're ready."

"Ha ha. Don't try anything funny."

Whatever situation this woman has been through, she really has trust issues, Trevan thought. *Kata . . . since we don't have a Patron Deity yet, I'll still pray to You . . . help me teach her that I'm trustworthy! I mean, if she's meant to be my Destined bride, trust kind of has to be a factor in that, right?*

A flutter of wings presaged the small shape of a bird darting up from the ground. It flew past him, landed on a branch above and beyond his head, then rippled and shifted shape, swelling into a larger sized bird. Proof that this was the woman Amara, and not some random bit of wildlife. Trevan wasn't familiar with the hawk form she had chosen, beige with brown speckles, but she looked quite real. No doubt the form was based on some hawk local to wherever she came from, as his was native to Katan.

Turning around, he scooped up the clothes left on the jungle floor. Neatly folding the garments, he tucked them into his belt, letting them drape over his hips. Lacing her boots together over the strip of leather as well, he turned back to her, giving the hawk-woman a smile.

"I look forward to flying with you; my brother Wolfer is also a shapeshifter—a mage-shifter—but he's afraid of heights. His wife, Alys, is a shapeshifter, too, but she only has an owl form, bird-wise, and prefers flying at night. So it'll be very nice to actually fly with a fellow sentient being. And we'll fly down the west side of the island. This time of year, the air currents aren't very strong, but we'll have some nice thermals to help on the sunny side of the mountain range, toward the end of our flight. Which, if we fly straight there, should take about an hour, more if we stop to drink or rest. Ready?"

Her head bobbed in assent. Trevan focused his energies inward, then outward, shrinking down. A strong thrust of his legs mid-transformation, a downbeat of his wings, and he took off, winging hard to escape the forest floor. She launched herself after him, and the two of them flew up through the canopy, into the sunlight that had burned through the last of the morning's haze.

It occurred to him belatedly that he hadn't done anything about his hunger. He thought briefly about swooping over the waves and catching a fish, of offering to share it with the specked hawk soaring at his side. Then thought about his protestations that Nightfallers were civilized and thought about fixing her a meal instead, once they were at the palace. He could begin a campaign to tame this wary woman flying at his side, pampering her, showing her she was special, and getting to know her.

His seduction skills might be a little rusty from lack of use, but they did exist, and he now had a viable target for them. That she was a fellow shapeshifter pleased him; it would be a symbol of symmetry between them, like Wolfer and Alys, even if their modes of shifting were different. Beak slightly agape, Trevan soared higher, guiding her toward his—and soon to be her—home.

Amara followed her feathered guide. He knew how to fly, despite being a mage. If he had been Shifterai, she would have been impressed with the realism of his reshaped body, with the deftness of his muscles as he switched between flapping and soaring, depending on the air currents. He also hadn't made any gestures, hadn't spoken any words; she thought that mages normally had to say or do silly things in order to cast their spells. In that regard, he was *almost* like a Shifterai male, melding smoothly into this golden-feathered hawk shape.

But he wasn't a real shapeshifter. Nor was he Shifterai, nor even an Aian.

It irked her that he was right; she *had* prejudged him just because he was a mage. And it had embarrassed her a little, shamed her, when he had pointed it out. Whitetail Family was considered a courteous tribe, among her people. It had only become necessary to be so wary of strangers when outsiders had discovered her sister's powers and coveted them.

At least Arora is safe, she thought with some satisfaction. *Hidden in that damp cave, she'll be a little chilly, but she'll be safe. I'll scout out these people, discern their intentions, and see if it's reasonably safe to bring her closer to them. I might keep her hidden in the jungle, if the nearest "civilization" is indeed an hour's flight away, but I should be able to take food to her, and a fresh change of clothes . . . which I'll have to steal.*

That wasn't a happy thought. She was many things, now that her twin's situation had exiled them both, but Amara was not a thief. Unfortunately, their money had been in their luggage, which had gone down with the ship. That left them with nothing but their clothes, the knife her sister carried, and that scrap of ship they had turned into a raft.

Not that they'd had much to begin with; passage to Fortuna was expensive. They'd saved money by foraging on the way south to the coast of Aiar, but that only solved the problem of food. It did nothing to cover the other costs of living.

Spare clothes would be needed for her sister in this reversed, southern climate of winter instead of summer. Soap would be nice, too; real soap, not just mashed leaves. A place to stay would also be good, but renting cost money, whether it was a room at an inn, or a room in someone's home. Ideally, she would buy a house on the fringe of the occupied stretches of this land, some place isolated from others where her sister could stay and not risk literally bumping into anyone, especially a mage, which was how their nightmarish exile had begun. But even just renting a single room was beyond her budget, never mind buying a house and enough land to keep their neighbors at bay.

I'll have to find some way of making coin. Perhaps hunting. I can spot deer and rabbits and game birds from above, and either stoop on the smaller ones, or land and shift into a predator for hunting the larger prey. If there are any sheep on this island, my sister could become a shepherdess; they live isolated lives, and there isn't a single member of the Shifterai

*worthy of the name that couldn't herd animals of all sorts—Father Sky,
even a job as a cart driver would suffice for one of us . . . though how low
I've come, considering the life of a wagoneer for my wage, when I should've
been a queen!*

*No, to be a hunter would be better. A hunter's hut in the woods, far
from strangers. That might keep her from being noticed. Arora says she
found us a land where both of us can be safe. I hope she's right. Now that
those mages chasing us have hopefully drowned in the sea, we should be able
to start all over again with a blank page, since no one down here knows
what she is.*

I just have to make sure it stays that way.

Her guide squawked, then dove. Curious, Amara followed him
down, searching through the leaves of the trees for whatever had
caught his attention. She thought it was a field mouse, until he
alighted on a bank at the edge of a quiet pool, shifting his shape.
Her clothes were still tucked around his waist. Landing on a branch,
she watched him as he glanced around for her.

He smiled when he spotted her, making her wonder why he was
being so nice to her. "There you are. I was thirsty, and knew this
stream was here. I thought you might be thirsty, too."

Watching him drop to one knee and scoop up a palmful of water, Amara debated whether she should shift shape or not. As she
debated, he scooped up a double handful and rose, approaching her
with the liquid. That surprised her. Raptors had sharp, strong beaks
and swift reflexes; even a shapechanged raptor could succumb to a
self-defensive instinct or two. But he approached her confidently,
still smiling, and offered his hands.

Struggling with her instincts, Amara carefully dipped her head,
catching a mouthful of water in her beak. Tipping her head back,
she swallowed it down. A second dip allowed her to drink, but too
much water had dripped from his hands to get another swallow.
When he turned away, she dropped from the branch, landing on

her feet. Feathers still covered her skin, but she didn't take any chances.

"Keep your back turned. I'll not have you gawking at me," she ordered. Away from the Plains, men weren't very respectful of women. They didn't follow the very sensible and highly civilized rules she was used to following. Of course, that was on the Aian continent. This place . . . she would have to wait and see.

Twisting just a little more to his left, he put his back to both her and the stream, giving her the privacy she wanted. "Just let me know when you're ready to fly again."

Does he have to be so cheerful? Suspicion had become an uncomfortable way of life for her. Unsure of his motives, Amara drank quickly, then shifted shape. A squawk of her own let him know she was ready. He turned, knelt, drank again, then grinned at her and changed, leaving him with his beak gaping slightly. A fast flutter of wings launched him upward, almost as if daring her to give chase.

Fine. Be that way—I can out-fly any spell-wrought shapechanger, any day.

Launching herself from the ground, Amara strove hard to overtake him. Or at least to catch up quickly. He knew where they were going, after all.

FOUR

❧❧❧

By the time they reached their destination, Amara itched with curiosity. There were signs of habitation in the jungles they flew over, but most of it was old, swallowed by the forests until only a few beams, a stray pillar, a bit of stone stairwell and the like scattered here and there remained visible to her hawk-sharp eyes. She did see a harbor in the distance, just before they veered eastward to a saddleback pass between what had turned out to be two distinct granite ranges, but it, too, showed signs of great neglect.

There were signs of land having been cleared, yes, but there were still more signs of neglect and abandonment lingering from untold years ago, and no signs of settlements. In fact, the only things that looked recent were strange, twisting, crystal-topped spires spaced every few miles along the ridge of the mountains and the meandering coast. No, the only building still intact within her field of view was a sprawling, multilobed structure that she didn't see until they were literally almost over it.

How she could have missed it, Amara didn't know, but one moment she was looking at gray granite and green forest, the next, blue roof tiles and polished gray white stones. Light glinted from a large, faceted crystal perched on the top of a cupola-topped dome; the crystal looked very much like the ones perched on the spires she had seen, making her wonder what its purpose might be. She didn't know enough about magic to be sure, but wondered if it was responsible for her not seeing this sprawling, multiarmed structure until the last moment.

Is that what those spires are for? Hiding their settlements? If so . . . Gods! There would have to be thousands of mages to disguise everything. Arora said this land would be safe for her, but if that's what those spires do, nowhere on this island is safe!

She almost missed her cue to land, and fluttered down onto the parapet edging the roof of one of the wings. Even as he landed, the redheaded mage transferred out of his golden hawk form. He flashed her a grin and gestured at a nearby door recessed in the tiled slope behind him. "Come; we go in this way."

Giving him as dirty a look as she could manage—avians weren't really configured for facial expressions—Amara squawked, mantling her wings.

"What?" He frowned at her a moment, then blinked, eyes widening in remembrance. A blush stole across his cheeks. "Oh, right! Clothes. Here—if you stay back from the edge, you won't be seen from below. Not that there was anyone down in the gardens that I could see, but still . . ." Removing her garments, he set them on the stones of the walkway. "I'll be inside, waiting for you."

The spellchanger opened the door and stepped inside, closing it behind him. Amara waited a moment, craning her feathered head to peer at the rest of the palace serving as her perch. There *weren't* any people outside in the garden, at least not on this side of the building. Even among her own people, who preferred tents to buildings in all but the coldest months, there would be people outside on a day like today, enjoying the mild sunshine.

Hopping off the parapet stones, she landed in her human form and quickly slipped into her things. As tempting as it was to slip off and do some exploring of her own, to try and figure out where all the people were, Amara didn't think the locals would look kindly upon it. Her current objective was to observe the people of this land to see if they were a high-level threat, not to give them a reason to want to observe her more closely.

He was lounging against the wall of the corridor, when she opened the door. The wall distracted her for a moment; it had been painted with a profligate use of magic, for the wall—indeed, the whole corridor for as far as she could see in the light from outside—looked like it was a windswept field of wheat, replete with fuzzy ripening heads rippling slowly in that wind. Dragging her attention back to her host, she found that the smile Trevan gave her was warm and friendly. It wasn't easy, resisting his charm; he seemed genuinely pleased to see her walk through that parapet door, even though he'd been with her moments before. He even took her hand, clasping her fingers in his warm palm and tugging her into an archway.

"I think Kelly will be in the sewing hall; you should probably meet her first."

"That would be the Queen?" Amara wanted to confirm, and felt rather grubby and underdressed when he nodded. Especially in a land where they used magic to paint their walls, of all things. One of the things she had lost when the ship had struck the reef, forcing her and her twin into the water, was her pectoral. Regardless of whatever else Shifterai might wear, if they were a shapechanger, they had the right to an ornamental pectoral collar. Each row was decorated with a repeating motif of one of the pure-shapes a Shift-erai could assume.

Being without hers and about to be introduced to foreign royalty left her feeling unsettlingly underdressed. Not quite naked, but close. But it was too late to protest; they had already emerged on the next floor, where the walls were a soothing shade of blue sky dotted with the occasionally fluffy cloud. Those clouds drifted past them, playing gradual peekaboo with the unpainted door frames they passed. Before she could ask him about it, he pulled her up to a doorway, rapping on it briefly with his knuckles before pushing it open.

"There you are, just as I thought. Kelly, meet Amara. Amara, this is Kelly, Queen of Nightfall. I found her in the forest," Trevan stated, flourishing his hand between the two women. Then added cryptically, wrinkling his nose, "Remind me to trounce Morg later for being so annoyingly right."

The woman rising from the chair placed at the long worktable was not what Amara was expecting. She had envisioned someone tall, stately, dressed in fine clothes, with some sort of crown perched upon thick, dark locks, much like her own people's sovereign, Aitava of the Sixteen Shapes. Instead, Queen Kelly of Nightfall was shorter than her by a finger-length, modest in build, with freckled skin and reddish blond hair free of any coronet, and clad in a blouse, laced vest, and skirt, all dyed in vague shades of visibly worn and faded blue. She almost blended into the background, for the walls in here were also shades of blue, though the clouds gathering in one corner of the painted walls were grayish and anvil-shaped, slowly forming a silent thunderhead.

The sight of the other woman's plain, unremarkable outfit made Amara feel a little better about arriving in her travel-worn clothes, even without her pectoral. It also made her feel rather disappointed, since the shorter woman had risen from what looked like a pile of garments in need of mending. *That* was a job for someone of far lesser rank, not the task of a sovereign.

What kind of a kingdom is this? she wondered, as the shorter woman held out her hand in greeting. Amara clasped it briefly, eyeing the other woman.

"Welcome to Nightfall. Amara, is it?"

"Amara Fen Ziel, of Family Whitetail, Clan Deer of the Shifterai," Amara stated, feeling the urge to establish her importance in the face of such a grubby queen. Glancing around the room, she found it empty of anyone else. "Where is everyone? Your retinue, your servants?"

That made the other two exchange quick looks. Trevan shrugged, silently deferring to the redheaded sovereign. Kelly lifted her chin slightly. "We're an incipient kingdom. I 'Rang the Bell' to start forming it less than two months ago."

Amara knew what that meant. It was still happening here and there in Aiar as regions pulled themselves out of the chaos that had followed the collapse of the old Empire, though most places had settled into distinct states. Ringing the Bell meant that a people had selected a leader and had chosen to petition the Gods for a Patron Deity to provide them with unity and a religious identity. Her people had gone back to the ancient, nature-revering faith of worshipping Mother Earth and Father Sky, with minor homage given to Brother and Sister Moons.

It made sense for two reasons: The shapeshifters among her people took on the form of nature itself through the animals they copied; and the majority of terrain that survived the magical explosion centered in the capital had divided itself into earth and sky, visual reminders of the most ancient of Gods. Of course, there were those who would contend that Fate, the Threefold God, was even older than Earth and Sky Themselves, but Amara preferred more practical debates. Still, the question of theology was an important one for an incipient kingdom and would give her a potential clue or two as to what the local customs might be.

"Who, then, is your Patron?"

Again, the two Nightfallers exchanged a quick look. The red-headed woman wrinkled her nose. "We're still working on that. But we have time. How did you end up on our island?"

One of her black brows arched. *They haven't chosen a Patron Deity yet?* Amara wasn't sure what to make of that. She also hadn't heard a good explanation as to where all the servants were, but let it pass for the moment. "A shipwreck. This man found me out in the forest, after I had gone looking for fresh water. He insisted that I come and meet with you."

"Actually, I insisted she should come and *stay* with us, seeing as she has no resources of her own to draw upon," Trevan corrected. "Being shipwrecked and all."

Kelly grinned. "You mean, being Prophesied and all."

"Prophesied?" Amara asked, confused by the reference. To her bemusement, the mage who had brought her here blushed, while his sovereign—incipient sovereign, rather, laughed softly.

"I know I shouldn't tease him, but . . . well, *your* presence on the island was predicted by an ancient Seer of Katan, the land this island broke away from," Kelly enlightened her. Or rather, confused her.

"*My* presence?"

Trevan, still a little flushed, nodded. "Yes, the Seer Draganna predicted a certain set of circumstances a thousand years ago. It's one of her few remaining Prophecies that hasn't completely come true yet."

"But which is fulfilling itself at a nice pace," Kelly agreed. She flicked her hand at her chest, then at Amara. "It turned out that I was the start of that Prophecy, and you are now a continuation of it."

Amara glanced between the two of them. "I don't understand."

Rubbing the back of his neck with one hand, Trevan cleared his throat. "Yes, well . . . there are eight verses in the Song of the Sons of Destiny—she was a rhyming Seer—and my seven brothers and I are fulfilling her Prophecy that certain events would happen in our lives, and, well . . ."

"It's a Love Curse," Kelly explained blithely when he hesitated. Her blunt words made him flush again. They also made Amara stare at her askance. The shorter woman shrugged. "I didn't believe in it, either, but your presence potentially makes you predicted bride number five. I was the first, Alys the second, then came Serina and Mariel . . . and now you."

The thought of being *predicted* to be someone's bride, without consulting *her* first, made Amara stubbornly skeptical. Hands shifting to her hips, she eyed both redheads warily. "Predicted bride for *whom?*"

Trevan lifted and wriggled his fingers in silent admission, his green eyes locked steadily with hers.

"That's not possible," Amara denied.

"Why not?" Kelly asked her.

"Because . . . because he's a mage! Because he's not Shifterai— how do I know he's truly worthy of me?"

"By getting to *know* him before you make such a snap judgment?" Kelly shot back, palms planting on her own hips. "He happens to be a very nice man! He's smart, creative, intelligent, funny—"

"Then why don't *you* marry him?" Amara retorted flippantly.

"I'm *already* married. And I'm not saying you *have* to marry him. There *are* two other brothers unspoken for on this island," the redheaded queen added tartly. "Of course, unless you're an Aquamancer, I doubt you'd be Koranen's type, and somehow, I don't think Rydan would appreciate an argumentative woman in his life."

Amara frowned, tallying up names and numbers. "But there are *eight* brothers. You say there are only three who are bachelors, yet you mentioned only four women. If there is one man per woman, as the Gods designed, then that leaves one brother unaccounted for—and who says I have to fall for one of these brothers? Surely there are plenty of other women in this land who could take my place?"

"Actually, there aren't," Kelly told her. "We are a very small incipient kingdom. We have the eight adult brothers, five women if we include you in the count, and one nine-year-old boy."

"That's *it*?" Amara asked skeptically, taken aback.

"That's it," Kelly confirmed.

"Well, there *are* the citizen-chickens," Trevan offered in a non sequitur. "But they sort of don't count."

Amara glanced back and forth between the two redheads, one strawberry blond, short, and female, the other coppery blond, tall, and male. She couldn't believe they were serious, and yet they looked as if they were. "I've landed on an island of madmen . . ."

"It's a long-standing joke," he reassured her. "Nothing more. And we're not madmen. We're actually quite nice, once you get to know us."

"And we're mostly harmless," Kelly agreed. Then wrinkled her nose again. "Well, except for the chickens. They're vicious."

"Look, why don't we get you settled in a room of your own and get you some food?" Trevan coaxed her. "You can have a nice bath, and I'm sure Her Majesty can find you some spare clothes to wear."

"Something of Serina's might fit; you're almost the same height, though a bit more curvy than she is," Kelly mused.

The thought of a room of her own—and not a residence of her own—made Amara uneasy. "Isn't there a cottage, or a hut, or something I could stay in? I don't want to put anyone to any trouble."

"Oh, it's no trouble. We have plenty of rooms just waiting to be filled," Kelly reassured her. "Trevan, I'm sure you could find her something in the northwest wing?"

"You mean the northeast wing; I don't think it would be a good idea for her to stay in the northwest one," he countered, shifting to touch Amara's elbow with one hand, the other gesturing toward the door.

Kelly's freckled face flushed with embarrassment. "East, west . . . right. I *meant* the northeast one. Go on and get her settled in, either way."

"What's wrong with the northwest wing?" Amara asked, worried. This really was a house of madmen—a miniature kingdom of madmen, if there were only fourteen residents on an island stretching many miles long.

"My twin lives there. He's a little antisocial at the moment. But don't worry; so long as he thinks you're Destined for me, he won't bother you," Trevan told her, escorting her out the door. "Ah— Evanor! Ev, this is Amara, the latest addition to the island. Amara, this is Evanor, my fourthborn brother. He's the one married to Mariel, our Healer."

Amara eyed the blond male who had been reaching for the doorknob when Trevan opened it. He was about as tall as Trevan and just as lean, but with light blond hair and brown eyes instead of copper and green. Despite the difference in their coloring, they shared the same facial shape, oval with firm jaws, high cheeks, slanted eyes, and straight noses. His tunic was cream, his trousers brown, and his boots tan, but otherwise he was dressed much like his brother.

The blond man's voice was also smoother than Trevan's when he spoke, almost melodic. "Greetings, Amara, and welcome to Nightfall."

"I'm going to get her settled in, then find her something to eat," Trev stated. "She washed up on the northern shore with just the clothes on her back, nothing more."

"Ah. I'll see what I can find for her in the way of supplies, then. Kelly set aside a few chests of clothes for Alys to go through, and there should still be a few things left in them, at least until new garments can be made." Giving them a slight bow, he entered the sewing hall.

Amara stared after him. She didn't like the thought of secondhand clothes, though she knew she didn't have much of a choice at the moment, and she wasn't going to complain. What puzzled her was the other man's motivation for such a thing. "Why would he go looking for clothing for me?"

"Because he's the Lord Chamberlain, and it's his job to make sure we're all clothed and fed. He'll also put you on the chore roster, to ensure you earn your keep," Trevan added.

"I . . . was thinking I could do that by being a hunter, or a shepherdess," Amara offered, wondering how the latter would be possible on an island with so few people. The former, maybe, but with only fourteen people, one of them a boy, she doubted they had need for a flock.

"We already have two hunters in the family, my secondborn brother, Wolfer, and myself," her escort informed her, guiding her down the hall. "You're welcome to add your efforts, of course, but we have to be careful to not over-hunt the deer herds . . . uh, that is . . . You said something about a Clan Deer? Is there some significance to that, such as being forbidden to hunt or eat venison?"

Amara shook her head. "I come from the Shifterai, where most of the men are natural shapechangers, and a few of the women, such as myself. We live in wandering tribes with our herds most of the year. Each tribe is called a Family, and each Family is associated with a larger group, called a Clan. Clan Deer has Families such as Whitetail, Blacktail, Caribou, Antelope, and so forth. Clan Cat has Families Tiger, Lion, Puma . . .

"Within each Family, the shapeshifters often first learn to take on the shape of whatever their Family animal is, or a related animal from within their Clan. If they take up another shape, they're often welcome to move to that Family once they're accounted an adult. It's considered a propitious sign of allegiance and a way to freshen the bloodlines," Amara explained. "We're not forbidden to eat any particular meat, just that we tend to avoid the flesh of those animals that don't taste very good."

"That's a sensible arrangement for your communities and a sensible approach to your diet," he observed, gesturing for her to take the right-hand fork in the hall. "I'm not very familiar with a nomadic lifestyle, though. I hope you'll feel comfortable staying in the palace, instead of . . . whatever. Tents, right?"

"*Geomes.* They're a special kind of tent, found only on the Shifting and the Centa Plains."

"Let's go down one floor; there are some nicer rooms on the second level in this wing," Trevan told her. "It won't be a *geome*, but it should be comfortable. And you'll have your choice of suites, too, given the ratio of rooms to occupants."

"Trevan . . . *why* are there so few of you?" Amara asked him, following him into another spiraling stairwell. It was a little disorienting, because it was painted to look like a running stream, only the stream didn't move quite as fast as one would expect. "This is a huge building, in good repair, clearly infused with magic given all these wall illusions. There are signs of old ruins out in the forests we flew over, enough for hundreds, even thousands to have once dwelled here, yet you said there are only fourteen of you on the whole of this island. Why?"

"When Aiar Shattered, the original inhabitants were trying to close down the Portal on Nightfall. They didn't quite get to it in time. The local ruler, a duchess and a Seer, managed to channel the energies into a Curse that prevented large numbers of people from living here, forcing everyone to relocate to the mainland. Since then, the island has been a convenient place for Katan to exile people to," he admitted.

That earned him a dubious look as they emerged on the next floor down. The walls here had a pastoral scene of rabbits grazing in a meadow. Amara was beginning to get used to walls with pictures that moved, though it made her all the more determined to protect her sister from any of the local, and clearly powerful, mages. "So how did *you* come to be here, or dare I ask?"

"The other Curse had a hand in it, the one Kelly mentioned. It was ascertained that if my eldest brother fell in love, some unspecified Disaster was supposed to happen, and the Empire thought it would happen to *them*," he emphasized, "so they exiled all eight of us to the island as soon as they had enough clues to pinpoint us as the brothers mentioned in the Song of the Sons of Destiny."

"I thought you said your putative queen married your eldest brother. Wouldn't that have precipitated the Disaster?" she asked next, then wrinkled her nose at a thought. "Or was theirs an arranged marriage?"

"It did, but the Curse talked about Katan failing to aid us . . . which they did, by refusing to help us when a bunch of misogynists from another continent came to the island thinking they could claim it for their own. The Council of Katan had interpreted it to mean that some huge Disaster would *prevent* them from helping us . . . but they willfully refused when we asked for help."

"Wait; I'm confused," Amara stated, shaking her head. "There's a Seer's Curse about you and your brothers that exiled you here, where the island was Cursed by another Seer, so that very few people could live here anymore. Yet you claim you're an incipient kingdom . . . but you don't have a Patron Deity, and you don't even have a full score of people living here, yet. *How* can you be an incipient kingdom with only fourteen citizens?"

"Numbers don't matter; the Bell was Rung, and the Gods answered it," he dismissed lightly. "That's all that was needed to sever the last of our ties to Katan. Besides, the Curse of Nightfall and the

Curse of the Sons seem to be dovetailing, and both seem to be coming true. As soon as the island one lifts, we can settle as many people as we like," Trevan offered, opening a door for her. "Here, try this set of rooms."

She had to pass close to him to step inside. In doing so, Amara inhaled, involuntarily catching his scent. Warm, male, slightly spicy, he smelled remarkably good. Like a fur blanket, though it was a poor comparison. She breathed in again, but having stepped into the chamber, it was too late to get another whiff.

The room distracted her, thankfully. It was furnished in the typical outlander style for a sitting room, with chairs and waist-high tables, a padded window bench, paintings on the walls, a hearth off to her right, and a door to one side of it. It took her a few moments to realize the ornamental wrought-iron sculptures with their lumps of translucent white balls were actually lightglobes in artistically designed stands.

Lightglobes. How civilized. Though my people don't waste iron by fashioning stands for them. It's too expensive, too heavy, and too difficult to transport in the nomadic seasons, and too simple to just keep hanging the same net-bags in both our tents and our winter homes. At least when darkness came, she wouldn't have to beg for a way to light a fire for illumination. She thought one of the metal boxes on the mantel over the fireplace might be a tinderbox. She couldn't be sure without investigating, but there were plenty of other things still waiting to be examined in the chamber.

Returning her attention to the walls, Amara thought the way the portraits, landscapes, and the like hung on the painted surface was a bit redundant, like hanging a painting in front of a tapestry. Still, she couldn't entirely dislike the effect, for they hung in a butterfly-filled sky, surreal, yet lovely. It did make her curious enough to finally ask him about it.

"Trevan, why are the walls like that? Wouldn't that be an awful waste of magic?" Amara asked, glancing back at him, only to find him right behind her.

He didn't come any closer, but he did quirk his mouth up on one side. "We had some enemies, up until recent months. We *were* in exile, after all, simply for having been born. One of those enemies had a scrying mirror locked on this place and used it to send magical beasts our way, in the attempt to kill us from afar. When Kelly came along . . . well, we'd been living as bachelors for three years, and she made us clean up the place. That changed the look of things to the point where it was awkward for our enemy to send his beasts, and that's when Morganen—he's the youngest of us—realized that if we painted the walls with constantly changing images, no one would be able to get a scrying lock on the inside of the palace ever again."

"Ah. And the way this whole place looked like just another patch of forest, until we were flying over it?" she asked him, circling one hand. "Was that done to discourage scrying, too?"

He flashed her a grin. "You catch on quickly. That's very good."

"It is?" Amara inquired warily.

The redheaded mage had the temerity to wink at her. "I *like* smart women. Why don't you look at the rest of the suite? This one has a changing room, if I remember right. And of course its own refreshing room, replete with bathing tub. We don't have any rainshower pipes, though I've been studying the sketches Mariel made for me and am working on coming up with something appropriate, since she and Serina like that sort of bathing."

"Rainshower pipes?" Amara asked over her shoulder as she moved to the next door and opened it. "More magic?"

"Not really. Well, the water temperature is controlled by an enchanted lever, but that's about it. A rainshower is just a perforated pipe that crosses overhead, creating a sort of miniature waterfall on demand. Dominor—he's my thirdborn brother—says it's more efficient than a bathtub, if all you want to do is get clean." Trevan shrugged, following her into the bedchamber. "Myself, I like taking a long, hot soak, but then I *am* a bit of a hedonist."

Amara took in the way the walls showed rolling hills filled with yellow and pink flowers on rich green grass. It sort of went with the age-yellowed curtains hanging from the posts of the bed. There was a fireplace in one wall, positioned so that it was back-to-back with the one in the front room, but it was unlit, leaving the room a little chilly. And a little dusty, she noticed, touching the top of a bureau of drawers only to leave a darker streak when she removed her fingers.

Trevan cleared his throat. "Sorry about that. It's been a while since we cleaned in here—*spessula dormundic!*"

The patina of dust swirled off the dresser, the nearby vanity table, the cheval-mirror in the corner, and the floor. The bed curtains fluttered and flapped, and the bedding *flumped*, plumping up visibly. So did the cushions lining the window bench in this room as well. In just a few moments, all the visible dirt and grime had gathered in the center of the room, compacting into a coin-sized ball that hovered in midair. Crossing to one of the square-paned windows, Trevan pushed it open. A flick of his hand caused the ball to fly out the window, vanishing somewhere into the garden below.

"There, nice and clean. That room should be the dressing room, and that one the refreshing room."

She wasn't comfortable with him being in a bedchamber with her, but it wasn't *her* bedchamber, yet, and he was merely showing her a possible choice for her quarters. Amara dutifully opened each door; the refreshing room was on the outer wall, with frosted-glass windows to protect the bather's privacy, since the stone-carved tub was placed below them. There was a water-flushed privy, another stone-carved sink set in a wooden counter, and nothing else.

No linens, no soaps, nothing. The dressing room was dark, but seemed to be filled with empty shelves along its edges.

Trevan reached past her shoulder, rapping on a white glass ball almost the size of her head hanging in one of the holders. Instantly it lit, startling her. His hand touched her shoulder, accompanied by a reassuring smile.

"They're just lightglobes. However hard you strike them once, that's how bright they'll be." He demonstrated with a harder rap of his knuckles on the glossy surface, and the sphere brightened correspondingly. He rapped it twice, quickly, and the glow winked out. "And a double-knock shuts them off. Simple, yes?"

"Your people use a lot of magic," she muttered, uncomfortable with the idea for two reasons. For one, her people didn't use a lot of magic; they *were* magic. At least most of the men were. A few of the women were blessed with mage-style magic, but they invariably became priestesses to ensure that all the Families and Clans benefited from their powers. For the other . . . if these people used a lot of magic, they *needed* a lot of magic, and that would put her twin in danger. "Unless these were left over from before the island was abandoned?"

"Some of them were, but some of them were created by my second-youngest brother, Koranen. He's a Pyromancer, and lightglobes are one of his more common creations. Especially now that we have a reliable, cheap supply of the special oil that fuels the illumination spell. That reminds me—what do you do?"

"I beg your pardon?" Amara asked him, confused.

"Well, you said you could be a hunter, but is there anything else you're trained to do?" he asked her. "Alys is our Mistress of the Herds—she's the wife of the second-eldest of us, Wolfer—and Serina, the wife of the third-eldest, Dominor, is our Exchequer. Mariel, wife of the fourth-eldest, Evanor, is our Healer, and of course you know what Kelly's job is. It just seems as if each woman who arrives here not only fulfils Prophecy as the bride of one of us, but also fulfils a particular role in building our own kingdom. So . . . what do you do?"

Taken aback by the question, Amara blinked at him. She had never actually considered what she *did*, just what she *was*. "I . . . It's different, on the Shifting Plains. There are cultural differences that I doubt I could explain."

"Try me," he countered. "But hold that thought; I promised you food, and *my* stomach is feeling a little hollow, right now. Let's go to the kitchen, where we can find something to eat as we talk," he said, catching her hand and tugging her out of the suite. "And then we can find you some bath linens and some softsoaps, and hopefully by then my next-brother will have found you something clean to change into, so that you can enjoy a nice bath. Assuming you like these rooms."

"What, do I stink?" Amara asked, worried about that. "And the rooms are acceptable, thank you."

"You're welcome. And no, you don't stink, but if you washed up on our shore, then you're probably longing for a real bath. I know *I* would be."

"Yes, but you said you were a hedonist who likes long baths, so you're clearly biased," she retorted, earning a grin from him at her teasing.

Amara felt her heart skip in her chest, and wondered uneasily at it. This foreigner wasn't the least bit intimidated by her, unlike the men of the Plains. Of course, he didn't *know* how powerful a shifter she was, or respect the conventions of her people . . . but it was nice to not be stammered at, blushed over, or worse, treated with arrogance. Not arrogance *toward* her, but the sort of arrogance wherein some Shifterai males thought they were good enough for her, simply because they were shapeshifters, too. But this man didn't know who and what she was; he was treating her like a normal maiden, wanting to hold her hand, to talk with her, to spend time in her company. Just because she was there.

It was refreshing, and flattering, and puzzling. And a little unnerving, with all this talk of Prophecies. *As if my presence here were foreordained by the Gods . . .* That thought made her mentally pause, even as she followed him down a stairwell two more floors, into an unpainted, stone-lined, windowless corridor. *Gods, did You actually arrange for this? My sister's situation is clearly by Your confounded will, but being chased off the Plains by greedy mages . . . the storm drove our ship to the south, but it was mage-wrought, trying to slow us down. My sister* chose *this place through her Visions . . . but her powers come from You.*

I'm confused!

Irritated, she let him pull her all the way to a large chamber with a quartet of cooking hearths—one of which was lit and had a bubbling, lidded cauldron hanging over the flames, making the room reek deliciously of beef—a trio of large worktables, and several tall stools. Guiding her to one, he disappeared through an archway, where she heard him opening and closing what sounded like cabinet doors. The copper-haired mage came back after a few moments with a pair of glasses, which he set on the table next to her before ducking back around the corner again.

"If you've been at sea for a long time, I'll not burden your stomach with anything heavy, since you probably didn't have much to eat," he offered from the other room, "but I think a little fruit and . . . ah, there's some of the soft-cheese that Alys made, and a bit of bread. That should do it."

"Actually, I had a lot to eat . . . if, by 'a lot,' you mean way too much raw fish," she added under her breath.

He leaned his head past the corner, peering at her. "What was that?"

"I said, I ate a lot of raw fish."

"I'll try to make sure it's not on the menu for the next few nights." He disappeared again, then came back a few moments later, his hands juggling a plate of cheese and bread, and a bowl of fruit. "You can wash your hands through that archway there," he directed her, nodding as he set his burdens on the table. "That's the scullery. The other one leads to the processing room, and to the stasis-cupboards and cold-cabinets where we store things. Do you cook?"

"I can," Amara admitted, rising and following him into the scullery.

"You make that sound as if you don't do it frequently."

"Well, no, usually others do the cooking. Or they did, back home," she amended, feeling homesick for the richer, more fulfilling life she had led before being forced to run. Once off the Plains, she had been forced to catch over half their meals, since staying at an inn ran the risk of her sister physically bumping into a mage in some crowded village street and being discovered. Arora had cooked more than her share of whatever game her twin had brought into camp, since she wasn't the huntress that Amara was, but Amara had cooked a few of their meals, too.

Trevan distracted her from her thoughts, showing her how to unplug the corks from the taps in the multibasined sinks, and how to adjust the heating lever. Amara played with the temperature a bit, enjoying the warmth, then felt guilty about her sister, stuck in a damp, cold cave behind a waterfall. *If only I could trust these people to not touch her, to leave her alone, to not covet her.*

He held off questioning her until they were wiping their hands on strips of linen, then accompanied her back to the table in the main kitchen. "So, if you had others cooking for you, what did you do with all your free time?"

How to put this in outlander terms, without giving away my own abilities? Amara drank a sip of the juice, finding it sweet and tart.

"Shifterai culture . . . is complicated. Half of it is run by the shapeshifters, since that is what separates us from other lands, but half of it is run by our women."

"By your women? Any particular reason?" he asked her.

"Yes. My ancestresses grew very tired of all the raping and pillaging that occurred in the wake of the Empire's destruction, and threatened to destroy everything if the men didn't settle down and return to civilized behavior."

She snuck a glance at him as she finished, wanting to see his reaction. He looked thoughtful, but not offended. In fact, he nodded slowly, proving he was quick-minded with his next comment.

"So, to be a woman *and* a shapeshifter . . . that gave you a lot of cultural status and political power among your people, didn't it?"

"Yes. I was being trained to be a leader of our people—you have to be at least twenty-five years in age before you can be a Family leader; until then, you learn under a mentor, or a series of mentors. That way, we aren't led by someone young and inexperienced."

"A wise policy," he agreed.

"Do you have a mentorship system for your leaders?" Amara asked, curious. She doubted it, because of the sheer lack of people in this place.

Trevan shook his head quickly, his copper locks sliding over his shoulders as he confirmed her thoughts. "No, there aren't enough of us to bother, yet. Though you could suggest the idea to Kelly; she likes planning for the long term. What did you study in your mentorship? What parts did you enjoy the most?"

Again, Amara had to think, nibbling on a bit of cheese-smeared bread. No one had ever *asked* her these things; everyone in the Family had assumed she wanted what she was doing. She had wanted it, of course, but no one had stopped to ask. She had simply *done* it.

But she had to be careful how she phrased things. Until these people, small in number but rich in magic, proved themselves trustworthy, she couldn't give away too much. "I studied the cycle of life on the Plains. Every four years we roam, and the fifth year, we farm, to grow the foods we cannot forage for during the winter months. The farms are owned by each Clan, and the farming duties are shared out from Family to Family within a Clan—the land itself is farmed once every other year, allowing it to lie fallow in between. There are supervisors who stay on the farms each year, ensuring that each incoming Family will know what to do and when to do it, but by allowing the Families to rotate, it prevents anyone from being forced to do nothing but farm, and it guarantees the food will be shared equally by all, when it comes time to take shelter from the winter storms."

"Why so much fallow time?" Trevan asked her, frowning in confusion. "Katan rotates its crops and rests its fields only once every four years over most of the Empire, and only rests once every three years up in the northlands, where the soil is drier."

"The soil of the Plains was badly damaged by the explosion that destroyed the capital. What used to be some of the most fertile valleys and hills in the old Empire, filled with the estates of the rich, became flattened land dotted with the occasional ruin from among the stouter buildings." Her mouth twisted wryly. "In that regard, I think it isn't that far off from your island, here, only your ruins were swallowed by the forest and time. Ours were knocked down by pure magic."

"How much land was affected?" Trevan asked her. "And what caused the explosion? Katan never heard the full truth of what happened, only that the Empire had Shattered, and most of the land was cast into chaos."

"We're not sure. Most of those who survived came from the estates, not the capital. There were tales of some important visitor from another continent come to petition the Gods at the Convocation, something about a grievous wrong—the usual tales of such things," she dismissed, picking up her cup. "The stories weren't even sure if it was a man or a woman, and some of them even said it was both, though all of them contradictorily agreed it was a single person. Which is impossible, since you cannot be a man and a woman at the same time."

"Actually, there are enchanted potions that can allow one gender to take on the characteristics of the other," Trevan told her. "I even tried it. Twice."

Amara choked on her juice. Rising, he fetched her a scrap of cloth to wipe her face and sat again, smirking. Blowing her nose, she eyed him over the linen. "That wasn't funny."

"Yes, it was. Actually, it was . . . enjoyable," the redheaded mage admitted, still smiling.

"Why?" she demanded, needing to know what could have prompted him to try such a bizarre thing. "The Gods made us who and what we are!"

"Because I wanted to understand women better. I wanted to know how a woman's senses interpreted her world . . . and how she experiences *pleasure*," he confessed softly.

The depth to which his voice dropped on that last word stirred something inside of Amara, a nervous sort of whirling in the pit of her stomach. It wasn't nausea, but it wasn't anything else that she'd ever felt before. Uncomfortable, she moved her hand away as he shifted his to touch it. If her sister were here, she could have asked Arora to read his intentions, to see if he was attempting to court her in some outlander way . . . but that would risk an entirely different set of problems.

In the next moment, he smacked his forehead. "Of course! Why didn't I think of *that* option? No, wait, that wouldn't work. It would involve one of us having to . . . um . . . never mind." Face reddening, he cleared his throat. "I just . . . have been having a problem with my work, and thought I had a solution for a moment, only to realize it wouldn't have been possible anyway. Forgive my ramblings, please."

She wasn't sure that she wanted to be courted by a strange outlander. She was a powerful shapeshifter; it was her duty to breed those talents back into her people, to ensure that they would always be strong enough to keep foreigners out of their lands, that they would always be unique, blessed by Earth and Sky. That was her duty. Of course, it was also her duty to *remain* on the Plains . . . and she hadn't done that. *Thanks to my sister . . . whom the Gods made as she is.*

That was the confusing part. The Gods had made *her*, Amara Fen Ziel, the most powerful shapeshifter her people had yet to discover. Twin to a woman the Gods infused with a wellspring of magic so pure and so powerful, she would be hunted and coveted by mages for the rest of her life. The Gods created Arora in a land of very few mages, where one would think she would be safe—though the few mage-priestesses among their people weren't strong enough to withstand the forces Arora somehow safely cradled within her—but when mages had finally noticed her, lives had been lost. Family lives.

The duty of a princess was to guide and protect her people. She might have been only nineteen at the time, but Amara had chosen to take her sister and flee the Plains, to protect her people. Remove what the mages sought—and she had carefully laid a trail for them to follow, which they thankfully had—and they would not attack the Shifterai. Her people were adept at stealth, not at open conflict. Sometimes they fought, when there was no other way, and it helped that they knew their Plains like no one else; they were bound to them by blood and by Patronage.

Those first mages had been eluded, tricked into the wrong direction, lost and left behind. Others had discovered her sister, and those had to be left behind, too. Some . . . some had needed to be eliminated. Yet more false trails, yet more worrisome nights, fleeing in the dark through unfamiliar lands, fearing the moment when her sister would brush up against the wrong person in some marketplace or on some thoroughfare . . .

Fingers brushed her brow, startling her. Trevan tucked a stray lock of her black hair behind one ear, his green gaze concerned. "You're not happy. What troubles you?"

He was charming, he was kind, he was caring, *he was a mage.* Pulling back, Amara stiffened her posture, setting up a sense of formal distance between them. "Nothing troubles me. Thank you for the food."

"You're welcome. And you are welcome to more of it," he added lightly. "Though supper will be served in just a few more hours, if you can wait. It's not my turn to cook, but I can guarantee fish isn't on the menu. We're having beef tonight. Tell me, why did you leave the Plains, and how did you end up here?"

"I'd rather not," she stated bluntly.

"But how are we to get to know each other, if we do not talk?" Trevan pointed out reasonably.

"Maybe I don't *want* to get to know you!" Amara snapped, rising from her stool so she could back away from him. "*Or* for you to get to know me."

Charming, handsome, even exotic with that reddish gold hair, he was still a mage, and mages could not be trusted. There had been that one blond mage from the river kingdom of Mornai—Yarrin was his name—who had chatted at her while they were traveling southward on that barge. He had seemed charming, until her sister had Looked at him and told her he wasn't nice. That he scared her whenever she Looked at him. No, mages were not to be trusted.

Trevan rose as well, brow furrowing. "Your presence here is my Destiny. I am merely doing what the Gods have asked of me!"

"The Gods, the Gods!" she scorned, slashing her hand between them. "It's always the Gods! Well, the Gods *made* me what I am—and then They had the gall to tear me away from everything I've known, everything I wanted, everything I *should* have become! Forgive me if I am *tired* of being yanked about by Their demands!"

"Then what do you *want*, if it's not the path They have selected for you?" Trevan asked her.

The tone of his voice, while heated, somehow managed to quell some of the anger that had arisen within her. Amara had the feeling he really did want to know, that he was concerned for her—*concerned for a woman he's only just met, because, if I understand his comments right, the Gods arranged for him to think that I came here to be his bride—as if!*

Resentment that had boiled up within her for the last year, and then some, finally spilled up and out of her. "What do I want? What do *I* want . . . I *want* the Gods to stop interfering in my life! I want all the mages to be swept off the face of the planet, because that is the *only* way they'll stop bothering us! I want the Gods to put everything back the way that it was and to leave us alone, because I *want* to be back home among my fellow Shifterai and not stuck on some Gods-forsaken piece of southern property a million miles from home!"

Into the silence following her words walked a tallish, slender woman with hair the color of moonlight, clad in a pink, *chamsa*-like dress. Instead of gathered *breikas*, however, she wore fitted dark pink hose on her legs, scandalously showing their shape. Her eyes, just a little darker in their golden hue than Amara's, flicked back and forth between the two of them, and when she spoke, her voice held the same flawless accents of Aian as Trevan's, though she looked nothing like him.

"If you want to have a crisis of faith, young lady, then you've come to the right place. If you want to have an argument, however, try to do it in a room without any sharp knives. Trevan, are there any of those pickled redfruits left? And did you see where the pot of honey went?"

He wrinkled his nose. "Honey and pickled redfruit? Are you at the craving stage already?"

"Mariel wants the redfruit and a small cask of beer so she can make some sort of snail-repellent for the garden. The honey is for me. Well, actually, it's for Dominor." She flashed both of them a grin, then held out her hand. "I'm Serina, your friendly, absent-minded Arithmancer."

Amara eyed the proffered hand, feeling a headache pinching her brow. "How many mages *are* there in this place?"

"It's easier to count the ones that aren't. Mikor—that's Mariel's son—and Kelly. The rest of us all have magic of some sort," Serina stated, even as Trevan made a quick slashing motion at neck level. It was too late, however. "Some of us are very powerful, too."

Lip curling in outward disgust—heart racing in an almost para-lyzing fear—Amara backed away from both of them. "Madmen . . . a whole island of mages and madmen!"

"Amara?"

Turning, she fled, fear spurring her into remembering which turns they had taken.

"Amara!"

Racing all the way up the stairs, Amara flung open doors at the top, until she flung open one that led to the walkway around the roof. Pounding footsteps spurred her into shedding her clothes and launching herself from the battlements in a single, swift reshape. Trevan shouted something behind her, even as she winged away as fast as she could. She side-slipped instinctively, felt magic puffing against her feathers, exploding in a shower of sparks, but she wasn't injured. Narrowing her shape from hawk to falcon, she raced to-ward the mountains and the tangle of the forest that would allow her to elude any pursuit.

FIVE

❦

G ods!" Trevan swore, slapping the top of the stone crenel between him and the bird flying off to the north. Frustrated,
he raked his hands through his hair, then tensed to leap after her.
Before he could, a voice caught his attention.

"Trevan? What's wrong? What did I say?" Serina asked
him, reaching the doorway onto the parapet. "*Was* it something I
said?"

Turning back to the mathemagician, Trevan flipped his hand in
the direction of the departing bird. "She has this . . . this *fear* of
mages, and she won't tell me why!" Needing something to do, he
stooped and picked up her fallen clothes, draping them over his
arm. "And now she's run off, and probably won't be reasonable
about anything. Gods—I'm *supposed* to find a woman to fall in love
and be happy with, not one to frighten off!"

Craning her head, Serina looked all around her, stepping out of the doorway. "Um . . . am I missing something? If those are her clothes, then where is *she*?"

"She's a shapechanger—a natural one, as opposed to a spell-caster. She flew off as a bird." He gestured again to the north, and Serina put her hands on her hips.

"Then why aren't you *chasing* after her? Isn't that your verse in the Song of Destiny? '*Before you in the woods she flees* . . .'? Shouldn't you go '*Catch her quick and hold her fast*,' before she gets completely out of sight?" his sister-in-law asked tartly.

"I tagged her with a tracking spell when I realized she had flown off," he dismissed, frustration giving way to disappointment and a touch of disgust. "If I chase her right now . . . she could injure her-self in her panic, trying to flee from me. Besides, she doesn't *want* me. I'm a *mage*. It's very difficult to court a girl if she loathes who and what you are!"

Serina flicked her hand at the mountains. "Trevan, *go chase her*. Catch her, hold her fast, and don't let go until she tells you *why* she fled. Remember all the communication problems Dominor and I had? Don't let that stop *you* from finding your happiness. Here—let me get you a Truth Stone, first. It's obvious she's not going to tell you the truth of her own volition. If nothing else, you can use it to show her that *you* are telling the truth when you say you don't mean her any harm. Wait here."

Ducking back inside, she left him alone. The redheaded mage squinted at the mountains, but didn't bother to evoke his tracing spell yet. Pacing, he waited for Serina to return, wondering why the Gods were laughing at him. *First I don't believe she's ever going to show; then she does. But when she does, she hates mages and fears me! I long for the kind of close intimacies my older brothers get to share, but she lied to me about there being someone else in the forest with her . . . and didn't she say "us" just now, when she was talking about how she wanted all the mages in the world to go away and leave "us" alone?*

Tipping his head back, he glared at the sky. *I don't appreciate being laughed at, You know!* Closing his eyes, he reached for a sense of patience. *Sweet Kata, I know You aren't our Patron anymore . . . but can You nudge Amara just a little, calm her down and let her* listen *to me, get her to believe* me when I say I don't want to hurt her? You're the Goddess of Lovers! Just because we've broken away is no reason not to honor all that You stand for . . . but how can *I be a lover, if the woman You brought to me fears me?*

Footsteps alerted him to Serina's return, but when he opened his eyes, it wasn't the willowy mathemagician. Trevan gave his youngest brother a chiding look. "Hello, Morg. You knew this morning she was already on the island, didn't you?"

Morganen shrugged blithely. "Of course. I'm the Prophesied matchmaker of the family. How do you think they arrived on the island without setting off any of our detection wards?"

Trevan drew in a breath to berate his youngest, light brown-haired sibling for being so careless, then let it go. Morg wouldn't have been careless, if he had been watching closely enough to see the . . . He glanced sharply at his sibling. "*They?* Then there *were* two of them that came ashore together?"

Morg cleared his throat behind an upraised hand. "Yes, well, I couldn't exactly announce *that* at the breakfast table, either, and we all know why. Anyway, that situation is resolving itself, or it will. You need to focus on your own. I also know that you'll have a very difficult time catching and conversing with your Destined bride, Trev, if you try to use the standard containment spells."

"You really think I'll need to cage her?" Trevan asked skeptically, arching a coppery brow. "I'll remind you the Prophecy says catch her and *hold* her. I would presume that means in my arms. She doesn't like mages, Brother; putting her in a cage would only scare her further."

"I think you won't be able to hold her in any shape or form where she couldn't shapeshift into something that could claw, bite, scratch, or sting you. And a regular cage . . . well, to make the openings small enough that she couldn't shapeshift her way free, you'd almost have to leave her without any way of breathing.

"So when I realized just how skillful she was, I went through my books and found this spell for you," Morg told him, offering Trevan a folded bit of paper that he had been holding in his other hand. "It will force her into her true shape, and hold her in it until you speak the release-word. One piece of advice, though: *Don't* use it while she's in midair, or perched on a tree or something. The notations on the spell says it's quick to take effect, so you might want to wait until she's on solid ground, first, rather than, oh, thirty feet above the trees."

Flicking his fingers off his forehead in a salute, the slender mage strolled away, as if his main purpose for climbing to the top of the palace was to enjoy the view, not to meddle in his brother's problems.

Trevan gave in to irritated temptation and stuck out his tongue at Morganen's retreating back, then turned over the paper in his hand. Aside from being annoyingly meddlesome, Morg was a knowledgeable mage, more learned than his mere twenty-three years would suggest. Unfolding the sheet, Trevan studied the spell, marked carefully in Katani lettering with stress lines and pronunciation accents. His brother had included a handwritten description of the visualization a mage was to hold in mind while casting it, and—thorough to the last—had included a motion-enchanted diagram of the dual hand movements that would aid as a mnemonic as well as a shaping agent for the magic.

One set of movements for confining a female into her true form, the other for confining a male. How entertaining. Especially those *hand movements,* Trevan thought, amused out of his irritation. *Who comes up with some of these mnemonics, anyway?*

There wasn't a notation on the paper giving the identity of the spell's creator, or even what grimoire it came from. Giving it up as a lost cause, for the universe was filled with too many mysteries for a mere mage to comprehend, Trevan waited patiently for Serina to return. He spent his time tucking Amara's clothes around his belt as he had done earlier in the day, then paced some more. She reappeared after several more minutes, looking a little greenish about the mouth.

"Sorry . . . I can't wait until I get past this stage." Handing him the flat white disc, she sagged against the crenellations beside him. "Why the Gods invented morning sickness and then made it midday and evening sickness, too, I'll never know. Go on, fly off and find your ladylove. Catch her, hold her, and be very, very kind to her, if you ever do *this* to her."

She patted her stomach in emphasis, which, at the angle she was leaning, was beginning to show the growing curve of her pregnancy.

"Since when am I *not* kind to a lady in distress?" he quipped archly, tucking the Truth Stone into the pouch hung on his belt. He had to shift some of Amara's clothes out of the way to get to it, of course. Nodding politely, Trevan muttered the tracking spell trigger and launched himself from the rooftop, his hawkish eyes firmly fixed on the glittering trail that now led to the north.

Amara huddled in the hollow crook of a lightning-forked tree and struggled to still her fear-induced panting. She didn't know if squirrels were common in this corner of the world, but it wasn't a bird form, which her pursuer would undoubtedly be looking for, yet it was agile enough to hide among the trees. She hadn't actually flown very far; in fact, when she had dipped into the forest canopy, she had reversed direction as soon as she had ascertained that she wasn't being followed. Hopefully, if he pursued her, the mage Trevan would think she had flown straight back to the raft on the far north shore, her entry point to this land.

That would only lead them to Arora, and that, I cannot do . . . Gods, Gods, why did you lead us to this land? Father Sky, Mother Earth, is there no place on this world that is safe *for us?*

Crouching near the edge of the forest, just within sight of the wall surrounding it—which didn't look like a wall at all on this side, but instead a section of cliff wall bordering just on the too-smooth-to-be-scaled side of rugged—she shook her furred head at the insanity of her life. *A year and a couple turns of Brother Moon ago, not even a full turn of Sister Moon, I was riding the Plains, wondering if I should have stayed in the City instead, like a supervisor at a farm.*

I was carefree and happy, apprenticed to Aitava herself, being groomed to be the next Queen of the Shifterai as soon as I should grow old and wise enough . . . We rode out to the edge of the Plains to conduct some trade, and that mage-woman, the Amazai, brushed up against my sister.

That started it all . . . her claim that my sister had to go with her to "resurrect the Empire." It wasn't possible for squirrels to snort, though Amara tried. *Resurrect the Empire, my fuzzy fat tail. What the Gods destroyed, mere mortal man cannot resurrect! Everyone on the Plains knows that. And then the kidnapping attempt, when Arora wouldn't go with her . . . that nearly cost us a few lives, fending it off.*

Then, once we were back in the Plains, that raid on the Family by that group of bandits, augmented by magic. If Belon Shai Soun hadn't overheard the bandits talking about "sparing any girls with light brown hair" and taking them to "the southlander" during the battle, we would never have known why they attacked. They paid for it dearly—more of them died than us—but some of us died.

Gods! Why do you torment us so? she demanded, squinting up at the sky. *You made my sister the way that she is—why?* Why?

The words of that strange, pale-haired mage woman echoed back to her. *If you want to have a crisis of faith . . . if you want to have a crisis of faith . . .* Amara was undeniably suffering one! It made no sense, gifting a woman in a land of no traditional magic with the power of a thousand mages, yet that was what the Gods in Their insane version of wisdom had done.

About the only wise thing They did was make me strong and smart enough to keep my sister safe. But I can't keep her safe—Amara froze as she spotted a golden-hued raptor winging its way northward over the compound wall. She craned her head, following it as it flew northward, then relaxed once the trees obscured it from view. *I can't keep her safe if You keep directing us to lands where mages reside! Powerful mages, as that woman said.*

Wearied even further than she had felt just that morning—had it only been a morning ago?—Amara closed her eyes and rested her furry gray skull against the bole of the tree. *At least Arora will be safe, hidden as she is, until I can return to her at night. I can fly as an owl or a bat . . . no, not a bat; the weather is too cold at night to risk it, right now. I should*—

The tree shook, snapping her head up and her eyes wide, heart pounding with fear. Fingers manacled her shapechanged body, startling a squeak from her. A twist inside her furry skin allowed her to catch sight of reddish gold hair, leaf green eyes, and a triumphant smile. "Got you!"

Twisting farther in his grip, she did what her frightened instincts demanded she do: Bending her lithe little body down, Amara bit him on the knuckle, as hard as she could.

Trevan almost dropped her. Hissing in pain—it hurt too much to even cry out—he found the grip of his other hand slipping, torn as he was between the effort of not letting go of her and not tightening so much that he hurt the glitter-covered beast trying to sever his forefinger. Thankfully, the bough beneath his left foot became the bough beneath his buttocks, albeit with a jarring *thump*. A slithering shift of his weight, and he dropped the last eleven or so feet to the forest floor, cushioning the fall with his knees.

Amara released his knuckle, ready to bite him again. She squeaked in the next moment, finding herself flung into a pile of aging leaves at the base of another tree. Words thundered at her as she shook her head and righted her body, preparing to shift shape and charge him in the form of a great bear. Her body bulged . . . but fumbled awkwardly onto hands and knees, not raced forward on four paws.

Naked hands and knees. Gasping, she tried to shift shape again . . . and could not. Not even a hint of fur could cloak her naked hide, leaving her shivering in fear at the feet of her redheaded tormentor.

Grimacing, Trevan eyed his bloodied finger. He flexed it warily, and more blood streamed from the wound, but it functioned well enough despite the pain. *"Sukra medis esthanor,"* he muttered, using a common Katani skin-healing charm meant to seal and soothe minor to medium lacerations. *"Coajis epi demisor."*

Checking the wound to make sure it was healing, he turned his attention to his kneeling quarry . . . and blinked. Gone were her long black locks and golden eyes. Her hair was still long, waist-length as it had been before, but now it was a plain, ordinary shade of light brown. Her eyes were no longer a startling shade of gold, wrapped in black lashes; they were green, fringed in brown.

More than that, while she was still lean and had some reasonably decent curves, they weren't quite as pronounced as before. She was still lovely, but not nearly as exotic as she had been. Trevan stared at her, taken aback by the changes.

This . . . is her true form?

Leaves exploded as she lunged out of the pile he had tossed her furry shapechanged form into, but not in his direction. She bolted perpendicular to him, launching herself to the side, racing deeper into the trees. Rolling his eyes, Trevan loped after her, following the trailing glitter of magic that still clung to her skin, shedding like dust stirred by a wind.

It wasn't easy giving chase when his body admired the view of *her* body scrambling through the undergrowth—she had a very nice backside even in this "true" form of hers—but he didn't want to lose sight of her. She was naked, barefoot, and running through unfamiliar territory. Adjusting himself while on the run wasn't easy, either. Necessary, but not easy; it slowed him down, though his eyes could still follow her by the glittering trail she unwittingly left in her wake.

Panicked by her inability to shift, Amara ran as fast as she could, desperate to get away from him. How he had found her, she didn't know, though probably from some damnable spell. How he had *trapped* her inside a single skin, she didn't know, either; she had never heard of anything other than bluesteel being able to force shapeshifters to stay within their own skin, and that was a secret tightly held by her own people, reserved for punishing Shifterai criminals. It frightened her so much, she barely felt the slap of branches against her naked hide, didn't really feel the sting of rocks and roots underfoot. But he hadn't touched her with any metal, just flung those words at—

"—Aaaaaah!" The gully was unexpected, her fall unstoppable. She grabbed at the passing bushes, scraped her arm against one, her leg against another, bruised her shoulder, and banged her hip tumbling down the slope. She skidded to a stop, one heel digging into the muddy, cold trickle of water occupying the bottom of the ravine. The sharp smell of broken greenery was accompanied by the faint, metallic tang of blood, and her skin felt icy-hot in several places where it had been scratched and scraped raw.

She heard her pursuer shouting her name and felt a new sting, this time in her eyes. Trapped in this single skin, she couldn't even heal herself properly, let alone run. Not that there was a place for her to run *to*, anymore; this island had no cities, no ports, no ships—not even any decent roads to run along, when one was stuck in a two-legged form. She *hated* mages!

Amara shrieked again, startled by the golden hawk that swooped down in front of her. He shifted shape, landing by her knees in a crouch, and she flung the first thing she could get her hand on, a clod of muddy moss. The redheaded mage flinched, then blocked with his arm the broken branch she used to attack him next.

"*Stop* that!" His shout and his glare echoed through the small, steep valley, freezing her in place.

Cold, naked, injured, Amara shivered and blinked at the tears threatening to form. This was the closest she had ever come to feeling helpless, and she did *not* like it. She flinched back when he shifted forward, earning another disgusted look.

"I am *not* going to hurt you! You hurt yourself badly enough as it is," Trevan chided her, holding her in place with a stern stare before shifting forward once more.

"Don't you touch me!" Amara threatened him, glancing around quickly for something else to hit him with. Heart in her throat, she scrabbled for a thicker branch, not the whip-thin thing she had tried before, but he got to it before her, lunging half over her body and clamping it to the forest floor.

That left part of him exposed, and she lifted her knee for an attack. A twist of his hip was all he needed to block the blow to his groin, but the movement caused its own troubles, reminding Amara of the pain in her shin and her hip. Her breath hissed in through her teeth, and she held her leg carefully in place, trying not to whimper.

"*Stop*. It," Trevan enunciated, staring her down. "Lie still. I need to check your injuries. You don't need to make them any worse."

Blood pounding in her ears, the Shifterai woman couldn't be sure she had heard him right. Not his words—whatever translation thing he had claimed to be using, the words came across just fine—but the tone of his voice. He sounded . . . *concerned*. And when he rocked back onto his knees, one hand feathering over her still-raised shin, she heard his breath hiss inward. As if *he* were the one scraped and bleeding, not just her.

"*Cutimundic!*"

She gasped, flinching as magic washed over her skin, tingling it. Her wounds stung, then the pain lessened a little, though it still throbbed. "What . . . ?"

"I cleaned your skin. Try not to squirm in the mud again. And hold still; I need to check for broken or dislocated bones," he told her. "*Examostura!*"

Again, magic washed over her hide. Trevan peered at her body as dispassionately as he could. Nothing glowed, so nothing was fractured or displaced. Her skin was scraped and bleeding in several places, bruises already forming, but that seemed to be it. He wanted to scoop her up and carry her straight to Mariel, to let the professional Healer tend to her injuries, but he was capable of tending them himself. More than that, if he *showed* her he didn't mean to harm her, that he intended to *heal* her, maybe she'd finally lose some of her irrational fear of him.

But first things first. Since none of her joints were dislocated, he carefully placed his fingertips on either side of her knees, and gently pushed her thighs together.

"What are you doing?" she demanded, giving him a glare as she resisted.

"Nothing is dislocated . . . and I am but a man, milady," Trevan stated delicately. She stared at him, so he spoke a little more bluntly. "Unless you have scrapes or scratches on the insides of your thighs that need tending, I really don't need to be looking at that part of your anatomy. It's very distracting."

Her eyes widened, and her knees slammed together. She grunted when that moved her bruised flesh too fast for comfort, but Amara wasn't going to leave anything visible below the navel, whatever the pain. Belatedly, she braced herself on one elbow and covered her breasts with the other arm. He reached toward her chest, and she flinched back. "Don't touch me!"

Trevan stared at her. Pointedly. "Your arm is badly scratched and still bleeding. I have a spell to heal it, but it has to be applied to each wound individually. I'm not the Healer that Mariel is, but I can at least keep you from bleeding too badly to put on your clothes again. If you hadn't noticed, it is rather cold and damp in this ravine."

"Which you *chased* me into!" Amara lifted her chin belligerently.

"Which you *ran* into, of your own volition," he countered and hovered his palm over her scraped skin. "*Sukra medis esthanor . . .*"

Her skin tingled and went numb. Wary, Amara peered at her forearm. The blood visibly ceased trickling, the redness turned pink, and the skin closed. It took several heartbeats, and she was left with shiny pink skin, but it was the kind of shiny pink that existed after a scab had fallen off. Something that would be easily shifted smooth and whole again . . . once she had her ability to shapeshift again. Fear started rising again within her.

"What are you going to do to me?" Amara demanded as he shifted to take care of the raw scrape covering the full length of her shin.

"Heal you, talk with you, and take you back to the palace for supper." Hovering his palm over the wound, he muttered the spell again, pouring more energy into his concentration to heal the much larger, if shallower, wound.

"And then what—bind me in your dungeon? Experiment on me?"

Trevan had heard of such games, played consensually between adults, but was well aware she didn't mean it in that particular way. She still had an unreasonable fear of him, one that would have to be

cured. "Hardly. Though I'm beginning to share your opinion that
the Gods are a little insane. You're as obstinate, paranoid, and
proud as my twin, maybe even crankier, yet They apparently picked
you out for me—you're not at all how I pictured my Destined bride
would be."

Strangely enough, that stung at her pride. Amara didn't want to
be "chosen by the Gods," or told whom to marry. It was the maid-
en's *choice*, of her own free will, as to whom she picked to wed. But
being told she wasn't good enough, even if it was for some foreign
mage? "What do you mean by that?"

"Someone sweet tempered and not the least bit afraid of me. Roll
over; I want to check your back," he directed her.

"I'm not afraid of you!" Amara retorted, though she didn't budge.
She didn't trust him enough to put herself into an even more vul-
nerable position than she already was.

"Then prove it and roll over. If you're worried about the mud,
I'll cast the Skin Cleaning spell again when we're through."

"Just because I'm not afraid of you doesn't mean I automatically
trust you," she stated as firmly as she could, glaring at him.

Giving up on healing her other major scrapes for the moment,
Trevan dug the marble disc out of his pouch, shifting her clothes
aside. Holding it up, he displayed it to her, showing her both of its
clean, white, slightly curved sides. "This is a Truth Stone. In case
you've never heard of one before—though I understand they're found
in many kingdoms around the world, given how useful they are—it is
an Artifact enchanted to display verbally expressed lies. If I hold this
and tell a lie, it will show up as a dark blemish as soon as I lift away my
fingers, lasting for a few moments before it turns white again."

Twisting it, he showed her the clean, white sides, then gripped it
again.

"My name is Kelly, and I am the Queen of Nightfall." Shifting the
stone, he showed her the black imprints of his fingers and palm. They

dotted the surface for a handful of heartbeats, as surely if his hand had been dipped in black ink; then the marks faded. Gripping it, he stated, "My name is Trevan, and I am *not* the Queen of Nightfall."

Unblemished white showed when he displayed it to her once more.

"A lie and a truth, both of which you know are verifiable from your own experience." Giving her a pointed look, he lifted the stone between them. "As soon as your injuries are tended to, and you are reasonably cleaned and decently dressed once again, you and I are going to have a discussion using this Stone. You are going to tell me *why* you fear me—as absurd as I find the very idea to be—and you are going to be *truthful* about it. More than that, *I* will be truthful as well. Whatever you want to ask of me, I will answer.

"Maybe *then* you'll admit I'm not like whatever bastards-by-inclination you've encountered in the past, to instill such a fear of mages in you," Trevan told her. "Now, turn over so I can check your backside for injuries in need of healing."

Displaying the unblemished Stone, he gave her a pointed look until she grudgingly complied.

"Thank you."

"I still don't trust you," she muttered, trying to keep her knees together without smearing her front side with dirt as she rolled over on the muddy, mossy slope.

"I am eminently trustworthy."

He showed her the stone, holding it past her shoulder . . . displaying a surface that was stained with a smoky gray imprint of his hand. Amara eyed it askance. "It's gray. You expect me to trust you when it's gray?"

"Ah. Right. I suppose I do need to qualify that, as I *will* lie to my enemies. But I swear I am and will be trustworthy where you are concerned." Trevan redisplayed the stone, relieved to see it was pure white this time.

Amara wasn't ignorant of Truth Stones; her people couldn't manufacture them, true, but most Families had taken the trouble to purchase the expensive Artifacts from outlanders, including Family Whitetail. Trevan of Nightfall honestly believed he would be trustworthy around her . . . but she knew the weakness of the Stones. It was what he believed right *now*. If he learned of her sister's existence, that trustworthiness would change. The only ones who hadn't coveted Arora's power for their own use had been the priestesses back home, and most of that was because they couldn't even begin to touch it, let alone tap it.

The other part of it lay in her own formidable protective abilities . . . when she wasn't trapped in just one skin. Feeling him heal a scrape on the back of her thigh, Amara waited until he was done chanting, then asked tartly, "And does being 'trustworthy' include releasing me from this spell you've used to cage me?"

"I would consider it . . . except I think you'd rather flee than talk with me. Correction, talk *honestly* with me. And we *will* be honest with each other. There. That's the worst of it. Stand up so I can clean off the dirt again—knees together!" Trevan nearly squeaked the command, as she reared up on hands and knees in front of him. His manhood ached, blood pooling far too rapidly in his loins, to the point of making his head ache with dizziness. "Don't put *that* in my face!"

"What?" Amara craned her head over her shoulder—and turned bright red when she realized exactly where his face was located in relation to her body. "Oh! Oh, Gods!"

Scrambling upright, she faced him, then covered her breasts and groin. Not that he could see her, thankfully; as she stood there in awkward embarrassment, the redheaded mage, face buried in his palms, had slumped to the ground. He rolled onto his back, groaning under his breath as if being tortured. There was no mistaking why, either; the straining cloth below his belt spoke volumes as to his exact reaction to being presented with a faceful of . . . that.

Muscles tight, heart pounding in his chest, Trevan fought his body's response to that view of her femininity. *Picture something disgusting . . . mucking out the manure from the dairy stalls by hand . . .* bare *hand, wrist deep in slimy, mushy . . . ugh.* That *did it.* It helped that he was lying uncomfortably on one of her boots, still dangling from his belt and trapped under his hip and thigh. Feeling his lust finally recede, Trevan carefully kept his eyes covered, just in case another peek at her ruined his mental imagery. He did free his mouth, though.

"For the love of Sweet Kata, never, *ever* do that to me again. Unless you absolutely mean it," Trevan added, prompted by his inner honesty.

Amara stared at him for a moment, absorbing his words, then stooped and scooped up the fallen Truth Stone. Squatting—knees carefully together and angled to one side, away from him—she pressed the marble against the fingers covering Trevan's face and daringly demanded, "Are you planning on raping me at any point?"

"Gods, no! That's disgusting!" Trevan lowered his hands and glared at her as soon as she peeled the Stone away, peering at the unblemished side that had touched him. Reaching up, he caught the disc in his hand, half covering her own. "*Nor* do I intend to drug you, enchant you, or in any way coerce you, magically or mundanely, into making love with me against your free will! Any so-called man, mage, or otherwise, who tries something like *that* should be castrated!"

White marble met her gaze when he pushed the Truth Stone at her, letting her see the truth of his words. She was leaning over, crouched next to him, and that made her breasts hang enticingly, just the way he liked breasts to hang when suckling on them while lying underneath . . . *think about dung, think about dung . . . slimy, wormy dung . . .* Trevan shuddered and averted his gaze, pushing to his feet.

A double-cast of his favorite cleaning spell scoured their bodies.

It was less harsh than most cleaning charms, though repeated use rubbed the skin raw and wore out clothing that much faster. He definitely preferred bathing, but there were times when bathtubs just weren't available, and he doubted she would want to don her only outfit while muddy. Pulling her clothes out of his belt, he offered them to her, taking back the Truth Stone in exchange and returning it to his pouch.

"Don't bother running away," he warned her, turning around so that she could get dressed behind his back. "I'll just come after you again, and you might end up breaking a bone, or running into something with inch-long thorns, next time."

While she dressed, Amara contemplated grabbing a branch and knocking him on the head with it, then running while he was unconscious . . . but he *had* showed concern for her well-being, healed her wounds, and made it very clear he wasn't going to attack her. Even when provoked, he hadn't attacked her, just given chase. *She* had tried to hit him with a branch before, but that was all. Guilt pricked at her conscience. *So far*, he was proving remarkably nice, even tolerable to be around.

Amara couldn't quite let go of her wariness or her fear, but . . . *I'll give him a chance*, the shapeshifter decided. *I'll skirt around the topic. I can ask what-if questions while he's holding the Stone, and pretend that Arora is actually some fancy, power-granting Artifact, and see what color the marble is when he gives me his answers.*

After all, her sister *had* claimed that her powers said this was the perfect place for them to be. Arora had never been wrong before. At least, not completely. Sometimes in the past there had been a hidden catch, though her twin had later said something about learning how to be more careful in how she phrased her inner inquiries.

"I'm dressed," she told him, though she still had her socks and boots left to don. She didn't want to, at least not until the mud between her chilled toes had dried and could be brushed off, though she did long for the warmth of footwear.

Trevan faced her again, peered around them, then pointed at a fallen tree spanning the stream at an angle and a bit of the bank to either side. "Let's sit over there. We can be comfortable while we get to the bottom of your problem with 'all' mages."

Touching her elbow, he helped her over to the log. He had cleaned her body and healed some of the worst scratches caused by her flight through the forest, but hadn't handed over her boots. As soon as she sat down on the fallen tree trunk, he crouched and cleaned her feet one last time with a spell. Only then did Trev offer her the socks still tucked into his belt. Sitting next to her, he passed over her boots as well, then pulled out the marble disc, pushed it into her hands as soon as she was shod, and began the interrogation.

"Alright. You have a definite problem with mages in general. Let's start with that. What have mages ever done to you, personally?"

Amara looked between the Stone and him and gave him the truth. "They attacked my Family, attempted to kidnap some of my kin, and some even wanted to cage me for cruel experiments. And before you say these were isolated incidents, I have been on the run from *mages* for more than a year now. More than a dozen mages, I think, though I didn't always stop to ask names or count noses." Pushing the unblemished disc at him, she asked, "If you found out I had a way of giving you access to a vast quantity of power, what would you do about it?"

Trevan blinked at the blunt question. "Is this why you were on the run?"

"Just answer the question!" Amara snapped, nervous.

SIX

~·❦·~

He didn't answer it immediately, though he didn't relinquish the Truth Stone. Giving her question the consideration it was due, Trevan mulled through his answer silently for a moment, then replied. "Well . . . if I had a very specific need for it, I might ask politely if I could use it . . . but otherwise, I'd have no need for it. I have enough magic of my own to do most everything I need to do, and what I don't have, I can always borrow from my brothers. We always help each other, whenever we have a bit of energy to spare."

Dropping the Stone into her hand, he let her examine it, knowing she would find no blemishes, then asked the next question.

"Did those mages hunt you down because they wanted to steal this . . . putative source of power from you?"

She tensed a little at the question, but he had phrased it in a way that Amara *could* answer truthfully. If he'd said "Artifact," it would have been more difficult to be honest. "Let's just say I know where a great source of magical power is hidden . . . but that I am *not* going to tell you where it is. What about your brothers?" she demanded, pushing the white disc into his hand again. "Would any of them want to use that source of power?"

"Again, *if* they ever had a great need for it, I'm certain they'd ask politely . . . but my brothers *wouldn't* steal. Nor would my sisters-in-law," he added as she opened her mouth. From the furrow that briefly appeared on her brow, then vanished, he had guessed her next question correctly. "Amara, to be frank, we don't *need* outside sources of magic. Morganen, Rydan, and Dominor are among the most powerful mages in the whole of the Katani Empire. Serina has admitted that she was considered one of the most powerful mages in the Natallian Empire, which lies across the Eastern Ocean from here, and she's close to Dominor in power—she's not quite as powerful as he is, but she was a Guardian of a Fountain, that's how powerful she was. And Rydan *is* a Guardian.

"If any of us need magic, we need only browbeat my twin into sharing the energies he guards," he admitted wryly, touching the Stone. "And I'd do it preferably by asking Kelly to ask him. *She* has zero magic, yet she has a way of getting my twin to cooperate, even when I can't coax it out of him. Or rather, she has no magic that *we* understand, since the way he heeds her is rather magical to *me*."

Glancing between the unblemished marble and his amused expression, Amara had to clarify a point of confusion. "What exactly is a 'Fountain'?"

"It's . . . a natural wellspring of magic, a source of energy located in a special place, usually somewhere carefully hidden, and it is so powerful that only the strongest mages can risk tapping into it—at least a hundred times stronger than the average mage," he explained. "All Fountains have Guardians, special, strong, good-by-nature mages, who are carefully tested and selected to guard them, because that much energy in the wrong hands could be devastating.

"In fact, that much energy misused *accidentally* is how Serina and Dominor met. It's a long and convoluted story," Trevan dismissed, "but suffice to say, Serina's job was to correct the problem, and she coerced Dominor into helping her correct it. The Fountain in question is over in Natallia, not the one here, of course. She passed on the Guardianship to someone else, in order to come here and live with Dominor in the interim, but when it's time to finish correcting the problem, the two of them will return there and fix it. Of course, I have to point out that *their* courtship was filled with misunderstandings, mainly because the two of them didn't communicate properly."

Amara gave the redheaded mage a sidelong look, part amusement, part disdain. "And who said *we* were in a courtship, the Gods? You've heard my opinion of *that*."

"If there's one thing I've learned, watching my brothers fall in love one after another, you cannot avoid Prophecy," Trevan told her. At the skeptical arch of her light brown brow, he appeased her. "Look, I'm not saying either of us is in love with the other. I don't know you well enough, and you don't know me. But if your fear of mages stems from the greed for power that you've observed in others, I assure you, I don't suffer from that greed. I have all the power I need right here. I don't need any magical Artifact—and I, personally, have never needed my brother's Fountain.

"Frankly, he didn't tell any of us he was the Guardian of a Fountain, until Dominor's situation forced his little secret out into the open back in mid-autumn—and I'm his twin!" Trevan let some of his indignation show in his voice, though he gave it a humorous twist to let her know it wasn't because he coveted the Fountain's power. "You'd think he would have at least told *me*, but he didn't. So we've never been able to rely upon it, and have never *needed* to rely upon it. If we don't need his Fountain—and he's our own flesh and blood—why would we need a source of power found in the hands of outlanders?"

Amara wasn't thinking about that. She acknowledged the rarity of him having a twin, in echo to her own status, but she was think-ing about what he had said. "So these Fountains . . . are in a single location? They never move?"

"Serina's the expert in the family—or at least she's more talka-tive about it than Rydan is—but that's how it goes, as far as I under-stand. I'd show you ours to prove we have plenty of power, but . . . well, I haven't even seen it myself, though I've benefited from its ef-fects," Trevan admitted wryly, wrinkling his nose.

At her curious look, he lifted his arm, pushing up his sleeve. He displayed the gold and silver bracelet fitted onto his wrist, bearing what looked like a large, oval, creamy-white moonstone cabochon on the top. It was pretty, but Amara had seen far fancier jewelry in her travels.

"This is a cryslet; they're very much like a scrying mirror, only they're different from the usual sort. Each of us wears one—which is another long story—but basically we use them to communicate with each other. It helps us cover the whole of the island without having to track each other down, or wear out our voices shouting for help. Those spires I'm sure you saw, with the crystals on top? Those are the way the messages are relayed across the Isle, and they're empowered by the Fountain."

"Does that take a lot of power, then?" Amara asked, curious in spite of herself. She knew some things about magic, but not a lot, and nothing about communication mirrors. Since the Families and Clans lived nomadic lives, it was too difficult to ensure that a mirror would stay intact when bumping around in a saddlebag or rattling along in a baggage cart. It was far easier to ensure that at least some of a partic-ular Family's men had swift bird shapes that could fly from encamp-ment to encampment, if messages needed to be sent, even if that particular Family wasn't in one of the bird-associated Clans.

Trevan shook his head. "No; in fact, you don't even have to be a mage to operate one, so long as you know how to operate it. But it's a constant threat of a drain for the crystal towers, since they have to be ready for use. A Fountain is constantly producing energy effortlessly, unlike a mage, who must eat and sleep at regular intervals. We have to concentrate our powers and expend our life-energy to use magic, which can literally exhaust a spellcaster if they're not watching what they're doing. Of course, the more magic a mage has, the longer it takes to exhaust him, and some of my brothers are quite powerful," he allowed, "but the cryslets themselves are pre-enchanted and should last at least a year or two before needing to be re-enchanted.

"So if the reason why you fear my family is because you fear that we'll covet the source of power you know about . . . again, why would we covet it? Between our own abilities and the Nightfall Fountain, why would we want for anything more?" he asked her.

He had a point . . . but he only spoke for himself, and Amara pointed that out to him. "So *you* say, but greed doesn't always heed such logic. If it did, then there wouldn't be robbery and theft, which are prevalent all around the world. And what about the rest of your family? If I took this Truth Stone to each of them and asked them the same set of questions, would it come away from their touch unchanged? Or do they secretly covet whatever I know? Would they lust after what some of my Family *died* to protect, before I was forced to flee with that secret to preserve it?"

That upset Trevan, but not because she questioned his kin. "I'm sorry you had to suffer through all of that. I'm sorry you lost your kin, and I'm sorry you . . . well, alright, I'm *not* sorry you came here, because you seem like an interesting woman—when you're not being afraid of me," he amended wryly. "All I can say is things are different on Nightfall. And if you want reassurance that the rest of my family feels the same way before you'll feel safe enough to stay among us, I'll hold them down and make sure they answer personally, while you hold this Truth Stone to their foreheads.

"All I ask in return is that you give me the chance for us to get to know each other. Alright?" he asked, while she peeked at the Stone in his hand. Trevan shifted it so she could be sure he had spoken true. In truth, he couldn't blame her for her protectiveness. If she indeed had some sort of knowledge about the location of an unguarded Fountain, or maybe some sort of power-storing Artifact, he couldn't blame her for being wary of mages, period. "In fact, everyone will be at the supper table tonight, including my otherwise reclusive twin, and you can ask them your questions then. Agreed?"

Amara sighed. "Fine. But I ask *everyone* on this island, even that boy you said is too young to be a mage—and your Queen, too—and if I don't like their answer, or they don't answer at all, or try to force me to tell them what I know, I'm leaving. *And* you have to release whatever spell you cast on me." Wrinkling her nose, she plucked a strand of light brown hair off her chest. "Did you *have* to make it such a plain-looking body? I'd much rather look like myself."

Opening his mouth, Trevan closed it after a moment, thinking twice about what he had been about to say. *Morganen said this spell would confine a shapeshifter in their* true *form . . . which means that black-haired, golden-eyed version of herself is merely what she* thinks *is her true form . . . which tells me she thinks she's pretty damned special. And if I tell her* this *is the real Amara Fen Ziel . . . she probably won't like that one bit.* Arrogant, opinionated, wary . . . she might be a little abrasive, thanks to her paranoia and pride, but Trevan decided he kind of liked it.

At least she's not boring . . . "I didn't pick the body; the spell picked it. And that's the truth," he added, touching the Stone before displaying its surface. It was the truth, after all. "*Ashraka!* There, you're free."

Amara sighed in relief as she felt her body shift inside her clothes, but double-checked the color of her hair all the same. *Back to black, thank the Gods . . . though I don't know how much I should thank Them.*

They've been a pain in my life, this last year-plus . . . Trevan deserved her thanks for releasing her, if nothing else. "Thank you."

"Next time, listen to me, and it shouldn't be necessary," Trevan reminded her wryly.

Rising from the fallen tree trunk, he offered her his hand, assisting her to her feet. Thunder rumbled in the distance, though the sky was still mostly clear, making him wonder if something had upset his twin. Shaking it off, he focused on the woman permitting him to still hold her hand and gave her a smile. If she believed *he* was trustworthy, his courtship of her could begin. Her trust in his family could begin at supper with the use of the Stone.

"Now, since I'd rather not go to all the trouble of having to haul around your clothing yet again, today, I think if we go . . . *that* way," Trev decided, orienting himself, "we can climb out of this place easily enough, at a point where we should meet up with the western road. We'll have to backtrack, but we won't have to worry about trying to climb such a steep slope, either."

Having used his cryslet to let Mariel know she had a patient to attend to in the herb room, Trevan stayed long enough to introduce the two women and provide the simple explanation that Amara had gone wandering into the woods to think about things and had taken an unexpected tumble down into a ravine. Amara had given him a shuttered glance that said she was grateful for the excuse, curious as to his proffering it, and still a little wary of his motives. He didn't think Mariel was fooled by the excuse, but the Healer didn't call either of them on it as she tended to Amara's lingering injuries.

Trevan didn't let Amara's attitude get to him, though. *The first task is to fetch her fresh flowers*, he decided. *Something pretty to help cheer her up. Not too sweet smelling; I get the feeling she would appreciate a spicier scent . . . or at least isn't the kind to sniff at anything insipidly sweet.*

Leaving the basement in the north wing, he mounted the nearest set of stairs to the ground floor, intending to exit and fetch a vaseful of flowers for Amara's suite. Then smacked himself in the forehead and about-faced, heading for one of the ground-floor rooms in the east wing. Somewhere over there, if memory served him right, they had stashed several vases during that massive cleaning spree Kelly had sent them on shortly after her arrival last summer.

He had reached the eastern hall and had opened one of the doors a short distance down, when his ears pricked at the sound of an exclamation. It wasn't much, but the voice was female . . . and unfamiliar. *An unfamiliar voice?* After having paid close attention to Amara's firm alto, Trevan was positive this had come from a lighter, softer soprano. *That can't be right. Was it one of the others?*

Backtracking, he reached the archway into the donjon in time to see two things: a slender woman with hair the same light brown shade, bone structure, and clothing style as Amara's—at least, Amara's "true" hair color, not the black she undeniably preferred—and his own black-haired twin, stalking straight at him. Trevan glanced at the woman again, who was staring at Kelly's infamous floating crown.

He had almost forgotten about it. Everyone had grown used to seeing it since it had appeared almost two months ago, just as they'd grown accustomed to the sight of the spell-painted walls shifting from one anti-scrying scene to the next as each hour passed. Now, though, he was struck by how wondrous the phenomenon was, seeing the way this newest arrival marveled at it.

A moment later, Trevan blinked. *Oh! This must be the source of those other tracks! But . . . how did my brother find her, when he was supposed to be asleep in his room, and she was left behind at the northern tip of the Isle?*

Rydan stopped in front of him, just as the woman glanced his way. Trevan had a brief impression of a face very much like her sister's, but without the more dramatic contrast of black hair against suntanned skin. His younger brother's opening words shocked him into forgetting about her, for the moment.

"I am going to *kill* Morganen!"

The words were more hissed than snarled, taking him aback. "Morg? Whatever for?"

The emotions playing with the muscles on Rydan's scowling face formed an interesting struggle. Hatred, loathing . . . shame?

"He slipped me some sort of drug at breakfast," Rydan growled. "I *dreamed*. Somehow, our lying, manipulative brother slipped her past my wards and into *my* bedroom—the hidden one!" he added sharply as Trev gave him a confused look.

Trevan was actually confused over *who* had slipped into his brother's bedroom, though he realized now that Rydan meant Morg had slipped the *woman* into his bedroom . . . though *which* bedroom was now a point of contention. *Rydan has more than one bedroom?* His twin continued to rant, half-choking on the words.

"I thought I was dreaming, Trevan, and I *couldn't control* myself!"

Trevan stared at his brother. The conversation was making no sense. *What in the Gods' many Names is he going on about?* "I don't understand."

"I *touched* her!" Rydan hissed, face twisting with not just loathing, Trev realized, but self-loathing. "Just . . . just my hand, my lips—but I *violated* your woman! I don't care what the Gods have Prophesied—I have had *enough* of these manipulations, and I am going to *kill* that son of a . . . of a *shame* to his very own mother!"

He thinks . . . he thinks he violated my *woman? That* woman? Trevan gaped at his brother, glancing at the woman in the loose tunic-dress thing and gathered trousers in the middle of the donjon hall.

"He *deserves* to die," Rydan muttered, and Trevan could hear the disgust choking his voice. "As do I . . ."

"Whoa—get that nonsense out of your head!" Trevan demanded,

grabbing his twin by the shoulders before Rydan could do anything foolish. Rydan knocked away his hands.

"Don't touch me! And didn't you *hear* what I said? I *violated* the sanctity of your *bride!*"

Oh, for the love of Sweet Kata's Ass—! Grabbing his brother by the shoulders, Trevan forced him around, facing his dark-haired twin toward the so-called violated woman. She was looking at them with concern on her somewhat plain face, yes, but she didn't seem upset to be anywhere near his womb-mate. "*That* is the *second* woman to reach the Isle today, Brother," he asserted, pointing at her past his twin's shoulder. "The first one, I encountered several hours ago. Presuming you woke up only a short time ago, that means she is woman number *six* to grace us with her presence, *not* woman number *five*.

"You did *not* violate my woman," he added as Rydan flinched in his grip. "*My* woman is down in the herb room, getting some scratches treated by our Healer. *That* woman is *your* woman. You cannot violate what is yours—at least, she doesn't act like she feels violated. Go get her, Rydan. She's all yours!"

Releasing his brother with a hard shove in her direction, Trevan spared the foreign girl a last, brief look before turning and heading back into the eastern wing. He kept his ears open, in case his twin did something foolish—well, more foolish than fleeing, which was probably going to be Rydan's first choice of action—but he still had a vase to track down and fill. *He* wasn't going to balk and rail at the Gods for sending him a woman to know and love.

Of all of the brothers, Trevan had taken the lesson of the heavenly union of Kata and Jinga to heart: Women and men were made for each other, to be partners and companions, lovers and friends—

"*GODS!*"

BOOM!

The door he was reaching for jumped on its hinges, slamming itself against the posts holding it in place. It rattled backward, accompanying the shuddering of glass in wooden frames. Apparently his brother had just released some of his frustration in a massive lightning strike. Giving up on finding a vase for the moment, Trevan turned and strode back toward the donjon. A voice rang out from the third floor just as he reached the entryway, making both him and his twin flinch.

"*Goddammit, Rydan!*—I just ripped a *huge* hole in Saber's shirt! If you're going to go play with lightning, *take* it elsewhere!"

The source of the yell was the redheaded figure leaning over the third-floor balcony by the entrance to the northern wing. Glaring down at them, Kelly pointed her arm firmly at one of the banks of windows across from her, then whirled and stalked back into the sewing room, slamming the door shut a few moments after she vanished from Trevan's field of view.

That was when Rydan doubled over, as if in deep agony. Trevan started forward, reaching for his brother's elbow, but Rydan uncurled himself and took off, bolting for the northern wing. It wasn't the first time he had done something like this, run rather than stay, and it frustrated his twin. Trevan was further dismayed by the woman, who shouted in Aian for Rydan to not leave her all on her own.

Rydan stumbled, half-fell, then lunged up and sprinted out of sight, hands clamped to his dark head as if to hold it in place for the sheer fear of his skull flying apart. Since there was nothing Trevan had ever been able to do to help his twin, he let Rydan go. Concerned for the abandoned woman, Trev changed his destination to her.

Her fear had been wiped from her face, which was heart shaped and thus exotic—slightly narrower from forehead to chin than Serina's face, and broader at the cheekbones—but otherwise plain. With her eyes closed, Trevan wasn't sure what their color might be, but her hair was about the same light brown shade as Morganen's, and perhaps a shade or two lighter than her sister's . . . because he had no doubt, after staring at the lovely Amara, that this was the Aian woman's sister.

Discounting Amara's shapeshifted sable hair and cat-gold eyes, and remembering how she had looked in her *true* form, as forced by that spell of Morg's . . . Amara and this woman were undeniably related to each other. They even looked close to the same age, within a year or two, though this one looked younger. Stopping in front of her, Trevan lifted his hand to touch her, to wake her from whatever trance she had gone into.

Her eyes opened just as he moved, and she gasped and jumped back with an exclamation. "Gods!—Don't touch me!"

Her surprise was understandable, but it was the panic in those wide, green eyes that alarmed him. Trevan eyed her, wondering if all Aian women were mildly insane. "Why?"

Another shout, this time from the side, "Don't you *dare* touch my sister! Back off from her!"

He recognized *that* voice. Amara strode into the donjon chamber from the north wing. Whether or not she had seen the flight of his twin, she now stalked straight toward Trevan with all the furious grace of an enraged cat. He realized she had said something about her Family or Clan or something being a whitetailed deer, but she looked very much like a territorial cat hissing at a dog foolish enough to come too close to her . . . well, the other woman wasn't a food-bowl or a sunny-spot, but Trevan backed off carefully, letting the two women reunite.

"What, in all the Gods' *Names*, are you *doing* here?" Amara yelled at her unnamed sibling. "I thought I *told you* to stay at the waterfall!"

That was where the two paths of footprints had been headed, one shod and one not, that I saw—she was coming back when I found her, and hadn't made a third set of prints yet, Trevan decided, just as the other woman swallowed, clenched her fists, and shouted her own reply.

"*Stop it!*"

Amara jerked her head back as if slapped, giving Trevan the impression that she wasn't accustomed to being yelled at like that.

"We are being *disrespectful* to our hosts," the younger woman stated firmly, but more calmly and quietly, "by shouting like a couple of . . . of . . . Amazai seagulls! This is *not* the time nor place to have this discussion!"

Above them, Kelly had reappeared. She leaned over the balcony, listening and watching. Amara caught her sibling by the wrist and turned toward the north wing.

"Then we will *find* a place to have this discussion!"

"Shouldn't you introduce her, first?" Kelly called down, halting both women before the black-haired one could haul off her light brown-haired companion.

Trevan waited for an introduction, too.

Sighing, Amara released the other woman's wrist, gesturing at her. "This is my sister, Arora Fen Ziel of the Shifting Plains. You are all forbidden to touch her. Arora, this is Kelly, incipient Queen of Nightfall."

Arora whipped her head around, staring at her sister in affront. She whapped Amara with the back of her hand. "*Ai*kelly! Show some respect!"

"She is an *incipient* queen!" Amara retorted, flicking her hand at the crown hovering over the dais to one side.

"Then at the very *least*, that deserves an *Ah*," Arora retorted, glaring pointedly. Then dropped her voice to the point where Trevan, only a body-length away, could barely hear her. "But she *will* be a queen, and currently still outranks you." Smoothing out her features, she looked up at the puzzled woman on the balcony and shifted one foot forward, dipping in a version of a curtsy, hands folded over her heart. Voice raised, she stated politely, "It is an honor to meet you, Aikelly of Nightfall."

Her elbow, Trevan noted with a touch of bemusement, neatly and oh-so-accidentally *bumped* her sister in the bicep as she lowered her arms, straightening. Amara echoed the peculiar gesture, but said nothing. She started to grab her sister's wrist—apparently the no-touching rule didn't apply to her—then spotted Trevan and flushed. Sighing roughly, she flicked her hand between them. "Arora, this is Trevan of Nightfall. He is the *mage* I spotted on the beach. In fact, this is a whole *island* of mages."

"I beg to differ," Kelly interjected, amusement coloring her tone. "I'm about as far from a mage as anyone can get. I rule this land through sheer charm, a bit of intimidation, and good common sense. Why don't you bring her up here, so we can speak more comfortably?"

"If Your Majesty will forgive us, I really do need to speak with my sister, first. Alone." Dipping another of those foot-forward curtsies, if without the hands over her heart, Amara pulled her sister away. "Please do excuse us; we'll gladly see you at the evening meal!"

At least Kelly had the grace to wait until the two ladies were out of earshot before catching Trevan's attention with a soft whistle. "And I though *I* was blunt."

"She has . . . Amara, that is," Trevan clarified. "She has trust issues. Apparently they were driven from their homeland and chased halfway around the world because of some secret. I don't know about this other woman. I *knew* there was someone else on the Isle, but Amara denied it when I first encountered her." He glanced up the hall, where they had vanished. "She's very protective."

"Gee, I hadn't noticed," Kelly observed dryly. "And what was up with your brother? He's not normally that volatile."

"He's the one who found Arora . . . in his bedchamber. Which reminds me," Trevan added. "Rydan claims Morg spiked his last drink with something. If it's true, Rydan will probably try to punish him for it. With access to that Fountain of his . . ."

"Magical Armageddon, I got it," Kelly agreed. She shifted to open the translucent white lid of her cryslet. "Fine. I'll just call him up and have a little what-the-hell-were-you-thinking chat with my Court Mage. In the meantime, O Vizier . . . do they know you're a shapeshifter? Whatever secret they have, that woman came charging in here loaded for bear. I'd like to know what it is before we have to pry it out of them. Preferably before it tries to bite us on the butt, like so many other secrets have tried to do, of late."

Trevan had no idea what Kelly meant by *loaded for bear*, but allowed it as yet another outworlder eccentricity. "Yes, Amara knows, but she only knows a few of them." He flashed his sister-in-law a grin. "I'll go skulk around, look cute, and spy for both our sakes."

"*Both* our sakes?" Kelly asked, amused.

"She *is* a challenge, with all those trust issues," Trevan observed, spreading his hands. A silent pulse of his will, and he reshaped himself into his favorite form, a marmalade copper cat. Leaving Kelly to head back to the sewing room, he trotted into the northern wing. It was likely that Amara would claim the suite he had shown her for that talk she wanted, but he would follow her scent—their scent—just to be sure. In this more sensitive form, both women reeked of raw soapleaf and hints of imperfectly washed sea and sweat to his feline nose, and it was easy to track exactly where they had gone.

SEVEN

❧⊰❦⊱❧

Amara pushed her twin into a room chosen at random on the ground floor. She had a vague impression of chairs and tables, for the walls had been painted with the dizzying sort of view she normally only saw on those rare occasions when she had turned herself into a trout. Shaking it off, she rounded on her sister.

"Now, how in the name of Mother Earth did you get here so fast? Did someone find you?—Did anyone *touch* you?" she added, worried about that possibility. Whatever ability her sister had been granted by the Gods to conceal what she was only extended as far as a mage's eyes could see. What they could touch wasn't covered, unfortunately. One of the priestesses back home had described the feel of her sister's power as a sort of humming tone, like touching a large bell that had been struck, only the toucher was deaf to the tune and could only feel it thrumming into their bones.

Arora lifted her chin, and did not act contrite, which she normally would have done. "I explored the cave. There was a magical cart that had been sent to dump rock chips, and when I asked if it was a good idea to hop inside as soon as it was empty, the answer was yes. So I *did*," she stated almost belligerently. "I saw an opportunity, and I *took* it. And I will not apologize for it!"

"*How* am I supposed to protect you, if you run off like this?" Amara countered, spreading her hands to indicate the palace around them. "And you didn't answer my question: Did *anyone* touch you?"

Her sister blushed.

Amara narrowed her golden eyes. "Arora Fen Ziel, *Princess* of the People—*who* touched you?!"

Folding her arms over her chest, Arora lifted her pointed chin stubbornly. "I'm not going to tell you—you're just going to blow it out of proportion!"

"Blow it *out* of proportion? Dammit, Sister—only *one*—urrgh! Only *two* people on this island are *not* mages, from what Trevan said," Amara corrected herself roughly, "and unless *either* of them was that redheaded pretender or a . . . a little boy I haven't even met yet, *anyone* touching you would have to be a mage! *How* many times do we have to run?"

"He was drugged!" Arora blurted, then bit her lip in the awkward silence that followed. As her sister blinked, she shrugged, tightening her arms around her chest. "He said he thought he was dreaming, and since I was in his bedchamber—*don't* you give me that look! I went searching for a refreshing room, and didn't realize the bedroom was occupied until after I stepped out again! Since I was in his bedchamber, and . . . and had to pass close by the bed, he thought I was someone else in his drugged stupor, dragged me down . . . and . . . and *kissed* me!"

Pulling her head back in shock, Amara felt herself growing outraged. Not just for some unnamed male mage touching her sister—at least it wasn't Trevan, for he had been busy chasing *her* around—but for a man daring to touch a Shifterai maiden in such a manner, violating everything her people had laid down as law in the rules of proper courtship behavior!

"You look like a sour-faced aunty," Arora drawled, disdain edging her tone.

That pinched Amara's black brows into a scowl. "And *you* look like you . . . like . . ."

"Like what?"

"Like you *enjoyed* it!" she accused her lighter-haired twin.

Hands going to her hips, Arora lifted her chin just that little bit more, leaning into her sister's space challengingly. "I *did.*"

"Arora Fen Ziel—" Mara started to lecture angrily, only to be cut off by her twin.

"*Rora* Fen Ziel—I am *not* a princess of *any* people! Not anymore! Get it through your head, Sister," her twin ordered, enunciating each word. "We are *in exile.* For as long as I live, I will be carrying this . . . *thing* around inside of me—and as long as I am carrying it, every single mage around the world will be wanting to get their hands on it. *Except here!*"

"You don't *know* that!" Amara shot back.

"I do know it—I *saw* it!"

Flipping her hands up in disgust, Amara retorted, "That's what you *say,* but you're no Seer! The Gods didn't bless you with Divine Foresight—They *Cursed* you with that *thing* you're carrying!"

"I may not be a Seer, but I can *still See*! And I have Seen that our days of running end *here,* in this very place!" Arora lowered her hands from her own dramatic gesture, planting them on her hips again. "Open your eyes, *Mara.* We are so far from the land of our birth, they don't even know the significance of *Ai* and *A* . . . so why bother using them? Why bother dragging around the dust and the grass of the Plains, when we should be learning how to move through the trees?

"I am *not* going to hide behind the walls of Shifterai customs," her twin added firmly, jerking her thumb at her chest. "Not when I'm never going to return to Shifterai lands!"

Amara flinched away from that truth, only to have her arm caught by her sister.

"And *you* have to face the fact that, if you still want to protect *me*, that means *you* will never return to the Plains again! *Face* the truth and embrace it, Mara. As I have done." Arora released her, waiting for her sister to respond.

Rubbing her wrist, though her sister hadn't hurt her physically, Amara set her mouth firmly. "I am what I was *born*, Sister. A Princess of the People. I should have been Queen . . . were it not for you."

Arora bared her teeth in a grimace. "Then *leave* me. I *know* I will be safe here. Yes, I am not a Seer . . . but I *still See*."

"I gave my word! I gave up my *birthright* for you—try to show some gratitude!" Amara growled.

"Then lighten up your attitude!" Arora snapped back. She started to say more, but at her dark-haired twin's snort, she drew in a sharp breath and released it in a harsh gust, cutting her hands between them. "On this point—at least until you can see *reason*—we will just have to disagree. And don't think that you can run my life. You may protect my life, but you *aren't the one living it*."

Growling, frustrated beyond bearing—for the *damnable* thing was, her sister spoke the truth—Amara whirled and yanked open the door.

"Rraowrr!"

She jumped back, startled. As did the marmalade cat that had been right on the other side of the door. They stared at each other for several seconds, then the long-haired, green-eyed cat blinked, settled back on his haunches, and briefly groomed his chest and shoulder, smoothing down a patch of his fluffed-up fur. Shaking himself—for the feline had to be male, with such lovely copper-and-orange fur over most of his frame and sporting only a small patch of white on his belly—he fluffed out his fur again, then padded forward and head-butted her on the shin, rubbing against her from shoulder to tail.

Amara loved cats. Her people *were* cats, or could at least take on feline shapes if they were skilled enough, but they did have ordinary, non-shifting hunting cats that roamed with the Families during the migratory months, and house cats that stayed in the City and lurked among the farms, keeping the mice away. Some part of her had wondered if she should have been born into one of the Families of Cat Clan, instead of into Whitetail of Deer Clan, but kinship ties had little to do with her love for the small, furry hunters.

Stooping, she picked up the marmalade tom. He was heavy and thus a bit awkward, but his fur was the softest she could remember feeling, long and luxurious with an undercoat that lacked any matting. That alone told her that he was a pampered cat, constantly groomed and cosseted. Which explained part of his friendliness, for he purred happily in her grasp . . . and nearly fell out of it when he twisted into the touch of her sister's petting fingers.

"Mother Earth, he's fat," Amara grunted, lifting him higher on her chest, making her breasts take some of his cuddled weight in order to keep from dropping him. "Probably was spoiled with tidbits from the table, as well as mice from the granary."

"Probably," Arora agreed. "Look, I'm sorry we yelled at each other. This whole chased-into-exile thing doesn't sit well with me, either . . . but I *am* trying to make the best of things. All I ask is that you let me try to be happy, regardless of our circumstances. You *do* want me to be happy, don't you?"

"I want you to be *safe*, first and foremost," Amara corrected, allowing the warm scent of happy, purring feline to fill her lungs and calm her temper. "*Then* you can be happy."

"If I'm *happy*," her sibling chuckled, "then wouldn't it follow that I'm also *safe*?"

"Maybe," Amara begrudged. The cat in her arms twisted his head, peering at her upside down. It was a funny pose, and chased away the rest of her lingering irritation. Or at least most of it. "Fine . . . I'm sorry I yelled at you, too. It just . . ." She groped for the right words. "It seems like you don't take our predicament seriously enough!"

"Oh, I take it seriously enough," Arora countered. "I just don't want to be like *you* and take it *too* seriously."

She tugged impishly on Amara's dark locks, earning a brief, dirty look. Not wanting to get into another argument, Amara changed the subject. "Come, there's a set of rooms they've offered to me. If nothing else, we can at least rest in peace before supper . . . at which, I intend to interrogate everyone available with a Truth Stone, in order to discern exactly what kind of threat these people are."

Arora gave her a skeptical look.

"Well, let's just say I came up with the possibility of my 'knowing' the secret location of some powerful Artifact that most mages would want, and I'm going to be asking what everyone's intentions will be toward that possible source of power."

"That's a clever twist," Arora praised her sister as Amara readjusted her grip on the orange fluffball in her arms, "but where will you get a Truth Stone?"

"The redheaded man, Trevan, promised to loan me one. He promised it *on* the Stone," Amara added as she moved through the doorway, contented cat purring against her chest. She supposed she should let him down . . . but it had been a long while since she had last had the luxury of being able to hold a cat for more than a few moments in passing. A thought crossed her mind, prompted by the year-plus of caution now built into her reactions. "Are you *sure* this other man didn't notice anything?"

"If he did, he didn't say anything," Arora countered. "I think he probably mistook it for part of the dream. I suppose if he's at supper, you can always just get him alone long enough to interrogate him with that Truth Stone."

Mara nodded. It would have to do, even if she had to ask delicate questions, and prepare for a quick escape, just in case. "Make sure you point him out."

Trevan excused himself from the ladies by the simple expediency of jumping down from Amara's arms as soon as they reached the third floor. Darting back down to the second, he trotted up the hall, pausing now and again to sniff at doorways and rub himself against their age-darkened frames. Part of it was to keep up the pretense of being a mere cat, should they come down in search of him. The other part was to give himself time to get over the shock of what he had just learned.

Amara talks of having to hide a secret. She also claims mages chased her from her homeland, searching for that secret, which is the hiding place of a great source of power . . . Her sister was supposed to remain hidden, and Amara denied her presence . . . but then the two of them speak of a great powerful thing inside of Arora . . . and when she petted me, I felt it! Oh Gods, I felt it!

As to *what* he had felt, Trevan wasn't entirely sure. It was like bathing in summer sunlight, and listening to his second-eldest brother's deep voice while his ear was pressed to Wolfer's chest, with a bit of that prickly feeling Rydan exuded whenever a storm rolled over the island, all of it blended together and seasoned powerfully with the taste of sheer magic.

Pausing mid-rub against a doorway, he flicked his tail, considering the implications. *Whatever this Arora holds within her . . . I've never felt anything even remotely that strong, outside of group magics. Like when all of us enchanted the cryslets and raised the towers after Evanor got his voice and his magic back. But that was with Rydan's Fountain, and Serina lending her powers, too . . . Gods—this is just one person, and she's carrying around what feels like even more energy than that within her . . . ?*

Gods . . . how can she stand it? How can she survive *it?* There was no way of telling *what* kind of Artifact could hold so much power and be carried as a part of a person—they had clearly said the thing was *inside* of the brown-haired sister. *How is she carrying it, what is it, and why is she the one transporting it? More to the point, why couldn't I sense it until she touched me?*

Trevan tried to imagine the kind of wardings that could completely contain all signs of magic. Like his thirdborn brother, Dominor, he had a way of synthesizing different kinds of magic to create Artifacts and new spells. He didn't quite have the same level of power that Dom had, but he did have a similar level of education. But this, to contain something *that* powerful to the point where it could only be felt at a touch, not Seen with a magical eye—well, if it had a physical form, he gauged it would take up a scroll almost a body-length long and a forearm in width just to cover it in enough runes and glyphs.

Possibly there are runes embroidered on the inside of her clothes, or maybe painted with special inks made from specific, magic-infused plants . . . but that would run the risk of the power being exposed to mage-sight whenever she takes off her clothes to bathe. The only other alternative would be sheer willpower . . . and I'm not sure if anyone less than Morganen would have that much focus and mental stamina.

No, there is something about these two women that we definitely have to investigate, he decided, moving away from the door and trotting up the hall toward the donjon. *I can finally understand Amara's protectiveness and paranoia, having been touched by her sister, though. If that were my sibling running around with a . . . well, with the equivalent of a Fountain inside of him, instead of outside of him in his secret little lair, I'd be a little high strung, too. Especially coming to an island where the majority of the population are mages.*

Unfortunately, every time someone has come to the Isle so far, some sort of Disaster has happened. Well, okay, Serina's arrival was the fixing *of a Disaster, the miscommunication between her and Dom, but there was still trouble involved.* A thought checked his stride, fluffing the fur along his spine and dragging his whiskers downward in dismay. *Oh, Sweet Kata . . . there are two of them on the Isle—does that mean* twice *the trouble?*

Shivering, he hurried to report to Kelly. For now, Trevan would keep quiet on whatever it was that the woman Arora carried. He only had a few chance-spoken comments and a sister's overprotectiveness to go on, after all. More would have to be learned, and so long as his family didn't give away that a house cat was one of his other favorite forms, he should be able to spy on both ladies fairly easily over the next few days. Not just for the Artifact-thing, but also to figure out how best to court his Destined bride.

What his seven brothers had never realized was how much *work* Trevan had put into learning how to court a woman. Once he hit puberty and started mastering his magics, he had discovered how much young ladies enjoyed having a pretty little kitty to dote upon and confide in when one was available. Many secrets had been whispered into his fur, many murmured hopes and dreams, and many giggles over crushes, too. Older women might be more discreet, but these two were around twenty or nineteen, if he was any judge, still young enough to confide in an affectionate, companionable cat.

Hm. I should use the cryslets to remind everyone to not *mention my ability to turn into a cat . . . and get Evanor and Mariel to sit on their excitable young son.* Shifting shape at the sewing room door, he slipped inside to make his first report to his Queen.

Summoned to Rydan's tower, Morganen waited in the gong chamber, the only room in the tower the rest of them were permitted to enter. It was bare of everything except whitewash on the walls, black curtains hung at the few windows, and a black lacquered frame supporting a large steel gong. He didn't bother to ring it, since he was the one who had been summoned.

Rydan emerged from the doorway that, similar to the one in Morganen's own tower, led down to the lower levels. Striding up to Morg, he stopped within reach, unusually close, and said, "Hold out your hand."

Curious, Morg complied, only to find his brother dropping a Truth Stone into his grip.

"Did you, or did you not, put some sort of *drug* into my breakfast drink?"

Morg eyed the Stone wryly. "How clever. You call me out to help you, only it's to help you interrogate me. How very clever."

"Answer the question!" Rydan ordered tersely. "Did you put some sort of potion into my breakfast juice, yes, or no?"

"Yes. For your own good," he added, before displaying the white marble disc. Nothing darkened the Artifact's surface, proving his words true. "You have this asinine idea in your head that love is something to be avoid—"

"*Did* you slip that woman past all of my wardings?" Rydan demanded, confusing his sibling. "The *woman*. Rora, with hair the same color as yours," he clarified sharply. "You had to have slipped her past all my wards! You're the only mage on this island who'd be strong enough."

Damn, caught in the act. Tightening his grip on the Truth Stone,

Morganen picked his words carefully. "Since you insist upon know-ing the truth, I *allowed* her to slip past the wards around the island as a whole, so that she could arrive undetected. Any wards she en-countered after she landed were her own problem to surmount, and I did not assist."

He didn't bother looking at the disc, though Rydan did. What he saw didn't make him happy. "So you say you had no idea that, after you *drugged* me, she managed to make her way into my most private place on her own?"

"Well, I knew that she was wandering around under the moun-tain at one point," Morganen admitted, "but no, I didn't know that."

"So you did not see me in my bed, suffering the effects of your little *prank*."

"No, I didn't see that part, either. Why don't you get to the point, Rydan?" Morg asked his glowering sibling. Not that there was anything new about Rydan glaring at life in general.

"Did you know what effects that drug would have on me?"

"Yes. You were supposed to dream about being happy, for once—happy in a relationship with a good woman."

Thunder rumbled on the heels of Morg's statement. Rydan snatched the disc from his hands, gripping it tightly. "Oh, I *did* dream about being happy, Brother. I dreamed about being happy with my wife, *very* happy. I was so happy," Rydan added in a growl, "that when I woke up, I thought it was just another part of that dreaming, and being *eager* to continue being *happy* with my 'wife,' I pulled her down onto my bed . . . *and I violated her!*"

Gods! Shocked, Morg barely managed to catch the Truth Stone as lightning cracked, deafening him. It was all-white, unblemished by even a hint of a lie. He groaned as the implications hit. The world felt like it dropped out from under the youngest brother for a very long, sickening moment. Squeezing his eyes shut, blocking out the literal truth visible in his grip, Morg cursed himself silently. He felt Rydan snatching the Stone away, and forced his eyes open, shame making his face freeze and burn in alternate waves.

"*This* is what your meddling led to, Brother. Because of *your* stupid act, I forced myself on the woman *you* thought was meant to be my bride! Next time you get the urge to meddle in my affairs, Morg? Prophecy or no Prophecy, *don't*!"

With a last crack of lightning and rumble of thunder, Rydan returned to the depths of his tower. Shaken, Morganen turned and stumbled out onto the ramparts. He didn't get far. That all-white surface tumbled over and over in his mind, mixing with his brother's harsh-flung words. *I violated her! I violated her! I violated her!*

Bracing his shaking body against a crenel, Morganen lost what little there was in his stomach. *He* had set this chain of events into motion. It was *his* fault, all his fault!

Knocking on the suite door, situated across the hall from his own, Trevan waited patiently for a reply. He knew they were still in there, having walked up in cat form for a sniff a little while ago, before padding off beyond any potential witnesses, changing, taking the stairs to the next level and coming back down again on the original side, as if following in the cat's—being his own—footsteps. His patience was rewarded after he knocked again, when Amara opened the door, just in time to hear the carillon bells at the top of the donjon dome ringing out the call to the evening meal. Their cryslets were used for communication these days, but the bells were still handy for announcing the timing of certain things.

"Yes?" she asked. She and her sister had done their best to tidy their appearance; it had helped that the blond man Amara had met, Evanor, had stopped by a little while ago with a chest of clothes, dropping it off with a smile and a brief word about hoping they would find a few useful things that fit until something more suitable could be made. He hadn't lingered beyond that, leaving the two Shifterai women to gingerly explore the age-worn contents of the trunk.

"Supper is ready," he offered, glancing beyond her to her sister and back. Amara was still clad in her original garments, but her sister had donned an extra shirt underneath her split-hem tunic. "It would have been ready half an hour earlier, but the extra people required that a couple more dishes be added to the menu.

"That, and Evanor—the pale blond one you met—he realized we really needed a bigger table, so we had to get one into position and find extra chairs to fit around it. So it is just as well we had the extra time. As there is more than enough room for all of us now, would you care to grant us the honor of your presence in our dining hall?" Trevan asked.

He lifted his forearm and elbow, and the two women glanced at each other before eyeing him askance. It took him a moment to realize what the problem was. Clearing his throat, Trev explained.

"The common, local courtesy is that when a gentleman invites a lady to walk with him, he offers her his arm so that she may place her hand upon it as they walk side by side."

Amara lifted her hand, eyed his forearm, then grasped it hesitantly near the wrist. Gently prying her fingers free, Trevan looped her arm under and around his elbow, pulling her closer to his side. It was a little presumptuous to place her so close to him without clear affection between them, but he figured that what she didn't know wouldn't hurt him. Glancing over her shoulder, he addressed the other woman, Arora.

"I would offer you my arm as well"—he felt Amara tense as he said this—"but as I am attempting to court your sister, it would not be entirely proper. Besides, the three of us would never fit through the door."

Amara caught the wink he gave her sister and tightened her mouth briefly. She didn't want him flirting with her twin. Flirting led to touching, and touching was forbidden. Instead, she would keep his attention on her. For her sister's sake, of course. "Then you had best keep your attention on me."

"Of course. Come this way," he directed, and guided her out of the room and back up the hall. "Some of the most useful rooms are in this wing, in my opinion. The east wing," Trevan stated, gesturing in that direction with his free hand, "has the great ballroom, the grand salon, and the ducal gallery, consisting of moldering art leftover from when this place was still a thriving duchy, before the Shattering of Aiar caused the Isle to be abandoned. The south wing—"

Arora frowned, interrupting him. "—Abandoned? Why would a land so far away as this one be abandoned just because of something that happened all the way up in Aiar?"

"Because the release of whatever energy destroyed the Aian Empire caused all the active Portals around the whole world to also be destroyed," Trevan explained. "Luckily, most kingdoms managed to be warned in advance by their Seers and closed most of them down in time to prevent damage. Unfortunately, the last one to be visited by the Council of Mages—the ruling body of the Katani Empire—was the one here on Nightfall. When everything went to a Netherhell in a gifting box, the Seer who lived here at the time was able to channel most of the energies into a Curse.

"The Curse dried up the main water supply for the island, until only a few dozen people could be supported, so Nightfall was quickly abandoned. It became a place for exiles," Trevan continued. "My brothers and I were among those honored to be 'guests' of the Isle, simply for the crime of being born. But now . . ." He peered at the walls of the corridor, which had shifted to a pattern of painted butterflies. "Well, we're no longer exiles and are building ourselves a kingdom from the ground up. It's very exciting—you probably see this sort of thing all the time in Aiar, but for us . . . there hasn't been a political shakeup of this size locally since the original Katan merged with its neighboring kingdom of Jingarun in a marriage of the Gods."

"Oh! I've heard of that," the woman following them exclaimed. Her sister craned her neck, and Arora explained. "It was in the records in the sub-basements of Shifting City. Very few of the records were ever complete, which is utterly frustrating to a true scholar, but there was mention of a decision made on how to end an ongoing feud between the two lands. The Goddess Kata did not want war, but could not abandon Her people and was trying to defend them from the Jingaruna, while the people of the God Jinga were suffering from a terrible drought and were demanding the surplus of Kata's lands, or they would go openly to war.

"Only there wasn't enough of a surplus to go around, because the drought was affecting the southern land almost as badly as the northern one. A major miracle was needed, but neither Patron had the power necessary," Arora explained. "So the Emperor of Aiar proposed that the God and Goddess wed; each had one-half of the prayer power needed, plus a little extra. Combined into a single nation, they would have no reason to feud over food, and by promoting the wedding in both lands as a positive thing, they could raise more than enough belief to not only end the drought, but perform a tripling of the harvests and the herds.

"Unfortunately . . . the records ended there . . ." She trailed off. "The decision was made, but though I know it happened, the records didn't show how long it took to spread the decision, nor what it took to organize a wedding of two Deities. And I don't know why the resulting kingdom was named Katan, after the Goddess. I'd think it would be named something like . . . like Katinga, some sort of amalgamation of Their names."

"That was explained in the Legend of the Courtship," Trevan

said. Then reconsidered his own words. "A legend that may have been a construct, if what you say is true—it was said that Jinga was so smitten by Kata's wisdom as well as Her beauty that He offered Her His fealty in exchange for the grace of Her name given to bless His people with better fortunes for their future."

"I suppose that makes sense," Amara offered. "And it creates a gallant legend much more suitable for opening the hearts of both sides. Katan, after all, was the one offering up the greater share of a miraculous harvest, while Jingarun was desperate to eat it. Using Katan's name was a way of acknowledging Katan's generosity, which would soothe the nerves of the Katani being asked to give up all that extra food."

Arora stuck out her tongue at her sister. "You just took all the romance out of the tale."

"I was simply trained to see the practical side of solutions, and you know it. Besides," Amara added, glancing at the man holding her arm curled around his, which was something a Shifterai male would do, "it doesn't negate the romance of the gesture. There are often many reasons to do something, each one just as valid as the next, and few of them so rare as to negate all of the rest."

"Ah, here we are. Brace yourselves," Trevan warned the two women as he stopped in front of one of the doors close to the donjon. "My brothers and their wives aren't exactly a horde of people, but there are more than enough of us to be overwhelming at first."

Opening the stout wooden panel, he led them into the dining chamber. The long table that filled most of the room had enough chairs placed for twenty people, with elbow room to spare. As it was, more than half the seats were filled, though the occupants quickly stood. Trevan nodded to everyone genially, guiding Amara up to the head of the table where the first of his sisters-in-law stood. Arora followed by default, though she hung back from everyone.

"I realize some of you have already met, but this will go faster if I just do this as a group," Trevan stated in preamble, releasing Amara's arm so that he could turn and present the two ladies. "Everyone, these are Amara Fen Ziel, and Arora Fen Ziel, from the distant land of Shifterai . . . which is somewhere in Aiar. Amara, Arora, this is Kelly, incipient Queen of Nightfall." He gestured to the redheaded woman, then to the tall, muscular blond at her side. "And her husband and Consort, my eldest brother, Saber.

"Next to Saber is his twin, Wolfer—the big one with the plain brown hair—and his wife, Alys." Trevan gestured at the shyly smiling woman with dark gold curls. "I'm introducing my brothers in their order of age, from eldest on downward," he added in explanation. "Wolfer is secondborn. The ages of the ladies . . . well, it's considered rude to inquire unless the ladies volunteer, so I haven't bothered. Across from them, we have Dominor, the fellow in dark blue on this side. His wife, Serina, is the tall one with the long, pale hair next to him."

Amara eyed the woman, who was busy looking at something in her hands, a slateboard. The pale blond woman looked up only when nudged by her husband's elbow, but the smile she offered the Shifterai visitors was warm and genuinely welcoming. The moment Trevan moved on, her attention dropped back to whatever she was doing, while the dark-haired man at her side rolled his blue eyes in a way that said this was a common occurrence, and that the newcomers shouldn't take offense at it.

"Next to her is Mikor, our youngest resident on the Isle." He nodded at a boy with brown curls and a gap-toothed smile, indicating that one of his teeth had apparently fallen out recently. "On the far side of him is Mariel, his mother and our resident Healer—you've met her already, Amara, but I wanted Arora to know who to go to if she ever has a scratch or a sniffle. The light blond fellow next to her is her husband, Evanor, and Dominor's younger twin."

"Just how many sets of twins do you have in your family?" Arora asked, bemusement coloring her voice.

"Four sets. I'm next in age below Evanor . . . and my twin, Rydan, isn't here, yet," Trevan murmured, peering down the length of the table, then at the door. "Neither is Morganen. Hmm. Well, after me comes Rydan, of course, and since I'm not sure if you've seen him or not, Amara, he has black hair and a solitary nature. Next is the third redhead of the family, and the seventhborn of us. His name is Koranen."

The auburn-haired man standing on the far side of the table, on the far side of Alys from his secondborn brother, flashed Amara and her sister a grin.

"Morganen is his younger twin, and he has light brown hair about the same shade as yours, Arora, though a little bit shorter," Trevan finished. "I'm sure he'll be along in just a few moments. Again, everyone, these are Amara and Arora. Please make them welcome."

Murmurs of welcome filled the room, then Evanor, the light blond brother they had met earlier, gestured past his own seat. "If you ladies would each like to take one of the empty places . . . ?"

Amara guided her sister around to the far side of the table. There were two places set next to the blond, Evanor. She took the one nearest him and nodded for Arora to take the last one on that side. It forced their redheaded host to circle around the end of the table and take a seat across from them. As soon as they settled in place, the others started passing bowls and platters of food their way.

Amara passed the proffered dishes first to her sister, who would be able to judge which dishes would be palatable to their foreign tongues. Serving herself from the ones her sister had selected, she tasted each dish. The flavors were a little strange, but not unpleasant.

There was something alcoholic called "stout" available for a drink, but Amara chose to stick to cow's milk. The last thing she needed was to lose her head in a crowd of strangers. Arora, she knew, wouldn't touch anything fermented, and for good reason. The one and only time her sister had drunk a cup of something fermented, she had set her own clothes on fire. Alcohol and magic didn't mix well for her twin.

EIGHT

❦

For a while, the conversations were limited to requests for dishes to be passed, murmurs of appreciation, and half-cryptic comments about whatever work the others had been doing all day. Trevan listened with half an ear to his siblings' talk of clearing and readying yet more land for rebuilding the old port city down at the western cove. When most of his hunger had been sated, a natural lull in the conversation occurred, giving him a chance to speak.

"To change the subject," he offered, making his family and the two women across from him glance his way, "Amara has some concerns about staying here. Understandable ones, given her and her sister's recent, troubled history. I think it would be just and proper if we could give her a chance to ask all of us a few questions, and hopefully set her and her sister's minds at ease. Does anybody object?"

Heads turned and eyes glanced from face to face. A heavy sigh was heard, focusing the attention of the others on the young boy at the table. "I suppose I have to *leave* now," Mikor complained, "if you're going to be talking about *adult* stuff, again."

Glancing at Amara, Trevan answered him. "I don't think that will be necessary, Mikor. In fact, I think it would be fair to ask *all* of us the questions she has in mind. Which would include you."

The curly-haired boy perked up again, visibly pleased at being included in an adult conversation.

Amara felt the weight of everyone else's stare. Firming her resolve, she nodded at Trevan. "I have already asked him the questions . . . under Truth Stone. I would ask that the rest of you prove your own honesty as well."

"Under Truth Stone?" one of the two curly-haired women, the one named Mariel, asked. "Isn't that a bit extreme?"

"Given our recent history," Arora spoke up from the far end of the occupied seats, leaning forward so she could see the Healer, "I don't think it is. Most of the mages we have met in recent months have unfortunately proven themselves untrustworthy in the end."

"And now we come to a whole household of mages, minus only two of you," Amara added, glancing at the incipient queen and the curly-haired boy. Sweeping her golden gaze over the rest of the gathered adults, she quirked her own brow. "You may refuse, of course . . . but if any of you do, then I'm afraid my sister and I must leave, regardless of how favorably the rest might answer."

"Then I'll be the first to answer," Kelly stated. "Since it seems you're Destined to join us anyway, we might as well set any possible fears to rest right now."

"*Destined?*" Arora asked. "I keep hearing that word whenever someone on this island talks to me. What is all this talk of Destiny about, Akelly?"

The muscular, honey blond male next to Kelly at the end of the table cleared his throat. "My seven brothers and I are the fulfillment of an ancient Katani Prophecy. Each of us is Destined to fall in love, with specific things happening as each of us does so. It is called the Curse of Eight, or the Song of the Sons of Destiny, depending on who you ask."

"There is a second Prophecy involved, by a different Seer," the brother with the dark brown hair added. Dominor, that was his name. "It is the Curse of Nightfall . . . and it also seems linked to our presence here. When both Curses are lifted, the island will be capable of returning to its former glory as a center of trade and commerce. The sooner we all meet and marry our Destined brides, the sooner that day will come."

"And since we have less than a year and a day in which to make Nightfall its own kingdom, we're eager to see our brides appear," the darkest of the redheads, Koranen, finished for the others. "So ask us what you will. If the two of you are Destined for two of us, the sooner we can make you comfortable, the sooner the last two among us can find our own brides, completing the Prophecies."

Amara exchanged glances with her sister, then looked at the red-head seated directly across from her. "So that's what you meant. You expect me to be Destined for *you*."

"The way things have been progressing? Yes. I'm next in line, and I met you first," Trevan agreed.

"That doesn't *guarantee* I'll find you worthy of *me*."

At the head of the table, Kelly arched her brow, taking mild offense at Amara's comment. "That doesn't guarantee that he'll find *you* worthy of him, either."

Trevan suddenly realized that there were two strong-willed women in the room, both with prickly senses of dignity. He quickly fished the Truth Stone out of the pouch hung from his belt, distracting them from any chance of an impending argument. "Here, pass this down to Kelly . . ."

The Stone reached the redhead after a few passes. Turning it over, she looked up at the others. "What is this?"

She doesn't know what a Truth Stone is? Amara thought contemptuously as the others explained it to Kelly. *What kind of a would-be sovereign is she, if she's never seen one before? They're in use everywhere!*

". . . Okay, I'm ready for your questions, now," Kelly told the Shifterai twins, returning her attention to them. "Ask away!"

"Fine. If you had a chance to grab a huge source of power and use it, even though it wasn't rightfully yours . . . would you?"

Kelly blinked at her, frowning in confusion. "What kind of power are we talking about, here? Solar? Electrical? Thermal? Hydroelectrical?" At Amara's confused look, she broke off and clarified. "I mean, sunlight, lightning, heat, water . . . what kind of power?"

"*Magical.* What other kind is there?" Amara asked, her opinion of the other woman sliding even lower at Kelly's obtuseness. "If you had a chance to grab and use a vast source of *magical* power, even if it wasn't yours to use, would you do it?"

"Why would I need to steal it?" Kelly countered, confounding Amara. "If I needed magic for some reason, I'd simply go to someone who has it—like my husband or brothers-in-law—and ask one of them for their help." Lifting the disc, she displayed its white sides, then gripped it again. "For that matter, *how* could I steal it? I have no magic of my own, and unless it's enchanted to respond to a physical touch or a simple verbal command, I can't even use it. So, *no*, I wouldn't try to steal it." Again, the disc was white. "Is that your only question?"

"No," Amara stated firmly, determined to see this through. "If someone held the *secret* of where to find this vast source of power, would you try to get it from them? Even if you couldn't use it directly yourself?"

"Again, why would I need to?" Kelly asked rhetorically. "I don't need any extraneous sources of power, and I don't care what secrets you hold, so long as those secrets do not endanger this island or its people. Now, anything else?"

The disc was white. Amara didn't let herself relax. "Your husband, next. Same questions. If you heard of a source of vast magical power, would you try to steal it? Would you try to get the secret of its location?"

Saber gripped the Stone. "No, and no. I have enough magic of my own for most of my needs, and what more I may need, I can call upon my brothers for."

The disc was white. He passed it to his twin, Wolfer, who gripped it just long enough to truthfully state, "No, and no. Same reasons."

The curly-haired woman next to him, Alys, gripped it as well, if a bit timidly, until her answer proved also true. "Um . . . no, I wouldn't steal it, and no, I don't need to know any secret of its location."

Dominor was next; they seemed to be passing it around in order of introduction. "I have no need to steal any power, and you may keep your secrets. Provided they do not bring harm to this Isle."

His wife gripped the white disc, nudged into releasing the chalkboard she had been working with between bites. Amara expected an absentminded answer from the distracted, ivory-haired woman, but she actually lifted her head from her work, leaned forward to see past the others, and looked straight at the Shifterai princess. Lifting the disc in her fingers, she addressed the questions in a different way.

"I have been the guardian of a vast magical power myself. I have protected its secret well, and I have used its energies for the greater good while I was its Guardian. And though I am not that Guardian anymore, I have permission from its current protector to return to it and use it as I may, because my guardianship was true. So, no, I don't need to steal anything. Any secret I may learn about some other putative source of power will not affect my decision."

Flipping the disc around, she showed its plain white backside, before passing it to the boy at her side. Mikor gripped it and said, "Uh, I don't even know if I'm gonna—er, *going* to grow up to be a mage, yet. And stealing is wrong. So there."

His mother took the Stone, showing that her son hadn't lied, then used it herself. Her words had even more of a bite to them than the ones the woman on the other side of her son had used. "I am a Healer. If I suddenly needed a vast supply of magical power, regardless of ownership, it would only happen because one of my patients was two breaths from death, and that source was the closest thing I had to draw upon to help save my patient.

"Other than that, I wouldn't need it . . . and if you have a problem with my possibly needing outside power to save someone from the edge of death," she added, slanting a hazel-eyed look at Amara, though she had to lean forward to do so, "then you'd better pray to all the Gods you've ever heard of that you don't end up as my patient."

Amara wasn't overly happy about the Healer's answer, though at least the woman did clarify that, outside of an emergency, she wouldn't need any outside source of magic. Amara let it pass, though.

Evanor took the Stone from her as soon as she displayed her honesty. "No, I wouldn't steal it, and no, I don't need to know about it."

Catching the disc as Evanor tossed it to him, Trevan repeated his answers from earlier. "No, and no, as you already know. Kor?"

"No, and no, as the others have all said. Are you satisfied?" the dark redhead asked her.

"No." Defiant in the face of the others all staring at her, even her own sister, Amara explained herself. "There are *eight* brothers, yet I see only six of you here. Until the other two have answered—*and* yonder would-be queen swears upon the Stone that these are *all* of the inhabitants of this island," she asserted, "I am not, and will not be, *satisfied*."

She had the satisfaction of seeing the freckled queen tighten her mouth, and knew that her barb had struck home. Amara acknowledged then and there that it *annoyed* her to no end how some magicless, ignorant *nobody* was being allowed to become a queen, when she, Amara Fen Ziel of Family Whitetail—capable of more than twice as many pure shapes as Aitava herself—had been forced into exile and ignominy.

Rather than answering her challenge directly, the other woman pulled up her sleeve, revealing the same strange bracelet Artifact Trevan had used earlier. A glance around the table showed that everyone but Amara and her sister wore one. Even the boy, Mikor, had a smaller version fitted to his wrist. Kelly did something to the base that the lid had sat upon, then spoke.

"Rydan? Would you please come to the dining hall?"

Amara couldn't hear any response, but whatever this Rydan said, it turned Kelly's freckled cheeks a little pink. Setting her jaw, she tried again.

"I must insist that you come anyway. Immediately. Thank you."

Trevan could imagine what his taciturn twin thought of being ordered to appear. Especially after running off like that. More and more of late, Rydan had begun running off during certain moments of stress. Not all such moments; he had stayed throughout the confrontation with the Council back when they had formally seceded from the Katani Empire, before taking his leave of his family to go and sleep after all the excitement was through. Today's departure from the donjon hall had been far more dramatic. But more and more, Rydan would grimace and slip away just when the conversations started getting animated at the dining table.

Kelly used the cryslet a second time. "Morganen, your presence is requested in the dining hall. Immediately, if you please." Snapping the lid shut, she turned her hand over. "Pass me the Stone, so I can swear that everyone in this room, plus the two that are coming, are all the inhabitants on the island."

Koranen complied. Arora took the opportunity to lean close and whisper, "*See? I* told you this was the safest place for us. They use magic like it's as common as water—even the non-mages among them. They don't need any more of it, if they can waste it on giving a young boy his own bracelet, like that."

Amara gave her twin an annoyed look, but only a brief one, for the woman at the other end of the table had repeated her declaration and was now displaying both sides of the Truth Stone. Perfectly white. There really wasn't anyone else living on the island.

In the tense silence that followed, the blond mage sitting next to Amara cleared his throat. "Well. Why don't we enjoy dessert while waiting for the other two to arrive?"

Debating a refusal, Amara gave in after she saw the fruit-studded, iced confection he fetched from the sideboard. A vibrating note made her flinch, but the spell divided the round, layered cake into sixteen equal slices. Accepting one of the slices, she found it spicy-sweet, but didn't eat it with quite the same relish as her sister did. Normally, Amara liked sweets. Right now, her stomach was a little too tense for her to do more than pick at it slowly.

The door opened, and a man clad entirely in black from shoulders to shoes entered. Combined with his black hair and eyes, the effect made his skin seem rather pale. The brooding frown creasing his forehead and turning down the corners of his mouth didn't help the overall impression Amara received. Nor did he seem eager to rush to his putative ruler's side.

Even his speech was devoid of civility, being nothing more than a clipped, "What?"

"Take this, and answer the following two questions," Kelly instructed him. She glanced down the table at Amara. "Well?"

Waiting until he had the Truth Stone firmly in hand, Amara gave him the questions. "If you knew someone else had control of a vast amount of magical power, would you steal it away from them for your own use? If the location of that vast power was being kept secret by someone, would you try to wrest the secret of it from them?"

"I have more than enough powers and secrets of my own. I need *nothing* of you or yours." Dropping the Stone into Kelly's palm with a curl of his lip, he turned to go.

The redheaded woman turned it over, eyes widening. "Um, Rydan—would you care to explain this?"

The big blond, Saber, cupped his wife's hand, examining the Stone for himself. The angle allowed Amara to see a hint of gray smudging the otherwise white surface. The black-haired man, Rydan, peered over his brother's shoulder, scowling in annoyed puzzlement. Wanting to demand a clarification, Amara drew in a breath to speak, but her twin beat her to it.

"Perhaps if you rephrased your answer in a way more specific to the questions asked . . . ?"

Color tinged his cheeks. Snatching up the Stone, which had bleached itself white in the interim, he snapped, "I neither want your powers, nor have need to steal any secrets—does *that* satisfy you?" He displayed the disc, showing how both sides were now completely white. "Now, stay away from me—both of you!"

Tossing it at Kelly, he strode out of the room—only to bump into someone else just starting to enter. Light brown hair swayed, bodies *oofed* . . . and the black-clad man snarled, making the newcomer, the missing Morganen, by default, flinch and scramble back, giving him room to leave. Glancing back at Kelly to see how the woman handled such a brusque attitude in her presence, Amara was one of the few people to see the dark gray spots staining one edge of the disc. In specific, the place where he had been holding it during his demand that she and her twin stay away from him.

He lied about that? He spoke the truth about not wanting any power or secret of ours, yes, but he lied about not wanting to associate with us? Or rather, lied about not wanting to associate with my sister, Amara realized shrewdly, glancing at her twin. Arora was staring at the newcomer with a touch of horror in her green eyes. That immediately made Amara wary about the last and final inhabitant of the island.

Worse, rather than going directly to his queen, the blue-clad man turned the other way, moving down next to Trevan, across from her twin. He flicked his gaze up from the table a couple of times, swallowed, then managed to find his voice.

"I am . . . terribly, *terribly* sorry about what happened. I thought it would help, but . . . but it only made things a hundred times worse. It was entirely my fault; he wouldn't have done it, if it wasn't for what I did to him . . . Anything . . . anything you want in reparation," the light brown-haired man stated, swallowing again, "I will do."

Raising a brow, Amara turned to her sister, murmuring, "What in the Blessed Names of Sky and Earth is he talking about?"

"*None* of your business," Arora retorted under her breath, blushing.

"Everything you do *is* my business," Amara reminded her twin tartly. "If somebody caused an offense, it is for *me* to judge the severity of it!"

"Not in this case!—We have agreed to disagree on this subject, so *drop* it," Arora ordered. Dismissing her sister by turning to the man standing on the other side of the table, she lifted her chin. "You and I will discuss reparations for your part in all of this at a later point. Your queen has a request to make of you. I suggest you attend to her."

"Actually, *they* have the request, but I have the Truth Stone," Kelly interjected, drawing everyone's attention. "Come here, Morg, and answer these two simple questions. If you heard someone had control of a vast source of magical power, would you steal it from them for your own use? Or if they merely held the secret of its location, would you try to steal that secret?"

Clasping the Stone, he shook his head. "No, and no. Now if you'll excuse me . . . I'm not feeling very hungry, right now."

Amara craned her neck to make sure the Stone was white. It was, which both pleased and rankled her. It was a relief to know that her sister *was* right, that this place seemed to be a haven where the secret of Arora's hidden magic would not be coveted by anyone . . . but it annoyed her to no end that Arora, loving, trusting, innocent Arora, was *right* about there being at least one place in the whole, wide world where they *wouldn't* have to worry about the natives coveting her power.

But she didn't have time to dwell on her feelings, for Kelly's husband caught the wrist of the departing man, stopping him. His voice, while not quite as low as his twin's, spoke volumes through its gravelly depth. "It seems you have *too* much free time on your hands, Brother, if you are wasting it by getting into trouble. You've been neglecting your sword work. In the salle, in a quarter of an hour. *Don't* be late."

The younger man winced, but freed himself and left without a word. Trevan watched him leave, the only other person in the room besides Amara, her twin, and the departed Rydan and Morg, who knew anything regarding that little confession. In his opinion, Morganen had messed up to some degree and probably deserved to get trounced around the salle by their eldest sibling. But on the other hand, the professed victim sitting across from him just didn't look all that traumatized, despite his twin's claim that she had been violated. Not even when Rydan had been in the same room with her.

In fact, if I had to gauge her reaction . . . she seemed rather interested in him, he thought. *But her sister doesn't seem too happy in her being interested in anyone. That can be blamed on the secret they're hiding, of course . . . I'll have to sneak around in cat form a bit more, eavesdrop on their conversations, I think.* Trevan caught himself as he started to smile, keeping it to a mildly happy look rather than a blatantly amused one. *Not that getting petted and pampered by her when I'm a cat will be a hardship . . .*

Arora nudged Amara with her elbow, giving her sister a pointed look. Setting down her fork, ignoring the rest of her cake, Amara let out a sigh. "I think it is time we retired, and . . . think carefully about your answers."

Her sister slapped the tabletop with her hand, startling her.

"You *never* give an inch, do you?" Arora demanded, her green eyes narrowed with disgust. "I *tell* you this is a safe place to be. I *tell* you that these people won't hurt you or me! You even ask them yourself, under Truth Stone, and *they* even tell you!—You know what? I give up!" Shoving to her feet, Arora leaned over her twin. "I *give up*. You can go do whatever you want. *I'm* going to stay here and see what kind of life I can make for myself. Go back to the Plains if you want to, since that's all you ever talk about!"

That hurt. Amara had given up everything—her home, her life, her people, her *future*—to protect her sister. Shoving to her feet, she faced off against her sister, struggling to keep her words general enough to not give away their secrets, even in her understandable outrage. "I gave my word! And just because *these* people say they're trustworthy, it doesn't mean no one else will come to this place! I remind you, those were *mages* that were following us! How do we know they even drowned, at Sun's Belt? *We* didn't!"

"*Fine.* I'll concede you have a point. But *you* can spend your days looking for outsiders, all you want!" Arora snapped back. "*I'm* going to lead my *own* life. One that *isn't* joined at your hip, the last time I looked, so *stop* trying to tell me what to do. Until *you* remove the burrs from under your saddle, don't try to talk to me," Arora ordered her twin. "I'm not the one keeping them there, I'm not the one who refuses to admit when she's *wrong*, and *I'm* not the one to let *you* keep galling me!"

Face flushed with embarrassed anger, fingers tightened into fists at her sides to keep herself from inadvertently shifting claws in the face of such antagonism, Amara watched her sister whirl and stalk away. Arora rounded the end of the table, strode up to the head of it, and stopped, her own cheeks flushed with emotion.

"I apologize to all of you for forcing you to witness our little spat." Green eyes flicked to gold for a moment, then back to the freckled face of the local Queen. "My only excuse is that my sister and I have had to endure each other's company for far too long, under increasingly *stressful* circumstances. I'm certain we'll *both* try to behave in a more civilized manner . . . should you continue to let us stay here, in your graciousness."

"I'm sure we won't turn you out," Saber stated, twisting to look up at her, before giving his wife an odd, almost wry look. "You're not the first pair to pick a fight within these walls."

Amara knew her duty, even if it rankled. "Your graciousness is appreciated. I . . . offer my apologies as well."

Arora left the room before she could follow. Amara wanted to give chase and give her sister a piece of her mind. She couldn't rush out of the room, however; she and her twin had already scraped their dignity raw by fighting in public. There was one thing she could do, at least.

"I do ask one . . . favor . . . of you," Amara stated, trying to remember what was more important to address, her sister's tantrum, or her sister's safety. "My sister is sensitive to physical contact, particularly from strangers. It causes unpleasantness for her. Please refrain from touching her."

"Then she'll be *perfect* for Rydan," the auburn-haired brother, Koranen, muttered. "He hates being touched, too."

Trevan reached over and smacked the back of his hand against his brother's arm. At the same time, the woman Alys elbowed him, and his other brother on that side of the table, Wolfer, leaned across her back and bapped him on the other arm.

"I see someone *else* has too much free time on his hands," Wolfer rumbled, his voice deep with displeasure. "You and me, in the salle, same as your brother."

"I can't. I have dish-clearing duty tonight," Koranen stated, briefly sticking out his tongue.

"Then I suggest you *hurry*."

Since it seemed the others were getting ready to leave, Amara abandoned her plate. There was another door, she noticed, at the far end of the room from the others. It was in the wall perpendicular to the other, but even if it led to a closet, she would rather pick it than use the same door as the rest. Standing, she headed that way. No one stopped her, thankfully, and the room beyond the door she opened held stacks of the same sort of armless chairs that had been placed around the dining table, as well as a large octagonal table. The door to her left opened onto the hall when she tested it, allowing her to escape back to her rooms gratefully.

Behind her, an orange-furred cat trotted out of the dining hall under the amused gazes of the others. They had been warned before he had gone to fetch the two newcomers for dinner to keep their mouths shut about who the fluffy feline really was—or at least most of his family had been warned. Hopefully they would keep his secret quiet while he spied on the newcomers in their midst. Pausing to stretch his limbs and yawn, Trevan scampered into a lope, following the black-haired Shifterai woman.

Maybe if he "caught" her at her door, she'd bring him inside for a bit of petting . . . and perhaps even a bit of muttering about her frustrations and her secrets, allowing him to learn even more.

NINE

⚜

She didn't notice that the cat was back until after she had rapped firmly on the lightglobe resting in an iron ring mounted to one of the bedposts, activating its magic. She had entered the suite Trevan had offered her without noticing any followers and shut the door after lightly knocking her knuckle on one of the smooth globes just inside the room. It had helpfully cast a dim light that had been just enough to help her navigate her way into the next room, but not enough light to see any prowling felines. Now, blinking and turning away from the sudden, strong light, roused in direct response to the strength of her tap, she found herself flinching back from the sight of the largish cat leaping unexpectedly onto her bed.

"What? Oh, you!" Hand pressed over her heart, Amara willed it to stop its sudden race and frowned at him. "What are *you* doing in here?"

He blinked at her, then padded up to the edge and head-butted her in the stomach, seeking attention.

Sighing, she scritched her fingers through his fur, giving in to his silent demand. "You're as bad as that Trevan fellow. Assuming arrogantly that I'd want to give him my attention, never mind even so much as the hour of the day . . ."

As much as she wanted to brood over her embarrassing, public fight with her sister, Amara felt too tired. Tired of brooding, tired of arguing, tired of running and hiding and watching everyone and everything with suspicion. Yes, her paranoia and caution had kept her and her sister alive, but she resented having to do it. She resented always having to be the voice of doubt. She also resented being told she was wrong.

There was nothing wrong in being suspicious about these people! And the questions I asked them were all in theory, *not in confronted-with-the-actual-power reality. There is still a minor but real possibility that they could change their minds if they ever find out about her. And yet she has the gall to complain about my vigilance!*

I've kept the two of us safe *ever since we fled the Plains—I kept our people safe, luring those mages away from the Plains. Kept us safe while we were on the run . . . always running, always watching, always, always, always . . .*

Gods, *I'm tired.* Pushing the cat out of her way, she climbed onto the bed and twisted onto her back, relaxing into the bedding. The nameless pesky feline padded back up to her, sniffing at her shoulder and cheek. Giving in to his silent demand for attention, she rolled onto her side and scratched behind his ears.

"You're as bad as Trevan," she told the cat. Then corrected herself. "No, he's worse. *You*, at least, don't expect me to fall into your fuzzy little limbs, as if you were the Gods' personally delivered gift. He's as bad as all those would-be suitors I used to have, before having to run off into exile."

Her mouth twisted for a moment, remembering what it had been like. Having grown into her shapechanging abilities even before puberty, when it normally struck most of the other shifters, Amara had been cautioned by her parents from an early age to examine the motives behind any would-be courters. Her mother and father had urged her over and over to search for a man who was *worthy* of her. Not just in his shifting abilities, or in his wealth, but in his personality, his interests, and even his dreams.

She had taken their words to heart once she had been old enough to go into the maiden's *geome*, the special domed tent reserved for unmarried young ladies in a given Family. By that point, every shapeshifting male in all of the Families of Deer Clan had learned of her extraordinary abilities, and some from beyond the bounds of the Clan. They had to wait one year before courting her, and one year to the day after the first flow of her menses had shifted her from girl-child to maiden, she'd been inundated with potential suitors. Each one had been subjected to her careful scrutiny, and nearly all had been quickly turned away.

Most weren't worthy of her as fellow shifters. Certainly this Trevan fellow fell absolutely flat on that account; he wasn't even a real shapeshifter, just a spell-shifter. It was encouraged for a princess to take a strong shapeshifter for her mate, since that increased the odds of another female shapeshifter being born.

Even winnowing out the men who could only take on a handful or so forms, there had been many more whom she disqualified for the way they constantly talked about her being the future queen of their people, and how they would help her rule. Not that having a helpmate was a bad thing; Aitava's own mate was a very wise man, widely respected for his knowledge. But the ones Amara had discarded all talked as if they would be telling her how to rule.

I don't think I mentioned I could have been the next Queen of the Shift-erai around him, so I doubt Trevan has any ambitions in that direction.

*Besides, he seems content to live here, and he's definitely not the mate of
their current would-be Queen.* She snorted at that thought. *Not much of
a Queen, if you ask me . . . though at least she's not ruled by her husband,
as far as I could see.*

The last thing any land needed was a puppet for a sovereign,
least of all the Shifterai. So she had dismissed those sorts of suitors,
back on the Plains. In matters of wealth, Amara had been less picky,
though she had automatically rejected any suitor who gamed too
much, whether they lost or won. She also dismissed those who drank
too much, and any man who didn't care for his tent, his belongings,
his horses, and his herd animals. A man who didn't show consideration for such things was not a man who would show consideration
for her, which was a part of a man's personality as well as being a
sign of his attitude toward prosperity.

Trevan, at least, had shown care and consideration for her, even
when he had chased her. He had healed most of her injuries himself
and insisted that she be tended further by their resident mage
Healer. He had personally attended to these chambers with his
magic, ensuring that the rooms were clean and fresh, and had answered her questions about his home with a definite hint of pride for
his surroundings. Of course, she hadn't been able to ask about his
personal wealth, not even indirectly, but then her own wasn't exactly a topic she wanted to discuss, namely because there wasn't
much of a topic left for her to discuss.

Personality-wise, there had been a few men among the Shifterai
she had found worthy of further attention. A number had been honorable, honest, open, and charming without being manipulative. But
most of those had enjoyed wandering the Plains. Though she didn't
speak of it very often to anyone, Amara had loved her life in the City,
with its structure and its permanence, its plans and its possibilities.
Being apprenticed to their Queen and learning how to manage and
direct life in the Shifting City had given her more fulfillment than

she had ever experienced while roaming about with Family and Clan.

That was where her and most of her remaining suitors' interests had diverged. Even their dreams and goals had differed. She knew that, as Queen, she would be expected to visit with all the Clans and their various Families. But the Queen's job—at least, as she saw it—was better served by remaining centrally located, and thus easily found by messengers wanting to consult about such-and-such problem.

It would be just as easy to circulate among all of the Clans and Families when all of them were in their winter homes, and spend extra time among each of the Families that were taking their turn laboring on the farms scattered around the City from spring to autumn. That way, she could have quality time with each group without wasting her time in riding out to find them on the vast, undulating grasslands, yet still be centrally located in case of an emergency.

Most of the Shifterai, men and women, preferred roaming the Plains. They liked the freedom, and the men especially liked being able to shift shape and lope off to hunt something down on a whim. Wild animals were harder to find close to the City. In the City, she didn't have to hunt if she didn't want to, though occasionally even she had felt the urge to chase something down personally. She had preferred the excitement of hunting down solutions to the problems that plagued their one, permanent settlement . . . and not many of her would-be suitors had understood that managing the City *was* exciting, to her.

I'd have to say this Trevan fellow at least shows some interest in helping to build up this brand-new kingdom of his, more so than most of my fellow Shifterai have shown an interest in building up the City at the heart of our own land. In that much, he and I are more alike than the men who pursued me in the past. We both dream of making things better, of reclaiming the potential of our homes.

But where he gets the idea I'll just fall into his claims of Prophecy and Destiny . . . I don't fall for just anyone, and he's not even a real shapeshifter. He'd have to prove himself twice as worthy as the next-best candidate back home, just for that alone!

Her fingers had grown idle with the depth of her thoughts. Nudging them back into stroking his fur, Trevan wished she wasn't quite so introspective. Or rather, he wished she weren't so *quietly* introspective.

It was widespread knowledge among mages that the Gods had banned spells that could read another person's thoughts, for that was the last possible bastion of privacy in the world. There were potions and spells that could drug a person's mind into suggestible compliance and even control the body, but nothing that could permit a mage to read someone's mind. All he could do was wait and see if she deigned to speak again.

"I wish you could talk," she stated abruptly, startling him. *He'd* been thinking the exact same thing. Her fingers raked the wrong way through his fur, fluffing it pleasurably before she smoothed it back down again. "I'd ask you all about this silly idea of some Prophecy controlling my life. I'd demand all the details, so I could analyze them minutely. I've gone through all of it in my head, what little I know about your human . . . well, I don't know if he's *your* human, but I'll bet you know more about him than I do. Even if you're just a cat."

She's thinking about me, Trevan realized, blinking. *Yessss!* He purred and nuzzled her firmly in encouragement. *Think some more about me! Think positively! Think that I'm a wonderful man whom you'd love to get to know, and think about staying here happily on the Isle with me!*

Amara chuckled as the cat, being given more direct attention from her once more, went into a purring, pacing, writhing ecstasy against her fingers. He even licked her hand several times, his rough-raspy tongue tickling her skin. She scritched her fingers through his ruff, rubbed at his ears, and stroked him from scalp to tail-tip. From the kneading of his paws, the purring in his throat, and the narrowing of his eyes, he was in feline heaven under her hand.

All that purring and petting was relaxing her, draining away her stress. With it went the dregs of her energy. Her jaw aching with a huge yawn, Amara realized she needed to shed her clothes and slip into bed before she fell asleep where she was. Without a fire lit in the hearth, the room was chilly, and she had spent too many shapeshifted days at sea to want to sleep one more night in anything but her own skin, which meant crawling under the covers for warmth.

Patting the cat, she forced herself up out of bed. A bit of investigation in the other room proved that the metal tin she had seen earlier did indeed contain the tools needed for starting a fire, being a bit of flint, a scrap of steel to strike hard enough to shave off a spark, and some old, delicate char-cloth to catch that spark upon, giving her enough time to ignite whatever tinder there was. Whoever had stocked this room had generously provided old scraps of decoratively inked paper for fire-starting materials, she discovered when she examined the woodbin in the bedroom. It was dry and brittle, perfect for catching on fire with the contents of the tinderbox, and once mixed with thin sticks of wood for kindling, got it burning well enough to ignite progressively larger pieces of wood.

The movement and work to get a fire going woke her up, at least until the heat from the logs was warm enough to make her sleepy once again, kneeling as close as she was. Thankfully, the cat had remained on her bed, sprawled and patient as he waited for her to return and resume her petting. There was a fire screen available, which she set in place to prevent sparks from leaping out; she didn't want the cat coming close in curiosity and getting burned by a stray cinder. He was a sweet cat and deserved better than being injured while more or less in her care.

Investigating the refreshing room once the fire was secured behind the screen, she found the mouth-brush the blond man, Evanor, had brought in the chest of clothes and toiletries earlier. Including it had been a thoughtful gesture on his part, and the courtesy of it made her flush a little with shame for her less than courteous behavior, today.

Now that she knew these people—in theory—would leave her sister alone, she wasn't quite so stressed-out as before. Without that stress and its underlying paranoia, she could admit to herself that her behavior and attitudes had bordered on atrocious. Especially that final fight with her sister. But thinking about *that* threatened to restore her stress. Shoving it to the back of her mind, Amara used the facilities, scrubbed her hands and her face, and retired to the bed. Shedding her clothes, she piled them on the trunk Evanor had brought, tapped the globe very softly to reduce it to a dim level of light, and slipped into bed.

The cat, she noted, budged from his sprawled position of ownership when she lifted the covers, giving her enough room to slide beneath the blankets. He cordially waited until she had squirmed around, settling onto her side, then leaped agilely over her, turned around twice, and settled down in front of her stomach, perfectly placed for her to pet him once again. He even looked right at her, stretching out a paw to gingerly touch her elbow when she didn't do so immediately.

Smiling wryly, Amara shifted her hand down into stroking range. He twisted his head under her touch, purring firmly and happily. Doing so left her arm bared to the cold of the chamber, however. Even with the fire burning behind a protective screen, the room was still chilly. Tucking her hand under his backside, Amara scooted him higher on the bed, until he was next to her pillow, and off the blankets. That allowed her to cover most of her arm while still allowing her to pamper him with attention.

The sight of her undressing had reminded Trevan of how she had looked in the forest, naked and terrified of him. This time, she wasn't terrified of him, but she also didn't know he was a cat. That was why he had waited until she was covered before joining her. Now he had a ready view of her cleavage, plus.

Twisting around, he carefully put his back to her to avoid temptation. Now was not the moment to get distracted by the temptations of her flesh. Really. Her hand slowed its stroking, then finally just rested against his ribs and spine, cupping him limply. Her breathing evened out as well, letting him know she was indeed falling asleep. Until he gained enough of her trust for more, Trev would just have to content himself with being touched by her in his feline form for the time being.

At least it's better than an incompletely enchanted courtier illusion . . . even if this is all we get to have until we can get to know each other . . . If I could, I'd take a bet against my brothers about all of this, he thought with some amusement, settling his chin on his tail. *They'd probably be taking bets on how quickly I can get her into my bed, while I'd be betting on how* long *it will take. Not that I want it to take forever, but this is the most important seduction of my life . . .*

The conversation at breakfast took an unexpected, interesting turn, after Mikor had been excused to go play for a while. It happened when Kelly asked her sister what she was good at doing, and Arora explained how she used to manage the notes and records for the Councils that met in the City. That brought up the City itself, which was a topic Amara rarely found tiring.

"The Shifting City is our only permanent settlement," she explained as the others listened with polite interest on their faces. "Built into the cratered ruins of the old capital, and surrounded by farmland where we grow the things we cannot hunt, barter, or gather, it shelters all the Clans and their Families each winter. It gives us a chance to socialize regularly, too, since we scatter across the Plains for the rest of the year. Well, those Families that aren't assigned to farming duties—Families in this sense means a particular group of people, some of which are related by ties of blood or marriage, and some of which are related by ties of herdership, though that's more on the Clan level than the Family level, since a Family that farms doesn't have enough time or land to tend to their herds.

"We keep extensive bloodline records for our sheep, goats, cattle, and especially our horses," she added in an aside. "Of course, our horses aren't quite up to the quality of the Centarai herds, but they're better than most found in the kingdoms around the Plains. Those are some of the records my sister helped keep track of in the archives of the City, herd lineages, what animals were traded to which kingdoms, where incoming livestock came from. Every winter, a full accounting of breeding quality is left behind, to be organized by those who stay while the others roam nomadically."

"So what do these Families do if they can't tend to their flocks of sheep?" Alys asked her. "You said that's a Clan matter?"

"When a particular Family draws the farming year, they pass on their herds to the other Families in their Clan for that year—for example, my Family, Whitetail, would decide the preceding winter to lend its goats to Family Blacktail, its sheep to Family Springbok, its horses to Family Antelope, and so forth. The animals would then be further divided into individual kin-families' care, with the strength of the bloodlines being carefully considered in Herding Councils. The Family that chooses to care for a particular type of animal gets paid by being allowed to crossbreed their stock, keeping whatever their own mares, nannies, and ewes drop, and sending off whatever the ladies of the outsider herd drop.

"We also get half the cheese from the milkings of each, and if it's sheep or goats, we get to claim half the shearings for our own use," Amara explained. "Sometimes, to strengthen the herds, they get sent cross-Clan, too. The year we had to leave the Plains, Family Whitetail, Clan Deer, hosted silk-goats from Family Mustang, Clan Horse. Two years before that, it was dairy cattle from Family Tiger, Clan Cat."

"It sounds rather complex," Kelly observed, smiling wryly.

Amara gave her a slight smile in return. "The complexity of a culture is often an indicator of how advanced it is as a civilization. Just because my people spend nine months out of the year in tents doesn't make us primitives or barbarians."

Kelly lost some of her humor. "I never said that it did." Changing the subject firmly, she looked at the others. "We still have foundations to clear and streets to plan. I've told Hope to tell the architect firm to work only in stone, wood, ceramic, and glass, with a minimum of metal and no *synthetics*. We should be getting the first of the plans back within a week."

"What's a *sin thettick*?" Amara had to ask. She hated exposing ignorance, but the others seemed to take it for granted.

"Various types of material you don't have available on this world, such as *plastic*, dry wall, and insulation batting and foam," Kelly dismissed, tossing out more strange words. "Nor will there be any need for electrical wiring. I told her to tell the firm the designs are for a back-to-nature commune, only with running water."

"So that's why you needed to talk to Hope, yesterday morning," Dominor observed, glancing at Morganen. "So, how's your extra-dimensional romance progressing, Brother?"

"Better than *yours* did," the aqua-eyed mage retorted. "Hope says she can get what we need, but she also wanted to address a potential problem . . . one that I forgot to mention to the rest of you, in the distraction of our new arrivals."

"What potential problem?" Saber asked, while Amara frowned, trying to follow the conversation.

Extra-dimensional? Things we don't have available "on this world"?

"The balance between the universes. An exchange of matter and energy," the youngest of the brothers explained. "We've borrowed Kelly from her universe—"

"Borrowed, like hell! I'm *not* giving her back," Saber interjected, giving his wife a firm, stay-put look.

"Exactly the point," Morg stated. "Hope says she's worked out a way to address the disparity in bloodlines, since Kelly will no longer contribute to the future populations of her world, but there's also the matter of supplies. Some of what we've borrowed from the other realm, we've either returned or compensated for in terms of value, gemstones for goods and such, but she's suggesting that we send across something, even if it's just a few tons of sterilized soil—sterilized to ensure that we don't accidentally send across plant seeds or insects that aren't native to Kelly's world—to compensate for the imbalance in physical mass . . . and to allow her to bring across several of her belongings to this world, when she's finally free to join me."

He blushed as he said that last part, and some of the others muttered teasing words about long-distance courtships, but it was his other comments that made Amara stare. "This woman is from another world? In another universe?"

"Of course," Kelly stated. "Where do you think I came from?"

"I thought you were just another Katani upstart, rebelling against the mainland and claiming your own little kingdom." It wasn't the most diplomatic way for her to put it, but Amara was still trying to grasp that this woman came from Elsewhere and all that such a thing implied. Confounded, she found herself blurting, "Wait—who Rang the Bell, summoning that crown I saw? It couldn't have been you. According to you, you're not even from this universe! The Gods wouldn't allow *that*."

"It *was* me," Kelly retorted, "meaning the local Gods *do* have faith in my ability to rule this land."

"Why don't you tell us what you're trained to do?" Serina asked Amara quickly. "I mean, your sister said she's experienced in the scribal arts, trained to organize information and paperwork. What are your skills? What do you like to do?"

"From the age of fifteen to nineteen, I spent my years as an apprentice to the Council of Princesses, and to the Queen herself, learning how to manage the City . . . and rule the Shifting Plains," Amara stated, holding Kelly's gaze. "What sort of training have *you* had?"

A muscle in that freckled jaw tensed. "An entire lifetime leading and looking after others, from the time I could walk and talk."

Something hit her in her lower leg, hard. Since her twin was on that side of her, if one seat removed, Amara knew it was Arora's doing. Her sister thought she was behaving poorly. Even Amara knew it, but knowing that the Gods had arranged for an *outworlder* to be a queen, while taking that same option away from *her*, didn't sit well with the shapeshifter.

"You say you've learned how to run a city?" Trevan interjected, buffering the antagonism between the two equally strong-willed women with the suggestion. "Then perhaps you could do us the honor of bending your expert eye to our plans? I'm certain there were at least a few things about this Shifting City that you and your fellow administrators wished you could have done differently, had you been able to start over from scratch, as well as features that made you proud. Things that you've considered during your training that perhaps we've missed?"

The side of her shin still throbbed from her sister's kick. Amara could remove the bruise by changing her flesh back and forth, working the contusion out of her system . . . but it was a warning for her to behave. The worst of it was, her sister was right; her resentment over their exile was making her lash out at everything.

She *knew* what it meant to be the one to Ring a Bell. By the covenant implied in the Laws of God and Man, only someone who had an actual chance at being a decent sovereign could summon up the sort of blessed, glowing, floating crown Amara had seen back in the central hall of this place. *If Kelly . . . if Akelly*, she forced herself to think, adding the honorific, *was the one who Rang the Bell for this place . . . then she's got the vote of the Gods on her side. Even if They stole away* my *chance to rule . . . They gave it to* her. *And . . . I should* respect *her for that.*

I also owe these people for my food and my shelter, and their attempt at offering me clothes. What little had been in her size, she had passed to her sister to wear for warmth yesterday, before supper, but they had given her food and such little comforts as a brush for her teeth. Swallowing her irritation wasn't easy, but Amara tried. Reminding herself that she *did* know quite a lot about city management and did have numerous ideas about how one should be planned, she managed a gracious nod.

"I do indeed have ideas. I . . . will admit that I am not as *familiar* with the layout of a coastal city as one could wish," Amara even managed to admit, keeping her eyes on Trevan's face, since it was easier to look at him while confessing a weakness than at the freckled foreigner. "But the principles shouldn't be that much different.

"I saw a lot of ruins half-buried in the forest, yesterday. Do you have any old maps of what used to be there? Were those the foundations you said needed to be cleared, or are you starting with entirely new plans?"

"Right now, we're still clearing land and stockpiling lumber and stone for building materials," Trevan told her. "In some places, the foundations and basements are still functional, but in others, the roots of the trees that took over in the last two hundred years cracked and ruined a lot of the original stones."

"We also have a tangle of underground pipes that have to be investigated," Saber reminded the others. "The island gets its drinking water from a desalination system located in a set of buildings to the north of the harbor—they're part of a Permanent Magic erected hundreds of years before the Shattering of Aiar to ensure the island always had freshwater and a source of income from the blocks of salt and algae extracted during the purification process. The water doesn't run through those pipes anymore. Three of the four processing tanks are dry; they have to be filled and tested to see if they still function. But to do that, we need to be sure the pertinent plumbing still works, which means we need to know where all those pipes go. It wouldn't do us any good to have the one without the other."

"What about sewage?" Amara asked. It wasn't the most proper of breakfast table topics, but it was an important and often overlooked aspect of city life. It also earned her a set of puzzled looks. "It doesn't just dump into the bay, does it? That runs the risk of contaminating your drinking water, or at least your salt blocks, if it's magically filtered."

The brother with the light brown hair, Morganen, sighed heavily and lifted his hand. "I'll investigate that. I might as well volunteer, since I'm still in the dog kennel. I'll see if I have a spell for tracing the water pipes, while we're at it."

"I have one," Dominor said. "I found it among the Archives at Koral-tai and realized it would be useful, if we ever wanted to turn Nightfall into a real kingdom."

That confused Amara. "I thought you *did* turn Nightfall into a real kingdom, or at least the start of one. I don't understand."

"My brother was kidnapped before Kelly Rang the Bell," Evanor informed her. "The short, short version is that we had to claim ourselves a sovereign kingdom to repel an invasion from overseas, because the mainland wouldn't send us any aid. Ironically that fulfilled part of the Prophecy that caused us to be exiled here in the first place."

"Even more ironic, my kidnappers were in turn captured by the opposing side, the kingdom of Natallia," Dominor continued dryly. "That's how I ended up meeting my wife and eventually was free to come back home. But while I was in Natallia, staying with her, I had access to an extensive library filled with both arcane and archaic information."

"Then maybe you could help me," Arora stated, making her sister glance her way in confusion. "Um . . . in private, that is. You and your wife, since you say the archive was where she was located. There were a few old records that survived the Shattering, back at the City, and I'm hoping you could fill in a few blanks for me."

Amara relaxed at that. Arora had a bad habit of going on and on about ancient history, if given a chance; it was as much her twin's passion as Amara's own love of City management. Trevan distracted Amara from her sister's conversation.

"If you want, you can fly down to the western cove with me and get a literal bird's-eye view of what's there," he offered.

"There should be some maps of the old city in one of the rooms over in the west wing," Kelly added, making Amara glance her way. "I'll root around in there while you're flying around, and see what I can find . . ." The freckled outworlder trailed off for a moment, then chuckled, making Amara frown.

"What's so funny?" she asked warily, eyeing the redhead.

"Oh, the Gods of this world have a twisted sense of humor, that's all," Akelly observed, folding her arms across her silk-clad chest. Her garment today was the same shade as her eyes, corseted along her ribs, skirted over her hips, and parted into tailored pants that showed off her legs almost as much as the *chamsa*-like dresses that Mariel and Serina wore, with their thick but fitted hosiery instead of proper, gathered *breikas*. "You would *think* that, with the Gods being the source-point of all of these Prophecies, They would have also arranged for you and I to get along with each other."

"*Technically*," Morganen interjected, "the Prophecy states that only she and Trevan would get along. I should know, I've been studying them for years. Trust me, there's *nothing* in those verses about the two of you *not* wanting to kill each other . . . sorry."

The absurdity of it got to her. Amara found herself first gaping at him, then laughing outright, until she finally braced her elbows on the table and buried her face in her palms. Winding down into chuckles, she lifted her head just enough to look at her rival and ask, "Tell me, were the Gods of that other world of yours just as insane as ours? Or are we all alone in being inflicted with Their 'twisted sense of humor,' as you so aptly put it?"

"Trust me, They had Their own little quirks. Tell you what. You try to drop your attitude problems, and I'll try to drop mine. No guarantees, but that each of us at least *tries* to get along. Deal?" the Queen of Nightfall asked.

"Deal. *Akelly*," Amara added out loud, granting the other woman the honorific she was due. Not the *Ai* of a fully crowned queen, of course, but the *A* she could manage, for now.

From the relieved look in Trevan's eyes, he was pleased by her concession. He wasn't a Shifterai man, it was true, nor was he a natural shapeshifter. But he wasn't interested in the *A* of her own name, which was more than most Shifterai men had been able to manage. She still didn't know what to make of these so-called Prophecies . . . but the other woman was right. Nothing was guaranteed where they were concerned, other than that they existed and might be pertinent to her circumstances.

Arora looked like she was going to be in dry-as-dust heaven with her fellow historians in a few more minutes. Knowing that her twin was as cautious about others touching her as Amara could wish her to be, Amara decided she could leave her sister alone for a while. *And I will* try *to trust that these people won't hurt her or steal her power. If we're supposed to be Destined brides . . . I* suppose *stealing her powers would make her thoroughly disinclined to stick around, let alone wed one of these foreigners . . . so she should be safe with them.*

Now, if only she could be sure she would be safe with Trevan and his Prophecy . . . whatever that was.

TEN

Trevan transformed as soon as he landed. Placing her clothes on a chunk of fallen masonry at the edge of one of the clearings he and his brothers had been making around the western cove, he turned away from the other hawk and waited for her to change and dress. Politeness demanded he not look her way, even if he had seen her getting dressed this morning, while he was hidden in her chambers as a cat. Distracting himself from the thought of her curves, Trev cleared his throat and spoke.

"As you've seen, right now we're still just clearing land, to find the old foundations like this one. Lots and *lots* of land. It's exhausting work, even with magic, since we are using up our energy even if our spells can do the work of a dozen men at a time. Kelly wants the resettlement to be well organized, logically placed and arranged, with plenty of room for people to settle. She's thinking garden space for each house, and tree-lined roads, to keep the city looking green from a distance and provide shade for travelers in the streets."

Amara, reshaped, reclothed, and tugging on her boots, shook her head. "As ideal as that would be, a home for each family big enough to have a garden of its own is not practical. Even though the land in the City was collectively owned by the Shifterai as a whole, and no one pays rent as they do in other lands, each Clan and Family has a particular section with a set number of chambers and suites, a certain amount of stabling space. Beyond that is the province of overflow, and that requires negotiation. If there are too many people in Family Malamute, then they try to claim extra rooms in the Clan Dog's overflow space, and that runs into problems if Family Fox also has too many people for its assigned rooms.

"The best shelter, as I said at breakfast, lies in the hollowed-out crater of the old capital, where the snow might accumulate, but the winds aren't as devastating. There are some buildings up on the edges of the crater valley, but they're exposed to the winds, which leech away the heat of their hearthfires and are thus undesirable, even if they have more space per person and animal. It's like this cove," she added in example. "You may think you have the whole island to sprawl across, but the farther away you go from the center of commerce and activity, the less convenient it is. Giving every house a garden of its own doubles and triples the area between houses and reduces the density. If you have to walk an hour to get to the nearest market, it's inconvenient."

"So how do your people deal with the problem of space and distance constraints?" Trevan asked, glancing over his shoulder. She was dressed, so he joined her, sitting on the chunk of weathered stone. Their perch had a gently sloping view of cleared, dirt-and-stone-scraped land leading down to the harbor; it was easy to see where the old cobblestone streets had been, which foundations were too weathered and damaged to safely use, and which buildings had possessed enough dirt for a little garden or vegetable patch.

"First priority in land use goes to the animals, of course. We build them stables and fowl houses and kennels. We have exercise yards and pasturage. Above the stables and such, we build tene-ments, suites much like the wings of your palace, save that bathtubs are communal, since it's cheaper to heat large tanks of water that several people can use, and share the responsibility among those in each tenement to keep the fires burning. Cooking is normally done per kin-family when we travel," she explained, "but in winter, it's communally done like the bathing is, since it's more fuel-efficient. The kitchens are in the center of each building, with the hearth chimneys adding to the heat for all the rooms around the outside, which are usually bedchambers and such—we build in circles, you see, like the shape of the maiden's *geome*."

"The what?" he asked.

"*Geome* is the name for the special domed tents we use on the Plains," Amara explained, twisting to pick up a stray stick behind the weathered, square-edged stone they were using for a bench. Lean-ing forward, she sketched in the dirt. "The maiden's *geome*, where all the young women stay after they become women, but before they've chosen a husband, is one of the largest *geomes* in a Family. It's so large that its dome roof has inner support poles forming an inner ring, like this."

She drew a large circle, then poked holes, forming an inner ring. Then she drew wiggly lines between the holes and the outer line for the tent wall, and wiggly lines connecting the dots into a ring. Trevan frowned, concentrating on the map as she explained.

"Between the posts are horizontal poles, from which we hang curtains, dividing up the spaces into little walled chambers. They're usually just big enough for a bed, a chest or two, and a chair. That's the bedchamber for each maiden. The central area here contains the travel-stove, braziers for heat around the perimeter, and enough workspace for most of us to tend to whatever task needs doing if the weather's bad outside. A regular *geome* has room for the mated couple's bed, maybe a few cots for their children, chests and chairs, and a travel table or two, plus individual workspace, but it's smaller overall." She used her foot to erase the circles and little scratch marks she had made for furnishings and redrew everything. "For our tenements, we have the circle of the stables at the bottom, with grain bins in the center and hayloft around the edges, and a stairway spiraling up like so.

"Then comes the kitchen, and workrooms around the edges, with a refreshing room or two. The next floor is the bathing hall and refreshing rooms, with bedchambers around the edges. The attic above has storage space, usually for preserved foodstuff stored there by the Families working on the farms that year. There's an average of five or six buildings per Family, many connected by covered passages that in turn form the sheltering walls for that Family's exercise yards, making a little compound." She drew several more circles, connecting them with double lines. "It makes the outskirts of the City look sort of like a series of towered fortresses. Between each Family-ring are dotted the craft-halls and gather-buildings, providing places for people to barter and trade their belongings and foods, and storehouses for the cargoes that weren't able to be delivered across the Plains before the onset of winter."

"This is unlike any city I've ever heard about," Trevan admitted, shaking his head. "I'm not sure how much of it will be applicable to our own needs."

"Oh, I've studied other city types." Amara hastened to reassure him. "These are actually the ideal configurations we came up with for large numbers of transient populations, in two centuries of developing a way to successfully live on the Plains. You'll find the

Family rings on the outskirts. The Oldcity section was built in the first few decades after the Shattering along the same lines that had been there before—a rough grid of streets, buildings that are rectangular. There are entertainment halls, temple and palace compounds, and things like restaurants and forges, things that aren't easily packed up and moved away each spring.

"The Family rings are occupied and then abandoned each year, but the Oldcity section is never emptied. There are eight main roads leading into it, from the eight cardinal and ordinal compass headings, but beyond that, it's a typical maze of streets and alleys. Inefficient, in other words." Lifting her gaze to the roughly cleared landscape before them, Amara surveyed it with a critical but appreciative eye. "You had the same inefficiency of hodgepodge design here—each general area being built at a different moment than the rest, and not always in harmony with its neighbors. The terrain is a factor, too, since over to the north are steeper hills than down there to the south. But there was some logic to it . . . and being able to start over almost completely anew, we could easily plan for a city that grows in stages, yet remains unified in design. Because they *all* grow in stages."

"For a woman whose people are nomadic most of the year, you sound like you prefer city life," Trevan observed, eyeing her. "Or am I off the mark?"

Amara met his gaze. "No, you're right . . . and it's not an easy thing to admit, *because* most of my people love traveling around the Plains. *I* like stability and order. I like having things defined. I like knowing that if I arrange my furnishings just so in my bedchamber, that if I set up some task on a table, I don't have to pack it all back into a wagon ten days later and not be able to fully access whatever I was doing until we reach the next watering hole." She looked back across the half-cleared vista and muttered, "I *don't* like being in exile, forced to move from place to place."

"Then you're in luck," Trevan said, scooting a little closer, until their elbows and knees bumped, making her glance at him again. He smiled to reassure her. "You don't have to move from here, if you choose to stay. You're safe and among friends . . . if you give us a chance to *be* your friends. And, since you know so much about different kinds of cities, you could feel useful again. Because I have the impression that you, in your efficiency-happy way, hate being useless, or at least hate having nothing to do."

She let out a scoffing sound, but she couldn't refute it outright. Folding her arms across her chest, she gave him a lofty, "Maybe . . ."

Smiling, Trevan leaned a little closer, swept his hand over the view of the cove, and offered, "Just *think* about it. An entire city, built literally from the ground up. It's not a task that can be completed in a single winter. It cannot even be completed by summer, or within a year, and probably not even a decade. This Shifting City of yours, it's already mostly built, right? Where's the challenge in that? Plenty of headaches," he agreed quickly, "but most of those come from inefficiencies that cannot be changed, because they were *built* that way by preceding generations.

"This is a near blank slate you could help us draw upon," he murmured into her ear, enjoying the scent of her this close. Her clothes still smelled faintly of soapleaf, but the rest of her was sweet and feminine. Dragging his attention back to what he was saying, Trevan coaxed her some more. "Years and years worth of work. Hard work, and slow to bear fruit, given we're literally starting from scratch . . . but I think you'd love doing it. If you chose to stay."

"And *if* I can get along with your Queen, you mean?" Amara dared to tease, her tone dry, but her mouth curving in a wry, acknowledging smile.

Trevan took the opening she gave. "What is it about her that rubs you the wrong way?"

He would have to ask me that. Blushing, Amara looked away. "It's not admirable."

"Who said it has to be? How you feel is how you feel," Trev pointed out. "Once you acknowledge it, how you deal with it makes the difference. And if it's something I can help you with . . ."

"I doubt it," she returned dryly, glancing at him. He didn't look away, holding her gaze, until she felt compelled to admit the truth. "I'm *envious* of her. There. I've admitted it. There's nothing admirable about it . . . and I can't seem to help it. She just . . . she rubs me *raw* by her mere existence."

"What is it, exactly, that you don't like?" Trevan asked, wanting to know. "Her hair? Her freckles?"

"The Gods picked *her* to be your Queen. They made *me* with all that I could need to be a queen myself, among my people . . . and They arrange my fate so that I have to flee everything I was preparing to do with my life," Amara admitted bitterly. "I had *everything* planned out. I was *happy.* I liked my work. I was useful—and *good* at it. I was respected and admired, and then the Gods made my . . . made my whole world come tumbling down," she said, almost saying *made my sister what she is,* before finding a way to amend it and keep her twin's secret. "I don't have anything left . . . and to find out she's an outworlder, yet the Gods have favored *her* over *me* . . . it galls me."

"No wonder you cling to your pride, if it's all you have left," Trevan murmured. Deciding the moment was right, he shifted a little closer and looped his arm around her shoulders, pulling her close. She stiffened a little, then leaned into him, sighing roughly, allowing him to rest his jaw against the top of her head. Holding her in a one-armed embrace, he comforted her. "You know, it may be true that you arrived here with nothing but your sister and your clothes, exiled far from home by secrets and enemies . . . but there's nothing stopping you from starting over, except you. And all you have to do to start over is accept our friendship."

"Don't you mean I have to accept that Prophecy thing and marry you?" she countered sardonically, though Amara didn't move away from his embrace. Mainly because she hadn't allowed herself to lean on anyone, figuratively or literally, in a long time . . . and it felt good leaning against him.

"You don't have to do anything you don't want to. Of course, if you don't relax your death-grip on your pride and open your eyes to all the possibilities around you," he amended lightly, "you'll never allow yourself to *see* all the things you *could* end up wanting to do. I can understand being bitter about not being able to do what you were born to do. But that doesn't mean you can't find something else to do with your life. Something that might end up being far better than anything you may have originally planned."

That made her snort and sit up, pulling away from him a little. He kept his arm around her, though he let his hand slide down to her *chamsa*-covered ribs, where it made her nervous from the tingling feel it engendered. "What could *you* possibly know about being exiled and denied your birthright?"

He smiled wryly. "My brothers and I were born the heirs to the Corvis County. We had a grand future ahead of us—Saber would have stayed as Count of Corvis after our parents died, Wolfer would still be his huntmaster, Dominor would have gone into politics, Evanor would have continued an excellent castellan for Saber, and the rest of us would have had wonderful careers as crafters of various spells and magical artifacts. I was already earning myself a decent regional reputation as a budding Master Artificer four years ago, even though I was only twenty-one at the time. The same with Kor as a Pyromancer, though he's two years younger.

"Rydan or Morg might have even gone into politics, themselves, though that was more Dominor's ambition, and Dom probably would have made it all the way to being Sovereign, if Rydan and Morg weren't interested in it themselves—Katan is a magocracy, ruled by its strongest mages," he explained at her puzzled look. "Every five years, the top mages of the land may challenge each other for the chance to compete against the current Sovereign, and the stronger mage either stays on the throne, or becomes the new King or Queen. Anyway, when word got out about Kor definitely being a Pyromancer, the Council—the top mages in the kingdom's bureaucracy—took a long hard look at the eight of us, and decided we were the Sons of Destiny the Seer Draganna sang about in her Curse of Eight prediction from a thousand years ago."

"So what *is* this Prophecy?" Amara asked. "Everyone keeps mentioning it, but no one says what it is."

"Technically there are two, one by the Seer Draganna, the other by the last Duchess of Nightfall, who died during the Shattering of Aiar, when all the unshielded, still-active Portals around the world exploded," Trevan explained, tucking her closer against his side with a gentle tug of his hand. That forced her to shift her arm so that it looped around him, making him smile. "The whole text of both Prophecies isn't important, save for three things. The first is the verse about my brother Saber, and is what got us exiled in the first place. Basically, it says that, should he ever fall in love with a maiden, truly fall in love with her, and, well, *claim* her, some unnamed disaster would come at her heel, and Katan would 'fail to aid.'

"Now the Department of Augury interpreted this to mean that if my brother ever fell in love with an untouched maiden and bedded her, the Disaster would happen to the Empire, and it would be so huge, Katan would be *unable* to prevent it . . . and we are not a small kingdom by any means."

"Even the Shifterai have heard of Katan, in the heart of Shattered Aiar," Amara snorted, tilting her head to rest it on his shoulder again. "We haven't heard much, since we have plenty of other things to occupy our minds, but we have heard of it, and of other lands. Mostly because my sister has a bizarre affinity for digging through old records and sharing her findings with anyone she can get to sit still long enough to listen. But you were talking about the Prophecy . . . ? Your brother is clearly married, so what was the Disaster?"

"Right, well, that was the misinterpreted part. When the Mandarites arrived, looking for land to conquer and settle—they're in a civil war with the Natallians on the other side of the Eastern Ocean from here, and wanted to find new sources of wealth to back their war—" he explained, "we contacted the mainland for help, and *they* refused to send help. Thus failing to aid us."

"And the Disaster?" she prompted.

"Two interpretations. The disaster of the Mandarites' arrival was one. Dominor was kidnapped, and I was injured by one of their weapons, trying to rescue him. We got him back, of course, after he fulfilled his own Prophecy verse," Trevan shrugged, "which was after Wolfer fulfilled *his* verse, so on and so forth. The other Disaster interpretation . . . well, in the middle of Ev's verse happening—his courtship with Mariel—the Council of Katan finally got off their lazy benches and paid us a visit, looking for women on the Isle. Which they had declared to be an offense punishable by death."

"Because they still thought that the Disaster was something that would ruin all of Katan," Amara concluded.

"Exactly. Well, when Kelly said she was going to Ring the Bell, one of the Councilors challenged her for it, and during the combat, she ended up pinning him to the floor with her foot . . . and humiliated him until he yielded the fight to her. Thus fulfilling a Prophecy about *him* learning humility 'at the heel of a true leader,' according to *that* Curse," Trevan explained. "Which was his own personal Disaster, delivered literally at her heel."

Amara twisted her head to glance up at him. "Your kin-family seems to have a lot of Prophecies associated with it."

"I'd noticed. Anyway, that was Saber's verse, and it's the reason we were banished here, and when Kelly came and decided she didn't want to hide among us in our exile, we started seeing the possibilities of independence from the Empire. Now, *my* verses, in the Song of the Sons, and the Curse of the Isle, are what you really want to know about, because they do actually pertain to *you*."

"Do they, now?" Amara drawled, sitting up in her skepticism. "I've already told you how I feel about the Gods meddling in my life. Besides, it might *not* be me."

"Hush," he chided, tucking her head back onto his shoulder with his hand. Resting his cheek on her soft hair, he continued, resettling his arm around her waist. He couldn't give her his verse verbatim, since that would give away a certain fluffy hidden identity, but he could hedge around the exact wording. "My verse is very clear about referring to the two of us . . . and *you* caused it."

"Me?"

"Yes, you. Part of it reads, 'Before you in the woods she flees,' and 'catch her quick, and hold her fast.' You're the one who decided to take off into the woods, yesterday, forcing me to catch you and hold you fast so that you wouldn't injure yourself any further."

Again, she lifted her head, this time quickly enough to bump his cheek out of her way. "You're making that up!"

"Not at all!" Trevan countered, meeting her skepticism head-on. "It spoke of me roaming through the forest before encountering you—and I indeed met you in the forest on the north end of the Isle. You ran from me, and I gave chase."

"And what *else* does it say?" Amara inquired skeptically, arching one of her brows.

Trevan closed the distance between them, resting his forehead against hers so that all either of them could see were each other's eyes. "That I would find my sense of home in you." She tried to snort and look away, but he lifted his other hand to her chin, holding her in place. "You've been looking for a sense of home, because you've been exiled from everything you know. Why shouldn't I feel the same way?"

Her gaze dropped from his. "Because . . . because you're clearly not as bothered about it as I am."

"A traveler can still enjoy the delights of a foreign land, even if they're secretly longing each night they're away for the day when they can once again sleep in their own bed." Dropping his own eyes, Trevan gave her a confession his own family would have scoffed at. "You envy Kelly for having what was taken from you. I envy my elder brothers for having their wives . . . and it's the little things I miss most. The touch of a hand, the sharing of a jest, a compliment received with a smile and a blush. Being able to sit here, with my arm around you, *talking* with you, makes me feel almost giddy with hope."

Amara felt her cheeks warm at his words, but couldn't quite let go of her skepticism. He was a foreigner, and probably wanted things no proper maiden of the Plains would permit outside of the marriage bed. "With hope for *what*?"

"That you're enjoying our conversation and are willing to sit here and talk some more."

A strange sense of disappointment wriggled inside of her. "*All* you want is to sit and talk?"

Twisting his head, Trevan tucked hers underneath his cheek. "For now, yes. Too many people rush past the little things, searching for the bigger pleasures in life. And I told you, I'm a hedonist at heart. I like *everything* about courting a woman. I also find your company enjoyable."

That made her snort derisively again. "I know very well I haven't been enjoyable to be around!"

Trevan chuckled and squeezed her a little. "You've had good reason to be prickly, after all that you've been through. But *now* . . . you're being enjoyable, aren't you? And, if you like, you can choose to continue being pleasant, now that you know there's little need to remain paranoid around us. That is, assuming you were satisfied by all of our answers last night?"

"For now," she grudgingly agreed.

He laughed outright, at that. "Your sister was right—you *don't* give in easily."

She elbowed him, since he was holding her too close for her to pull free. "Just for that, I'll make you work even *harder* at courting me. I have high standards, you know—and high expectations!"

"I'd expect no less from a woman who was expecting to be a queen. But since the Gods have something *else* in mind for you . . . how about being a mayor?"

Lifting her head, Amara stared at him yet again. "Mayor?"

"Why not? Kelly may have a knack for ordering the rest of us around, but she can't be everywhere, or do everything. She knows this and admits it. Running a town—once we *have* a town to run," he amended, shrugging, "will be a full-time job. A *stable* job, where you won't have to pack up and move every ten days, spring through autumn. You'll have a permanent home, a permanent career, and a chance to prove just how efficient all of your ideas about city management can be. Plus, you'll have the best of all possible perks at your fingertips."

"What would that be?"

"Me." He grinned as he said it.

It was her turn to laugh. "You're full of yourself . . ."

"Perhaps, but I'm rather charming all the same."

He was, but Amara wasn't going to let him know it. Not that

readily. She gave him a mock-stern look and dragged the topic back to its earlier place. "You never said what the other Prophecy had to say about me."

"Well, it doesn't actually say anything about *you*," Trevan hedged. "It's just two lines, about swiftness being slowed, and bound to please one."

"And that relates to you, how?" she asked.

"To be honest . . . I used to chase a lot of women, in my past," Trevan admitted. "But I was the one who did the chasing, and while I had fun chasing the others . . . I never let myself be caught. So I should put *you* on notice that *I* won't be easy to catch and hold, even if I do court you. If you want me to keep courting you, I'm afraid you'll have to prove that you're worthy of my attention."

Amara stared at him, taken aback by his words. But not for their arrogance. In all her past courtings—brief but many—*her* worth had never been in doubt. In fact, it had been the primary reason why so many men had sought her hand, because her *worthiness* as a Shifterai woman had never been questioned. She was a shapeshifter, a princess, and thus among the most desirable of all women.

Trevan of Nightfall simply didn't *care* that she was a shapeshifter. He didn't know that she was the most powerful shapeshifter her people had seen in their two centuries of existence. It did not matter. By whatever measurement he would be judging her, he would be judging *her*, not her abilities or her reputation.

As much as that was a relief to realize, knowing that he wasn't courting her for outside gain, it was also an embarrassment. She hadn't exactly been acting *worthy* since their first meeting. Unable to look at him, Amara lowered her gaze, wondering what he could have possibly seen in her that interested him, aside from some Seer's vague ramblings.

Seeing her flush and look away, Trevan lifted her chin with his finger, urging her to look him in the eye. "Never doubt that you can hold my attention, Amara. If you put your mind to it. The Gods Themselves had no doubts, otherwise you'd still be back on the Plains. Unless . . . You said you had your life planned out for you, before it all went astray," he recalled, frowning softly, worriedly. "Did that include the man you planned to marry?"

She scoffed at the idea, her embarrassment broken. "Hardly. A Princess of the Shifterai is sought after by every eligible male, young and old, simply because she's a princess, a fellow shapeshifter . . . and is a potential heir to the current Queen." At his questioning look, she explained. "Our culture is somewhat like yours, in that every winter, any princess of the age of twenty-five or older may challenge the current Queen in a shapechanging contest. The contestants are judged by the purity of their shapes, how closely they can match a particular type of animal, and by the number of shapes they can take.

"Our Queen is known as Aitava of the Sixteen Shapes, because that's how many pure forms she managed to shape—most shapeshifters can only manage six to eight shapes, and no more. It's refreshing to be wanted by someone who neither knows the extent of my abilities, nor cares about my political chances."

"Well, I'll admit I neither know nor care, as you say, about your political affiliations. But I will admit I'm curious about your shapeshifting," Trevan admitted. "If the average Shifterai can manage about seven shapes, and your Queen more than twice that, where do you fall on the scale? What's your limit?"

Amara smirked, realizing that, for once in her life, she was free to boast about her abilities, because her audience wouldn't care. Or rather, wouldn't covet or feel the bite of envy. "The only limit I have found is the length of time it takes me to study an animal and shift myself to match the function and purity of its form."

"So how many . . ." Trevan broke off as two wolves loped into view, swerving their way. "We have company."

"Company?" Amara asked, tensing as she glanced between him and the approaching animals. "I thought your kin-family were the only ones on this island. Since when did you start having Shifterai for visitors?"

Trevan chuckled and shook his head. "Not Shifterai. Spell-shifters. The darker one is Wolfer, and the lighter is his wife, Alys."

The wolves trotted up to within a few body-lengths, then rippled, rising up onto their hind legs and resolving into their natural forms. Wolfer grinned at his brother. "There you are, you lazy beast. Morganen's heard some interesting news from the mainland, via mirror. There was a sailor who visited us a couple weeks before the Council did, a man named Marcas. He said he'd be interested in moving to the Isle and turning fisherman, once he settled his affairs on the mainland.

"Kelly suggested a better offer yesterday morning, offering for him to be the official ferryman of Nightfall, running a boat between here and the mainland and carrying cargoes and passengers for a modest but profitable fee, and he has accepted. He'll be arriving within the week to set up house and start his ferry-service between here and Orovalis—that's a major port city on the coast a little north of here," Wolfer added to Amara in explanation. "The Council has grudgingly agreed to allow us to begin importing settlers from Katan openly *and* has announced officially to the whole coast that we're no longer considered in exile. Visitors, both male and female, may come and go without penalty of death."

"About Gods-be-damned *time*, considering we Rang the Bell in front of half the Council *weeks* ago," Trevan muttered. He shook off his irritation, addressing his older brother. "Let me guess. Our first priority is building a house down by the harbor for this Marcas?"

"Of course." Wolfer glanced at Amara, his wolf-gold gaze meeting her amber one. "If you have any ideas on where to put it, you'd better start consulting with our Queen—politely—so that we'll know where to focus our efforts."

"Why don't we go down to the harbor and have a look, before going back up to see if Kelly has found any useful maps?" Trev offered, glancing at Amara.

"I wouldn't mind a second view of what we have to work with," Amara agreed. She glanced at the other two and said what she hadn't been able to say to anyone since leaving the Plains. "Shall we all fly there?"

Wolfer blushed, and Alys choked on a laugh, earning her a dirty look from her husband.

"Wolfer doesn't like to fly," Trevan explained briefly as his sister-in-law only laughed harder. "Why don't *we* fly, while they do whatever they like?"

Stepping forward, Trevan put his back to her and whapped his brother on the arm. Wolfer frowned at him. "What was *that* for?"

"Be polite and turn your back—she's a *natural* shapeshifter," the redhead explained. "Her clothing doesn't shift with her."

Wolfer grunted. "*That's* highly inconvenient."

"Isn't there a way to make her clothes go with her?" Alys asked, glancing between the three of them, since Amara hadn't moved yet. "Some sort of charm or spell?"

Trevan glanced at her, then turned to look at Amara. "That's actually not a bad idea! I think I know of a way to pull it off, too. Some sort of jewelry, such as a necklace or a ring, or maybe an earring, something that has a resizing spell on it so that it won't be lost if you shift into something too small or too large. The only thing that may have prevented your own people from coming up with such an idea is because you've implied you don't have many mages born among your people—most of your magic is bound up in your shapechanging abilities.

"You know," he continued thoughtfully, mind racing as he studied her, "an earring *might* actually be the best idea, or at least some sort of body-piercing. Kelly was telling me about the way some of the people of her world would pierce eyebrows and such, and while fish and snakes might not exactly have ears, they *do* have eyes, and by default, eyebrows.

"And it doesn't actually have to be a very big Artifact, no matter how many clothes you might end up wearing. Serina was showing me the other day how a thumb-sized nutshell has the power to hold three or four chests' worth of belongings. If I incorporated a *myjii* shell into the crafting of the Artifact, using silverthorn extract to blend it into an alloy of gold and silver—"

Rolling her eyes, Alys interrupted him. "—If you don't mind, Trevan, we *do* have more important work to do. Or at least more immediate. Try to focus?

"Whatever you do," she warned Amara, turning to address the other woman, "*don't* get him started on a new Artificing idea when there's other work to be done. He's *always* been this bad, even when we were children. Honestly, I don't know why the others keep thinking his best talents lie in the courting of women, when his *real* obsession is coming up with brand-new toys to play with."

"Marriage has made *you* rather bold and sassy, young lady," Trevan shot back, eyeing Alys warily. He smirked after a moment. "I like it. Keep it up."

Wolfer groaned and hustled his giggling wife away from the two of them. "We'll meet you down at the dock."

ELEVEN

"These are *really* good plans," Akelly told Amara, eyeing each of the sketches the Shifterai woman had come up with in the last three hours.

"You needn't sound so surprised," Amara retorted dryly. "This *is* one of the things I'm trained to do."

"I *am* surprised. You've managed to come up with some very good ideas in a very short period of time."

Trevan had stayed with her just long enough to help smooth over the initial meeting with Akelly before both of them had left Amara to her self-appointed task. She had worked hard and fast after returning from the cove to find five different maps of the streets and buildings that used to exist, along with a goblet of a nasty, bitter, milky-white brew called Ultra Tongue, something that the youngest brother, Morganen, had insisted she drink. The potion was supposed to grant her the ability to speak and be understood in

any language, though its most blatant effect so far was the very useful ability to read old languages.

It made her eyes twitch, but Amara could live with that, since it
allowed her to read the local writings flawlessly. Being able to read
that writing had helped immensely in her work. Having the original
maps, replete with notations of things like warehouses, taverns,
marketplaces, and the like as recorded during different periods over
the course of several centuries of city growth, had given her a very
good idea of what a coastal city needed.

Now, alone together in the main map room, Amara eyed the
freckled outworlder. Her envy was still there, but Trevan's suggestion about finding a new purpose in spite of his and his brother's
exile mingled in her brain with the suggestion that she try being in
charge of the city-to-be . . . which she was already designing, admittedly. Now, looking at the incipient Queen, Amara gave in to
her curiosity. "Would you answer a question, for me?"

"What do you want to know?" Akelly returned, tugging one of
the older maps back into reach so she could trace some of the water
pipes, or maybe it was the sewage system.

"Why did you abandon your world for this one? Why even come
here in the first place?"

"In the first place, I didn't have a choice. I was kidnapped out of
my bed by Morganen." Akelly gave her a sidelong look. She smiled
a little at Amara's blatant confusion. "I had enemies, in the other
realm. After failing to run me out of town through petty harass-
ment, they decided to burn me out of my home . . . while I was
asleep in my bed. Morg saved me. For whatever reason, he was looking for Saber's Destined bride in other universes. I was one of a
handful of possible candidates. When he saw me endangered that
night, he plucked me to safety. And then refused to send me back
until Saber and I both got past our stubborn dislike of each other
and realized we had a lot in common."

"You're from different universes, and you have a lot in common?" Amara scoffed.

"Well, certainly not the superficial things," Akelly returned smartly. "For one thing, my world has no magic whatsoever, while this one is steeped in it. For another, I'm an only child, and he's the eldest of eight. But those aren't the things that matter. We're both overly responsible, we're both highly independent, we're both determined to do what is right and make those around us also do what is right, and we're both used to herding cats, as my people like to say."

That distracted her. Amara frowned softly. "That reminds me. There's a cat running around here, big, orange, and fluffy, a long-hair. Whose cat is it, and what is his name?"

Akelly smirked. "He's no one's pet, though I suppose you could say he has a special relationship with Trevan, one the rest of us don't get to share. As for his name . . . we all just call him Cat. Why, has he been bothering you?"

"No. In fact, he's been rather affectionate. What are you looking for?" Amara asked, lifting her chin at the maps Akelly was tracing.

"Where the sewage waste for the castle and the city all goes, but I can't tell which direction it flows."

Reaching across the map, Amara traced it straight to the desalination complex. "These symbols here show the flow."

Akelly blinked twice rapidly, then rubbed at her eyes with one hand. "I hate the way this stuff makes my eyes itch. The ear-twitching isn't too bad, since it only happens just once whenever I hear a new language for the first time . . . but it happens every damned time I encounter a different language in text."

"Don't your people have anything similar?" Amara asked.

That made the other woman snort. "Hardly. No magic, remember? Though I suppose *some* of the things we have could be considered magic by your standards, if you count the stuff that's very difficult to explain."

"Why don't you try? I might actually understand," Amara challenged her.

Lifting her wrist, Akelly displayed the bracelet-thing. "This is a cryslet, an enchanted communications device. You've seen me use it, right?"

Amara nodded, eyeing the gold symbols on the tapered bands that formed the arms of the bracelet.

"It's based on a device from my world. Or rather, a series of them. Back home, they're made from machines, not spells—just like a water-powered mill is a machine, only the machines in question are a hundred thousand times more complicated and meant for communication, not the grinding of grain," the redhead dismissed. "And that's only one of a hundred thousand other inventions, if not more. Some have analogies in this world, but many more do not.

"Conversely, some things in this world are equally unique, like the Ultra Tongue potion." She flashed Amara a quick smile. "If I could brew batches of it in the other world, either I'd make an obscene fortune selling it to everyone, or I'd start a hundred different wars, as adjacent nations told each other what they *really* thought of their neighbors."

Amara had to chuckle at that. "You're probably right. You and I can understand each other just fine, and it hasn't once guaranteed that we'll get along."

"Well, *this* isn't too bad," Akelly admitted, gesturing at their work on the maps. "And I do appreciate the work you've done. Let's take . . . these three sketches," she added, sorting through the alternate ideas Amara had come up with, "and pass them around at lunch. I'd like to get a consensus from the others. I may have the vision, and you the expertise, but they're the natives to this land and might see any flaws that we've both missed."

Amara nodded and started tidying the other maps spread over the table. Akelly was right; this moment hadn't been too bad between them. A nudge from her conscience made her face warm just a little bit. *No, it wasn't bad at all . . . not when you stopped being so annoyed with everyone, and thus annoying to them.*

Her people called it *the eating of grass*: choking down one's pride and bowing to the winds of circumstance rather than trying to argue and fight against fate. Grass didn't taste good, and didn't go down easily, nor did it always stay down easily if the other person didn't accept the apology graciously, but it had yet to kill the eater that tried. Following the shorter woman out of the map room, Amara found herself hoping that things in this place really were as they appeared. That her sister's secret *would* be safe among these people, should it become known. That she could indeed find fulfillment and purpose running the as-yet unnamed city, filling the void that had been ripped into her life when she and Arora were forced to flee the Plains.

And that Trevan really might be worthy of her as a potential husband. Free will was the first and foremost gift of the Gods to mortals, even if They had also given the world Seers and their Prophecies. *But independence and self-determination aren't enough, if you build yourself a life that has no one to share your triumphs and miseries with*, the same corner of her mind prodded her. *Which is why you were so annoyed with all those would-be suitors, back home. All they wanted to share were the triumphs. Your triumphs, for the most part.*

"Ah, there you are!" The relief in Trevan's voice welcomed both of them as they entered the donjon chamber. He was up on the first-floor balcony to their left, at the entrance to the north wing, and leaned over the railing to address them. "I'm glad to see you're both alive and unharmed. I was about to come fetch you for lunch, since it's almost ready."

"That reminds me," Akelly stated, peering up at him. "When I asked you and your brothers to put a time function into the cryslets, you only put in the hours of the day. I'd like to see a spell added to that to divide the hours into minutes—*and* I'd like to see the spell adjusted so that it's controlled by one central chronometer spell, for accuracy in all cryslets across the Isle."

"What do we need minutes for?" he returned skeptically. "Nothing we do needs to be that precisely timed, save for spells—and those, we can time with enchanted hourglasses. Why would we need to know the exact minute of the hour?"

"Because it's more efficient?" Amara found herself answering before the freckled outworlder could. Out of the corner of her eye, she saw Akelly glance sharply at her, and met the other woman's gaze. "What?"

"I guess we *do* have more in common than I thought. She's exactly right, Trevan," the Queen stated firmly, looking up at him again. "It's more efficient! And because I said so. What's the point of being a queen, if I cannot be arbitrary and autocratic once in a rare while?"

"Once in a *rare* while?" Amara couldn't help challenging her, arching her brow.

"Watch it, or I'll make you feed the chickens," Akelly retorted.

"Hey! Be nice!" Trevan ordered from the balcony. He had to pause as the bells announcing the midday meal pealed overhead in a short, musical tune drafted by Evanor; then he spoke again. "I think I've finally found a use for gauging the minutes in an hour—it's to see how long the two of *you* can get along, before you go back to sniping at each other!"

Amara eyed him for a moment, then thoughtfully turned to the woman next to her. "A pity I don't have any money to my name, or I'd take that up as a bet. Care to front the stake for it and make a fortune with me on it?"

"Sixty for me, forty for you, since I'm putting up the money?" Akelly offered after tipping her head thoughtfully for a moment.

"Fifty-five, forty-five. You'd still have to have my cooperation in order to win, after all," Amara reminded her with a smirk.

"*Unbelievable*," Trevan muttered audibly. "Forget it, both of you! You're not extorting a single coppera out of me by colluding with each other under the guise of a bet. And I'll remind you, Kelly, that it's *your* turn to set the table."

"Spoilsport," Amara muttered, following Akelly toward the stairs. Her comment earned her a snicker from the outworlder, and that made her smile. Maybe they did have a few things in common, after all.

Two nights in a row of good, solid sleep had Amara waking with that strange but delicious feeling of leisurely energy, the kind best expended in a deep breath and a full, yawning stretch. Doing so, of course, dislodged Cat, who woke with a grumble, blinked dazedly at her, then flicked his ears and twisted around, putting his rump to her in what looked like a deliberate show of feline disgruntlement. She grinned and ruffled his fur, scritching and stroking him until he purred and kneaded under her touch, before stretching and yawning himself.

Hugging the cat, who grumbled for a moment before squirming and licking her cheek, Amara admitted she felt better than she had in recent memory. Good food—that wasn't fish after fish—plus good sleep in a warm bed, not having to swim for hundreds of miles while towing her sister on a raft . . . she felt *good*. Until she remembered how awful she had been behaving, lately.

Her good mood evaporated around the edges. Rolling onto her back, Amara grimaced at the ceiling. It was patterned in a forest snowstorm, matching the chill that nipped at the parts of her not covered by the blankets, though at least it was a pretty snowstorm. Reviewing her actions, Amara groaned and covered her face with her palms, wishing the world would go away and spare her any further embarrassment.

At least, until Cat nudged her, sniffing at her fingers. Lowering her arms, she sighed heavily. "I," Amara stated, deigning to scratch behind his marmalade ears, "am a member of Family Ass. Not that there is a *real* Family Ass, but that's what we say on the Plains when someone has been an unconscionable idiot. Rude, bad-tempered, behaving petulantly . . .

"Gods, I should kick myself from here to the ports of Amazai and back. How can these people still like me?" she asked the feline enjoying her caress. "Yes, I've been stressed—and with very good reason—but I'm a Princess of the Plains, and I *should* have behaved more nobly." She wrinkled her nose in distaste. "I suppose I should *apologize* . . . but I never liked the taste of grass."

She lay there, thinking about it as she stroked her fingers through Cat's fur and finally shrugged.

"I suppose I don't *have* to apologize immediately. Eventually, yes; it would only be proper. But I should make sure it's worth my while to bend that far. I'm still not entirely sure if I should stay." Craning her neck, she peered at Cat, who had stopped purring. "Not that it matters to *you*, so long as someone is here to love you . . ."

He blinked at her, then leaped onto her stomach, making her *oof* at the solidity of his weight, before turning his back on her and beginning his morning grooming.

"Hey! Get off!"

In the manner of all cats, he ignored her. Amara thought about shoving him aside, but she was too comfortable to bother. Sleeping in a feather-stuffed bed was a luxury she hadn't enjoyed since leaving the Plains. Judging by the dim light filtering through the curtains, dawn had begun and breakfast would be served soon, which meant she couldn't laze here forever, but she did have some time to spare before she had to rise.

The light blond mage, Evanor, had spoken of adding her and her sister's names to the chalkboard hung outside the dining hall, which served as some sort of magically adjusted chores roster. She could handle that. There were plenty of chores to do down by the shore, too, regarding the construction of a house for this Marcas person who was coming to the island—a man who would have to be questioned, too. There was plenty here to keep her occupied, enough to see if it was indeed worth her while to swallow her pride, eat some grass, and apologize for her behavior. Because if it was worth staying here, it was worth apologizing.

If. There was the question. She wasn't sure if she *could* stay on the island; that would depend on how the others reacted to her sister's secret being exposed. Amara didn't try to fool herself on that point, because at some time, somewhere along the way, someone who was a mage *would* bump into Arora. How these people reacted at that point would show just how safe it really was for the two of them to stay on Nightfall.

I suppose it is *possible that they actually wouldn't want her power,* Amara acknowledged hopefully, stroking her fingers down Cat's spine, as he worked on grooming one outstretched leg. *And if so . . . if she endears herself to them, if I don't make myself more of a Family Ass member*—she thought blushing—*then it might be possible they would consider defending her against others. Because if this city idea takes off, if people do start moving here . . . other mages will come. I can't question every single person who comes to this island . . . but if I had allies, mage-allies capable of helping me defend my sister . . .*

It was an incredible thing to consider. They'd been forced to flee most of the mages that had chased after them, because only another mage of equal power could thwart the spells of a determined foe. She was a shapeshifter, not a spellcaster. Stealth, she could do. Cunning, yes—and she had managed to be stealthy and cunning enough to catch one particularly nasty mage off guard.

Amara had ended the woman's life before she could follow

through on her plan to hurt her spell-captured sister. The mage's death had terminated the spell, freeing Arora in the only way Amara could manage. She didn't like to kill, but she was Shifterai; it was one of the ways her people made their fortunes, though they were always careful to pick lawful prey in righteous causes. Eradicating a single woman intent on torturing and possibly killing one woman for her power wasn't much different from hunting down and ending the lives of a band of criminals intent on stealing, raping, and slaughtering their victims. It was a lawful act of defending someone else.

Fleeing was easier than killing, of course, but if she had a *group* of mages to stand toe-to-toe against a magical foe . . . Amara and her twin wouldn't *have* to flee. Not to mention, if she stayed to see how they would react, she would be able to enjoy regular meals and a comfortable night's rest. "Yes," she decided aloud, making Cat pause mid-grooming to glance at her again. "I'll give them a chance to prove themselves . . . and I'll try to be nicer to give them more of an incentive to defend us, should anyone try to attack."

Cat sneezed and shook his head hard, making his pointy little ears flap. The act fluffed out his mane. He blinked at her, then padded up over her chest—threatening to bruise her breasts from the weighty press of his paws—and lowered his head, lapping at her lips with his raspy tongue. Laughing, wrinkling her nose, Amara pushed him away, sitting up so that he had no choice but to tumble into her lap. Scrubbing his fur in apology, she kissed him on the top of his fuzzy orange head. Then she pushed him to one side and abandoned the bed, finally ready to rise, bathe, dress, and find something useful to do.

Amara ended up spending most of her time alone in the map room, seated at an angled scribe's table suitable for scribbling lists and drafting more detailed plans than the one she had sketched. She was interrupted only by Evanor stopping by with a glass and pitcher of juice at about midmorning, by Trevan dropping by to tell her when lunch was ready, and a second time by his brother—this time, Evanor visited with a plate of fruit and cheese and a fresh pitcher of juice at midafternoon. But it wasn't a bad thing, being left alone. She had managed to be quite productive, once she had started. There were a couple more days' worth of work ahead of her, but she had made an excellent beginning, all things considered.

Kelly had told her to find whatever she needed in the main map room and its two flanking storage chambers. One of the storage rooms contained nothing but racks of rolled up maps, organized by some system that must have made sense to the island's previous inhabitants. Or perhaps the intermittent occupants exiled to the Isle had idly rearranged a few scrolls here and there; that was equally possible, she had to allow.

But it was annoying to Amara to find maps of orchards from the south end of Nightfall mixed in with drawings of temple placements across the island and a detailed series of blueprints for an entertainment house all rolled up together. Well, all rolled up together, save that the maps detailing the arrangement for the upper mid-level balcony seats and some of the backstage riggings were missing and had been replaced with a sketch of an herb garden, a market list, and a scrap of a scroll that, if she read the Katani markings right, were part of the lyrics to a particularly bawdy song. Worse, the bawdy song looked like it was building up to a joke, only the biggest part that was missing contained the punch line. How vexing.

The other storeroom had contained supplies. The ink had dried up, but the silverpoint pencils were still good, as was the framed drawing glass she had found to brace on the scribe's desk, the T square, a ruler marked in whatever local measurements had been popular a couple centuries ago in this corner of the world, and a resin ball, stored in a rune-carved box that had apparently kept it soft and pliable rather than petrified with age. It was sticky enough to hold a sheet of parchment to a surface just firmly enough to keep it in place, yet capable of erasing the marks made by the pencils she had found, without leaving streaks of resin behind.

After that, all she had needed to do was drag over one of the wrought iron lightglobe stands and brace the drawing glass so that one of the globes shone through it from behind. Using resin, she had hung an old map of the cove, a fresh sheet of preserved parchment layered over it, and traced the contours of the western harbor and the placement of the desalination plant. Doing that three times more gave her a total of four potential maps to draw, and a reasonably accurate coastline without having to find a way to measure the actual shore.

Replacing the drawing glass on the scribe's desk and adjusting the glow of the lightglobe, she had spent the rest of the morning referencing terrain features, sketching them in lightly when she was sure of general points of steepness that had forced roads and buildings to diverge from a particular path. After lunch, Amara took a different tack; finding spare paper, she cut it up with a pair of scissors she had found in the second storeroom, sketched various districts and types of buildings and amenities onto the different scraps, and used tiny pinches of resin to stick the scraps onto the contour map.

Parchment was reasonably common in a nation where the greatest wealth of a person was measured in the number of their herd animals, but not that common. And on the Plains, where the trees were limited to the few river valleys that coursed through the grasslands, plus the orchards sheltering at the edges of the crater of Shifting City, paper was expensive. Chalk and slateboards were even rarer, however, since the Plains were far from any sources of those two materials.

Rather than making sketch after sketch after sketch, wasting paper with designs that would be crumpled up at the end of the day, she had learned during her apprenticeship to start with little scraps like these, and use those to "draw" up different city plans. It not only saved on paper to do things this way, it saved on time, since once everything was cut out and marked, she didn't have to keep redrawing it, which even a chalkboard would have forced her to do. For all that it was time-saving and paper-saving, her work was also very effective. Within a couple of hours, she had gone through a full score of variations, noting on several sheets of paper which design variations seemed the most functional and which the most attractive.

It was satisfying work, too, even though it was painstaking. She had forgotten how much she missed making plans. Not the ones made up on the run, which had been the story of her and her sister's life for more than a year, but this kind of plan: meticulous, efficient, carefully considered in a dozen different ways, each for a dozen different needs.

Even though her work absorbed her attention, bringing her a sense of peaceful, satisfactory accomplishment, it was something of a relief to be startled by a knock on the door. A quick glance at the windows told her it was still late afternoon, not quite supper time. The door opened as she straightened, then groaned, feeling the stiffness in her shoulders and back. Trevan leaned his head inside, his green gaze searching for and finding her as she stretched.

Evanor had given her a new set of clothing to wear at breakfast, cut and stitched by his own hands. They were an ankle-length *chamsa* in a golden color, cut a little more like his wife's garment than a proper knee-length one, and an approximation of the gathered *breikas* she preferred, rather than the hose the petite, plump Mariel wore. The *breikas* had a fitted yoke at the waist, tied shut by lacings instead of the drawstring kind she was accustomed to wearing.

That was the style her sister wore, since Arora wasn't a shapeshifter; Princesses wore garments that could be easily and quickly dropped.

Amara didn't complain, however; the *breikas* were a darker gold that went well with the long-sleeved tunic-dress, both cut from a soft, fulled wool that kept her nicely warm despite the cool temperatures of the overcast day. Kelly, Ev had informed her, had taken the time to embroider black threads in scrolling geometric lines at the cuffs, throat, and hem of the *chamsa*. It wasn't very Shifterai in style, which leaned heavily on the animal shapes her people preferred, but the fact that the freckled outworlder had taken the time to make *her* clothing look nice had softened Amara just a little more toward the Queen of this land.

The moment he spotted her, with her scribe's desk positioned sideways to one of the windows on the opposite wall in order to take advantage of the light it cast, Trevan smiled and entered the map room. Nudging the door shut, he approached her, one hand clenched in a palm-up fist. His grin was infectious, making her wonder why he was so happy.

"I did it! At least, I *think* I did it," he amended, stopping next to her. His gaze roved over her body, taking in the new garments. "I like what you're wearing. Let me guess, Ev cut it out, and Kelly embroidered it, am I right?"

"Yes."

Trevan nodded. "I thought as much. Evanor has been making our clothes since we were exiled here, but Kelly has the better hand for embroidery. I don't know if you've seen the portraits she stitched of herself and Saber, but they're hanging in the donjon, on either side of the throne-bench. She puts it on almost everything, in fact."

Holding out his forearm, he displayed the three-color embroidery of black, green, and golden thread on the soft wool cuff of his off-white tunic. Then he turned his hand palm-up again and uncurled his fingers, revealing a small circle made from twists of copper wrapped around what looked like a hollow, curved tube of glass. Amara frowned at it in confusion.

"What is that?"

"I *think* it is a solution to your clothing-carrying problem. I've tested it on myself, but it's hard to find a spell that shapechanges just the body and not the clothes as well—here," Trevan said, setting the odd earring onto the flat top of her desk, next to the box of resin. Unbuckling his belt, he dropped it on the floor, then pulled his tunic over his head. He wore a linen undertunic, keeping him warm in the cool air of the room. "Take that off, and put this on; it's one of my older tunics, so if anything happens to it, I won't particularly care. It should be big enough to cover all the pertinent bits, too, since I'm taller than you, and it hits me at mid-thigh. As soon as you have it on, we can fit the earring into your ear, and you can try shifting shape and see if my tunic survives the process."

Amara blinked at him. Trevan was literally offering her the shirt from his back . . . to see if he had created an Artifact that could keep her clothing with her and still on her whenever she shifted shape and hopefully keep it intact? She looked doubtfully at the woolen tunic, decorated at its neckline with the same painstakingly embroidered plait.

"Go ahead," Trevan urged her. "Seriously, this isn't my best tunic. I've destroyed far better ones than this in previous experiments, through the years."

It *was* a little frayed and worn-looking, she decided, accepting it gingerly. Trevan stepped back and turned around, giving her visual privacy. Sliding off the tallish scribe's chair that went with the desk, she set the tunic on the seat and slipped out of her new *chamsa*. She quickly pulled his tunic over her head, feeling the leftover warmth from his body and smelling his masculine scent, almost as if he had enfolded her into an embrace.

She wasn't small; both she and her twin were a little above the average height for women of the Plains, who were considered taller than the average Aian elsewhere on the continent, but he was taller than her by a finger-length. The cuffs fell over the backs of her hands when she shrugged into it, and the hemline almost brushed her knees. She had to pause to unlace her boots, working quickly to free her feet. Worming her hands up under the hem, which didn't have the convenient side-slits of a Plains tunic, she worked the laces of her *breikas* loose enough to tug off the gathered pants, her undershorts, and the aging but still useful socks she had found in the chest of spare clothes Evanor had brought around the day of her arrival.

Standing there in nothing but his shirt, Amara felt her body tighten and tingle. She wasn't used to feeling this way. Admittedly, she had been courted by some rather attractive shapeshifters back home, but they had actively tried to snare her attention, touching her in spots that were close to but not actually improper, whispering suggestions into her ears of what they would do with her if she took them as her mate, some even going so far as to describe in eloquent detail. Sometimes her interest had been roused, but it had been deliberately aroused.

All *this* man had to do was offer his shirt to her for a potentially destructive experiment, and turn his back to her so that she could don it modestly. This act of kindness, this thoughtfulness on Trevan's part, somehow both intrigued and aroused her. She wasn't expecting any of it, and yet the tightening of her breasts, the clenching of her abdomen, the way she kept wanting to inhale his lingering scent all bespoke a visceral interest. Amara was fairly sure he hadn't cast some sort of spell on her, and she certainly hadn't drunk any potions, but there it was. Standing behind him in nothing but his shirt . . . she wanted him.

TWELVE

❧⸲❧

I t was with a bemused state of mind that she cleared her throat, indicating that he could turn around once again. "Um . . . how do I look?"

His green gaze swept down over her body, covering her from her dark scalp to her pale soles. Trevan, in his enthusiasm to test out his earring design, hadn't considered what it would be like to see her standing there in just his shirt. In *his* shirt. He felt territorially pleased by it and licked his lips, answering honestly. "Beautiful, of course."

She blushed and shrugged, folding her arms across her chest. Dragging the topic firmly back to his experiment, she tried not to think about whether or not he had seen the peaks of her nipples poking at the age-worn wool. "So, now what?"

Blinking, Trevan shoved his physical interest in her aside. It wasn't easy; choosing to chastely sleep with her at night in his cat

form and then spending most of his waking time either in courting her carefully or working on projects like this earring one, hadn't
left him with a lot of personal time in which to blunt the edges of
his desire for her. But he did it. Amara was finally beginning to
relax around him and his family, to show that she indeed had a
nicer side. The others may have deeply doubted it, but the moment he had seen her, picking her way through the northern trees,
he had flung himself into believing his verse of the Prophecy
wholeheartedly.

Amara Fen Ziel, formerly of the distant land of Shifterai, *was* his
perfect woman. He just had to explore her personality and encourage all of her best traits to the surface. Firmly reminding himself
that he had time to court her, Trevan cleared his throat and stepped
close to her. That allowed him to reach past her arm and touch the
tiny piece of jewelry on the top of her scribe's desk. "Now, we at-
tune the earring to your personal magics.

"That was the hardest part, you see. There are a number of
storage-style Artifacts, and with the blending of *myjii* shell powder
into the glass of the tube as a stabilizing agent for the silicon, I knew
I could create a tiny container capable of storing a much larger volume of matter." Licking his lips, he looked at her again. She was
close enough to kiss . . . if he gave in to that urge. Drawing in a deep
breath, he refocused his thoughts. "But the, ah, hard part"—*aside
from myself*—"was finding a way to control the containment and release of your clothes. I finally got the brilliant idea of using your
own magical signature.

"You're not a traditional spellcasting mage, it's true," Trevan
added honestly, "but you still have magic, and you exercise your power
whenever you shift your shape. So, the copper lacing the tube and
forming the hook that fits through your ear will be harmonized to
your personal signature. I just put it through your earlobe, and
while I enchant it, you shift your shape a bit. Nothing too far from

human, so you remain, um, decently clothed, but something that still alters you all over."

"A non-pure form?" Amara asked, wrinkling her nose. She could do it, and had done it at need, but a Shifterai's pride lay in their ability to make themselves indistinguishable from the real thing.

"Well, I have to set the threshold of the spell," Trevan explained. "If you just, say, grew your arms and legs a couple inches longer to be able to reach something on a high shelf, it wouldn't do for the magic of the earring to activate and suddenly leave you . . . naked."

His gaze slipped back down over her body, and again Amara felt her flesh tingle a little. There was something about the way he had hesitated before saying that word that made her aware that she *was* naked, beneath his tunic. His tunic, and not her own clothes.

That made her flesh tingle and ache again. Amara blinked and looked away, focusing on that thought. *Trevan's tunic, wrapped around me . . . yes . . . Trevan's* arms, *wrapped around me . . . oh yes. Yes, I'd better stop* that *line of thinking—what would he think of me, if I abandoned the self-control of a maiden?* Hoping her cheeks weren't as visibly pink as they felt, she cleared her throat and nodded. "Right. Put the earring in, shapeshift a bit, and then once it's set . . . give it a full test. Right?"

"Correct." Picking up the earring, Trevan ducked his head a little, peering at her ears. "I don't see any holes in your ear. This might hurt."

That made Amara snort, eyeing him with a touch of impatience. "I'm a shapeshifter, Trevan. I *make* my own earring holes—why should I endure the pain of a piercing, if I don't have to?"

"Good point." He waited while she tilted her head to the side, scraping her black locks behind her left ear, then her lobe rippled slightly, dimpling into a hole. Lifting the earring, he gently slotted the wire of the post through the hole she had formed. "Alright, I'm going to hold the clasp closed and chant. While I'm chanting, I want you to shift slowly from this body to some . . . some two-legged animal form. It won't be a 'pure' form, but if you turn yourself into a bipedal, fur-covered cat or something, that will be a good calibration of just how much magic it will take for the earring to need before activation.

"And then shift into a four-legged form—but go slowly, both changing into it, and changing all the way back to your human form," he emphasized. "I'll have to keep holding the earring closed and chant while you do so, to infuse it with the gauging spell. Ready?"

Amara nodded a tiny bit, hyperaware of his fingers against the side of her neck. She was very ticklish around her neck and didn't want to startle him into touching her lightly there. "Um, ready. Give me a three-count, when *you're* ready."

"Three . . . two . . . one. *Annanou disek courou jam. Annanou disek courou zham* . . ." Trevan recited in a flat, unmusical monotone, focusing his magic through the mnemonic words, changing them as gradually as she changed. It wasn't *his* power he was trying to match to the earring, after all, but hers.

Slowly, the soft skin under his knuckles sprouted velvety-soft fur. He managed to keep his grasp as steady as his chanting, until she lifted a claw-tipped hand, pointing downward in silent warning that she was about to shift to all fours. He chanted steadily, but poured more of his own energies into the spell, infusing the copper with a tingling awareness of the life-energy she was using with her transformation. Stooping carefully, matching her movements, he followed her as she dropped into a crouch, then into a four-legged stance, becoming a lean, long-legged, spotted hunting cat draped awkwardly in his tunic.

Staying with her, ignoring the ache in his back, Trevan kept chanting while she shifted gradually back. Her body straightened into an upright stance, her bones shifted from lean predator to lean woman, and the fur retreated back beneath the smooth expanse of her skin. Bringing his chant back to a close in reverse order wasn't easy, but he managed. His fingers protested with little cramped twinges when he released her earring, but when he twisted her lobe slightly to look at the back, the copper wiring had fused itself into a solid piece.

"There. That should do it. You'll have to shapeshift the earring free to take it off, but it should function. Presuming it passes the full-shift test."

"I don't think it did," Amara told Trevan, giving him a dubious look. "Your shirt stayed in place, in spite of my change."

He shook his head. "This was just the calibration spell. The next time you *don* a garment, that garment should go into the earring when you get to the stage in the transformation where it's necessary to remove it. I had you change into my shirt first to ensure that your own weren't risked by your transformation during the final stage of enchantment. All you have to do now," Trevan explained, "is take it off completely, put it back on, and the spell should work the next time you transform . . . I think."

Amara wasn't too reassured by his caveat at the end, but nodded, accepting it. She waited for him to turn around, and waited . . . and finally lifted her hand, twirling her finger. Flushing, Trevan cleared his throat and turned his back to her. Quickly stripping off his shirt, she hesitated for a moment, then set it on the ground, to be absolutely sure she had removed it completely, waited for a few heart-beats, then snatched it up and shrugged back into it.

"Alright. I'm ready." She started to flex her power, then paused. "Ah . . . do you have to watch, or should you watch, in case some-thing goes wrong?"

Craning his neck, Trevan glanced over his shoulder. "If some-thing goes wrong, you might end up naked. The choice is yours."

"Or strangled in folds of fabric—go ahead and watch," Amara ordered him, though her cheeks heated. "Just in case you need to rescue me."

Trevan grinned, turning back to face her. "Somehow, I doubt you're the type of person who often needs rescuing."

"I should hope not," she scoffed. Drawing in a deep breath, she braced herself mentally and shifted back into the shape of a swift, spotted Plains cat. Her clothing vanished, leaving her naked . . . on four properly formed, fur-covered legs. Amara twisted her head, eyeing herself, then peered up at him.

Stooping, Trevan touched her tuft-tipped ear, which still bore the earring she had carefully kept attached during the shift. He nodded and straightened. "It seems to be in there, though I can't tell if it's all right, just yet. Go ahead and shift back."

Releasing herself back into her normal form, transforming quickly, Amara winced in expectation . . . but the soft scratch of fine-spun wool enveloped her from neck to knee just as quickly. Letting out a relieved breath, she smoothed his tunic over her body and gave him a smile. "It worked!"

"For a full shift," Trevan cautioned her. "I tried to include a gauge of physical privacy. If you're still in a human-like, adult-sized form, you'll be clothed. But if you grow significantly taller or shorter . . . your clothing will probably disappear, even if you're still fully human in shape. The earring only stores your clothes. It doesn't resize them."

Amara nodded. "Understood. I should try this in my own clothes, next."

"Right. I'll just . . . I'll just turn around while you change again," Trevan agreed. He closed his eyes as he did so, resisting the urge to peek. Not for the first time, he saw her as he had seen her—and tried *not* to see her—out in the jungle. Naked. Scratched and dirty, but naked all the same. Breasts just large enough to curve his fingers around. Thighs that were both soft-looking and strong, with muscles hidden under velvety soft skin. That thatch of brown hair concealing her secrets . . .

It would be black now, of course, since she seemed to think her "true" form had night black hair and honey golden eyes. The spell Morg had given him, however, was supposed to trap her in her *true* form. *Which looked remarkably like her sister's, though I didn't know it at the time*, he realized. *In fact, I'd hazard a guess that, unlike the four sets of my brothers and I, Amara and Arora were born identical twins. Somewhere along the way, though, Amara rebelled, developing this exotic self-identity.*

Probably as a part of that self-pride she wears like a ceremonial cloak, he decided, listening to the rustle of fabric behind him. *Her sister isn't ugly by any means, but aside from a reasonably nice figure and eyes almost as green as my own, she's rather ordinary looking. Well, her Aian facial features are exotically pretty, in and of themselves*, Trevan acknowledged. *But that's here, where oval Katani faces predominate. Back on the Shifting Plains, both of their heart-shaped faces are probably a silvara a dozen.*

Add in a normal, average shade of light brown hair, and Arora probably blends into the background. Unless . . . black hair is common on the Plains and light brown is unusual? He remembered something his sister-in-law Serina had once said, about nearly everyone back in the Moonlands having platinum-pale hair. It might be that only on Katani soil light brown was the average, common hair color.

Behind his back, Amara finished lacing her boots in place. Picking up his tunic from the chair, she fingered the soft-scratchy wool. Traces of her own body heat still lingered in its folds, but it wasn't for that reason she curled her fingers into the fabric. A quick glance showed Trevan still standing with his back to her. Lifting the tunic to her nose, Amara inhaled silently, enjoying the warm, male scent he had left behind. It did something to her, invoked thoughts of comfort, even a touch of happiness. It also smelled like wool . . . and a hint of Cat.

He shifted, folding his arms across his chest. Realizing he might be cold, Amara relaxed her grip on the cloth and cleared her throat. "Here. I'm done with your shirt. Thank you."

Turning around, Trevan accepted his shirt. He shook it out and pulled it on and surreptitiously sniffed as the material passed his nose. It now smelled like her, just a little bit. Perhaps he wouldn't put it into the laundry basket in his bedchamber. At least, not immediately. Of course, he did have the real thing to cuddle with at night, even if he was stuck doing it as a cat for the time being. Refastening his belt, Trevan smiled at her and opened his arms.

Amara eyed him askance. *Is he asking for a . . . ? Yes, I think so.* He had just given her a wonderful, useful gift, and hugs *were* allowed in courtships. If Trevan wanted a hug, she would gladly give him one. It also allowed her to smell the real thing as she moved into his arms and tucked her cheek onto his wool-covered shoulder, her nose tickled by the strands of his hair.

With her arms hugging his ribs, she could feel the muscles of his back shift as he wrapped his own limbs around her. Amara silently admitted it felt surprisingly good to hold and be held. Back home, she hadn't allowed many of her would-be suitors to embrace her, even if it was one of the acceptable courtship touches, but this was nice.

Actually, *nice* was a bland word for it. He was warm and comfortable, yet solid. Firm, without being hard. Amara decided he felt kind of like a vertical bed; she just wanted to relax into him and let herself happily drift off into sleep, except she wasn't sleepy. And he wasn't a bed; he was a man.

One didn't live among natural shapeshifters, who were constantly having to drop their clothing in order to change their bodies, without becoming aware of anatomy. She was now quite aware of Trevan's anatomy. Pressed together as they were, from head to thigh, she could definitely feel his anatomy. Aroused anatomy.

It wasn't appropriate for that part of his anatomy to be brushed against her, even if they were both fully clothed. She had to be fair and admit he wasn't actually doing anything with his hips; his erection was just *there*. Still, proper courting behavior demanded self-control on the part of both man and maiden, which meant she had to change that part of their bodily contact.

Normally, she would have shaped claws and prickled him through his clothing in subtle warning to let go and back off. But Trevan wasn't her normal sort of suitor . . . and she wasn't reacting to him like she had all the others. His reaction to her wasn't offensive. Startling, and unallowable, but she wasn't offended by it. Flattered, rather. Unfortunately, that left her with trying to figure out a way to extract herself from its proximity without making it seem as if she were rejecting him. She knew quite well how to reject an unwanted suitor, but not entirely how to treat one that *was* wanted, and that made her hesitate.

Marveling at how such a hard-minded woman could feel so soft and giving, Trevan loved the fact that he was finally holding her in his arms. It was true enough he had only met her a few days ago, but Amara wasn't an ordinary woman. Stubborn, prideful, vexing, beautiful, fascinating, intelligent, wary, and a dozen other things he could have named, but not ordinary.

For all that she was indeed stubborn, proud, and wary, though, she was now in his arms. Warm, soft, feminine, sweetly scented . . . delicious. He gathered her closer, inhaling the scent of her soft black hair, then pulled back a little so that he could look at her. She pulled back as well, golden eyes wide, though he didn't let her move back far. Trevan didn't want to lose the heady feel of her in his arms.

Her tongue made a brief appearance, wetting her lips. He watched the flick of that pink tip, and he knew he couldn't resist the implicit invitation. Dipping his mouth to meet hers, Trevan caught her lips while they were still partly open and nipped softly, parting them farther. She tasted sweet enough to eat; hungry, his own tongue darted out, savoring the soft, full curve of her bottom lip before slipping inside the moment she gasped.

Shock held Amara still. He was—he just—wrong, and yet—the touch of his mouth, the sweep of his tongue, the sheer *intimacy* of being . . . ! Her nerves twisted inside her body, but it wasn't like shapeshifting, and it wasn't painful. It felt *good*, confusingly good. Amara *knew* this was wrong, but—

"How are the city pla . . . oh! Uh, sorry. I didn't realize . . ."

When she heard Kelly's voice so suddenly, not even aware until that moment that the other woman had entered the map room, Amara's face burned with an unbearable shame. Jerking back, she slapped Trevan, belatedly doing what she should have done the moment his mouth touched hers. No self-respecting maiden of the Plains would dare let a man touch his mouth to hers outside of marriage!

Trevan, jaw burning from the sharp impact of her palm, staggered back from Amara, utterly confused by her attack. He could have sworn she was enjoying his kiss! Yet she *slapped* him? Confusion warred with hurt inside of him, both physical and emotional, but his sister-in-law's reaction claimed the majority of his stunned attention.

"What the hell did you just *do*?" Kelly demanded, grabbing Amara by the arm and hauling her around to face her.

Skin still burning, Amara responded with the truth. "I slapped him!"

"Yes, I *saw* that! I want to know *why*," Kelly demanded, glaring at her.

"Because he *kissed* me! Men aren't allowed to kiss maidens—it is *forbidden*!"

Both of the Nightfallers blinked at her. Trevan still looked a bit dazed as he rubbed absently at the reddening handprint on his face, but Kelly looked increasingly furious. Aquamarine eyes narrowing, she repeated, "You slapped him . . . because of some . . . *foreign* custom?"

"It is not a foreign custom!" Amara protested, flushing again. Somewhere, things had started to go terribly wrong. The only thing she could fall back on, to cling to in her confusion, was her position and her rank. "It is *my* people's custom! I am a Princess of the People, and I will *not* be disrespected!"

For a moment, Kelly gaped at her—then her hand whipped up, *cracking* across Amara's cheek. "*That* is disrespect!" she asserted, jabbing her finger at the stunned Shifterai woman. "Whatever land you are in, *those* are the laws and customs you abide by—when in Rome, you do as the Romans do, and when on Nightfall, you do as the Nightfallers do! This is *not* the Shifting Plains, and unless you want to have your butt kicked all the way *back* to them, you will abide by *our* laws!

"The *only* disrespect I see here is how *you* keep insulting *our* way of life! Get out of my sight," Kelly ordered, revulsion twisting her freckled face. "You disgust me."

Amara fled, shame burning through her. Darting through the open door, she lunged to her left, running up the hall. At the first archway to a stairwell, she dashed inside and scrambled up the steps, desperate to reach the roof and fly away from her embarrassment . . . though she knew she could only flee the scene of it.

Back in the map room, Trevan shook off his bewilderment and moved to follow her. Amara *did* have a reason to slap him by her cultural standards, but he did want to talk to her about maybe adopting his. Certainly it would be less painful. Kelly blocked him with her arm, however. He frowned and moved past her, but she grabbed his wrist, halting him again.

"Let her go, Trevan. Let her run away! She's been insulting us from the moment I met her, and there's no way in hell the Gods meant for *her* to be the perfect woman for *you*—you deserve far better than that!" Kelly told him, lifting her chin at the empty hall Amara had used.

"And *you* aren't giving her a chance," Trev shot back, freeing his arm from her grasp. "She has every right to be tense and nervous—we're nothing more than strangers to her, still!"

"That doesn't give her any right to impose *her* values on *our* culture!"

"Why not?" Trevan challenged her. "*You* did. The first time I met you—the first time you were conscious—you laid down a whole list of rules on how the rest of us were supposed to behave around you. Or did you *conveniently* forget that?"

His words took her aback, making her blink and blush. "Well, I . . . That's not the *only* reason I don't like her," Kelly recovered, choosing to ignore his words, since she was unable to refute them honestly. "She disparages my rank and my right to be Queen, she goes around acting like we're all beneath her, and she hasn't done more than two things to *try* to get along with the rest of us! She's disrespectful, arrogant . . . I *don't like* her!"

Leaning in close until he loomed over her, Trevan ordered, "*Learn*. Being a queen isn't just about giving orders. It's about *diplomacy* and finding and encouraging the *best* in people, not in dragging out their worst!"

Kelly paled, then reddened again. A muscle flexed in her jaw, and Trevan could have sworn he heard her teeth grinding, but she dragged in a rough, deep breath, held it, and let it out slowly. Under control. "Until she *apologizes* for her misbehavior . . . I do not think she will be *capable* of showing her 'best.' Regardless of whether or not she has it!"

"She slapped *me*, Kelly. As the person who was struck, it is up to *me* to decide whether or not she should apologize—and by *her* way of thinking, I did deserve it! Had one of us kissed *you* without advanced permission, that first breakfast together, you *would* have slapped one of us, whether or not you liked it," he reminded her. "Jinga's Tits! You pinned Dominor to the floor on that very first day, just for being insolent about following your orders, which *you* imposed upon us!"

She couldn't meet his gaze at that.

"Kelly, *give* her a chance," Trevan half-ordered, half-coaxed. "If she can be convinced to trust us, I think there's a woman hidden inside of all that protective armor she wears that *could* be worthy of joining us. But if you keep *jabbing* at her, forcing her to remain on the defensive, she'll never open up! As for Nightfall customs, we don't *have* any, yet. Other than the ones about being polite and civilized."

"As soon as *she* starts being polite and—" Kelly began.

Trevan lifted his hand between them, cutting her off. "—Enough! That goes *both ways*, Sister. Sometimes *you* have to bend first. It's called leading by example. Maybe you ought to try it?"

Brushing past her, he stalked out of the map room. Amara was long gone, probably running back to her rooms, or maybe out into the forest again. He didn't have a tracking spell on her, so there was little he could do about catching up to her. There was, however, something he *could* do, and that was learn more about Shifterai customs.

The fact that her people didn't seem to believe in kissing outside of marriage ran contrary to all the mating customs *he* knew about. Admittedly, Trev knew mostly just the Katani customs and some

Natallian and Moonland ones from stray conversations with Mariel and Serina, but he had heard rumors of how other lands handled courtships. Furthermore, so long as a person could afford a contraceptive amulet, he didn't think a culture with access to them would feel the need to make their people refrain entirely from even the most casual of intimacies, such as a mere kiss.

Detouring into the north wing, Trevan headed for Arora's suite. He didn't actually know where it was, but odds were, it was somewhere in his twin's branch of the palace. A quick shapeshift would allow him to sniff her out. Right now, she was supposedly napping to recover her strength from her and her sister's ordeal at sea, though he suspected it was as much to alter her waking hours to better match his twin's.

He didn't envy Arora the task of fulfilling *that* Destiny. Trev loved his brother dearly, but he didn't quite understand the man Rydan had grown into over the last several years. If Arora could manage to understand him, if she could manage to draw Rydan out of his strange, protective shell, he would wish her a blessing from every God and Goddess out there. In the meantime, she was the only person who had a clue about what was going through her sister's head, and she was his only other source of information on the customs of the Shifting Plains.

Shifting into his cat form, Trevan trotted along the second-floor corridor, guessing that she might be on the same level as his brother's rooms. Someone would have put her there to try to force the two of them into proximity, since not even Rydan the Stubborn could avoid his Destiny forever. Sure enough, he spotted someone standing at a door, conversing with someone else on the other side of the almost-shut panel. The light brown hair of the first figure proclaimed immediately that her visitor was Morganen. Curious, he moved closer, approaching just in time to hear Arora giving a reply.

"There are things about your brother which *none* of you

understand," Trevan heard her say, and he flicked his ears forward, straining to hear more. She continued, addressing his youngest sibling with a hint of sharpness in her otherwise gentle tone. "Until I can find a way to fix those things, pressure from his family would only make them worse!"

So the soft-spoken twin has some of the same inner steel as her sister? Trevan quickly decided that was a good thing. Arora would need to be strong, to be able to break down the layers of defenses his own twin had built up over the years. *But what kind of pressure, aside from the stick-of-obviousness smacked into his stubborn head . . . and what would be made worse for Rydan?*

"Now, if you don't mind," he heard her add tartly, distracting him from his silent questions, "I'm going back to bed. Good night! Or good afternoon . . . whatever!"

Morganen pulled back from the door quickly, avoiding being bumped by the panel as it *thumped* shut, firmly barricading him from further conversation. Trevan didn't know what the two had been talking about beyond Rydan, but it looked like his own conversation would have to be delayed. He turned to go, only to find himself overtaken by Morganen, who scooped him off the floor, startling a *mrraurf* out of him.

"Hello, Cat," Morg greeted him, cradling his transformed brother against his chest with one arm, freeing the other so that he could scratch at Trevan's ruff. "What brings you nosing along here? Did you lose your own bride?"

That narrowed Trevan's eyes, but he didn't bother to comment, otherwise. After Kelly's interference, he didn't need Morg's style of meddling to add to his problems. Not today, at any rate. As soon as they reached the junction in the *Y*, he squirmed and leaped free, padding into the northeastern wing.

"Fine," Morg muttered. "See if I tell you where your quarry went, you fickle feline!"

That almost made Trevan turn around, but until he learned more about the Shifterai ways that Amara expected, he knew it would be useless to track her down. Tail jauntily raised, with the perfect insolent droop curling its fluffy tip, he ignored his brother and trotted onward.

Dinner was a strange affair. Kelly was still upset, though she somehow held her tongue. Amara, having returned from wherever she had gone, was incredibly subdued, only offering up a please or a thank-you when dishes were passed her way. Neither female glanced at the other, and even though Amara sat across from him, she didn't look at Trevan, either. As soon as the meal ended, she stood, murmured an excuse, and left.

Her twin stood as well, but not to leave; instead, Arora fixed a plate of leftover food. Trevan didn't have a chance to ask her for an hour of her time. The plate was for his twin, and she seemed determined to go straight to him, since Rydan hadn't shown up in time for supper. Trevan wanted to ask her *how* she thought she was going to find his twin . . . but she had apparently found him once already, he reminded himself, watching her leave through the door his eldest brother held for her.

Found him, got through his wards, and was "attacked" by him . . . in such a manner that she herself wasn't all that upset by it. Gods . . . why did I end up with the confirmed maiden of the pair?

Guessing she wouldn't get far, Trevan decided to stake out her suite and catch her when she returned. Whatever power she held, it had allowed her to sneak up on Rydan the other day. It would no doubt get her past his wards a second time, but that was no guarantee she'd get past Rydan himself. His womb-mate could be quite stubborn at times, and rather bullheaded when it came to his own good.

No, she'd be back within an hour or two. Trevan would transform, wait outside her room with the patience of a real cat stalking a mouse hole, and would simply knock on her door once she had returned and was inside. Once he learned exactly what sort of expectations Amara had, he would be able to court his Destined wife much more effectively.

He'd also find some way for Amara to apologize for slapping his cheek. The side of his jaw still felt a bit tender, though the red had faded. *Or at least find some way of getting her to kiss it and make it feel better . . .*

Ever since running out of the map room, Amara had been unable to outrun her thoughts. They whirled and circled, jabbed and poked. She had found herself flying through the forest, seeking the ravine where she had fallen. It had been a little hard to find, but eventually she had found the right fallen tree, not far from the marks her body had gouged in the steeply sloped earth during her uncomfortable fall. There, it wasn't Queen Kelly's anger or Trevan's shock that had haunted her for nearly an hour, but her own sister's words.

Words of truth, about never again being able to go home. About having to give up the Plains even in her heart. As much as she longed to deny it, even Amara knew that the Shifterai would never be able to help Arora. Not to control her power, or to explain it, or somehow make it completely unattractive or at least unavailable to mages. It was magic, pure power on a level she couldn't understand. Something that only a mage could comprehend, let alone handle. Which meant that, as long as her twin lived, Arora would have to search for mages who could help her somehow.

Running wasn't the right solution. Staying on the Plains had proven worse than running, for it had endangered their kin, but a lifetime of running wasn't a life! This place, these people, had sworn they wouldn't covet her sister's powers. They might even be able to help, either in containment or in finding a solution to Arora's dilemma, though Amara wasn't going to hold her breath over the latter.

But if this was a safe place to stay, as her twin kept claiming . . . her own protective attitudes had clawed and scratched the surface impression she should have been making. Amara couldn't escape that singular fact. Time and again, she had heard the Lords of the Families caution their warbands to *heed* the laws of other lands, so that all Shifterai would be welcomed . . . and customs were very much like unofficial laws.

When in Rome, do as the Romans do. When on Nightfall, do as the Nightfallers do . . . She had no idea where this Rome place was, but she *was* on Nightfall. Living among Nightfallers. She had always been the dutiful daughter, the good daughter, the one who heeded every custom, obeyed every law, and made her parents proud of her. Whether or not they were Plains laws should not have mattered . . . if she were truly interested in being a good and dutiful person, keeping her parents proud of her.

Returning to the castle at sunset, when the bells for the evening meal rang, she had washed away the tears that had escaped onto her cheeks at some point and forced herself to join the others for dinner. But everything she tasted, from the tender beef to the mashed roots with garlic sauce, tasted like grass in her mouth. No one tried to talk to her, either, other than to ask for something to be passed their way. Unable to eat more than a few mouthfuls, Amara retreated as soon as she could leave without giving insult and hid in her room. Which these people had given her, along with the food and her new clothes, without any expectation or at least direct mention of repayment.

Even the cat seemed to be avoiding her. The first night, he had joined her without her noticing it, and the second, he had brushed against her calf deliberately before trotting into her suite as if he owned it, letting her know he was there. Tonight, nothing. She was left alone.

Uncomfortable from being ignored, feeling like she had been stuck in a second exile, Amara could do nothing but pace in her sitting room and think about her actions, ears straining to see if Cat came by and mewed at her door. It wasn't a comfortable thing to do; the more she thought about her actions, the more she could taste the grass she knew she would have to eat. As much as she might use the excuse of the stress she and her twin had been under, it was only an excuse, and not a good enough reason for bad manners.

A knock at the door startled her. For one wild moment, she thought it was Cat—but that was a silly idea. Cats didn't knock at doors; they were cats. They meowed or scratched. Crossing to the door, she opened it and found herself surprised a second time. Akelly stood on the other side, but she didn't look angry. In fact, her words startled Amara a third time.

"I came here to apologize," Akelly said, holding Amara's gaze steadily. "I shouldn't have yelled at you. I certainly shouldn't have slapped you, and I should have been more understanding of your culture, even if it isn't our own." Her mouth quirked up on one side, though it wasn't exactly a smile. "I, um, actually know exactly how you feel, since I came here still clinging to my own people's ways, as a way to not feel so lost and adrift . . . but I've had to let go of some of them, so that I could blend in better.

"I shouldn't have yelled, and I shouldn't have struck you," she repeated. "There were far better ways of discussing the problem which I could have used, but I didn't choose any of them. I handled the moment in the map room very badly . . . and for all of it, I apologize. I hope you can forgive me."

Amara could only stare at her for a long moment, a strange and uncomfortable realization dawning within her. *She* couldn't have apologized this quickly, yet Akelly had managed to do so. Worse . . . her first instinct was to accept the apology as her due. But her sister's words still haunted her, as did the shame of her own actions, and the taste of grass lingered on her tongue. Amara acknowledged the worst realization of all. *She* wouldn't have made quite as good a queen as this woman, who was the first to swallow her pride and admit she was wrong, even though Akelly technically had been right to chastise her for demanding that the others heed foreign customs, ones that they didn't even know about in the first place.

Amara did what she had to do. She already had the taste of grass in her mouth, so it was simply a matter of chewing on the words and swallowing down her pride. "No, you were right. I was wrong. This . . . this place isn't the Plains, and I have no right to demand any of the treatment I'd be getting if I were still among my people. I shouldn't have slapped Trevan, especially since he doesn't know any Shifterai customs and cannot be held accountable in his ignorance . . . and . . ." She swallowed physically, forcing the words out. It wasn't easy, and her face burned with shame, but she said what she had to say. "I *shouldn't* have disrespected you from the moment we met.

"The Gods were . . . were right to take me out of the Plains as They did. I don't think I would have made a very good queen. Not when you'll make a much better one."

Akelly startled her with an abrupt, amused laugh. "Ha! You think *I* would make a better queen? When I'm clearly just as bad as *you*? Please—we both have a ton of things to apologize for. Why don't we just consider our apologies exchanged, wipe the slate clean, and start all over? Hi," she added, sticking out her hand. "My name is Kelly, I just happen to live here in this madhouse with my husband, and I'm pleased to meet you, whoever you are."

It was utterly absurd, yet Amara couldn't help the chuckle that escaped. Clasping hands, she swallowed again, and managed a smile. "Hello, Akelly, I'm—"

"—*Just* Kelly. Unless I *have* to be all formal and queenly, which usually means only around visitors, I prefer to just be myself," Kelly insisted. "I've been just Kelly for longer than I've been Queen Kelly, and I'm rather used to it."

"Ah. Well . . . Kelly," Amara managed, "I've been Amara for longer than I've been Mara, but if you would rather . . ."

Kelly shook her head, still holding hands. "Amara is a nice name. Keep it. Besides, all I'm asking is that *both* of us drop the attitudes. Neither of us have to drop any titles."

"But you said you use yours around visitors," Amara pointed out, releasing Kelly's fingers.

That earned her a skeptical look from the freckled woman. "Trevan insists there's something inside of you that's worth keeping around. That means you'll probably end up as family, which isn't the same thing as being a visitor. Since the Gods of this world seem to meddle a lot more closely in the affairs of mortals than back in the other world, I've given up trying to fight against fate—it's like trying to swim upstream, when swimming downstream isn't as exhausting and gives you more control over where you might land.

"Since we were a bit distracted earlier, would you like to come back to the map room with me now and go over what progress you've made on those city plans of yours?" Kelly inquired, tilting her head toward the donjon end of the hall. "I know where my strengths and weaknesses lie . . . including my unfortunate temper . . . and mapping a workable city isn't the strongest of my talents. But you do seem to have a knack for it, and if you'd like to lend your talents to us, I wouldn't object."

Amara nodded. They *had* gotten along earlier when discussing ideas for the port city. By returning to her work, she knew she could start repaying the hospitality she had been shown. In the morning, though . . . in the morning, she would have to apologize to everyone at the breakfast table for her attitude in general up until now, and a private apology was due to Trevan. Leaving her suite, she followed Kelly up the hall.

"If I may ask, what *are* the local courting customs?"

"Technically . . . we don't have any," Kelly admitted. Her cheeks pinked with the confession, but she shrugged it off. "I certainly wouldn't go by my and Saber's courtship. We yelled at each other a lot, before circumstances forced us into spending a lot of time together, allowing us to finally get to know each other rather than just ranting and railing at our situations. We were attacked by water-snakes, you see, and the cure for the poison is literally spending hours upon hours in a bathing tub. Which we had to do together, since it was the closest tub at hand."

"I'm not sure I could stand spending hours upon hours with you in a tub," Amara muttered. "No offense, but he has my admiration for it."

"None taken. Wolfer and Alys . . . they were childhood sweethearts, so when they got back together . . ." Kelly shrugged eloquently. "They had an easy time of it. Dominor was kidnapped and taken to another continent, where Serina bought him and put him under some sort of mage-oath to help her undertake a task. They fought a bit, too, mainly over some misunderstandings that grew out of control for a while, but Mariel and Evanor got along fairly easily from the start." She flicked a sidelong look at Amara, her aqua eyes bright with amusement. "It certainly seems the pattern of the elder twins having rocky starts to their relationships is holding, isn't it?"

With great self-restraint and dignity, Amara did *not* stick out her tongue at the other woman.

THIRTEEN

❊

Cat wasn't around when she returned to her rooms the second time. Even though she had only enjoyed his company a few times, Amara missed him. Her night wasn't easy, either. Though she did sleep, the Shifterai woman slept restlessly at best and needed a hot bath to wake herself up when morning finally arrived. As she did so, she knew what she had to do this morning.

She *had* done wrong and *had* to apologize. Not just to Ak . . . to Kelly, but to everyone else as well. Including her sister. *Arora is right*, Amara admitted reluctantly. *We'll probably* never *return to the Plains. Even I admit freely that a life on the run isn't a real life, and we do need to settle* somewhere.

Here is no worse than anywhere else . . . and perhaps a bit better. Scooping water up over her head to rinse away the softsoap, she prayed with her eyes shut. *Father Sky, Mother Earth . . . or rather, whatever Gods rule this land . . . please make sure these people* are *as safe to live among as You've led my twin to believe . . .*

That reminded her that she didn't know much about this land. She knew a little bit about how its occupants came to be here, but only a little. If she needed to make a life for herself—if she *wanted* to make a life for herself—Amara knew she would have to learn more. Especially if she was going to design them their first official city.

After I apologize. Making a face as she reached for one of the nubbly toweling cloths Evanor had left for her, she scrubbed it dry, then climbed out of the tub and dried the rest of herself.

Her clothes were in the changing room attached to her suite. The blond man had brought several quickly made pairs of undergarments, but only one set of new outerwear. Donning fresh undershorts, she pulled on the gathered trousers and *chamsa* of the day before. For a moment, she remembered what Trevan's tunic had felt like on her skin, enveloping her with its soft but scratchy, scented warmth, and she felt her skin respond with a tingle of memory.

Reaching up, she touched her ear, where the earring still hung from her left lobe. Since her suite had a mirror in its changing room, she padded over to it, stared at herself for a long moment, then transformed. Between one breath and the next, a bright-eyed, light brown-furred doe, sporting a touch of white on the tip of her muzzle, stared back at her. No sign of her clothing existed; one moment she had been human and clothed, the next, they had vanished.

Shifting shape again, she shortened herself into a house cat, this time with fluffy cream fur and golden eyes. From that, she morphed back into her human form, then cautiously and experimentally expanded her size, but without changing her shape. Her clothing grew tight within moments . . . and then vanished, leaving her naked as soon as she was just over half a foot taller. Shrinking back down brought her clothing out of hiding, so she kept going down. Only when she was shorter than that boy, Mikor, did her clothing vanish again, leaving her with almost two feet of leeway for making herself smaller than her natural height.

Pleased, Amara returned to her natural size. She fingered the ring again, smiling at her image. That smile faded after a moment. Trevan had given her this marvelous piece of modesty-retaining magic . . . and she had slapped him. An apology was definitely owed to him, and more than an apology.

Kelly's words returned to haunt her, the ones about that unknown place, Rome, and about Nightfall. *When on Nightfall, do as the Nightfallers do.* The shorter woman had admitted last night that almost anything was permitted in a courtship, provided the couple used magic for a contraceptive.

Her own people didn't usually have that recourse, since they didn't have many spellcasting, Artifact-crafting mages among their numbers. What few contraceptive sigils could be made usually went first to the widows who joined the priesthood, serving as honorable, respectable pleasure-instructors of young men. It was another reason why abstinence was the rule in courtship on the Plains.

The woman Mariel, Amara thought suddenly, staring at her reflection. *They've said she's a Healer—trained in Healing magics, that is, not just in herbal medicine. She might know how to craft some method of contraception. If . . . if I am to stay here, and make a life for myself here—Arora and me, that is—we'll both need to . . . Gods, I can't believe I'm even* thinking *about this . . .*

Firming her courage, she eyed her reflection and squared her shoulders, lifting her chin a little. *If we stay and make lives for ourselves . . . that means following the local courtship rules. And* that *means talking to Mariel about courtship methods and contraceptives. Especially the latter, since I have yet to cross a kingdom that encourages children born outside the bonds of marriage.*

So that's what I'll do. Apologize profusely, eating as much grass as I can stomach, she silently told her reflection, watching her nose wrinkle a little in distaste, *and talk to the Healer about courtship and so forth. The herb-healers back home knew all about sex and midwivery, so I've no doubt a magically trained one should know of such things, too.*

Bells rang in the distance, announcing breakfast. Nodding to herself, she turned away from the mirror, exiting the room. Time to swallow some grass.

Trevan smothered a yawn over his porridge. Nothing had awakened him from his cat-shaped nap in the corridor outside Arora's room, mainly because she hadn't returned. He had plenty of faith his twin hadn't killed her, or locked her up—well, not permanently; Rydan did know most of the same catch-and-hold wards that Trevan did, which were effective, if laborious to enchant into place—but he was curious to know why she had been gone all night and where she had been all this time.

The moment his twin entered the room, floating a handful of food-laden dishes to the breakfast table, Trevan managed to snap himself a little more awake. Rising, he abandoned his breakfast long enough to catch Rydan's attention, pausing his younger sibling. Leaning in close, he whispered, "Arora said she was going to go looking for you last night. She's not here this morning, and I'm fairly sure she didn't return to her rooms in the night. Do you know where she is?"

"Yes." Turning away from him, Rydan headed back through the door, no doubt to fetch more of the food he cooked, breakfast being the most frequent of his chores.

"Rydan." Catching his twin's elbow, Trevan stopped him. Rydan stiffened, glancing down at Trevan's hand pointedly. Removing it, Trev arched his brow and wriggled his fingers just as pointedly. "Either tell me where she is, or I'll touch you again."

"She is asleep. In my bed."

"In your *bed*?" Amara demanded, standing in the doorway behind him. Her hands went to her hips, and Trevan could have sworn she gained two inches in height as she glared at his twin. "*What* is my sister doing *in your bed*?"

"Yes, *explain* yourself," Trevan ordered, as the handful of others already in the room looked up from filling their plates.

"She is sleeping. *Just* sleeping," Rydan added over his shoulder to the enraged, black-haired woman behind him. "She brought me dinner, and we talked. A lot. Then she fell asleep. As there is only the one bed in that area, I carried her to it and left her there. *Alone*." Turning to face Amara, who had paled, her body visibly tensing, he arched one of his brows at her. "If you will move, I will fetch the rest of breakfast, make myself a plate, carry it down to my quarters, wake her from her slumber, and send her up here. *If* you move."

"You *touched* her. I *told* you not to touch her!" Amara argued, growing a couple more inches, until she was visibly taller than him.

Rydan wasn't intimidated. He folded his arms across his chest. "*She* touched *me*. Of her own free will."

"You had us all swear on a Truth Stone that, if we were presented with a vast amount of power, we wouldn't be interested in grabbing it," Trevan interjected, reminding her of it. "*All* of us swore to that with full honesty. When your sister comes back up here, you will see for yourself that she is unharmed."

Amara flushed. "How . . . you . . . !"

"We're not stupid, you know. You talked about a great source of power, and warned us practically in the same breath to not touch your twin," Morganen told her, appearing in the corridor at her back. A couple of the others had arrived behind him, though he blocked most of Trevan's angled view. She twisted to face him, as the youngest of the brothers continued. "The most logical conclusion to draw is that, somehow, she is carrying that power, or at least the secret of it. Which none of us are interested in. Now, if you'll stop blocking the doorway, we can all break our morning fast."

Flushing, she tightened her mouth for a moment, then stepped into the room, sidestepping to avoid brushing up against Rydan. No one else said anything to the black-haired brother, but then they didn't have to. If Rydan was finally succumbing to his Destiny, no one was going to be stupid enough to make a big deal of it and risk making their stubborn, sixthborn sibling dig in his heels over the matter.

For her part, Amara surreptitiously pressed a hand to her chest, where her racing heart was finally slowing down again. The thought of *any* mage touching her sister alarmed her and brought out her protective instincts. But as hard as it was for her to grasp, these people honestly seemed to *not* care about Arora's powers. It was a strange concept and one she would have to struggle with before she could accept it in full. Moving around the table, she took her seat and began serving herself food.

Eventually, Rydan came back, deposited a couple of platters, flicked his hands to fill a plate with food, and levitated it out the door without acknowledging the others.

It was hard to think of her twin enjoying the company of such a dour man, but then Amara had always had a hard time thinking of any man being worthy enough for either of them. Now, thanks to the idea of a Prophecy or two having an actual impact on her life, she had to consider Trevan as possibly worthy. But until now, it hadn't really occurred to her that Rydan was a Foreseen possibility for Arora, too. The idea of the dark, brooding man being someone's mate only made his redheaded twin seem all the more appealing in contrast.

Unfortunately, thoughts of Prophecy led right back to thoughts of actually settling and staying here . . . and that led to thoughts of how poorly she had behaved in the last few days. Midway through the meal, when she had eaten all her nervous stomach could handle, Amara set down her fork, stood up, and cleared her throat. The others—minus her sister and Rydan—glanced up at her. Keeping her gaze on the table, she addressed them.

"I would like to . . . *apologize* . . . for my ill behavior since our arrival. I can explain it all I want under the guise of stress, and being in unfamiliar territory, and a certain, justifiable paranoia . . . but I still displayed bad manners. You have been kind to my sister and me, and I have repaid you poorly. I am sorry for that." She forced her gaze up, high enough to glance at the green-eyed man seated across from her. "And to you, I must apologize in specific. I should not have done what I did, yesterday. It was wrong of me, and I hope that you can forgive me at some point."

Pausing, unsure what else to say, she finally sat down and picked up her fork. Not that her sausage-and-root hash was all that appealing anymore, but at least poking at it gave her something to do. Until Saber spoke, addressing her from his position beside his silently watching wife.

"It takes great strength to admit when you have done some wrong," he stated, assessing her with his gray gaze. "But it takes even greater strength to acknowledge it openly . . . and you have my admiration for that."

Amara flushed, unsure if she deserved his praise.

"On that note," Kelly stated, drawing the attention of the others away from Amara, "I owe everyone an apology as well, if I have been a bit . . . brusque in my attitude since arriving here. I'm sorry, too."

That made the other adults exchange looks. Of all of them, only Mikor was unaffected, but then he seemed to be preoccupied with the very important task of picking the bits of icing from his sticky roll. Serina cleared her throat, focusing the group's attention yet a third time.

"While we're on the subject of . . . familial troubles," she hedged carefully, "this family is in trouble over a different matter. Very few of us have been producing anything in the last few months, and that is putting us into serious trouble."

"How do you mean?" Trevan asked her.

"We've been preoccupied with clearing land, that's what," Saber observed, catching her meaning. "Clearing land, and planning a city, and preparing to build a house for the arrival of our first non-family citizens. I've been selling off spare stock from my armory collection, and we still have several lightglobes, plus the salt and algae blocks from the desalination process . . . but we haven't been making anything new, and we're running out of things to sell to the traders. We may have wild orchards to pick and preserve fruit from, but we *don't* have wild grain fields for harvesting our rye and wheat needs. If we had more Artifacts to sell . . ."

That stung at Trevan's creative pride. He did have the clothing-holding earring design he had made for Amara, a brand-new, successfully enchanted Artifact ready for reproduction . . . but even he had to admit the prime market for that was an ocean plus half a continent away, and there were no trade routes established between Nightfall and the Shifting Plains. Yet. He tried to soothe his pride with a reminder of their schedule. "Well, once we get the house finished, we should be able to find a little more time."

"That doesn't help us right now, though," Serina pointed out. "And soon enough, *more* people will arrive, and *they'll* need houses, and craftshops, and other things. The regular trade ship—with our staple supplies on board—will also arrive in two more days. If we're trying to hoard our incoming coin for restamping with an official Nightfall imprint, that means we need *things* to sell. Between the official traders and the smugglers daring to visit us for tax-free goods, we're going to run out of enough things to sell very soon."

"How bad is it?" Kelly asked her.

"I've already estimated that we have maybe three months before we'll run out of trade items to sell, between the Katani trading ships, legitimate or not, and the Natallian nuns and their own trading needs," Saber told her, speaking for Serina. "It's a conservative estimate, based on none of us making anything new, whatsoever."

"You don't really need *me* for land clearing, do you?" Koranen offered, glancing around the table. "We still have plenty of *comsworg* oil for crafting lightglobes, and I can make panes of glass for windows in between sets of globes, while the forging kilns are still hot. Glass is always a good trade commodity, provided it's packed with cushioning spells. The quality of the sand for a window doesn't have to be as high a mirror, either."

Trevan realized suddenly that his auburn-haired brother was looking a little worse for wear, with dark circles under his hazel eyes. He winced internally. *He* had Amara to pursue, and while he hadn't yet pursued her into a bed, he at least had the *hope* of doing so.

Koranen, however, was still all alone, unable to touch or be touched by a normal woman long enough to relieve at least some of his sexual frustrations . . . and unable to enchant the illusionary courtiers into responding like a real woman would in the presence of a lover. Both of them had learned the hard way that if the woman didn't respond right, it didn't *feel* right. Trevan couldn't speak to his younger sibling about it, though; not at the breakfast table, and not during an otherwise important conversation about their overall finances. He refocused his attention on the others.

The mathemagician in their midst shook her head, her pale braid sliding across her shoulders.

"Lightglobes won't bring in enough money; from the records I've perused, the traders only buy so many at a time and no more, because it's a luxury item. In order to sell more, we'd have to cut our costs down to a nonprofitable level. Considering we'll still need to buy certain building supplies from the mainland, such as nails, it's not going to be enough to offset rising costs," Serina countered. "We also can't increase the salt production until we've repaired a lot more of those street pipes and got them flowing again. What we need are more Artifacts to sell."

"My uncle has a lot of Artifacts," Alys offered, before anyone else could speak. The others glanced her way, including her golden-eyed husband. "Well, he *did*. Some weren't all that expensive, but then some were ones that he designed himself, while others he paid dearly for. Lots of them were made to gauge the turbidity of the aether, so that he could send all those nasty beasts your way, plus many other things that he collected over the years. Cousin Barol had a few of his own, too . . . I think."

"Nasty beasts?" Amara asked, confused. Somehow, she didn't think they were referring to feral livestock, which were the kind of nasty beasts her own people usually ended up fighting.

"One of our kinsman by marriage was trying to kill us with magically created war-beasts for the first three years we lived here," Trevan dismissed. "He's been dealt with, so there's nothing more to worry about."

"My cousin Barol also had a number of Artifacts, the few times I visited the Devries estate," Alys repeated more firmly. "I'm sure of it, now that I've given it some thought. He had a number of scrying mirrors, I think some enchanted armor, expandable bookshelves, and a collection of animal figurines that you could call into life-size to do your bidding for short periods of time. All of his belongings, and Uncle Broger's and Uncle Donnock's, technically now belong to me as the sole surviving Devries heir. Plus there are spellbooks and other things that the estate managers don't need to use. They can be sent here and sold to the traders quite easily."

"That sounds like some of it might be helpful," Wolfer agreed. "But are you sure you want to sell it all?"

"I don't want *any* of it," Alys emphasized, "and I doubt I'd even know how to use it, but if we had the estate servants pack it all up and ship it out to us, the rest of you could figure out what the stuff is, what it does, and what you can sell it for. Or keep it for your own use. I'd rather pay the expense to ship it all here and have the useful things go to family members first, rather than having the government auction it off and pocket part of the sale price," she added candidly. "Otherwise, it's just gathering dust and cluttering up space back there. As far as I'm concerned, my life is here. Why shouldn't I have all of that shipped here to see if any of it is useful, when there's no other reason for me to return to the mainland?"

Watching Wolfer smile and kiss his wife on the top of her dark gold curls, Amara wondered at how simply the woman accepted her presence on the island. If she was wealthy enough to possess all the goods of so many relatives' estates, the curly-haired woman could undoubtedly sell quite a bit of it and make herself a comfortable life elsewhere, with servants to do all the hard work . . . rather than stick around, clearing land and feeding chickens all the way out here. It made her uncomfortable once more about her own attitude.

"That's a good idea, and an easy way to get supplies relatively quickly," Kelly agreed. "But we need more in the way of income . . . and *one* of us has more than her share of wealth. Isn't that right, Serina?"

The same woman who had started the discussion had the grace to blush. "Um . . . right."

"Did you not say you were going to work on a taxation system based on a percentage of a person's income?" Kelly asked her. "And don't you own more than a kingdom's ransom in those fancy pearls of yours?"

"Well, it's pre-owned, not *income*, per se," Serina hedged, until her husband elbowed her. Sighing heavily, she gave in. "Fine. But you're not appropriating *all* of them. You can have *one* of the smallest rainbow pearls to negotiate with the traders in two days. But only one, for now. I'd rather hold off on how many we sell, since it's bad to glut the market and drive down their value, and I'd like to hold some of those pearls in reserve for when we really and truly need a sudden influx of supplies."

"One very small rainbow pearl will probably pay for everything we'll want to trade for this time around," Saber reassured her. "Including nails for the house we'll be building, plus a bit more. Speaking of building things," he added, turning to his wife. "When will we get the first designs for the structures you wanted?"

Morganen answered for Kelly. "Hope says the architect firm will have the first of the rough drafts ready in two more days. And they've said they can implement a design using frame and peg construction techniques. I have a spellbook that uses wooden pegs in place of nails and tongue-and-groove designs for the timber frames. We'll still need to buy a few nails but not as many as you'd think. The pegs themselves can be spell-crafted from the hardwoods found right here on the island. Remember, we have plenty of energy, and plenty of raw materials, if we use the right building techniques."

"Which is why I chose to ask for designs that use mostly stone, wood, and glass," Kelly agreed. "Amara, how much more time do you need for the first draft of the northern edge of the cove?"

"About . . . two more days," she calculated, giving it a quick thought. "Maybe three."

"Good. Get on it. We'll focus our work on the foundations, streets, and pipes on that side of the harbor, since it's closest to the desalination plant. We'll also eventually need a new dock built for this Marcas to moor his ship to, so that he won't run into docking problems with the trade ships. Who wants that one?"

The conversation broke into different segments, as the brothers and their wives argued over who would be responsible for what task for the day. Waiting for Mariel to finish telling her son what lessons he had for the day, Amara ate some more of her breakfast, her stomach settling now that her apologies had been so readily accepted. As soon as she gracefully could, she would ask the Healer for a private moment in which to hold a frank discussion covering what courtship meant around these brothers.

Even if they didn't have any "official" courtship customs, yet, Mariel was not only a Healer, she was also the most recent to be courted and married, and would surely be able to extrapolate Trevan's preferred style from what she had experienced of Evanor's. And she *was* a Healer; surely she'd keep Amara's awkward questions private if asked to do so. Most Healers had a code of ethics about such things, regardless of their origins.

When no one gave her any odd looks when she left the room, following in the Healer's wake, Amara figured she was finally on the right path to getting along with these people. She really didn't need another double-slapping session of misunderstandings and badly crossed customs on her plate.

Trevan left Arora's suite feeling about as frustrated as Koranen had looked this morning. According to Amara's levelheaded twin, Arora, Shifterai courtship practices were . . . were *unnatural*. No kissing, no touching of genitalia—loins *or* breasts, male or female—and no copulation whatsoever. Exposure of body parts wasn't anything special or titillating by their standards, but then half of the population were natural shapeshifters, and didn't have access to the clothing-storing earring he had made for Amara. Of course, they usually tried to cover up the affected areas with a layer of fur, feathers, or scales for a semblance of decency, but otherwise it was politely ignored.

No, the worst of it was that most of the courtship touches *he* was used to indulging in, up to and including intercourse itself, were forbidden for a man and a maiden to practice. For a man and his wife, yes. For a man and a duly ordained priestess, yes. But maidens remained maidens, especially if they wanted to be highly regarded for their self-control. Even the widowed wives who chose not to go into the priesthood usually returned to "maiden" status, meaning they had to be courted properly by custom all over again. Because of this, the power in moving from a courtship to a marriage was entirely in the woman's hands.

In fact, it was literally by her hand. According to Arora, all a woman had to do was hold out her hand to her chosen man from the far side of a fire, and if the man accepted, he simply had to leap across the flames to claim his rights as her husband . . . but only if she held up her hand from the far side, through the flames. Girls therefore learned to either hold out their hands to either side or walk around the fire when asking for something. Amara—according to her twin—had always chosen scrupulously to walk around a fire, rather than let there be any doubt about whether or not she was offering her hand.

Of course, that was in a culture that was distinctly nomadic roughly nine months out of the year, where campfires were frequently encountered in Family encampments. All one needed to do was peel back the sod in a big circle, or set up an iron brazier-pan on its stand, which was usually low enough to leap over. Here on Nightfall, fires were safely confined to actual fireplaces, making them impossible to leap. Unless he could convince Amara to court the Katani way—which he highly doubted, given how she'd instinctively slapped him—Trevan was out of luck in the physical pleasure department for the foreseeable future.

Pausing just short of the junction where the two end wings joined the main trunk of the north wing, he turned, gripped the posts of the nearest doorway, and thumped his head slowly and repeatedly against the wooden surface. After about seven or eight thumps, when it actually began to hurt, Trev rested his forehead against the age-darkened wood. The Gods had to be mocking him, teasing and tormenting him for all those years he had spent bounding from lover to lover as a youth, to deny him even now, when he was so close to ending his celibate exile.

But at least I have *a chance at ending my exile*, he acknowledged after a moment. *Poor Kor, shut out yet again.* Pushing away from the door, Trevan headed for the stairs to the ramparts. Now that his primary task had been managed—pestering Arora for advice on how to court her sister—he had work to do. Though he did far more than just work with wood, it was one of his favorite materials, and his family would eventually need stout beams and planks shaped from the trees they had been clearing from the ruins of the old port city. That meant his task was to strip off branches and bark and shape the boles for eventual use as lumber.

Amara had her task, drawing up plans for the city, and he had his, preparing the materials for its construction. He would have to court her later.

I don't know how many women he's been with," Mariel confessed. "Obviously, none of us women on the island. But from what Evanor and the others have mentioned, before their exile, Trevan was definitely known as the lover of the family. And a precocious one, since apparently he was flirting with women before he turned sixteen, the age of adulthood among the Katani.

"But you needn't worry that he's carrying around what we in Natallia like to call a bedbug," the short, plump Healer added, briefly confusing Amara. "When I examined him shortly after my arrival, I found him to be clean and illness-free."

Oh. Bedbug . . . right. Shifterai men could and occasionally did seek the services of outlander women for relieving their needs when traveling outkingdom in a warband, but it was discouraged for one very important reason: If an outlander woman wasn't protected thoroughly against pregnancy, it was possible that woman could give birth to a shapeshifter son, or that one of her children would bear a shapeshifter son. Without the training and the discipline her people had learned through painstaking practice in their first few decades, such children were destined for awkward lives.

Avoiding sexual ailments was a side benefit of disdaining outlander women. The only exception to that cultural disdain was the occasional adoption of an outlander woman into a particular Family. It freshened their bloodlines and allowed a Family to create ties with outkingdom kin, which could be quite advantageous when looking to make a trade. But to be so casual about sex, to not be dedicated to holy service, yet not quite be an outlander whore, either, that was confusing to her.

"And . . . everybody does it?"

"From what I've heard, so long as people have contraceptive amulets, they do it in Natallia, they do it in Guchere, they do it in Katan . . . and they even do it in that place Kelly comes from," Mariel offered, shrugging. "She was untouched by personal choice when she married Saber, not because it was a social requirement."

Part of Amara wanted to admire the redheaded outworlder for her self-restraint, even when it wasn't needed, but Kelly wasn't Shifterai. It didn't mean the same thing. But still, it was hard to wrap her head around all the other things Mariel had mentioned. Hand-holding, casual touches, embraces that ran from friendly to passionate, and the many different places that lips could touch. It was forbidden . . . but a part of Amara reminded her that if Trevan had practice in it, did it really matter if his skill came from the teachings of a sanctified priestess or a handful of women who were willing?

"He didn't . . ."

"He didn't, what?" Mariel asked her when Amara trailed off.

"He didn't . . . *hire* any of those women, did he?" she forced herself to ask. If he had, Amara didn't know which was worse, the promiscuous who did it of their own free will, ruled by their passions, or the promiscuous who did it for pay, ruled by their coin purses.

"From what I hear, he should have been hiring himself out, his brothers consider him to be that good." Catching Amara's recoil, Mariel frowned at the younger woman. "Do *not* think that wenching is dishonorable. Selling one's body is no different than selling one's sword . . . except that the person hiring a professional wench isn't asking her to kill or hurt anyone. Frankly, many men *prefer* going to a hired woman for their first experiences, so that they can be taught how to treat a woman properly."

She didn't know it, but the Healer had hit on the same argument used by the Shifterai priesthood. Subduing her internal objections, Amara sighed. "This is all just so *different*! Back home, everything was clear, everyone knew their place, and relationships progressed or not, at an openly understood pace. But here . . . *anything* goes. There are no rules, no boundaries, no guidelines!"

"So make it up as you go along," Mariel offered, patting her on the shoulder. "And *relax*. Not a single one of these brothers would harm a hair on your head."

At that, Amara had to arch one of her brows skeptically. "Considering how I've acted until now . . ."

The Healer laughed and patted her again. "For you, they might make an exception. *If* you backslide and turn sour again. To prevent that, I prescribe that you *relax*. That you tell yourself it's all right to kiss a man . . . and that you get Trevan to let you practice on him. I'm sure he's eager to teach you everything you'll want to learn.

"Just hold off on going any farther than a kiss, and don't fall into his bed within the next two days," Mariel added bluntly. "That's how long it'll take for me to craft a pair of contraceptive amulets for you and your sister to wear. Alys already wears one, as do I, while Serina is pregnant, and Kelly is trying to get that way. I forgot to consider making ones for other women coming into the family, but they won't take long to make.

"Now, if you have any more questions of a health-related nature, I'd be happy to answer them . . . but if you have questions on how to court a man in the local manner, I'd suggest talking to Trevan directly." A last pat on her shoulder, and Mariel nudged Amara toward the door. "Communicating directly, asking and answering questions openly, will do far more to teach you about local courtship practices than anything else I could tell you."

With that admonition, Amara found herself pushed out of the woman's herb room. Knowing from the discussion at breakfast that Trevan would be down at the cove all day, helping the others trace pipes, shape logs, and prepare the foundation for the house that was to come, she retreated to the map room in the west wing.

FOURTEEN

❧◆❧

nsure how to proceed when it came to the "relaxed" style of courtship, Amara was grateful when Trevan dropped by late in the afternoon to see how her drawings were progressing. That allowed her to talk with him, to ask how his own work had gone, and hear how much he and his siblings had done. Unfortunately, they were interrupted by his elder brother before she could work up the nerve to move close enough to touch him, let alone attempt something bolder and highly unlike the ways of the Plains.

Evanor rapped on the open panel of the door and poked his pale blond head into the room.

"Pardon the interruption, but you're now on the chores roster, Amara," Ev told her, glancing briefly at Trevan. "It's the chalkboard outside the dining hall. You're scheduled to help Trevan set the table tonight, and your twin gets to help clear it. If you know how to cook, and think you can handle preparing dishes with the local food, do let me know. The table will need to be set soon. Supper is at sunset."

He closed the door as he pulled back, leaving her alone with his brother. His comment about clearing the table reminded her she hadn't seen her sister since the black-haired brother had sworn he would send Arora back up to Amara this morning. Biting her lip, feeling guilty and worried from her thoughtless neglect, Amara headed for the door.

Trevan caught her arm. "We still have half an hour before sunset. We don't have to set the table immediately."

"It's not that—your brother said he would send Arora to me, and I haven't seen her all day," Amara retorted, struggling to keep herself calm. *I will not suspect Trevan's twin without true cause, and . . . and I haven't had a good enough reason yet*, she reminded herself silently, before adding aloud, "I should have gone looking for her, rather than wait for her to come to me."

"Relax, she's fine," Trev reassured Amara, keeping his fingers hooked around her elbow. "I talked to her myself, not more than an hour after breakfast. When we were done chatting, she said she was going straight to bed, and as far as I know, she probably did."

That made her frown. "You talked to her? Why?"

Releasing her, Trevan scratched behind his ear, stalling for time as he tried to figure out how much to admit. Finally, he shrugged and said, "I wanted to ask her some questions about Plains life."

Amara flushed with embarrassment. Turning away, she crossed her arms. "And I suppose *I'm* too prickly to ask."

"I have no problem with talking to you," Trevan countered, cupping his hands around her shoulders. This was a permitted touch, and he took advantage of it, gently rubbing her upper arms. "I just wanted to ask her some questions. Some of it," he added, leaning close enough to brush her ear with his breath, though his mouth was forbidden, "concerned *you*. And I figured she wouldn't mind telling me about you."

"Whereas I would?" Amara quipped. Her ear twitched under the warm caress of his breath, making her aware of just how many nerve endings she possessed on the side of her head. He was so close to her ear, she wondered why he wasn't trying to kiss it. Married men kissed their wives in such places on the Plains, and the Healer of this land had said men and women in this part of the world did the same things, only it didn't matter whether or not they were married. It made her doubt her allure . . . which was an unnerving realization. "I'm still not sure why you want to court me, let alone talk to me. I haven't exactly been enjoyable company."

Sliding his hands down her arms, he shifted them so that his forearms crossed and covered hers, allowing him to embrace her from behind. Not too tightly, since he wasn't allowed to do anything as crude as grinding his half-erect self against her, but he could simply hold her. Resting his jaw against her soft, black hair, he corrected her wryly.

"I'll remind you, I came in here, seeking you deliberately, *just* to talk to you. True, you're a little prideful, prickly, and paranoid at times," he daringly teased, "but you're also the first person in a very long time to *accept* that there's more to me than just what everyone says there is. Everyone thinks that I'm 'just' a woodworker, or 'just' a flirt. When I told you about my earring idea, you didn't doubt that *I* could do it."

"But, I did doubt," she had to point out in fairness.

"You doubted whether it could be *done*. That's not the same thing as doubting whether *I* would be the one to succeed at it. I'm not the most powerful of my brothers, and so they don't always pay attention to the cleverness of my contributions. It gets tiresome, being overlooked." Skimming his palms over her forearms, he rubbed them for a few moments more, then slid his hands to her hips. That bordered on forbidden territory, but after holding her warmth against him, after smelling her scent, Trev couldn't entirely resist.

The feel of his hands moving over her body, caressing her through her clothes, was startlingly pleasant. Actually, it was more than pleasant; her stomach twisted with a strange thrill of energy. She wasn't ignorant of pleasure; the women of the Plains had to exercise discipline when it came to courtship and men, but there was nothing stopping them from acquainting themselves with their own bodies. But this wasn't the same sort of pleasure Amara had known when she had caressed herself. This was different, more intense.

Yet it didn't go very far. *He* didn't go very far. Curious to know what more he could arouse in her, enough to bolster her courage, Amara reminded herself firmly that she *wasn't* on the Plains, that she *was* going to give this Nightfall place a chance at maybe proving it could be her new home, and turned to face Trevan. One of his palms slid across her backside as she twisted, an intimate touch no one had ever dared attempt. It was innocent enough—she had caused it—but it was also erotic.

Just as he shifted his hands back to the more neutral ground of her hips, Amara rose on her toes and pressed her mouth to his, holding her breath at her own boldness.

Startled, Trevan quickly grabbed her arms, pushing her back. It was for his own sake that he did so, since after Arora's lecture, he was very mindful that he *wasn't* allowed to grab her closer, that the woman always controlled the pace of courtship on the Plains. So, rattled by the touch of her lips, unable to believe she would do such a thing, he demanded, "What was *that* for?"

Amara paled at his accusation. The first thought that ran through her mind—shocked as much from her own impulsive actions as from his own startlement—was, *Oh, Gods . . . he thinks I'm an outlander whore!* Her first instinct was to flee. Whirling, she bolted for the door.

"Sh'kadeth!"

Even as she grabbed the lever, it locked in place with an audible *snick*, preventing her from using it. There was another way out, if she used the connecting door to the storeroom with the spare parchment in it—

Trevan caught her by the elbow before she could do more than whirl to head that way. "Would you *stop* trying to run from me when something goes wrong? Now, why did you kiss me? I thought you and your sister both said kissing was forbidden!"

He asked my sister about that? Amara wondered, cheeks heating at the implication. She stared at him in confusion. "You asked her . . . ?"

"I asked her how to court you, according to Shifterai rules. I didn't want to alarm you again with my outlander ways," he muttered.

"You mean, you didn't want me to slap you again," she corrected wryly, feeling the returning prickle of her shame.

"That, too. Look, the more I get to know you, the more I *do* like you," Trev told Amara. "And it's not because you're an astounding shapeshifter. Your sister told me how everyone back home used to chase after you simply because you have the best blood of your people. I couldn't care less about what you were born; it's simply a part of you. What I *like* is how brilliant you are."

"So brilliant, I get everyone mad at me," Amara muttered, only feeling worse.

"Please, Dominor does that all the time. Yet we still love him," Trevan dismissed, making her glance up dubiously. "You're passionate about your work, just as I am. You understand the joy of taking flight, just like me. You protect and shelter your twin from others, just as I do."

"You protect and shelter that sour . . . that man?" she corrected herself, giving Trevan an apologetic look for her rude slip. "Sorry."

"Yes, I do—and you're forgiven. I usually share chores with him, since he tolerates my presence better than the others'. I try to make sure I'm there to be a cushion whenever he has to work with the others on some magical project. And I've defended his right to be alone, to cling to his own ways and habits in spite of how different they are from the things everyone else in this family does," he explained to her. "I'm not as powerful a mage as he is, but I'm every bit as clever, and very economical with my own power, so that I can substitute for him in a pinch when the others need help in the daytime, when Rydan prefers to sleep. I also deliberately draw attention to myself, so that fewer people will plague him with their demands, making him less irritable.

"No, I don't protect him as openly as you protect your sister, but there are different ways to protect someone," he stated quietly, cupping her shoulders once more, though this time he was facing her. "The more I get to know you, the more ways I find that we're alike, while the remaining differences only make each of us all the more interesting . . . or am I not interesting enough for you?"

Amara didn't answer right away, but only because she was giving his question careful thought. "You *are* interesting," she finally admitted. "You're not awed by my abilities, for all that you're undeniably pursuing me. That's unusual, and flattering, because you *are* still interested in me. You don't seem to think I'm wasting my time on city planning. Everyone back home expected me to shadow Aitava every single hour of the day, even if that was not how it worked—apprenticing to the Queen was about learning how the *kingdom* works, which meant I spent as much time or more shadowing her advisors as I did her.

"But you don't expect that from me. And . . . and I *like* that you want to know how to court me the Shifterai way . . ." Amara trailed off.

"I hear a 'but' in that statement," Trevan prompted her. "You're pleased, but . . . ?"

Face heating again, she looked down and away, not quite able to meet his gaze, and mumbled something.

"What was that?" he prodded.

"I . . . wanted to try courting you *your* way," she forced herself to say more clearly, "to see what the outlander fuss is all about."

"I *knew* I should have kept hitting my head on that door," he muttered, closing his eyes for a moment.

"What?" she asked, confused by his odd comment.

"Never mind. Look, courtship according to Shifterai rules places all the decision making in the hands of the woman. If you decide you want to kiss me," Trevan offered her, lifting his hand to brush back a lock of her hair, tucking the soft, dark strands behind her ear, "then that is your prerogative, and I will comply. If you choose to *not* kiss me . . . I may go slightly insane from the wait, but I will also comply. There's no need to rush this. We have plenty of time to see if we fall in love, agreed?"

He was right; there was no need to rush . . . but that didn't mean it was forbidden, either.

Amara kissed him. Again, it was purely on impulse, but she did it, lifting herself so she could press her mouth to his. For a wonderful, long moment, his lips moved with hers, his hands coming up to her cheeks to tilt her head just a little farther for a better kiss. Then those lips stopped. A moment later, he withdrew, arching a coppery-blond brow at her.

"Did you just increase your height?" Trevan asked her warily. His suspicion was confirmed when she shrunk a little, face reddening.

Guilt and shame washed through her. "I'm sorry," Amara apologized, looking down and away. "I shouldn't have done that. It was thoughtless and crude."

Instinct told Trevan she was referring to some sort of Shifterai social mistake on her part, though it didn't make much sense.

Cupping her jaw, he lifted her face. "Look at me, Amara. I'm *not* upset. I don't find it offensive. Is that why you thought I was asking? Because you thought I was offended by you altering your shape? Isn't that what you Shifterai do?"

"*Pure* shapes," she explained, meeting his green gaze. "We're supposed to pursue pure shapes. Anything less is . . . sloppy. Shameful. It's considered a sign of weakness in a shapeshifter, of incompleteness, if all you can do is grow a cat's tail or a hawk's claws—the only exception is to grow fur, feathers, or scales for modesty, which is allowable for practical reasons."

"Amara, to spell-shape oneself, it's the exact opposite," Trevan chided her, releasing her so he could return to her desk. She had a mug resting on the flat top of the angled desk; a quick check proved there was still water inside. Picking up the half-full mug, he returned to her. "You start out with a pure shape and tweak the spells from there if you want to achieve only a portion of the transformation. Being able to control it to such a fine degree that you *only* grow a cat's tail or a falcon's claws is a mark of very high skill, among mages.

"As for your *pure* form . . ." He poured the water onto the age-worn stones beneath their feet with his left hand, and snapped the fingers of his right. "*Nucsolk!*"

The water swelled quickly upward, forming a large bubble as it scraped itself off the floor. It flattened after a moment, shimmered, and misted; the bubble squeezed itself into a thin, vertical oval, becoming a sheet of liquid much like a frameless cheval-glass.

"*Plulet*," he ordered, and the flattened bubble misted and turned reflective under the force of his spell-shaped will. Amara glanced at him, then at her reflection in the surface. A swerving slash of his hands, another mutter, and her shape altered, making her gasp.

"You—why did you do this again?" Amara demanded, staring at her now green eyes and light brown hair. She tried to change back, but like before, it was a futile effort. "Trevan, this isn't funny! Stop making me look like my sister!"

"*This* is your true form," Trev told her, moving around to stand behind her. "That is what this particular spell does. *You* make yourself look different from your sister. I suspect the transformation was gradual, altering more and more as the two of you grew up. I think you subconsciously chose to look different, because you wanted to *be* different."

"But I *was* different! She's not a shifter, while I am," Amara asserted, gesturing at the mirror. "This . . . this is nonsense! Why would I choose to look different when I was already different? The other is my true form, not this . . . *plain* . . ." She trailed off, flushing again, and tried to rescue her comment. "Not that my sister is *ugly*, but *this* isn't me. We're nothing alike! We're *not* identical."

"But did people try to claim that you were, when you were very young?" the redhead behind her asked, cupping her shoulders again to hold her in place. "Everyone kept expecting my brothers and me to end up identical to our twins. A lot of twins are, and with four sets of them, you'd think at least two of us would look like our fellow twin. Very young siblings often look like each other, even if they're not identical . . . but each of us grew up different. The people living around my family eventually accepted that we were different. About the only good thing is that each of us looks enough like both our mother and our father that no one doubted our parentage, despite the clear disparity in our hair color."

"That is a good question—how can one of you have black hair, and the next be a blond?" she asked.

"Father had golden blond hair, and Mother had black," he admitted with a shrug. "I suspect that some people kept telling you how you were nothing like your sister. That you were more attractive, because *you* were the shapeshifter in the family, and she wasn't. You had the allure and the appeal of a rare woman who could change her shape, while your twin was just a plain, boring, non-changing, ordinary woman." Wrapping his arms around her, Trevan met her gaze through the mirror, almost as green as his own. "And those few people who dared to point out how much you *looked* like your sister, and thus had to be like her, that made you want to rebel. I think you subconsciously made yourself match your physical appearance to that constantly asserted allure, gradually shifting your visage away from your twin as proof of your unique self-identity."

Releasing the spell with a word and a gesture, he let her shift back to her black-haired, golden-eyed shape, encircling her in his arms as she changed.

"Either way," Trev informed her, "I like *you*. Regardless of what you look like. You could turn your skin purple, your hair green, and grow tentacles for arms . . . well, maybe I'd have to get used to tentacles for arms," he allowed mock-thoughtfully, winking at her in the mirror, "but it's the woman inside who matters. Physical appearances can be changed by magic, by cosmetics, by accidents and injuries, by the rise and fall of one's health, and by the marching of time . . . but the person you are inside, that is what I find most important.

"So if you *choose* to have black hair and golden eyes, and look exotically beautiful . . . well, I'm not going to complain at the view, but I can find just as much beauty in you wearing your sister's plain hair and green eyes. Most of her beauty comes from her personality, anyway . . . and yours is no different."

Staring at her darkened hair, Amara wondered at how she had made the transformation of herself. She had never heard of a shapeshifter holding even such a small change for so long . . . and yet her hair *had* started its darkening at the onset of puberty. After years of being mistaken for her twin, lumped together with her twin, treated like her twin, it had been a relief to develop a distinct and separate visual identity. His explanation made sense.

It also came with a kiss, as he pressed his lips to her cheek, near her ear. Amara twisted to look at him. "I thought you said I'd be in control of how fast we progress."

Trevan smirked. "I figured it would only be fair if I could return to you everything that you do to me. So if you kiss me . . . I can kiss you back."

"And keep kissing me?" She decided to tease him, arching her brow. "I would think a one-for-one trade would be more in order."

"You said you wanted to try courting in the outlander style," he countered smoothly, pressing another light kiss to her cheek in between murmurs. "Once you've opened a door, it's been opened, and there's no closing it again."

Twisting free of his arms, Amara placed her fingertips against his mouth, pushing on his lips. That quirked his brow, even as it moved him back. "We didn't agree on *those* rules. Yet." Removing her fingers, she placed her hands on her hips while she considered his offer. "Alright . . . it's agreed. But we start back at no kissing, until I kiss you." Turning away, she glanced at him over her shoulder, unable to stop the small smile that was twitching the corner of her mouth. "And I don't feel like kissing you, right now."

It had been a long while since a woman had last dared to tease him like that. Catching her around the waist, Trevan pulled Amara against his side. She arched her brow at his presumption, but he only smiled. "*This* is allowable, by the courting customs of your people."

Now she was back on familiar ground. Men had tried something similar to this, before, and she knew how to play this particular game. Looping her arm around his waist, tucking it under his, she quipped, "Maybe, but all you can do is hold me."

"I wasn't referring to holding you." Leaning in close, Trevan pursed his lips and blew a thin stream of breath slowly up the side of her throat. The warm air stirred a few strands of her hair that weren't tucked behind her ear but otherwise tickled her flesh without impediment. And yet it wasn't the same as a real tickling. She didn't squeak, didn't squirm, didn't push him firmly away.

Instead, Amara shivered. No one had ever done this to her before. Breathed in her ear while speaking, yes, but breathed on her neck? Not this purposefully. He reached a spot at the corner of her jaw that seemed particularly sensitive, making her tremble again. He was so close to her ear, she expected him to sensually torment that next, but he didn't go there yet. Goose pimples raised on her flesh, joined by a swirl of desire in her belly, roused by his phantom touch and her anticipation.

Pausing for a slow, deliberate lungful, Trevan blew carefully again, but not toward her ear; instead, he trailed his breath along the edge of her jaw, craning his neck so that he ended at her chin. Her head tipped back, a subconscious invitation for him to breathe that thin, purposeful stream down her throat. He accepted her direction, but only as a momentary distraction.

Catching her free hand with his own, Trev lifted it to his lips, as he inhaled a second time. This time, his breath played over the back of her hand, slipping back and forth from littlest finger to thumb, then back again. With each snaking pass, he worked his way closer to her wrist, then onto it. A careful angle blew cool air up the cuff of her sleeve, re-fluffing the fine hairs that had started to smooth from their earlier prickling.

For the final touch, he ceased blowing along her forearm for a few moments. Turning back to her hand, he brushed the tip of his nose lightly over the same side-winding path, until he reached her wrist. There, he sent one last stream of cool air up her sleeve. When he lifted his gaze back to hers, she had let her eyes drift shut, and her lips had parted in that way that said she was still concentrating on the sensations he had given her. A glance down at the soft curves beneath her dress displayed the proof of her arousal pressing against the fabric.

Pleased with himself, Trevan smiled. *Nearly four years of exile, and I haven't lost my touch . . .*

Her black lashes drifted upward, and her amber gaze fastened on his face. Brows lowering, she came out of her reverie with a suspicious look. "Are you smirking?"

Trevan didn't answer. Amara, unnerved by how aroused she was just by some breath and his nose, eyed him warily. He ignored it and pursed his lips, leaning in by her ear. This time, he deliberately circled a cooling stream of his breath from just in front of it, under the lobe, around and up over the shell . . . and then breathed hotly into the center with parted lips. The tickling clashed with the heat, flashing through her in a streak of sharp arousal.

When he traced his nose up, around, and down the curve of her ear, making a return trip, the strength of her reaction caught her off her guard. She clung to him with her right arm, supporting herself, as her knees threatened to buckle. Chuckling, Trevan took advantage, shifting his left arm so that she dipped back suddenly. Held up only by his grip and the arc of her legs, she wasn't prepared for what he did next.

Placing his mouth just above one of her nipples, he blew *through* her clothes. The stimulation was too much for her. Every place he had breathed, from her throat to her hand, from her ear to her breast, connected itself to her loins. Crying out, Amara gave up trying to right herself, dropping her head back so that her breasts thrust up closer to his breath—his *breath*!

She could barely think. "Trevan, please! St . . . stop . . . you can't . . ."

"But this is allowable," he murmured, smirking openly now. "After all, there's nothing in Shifterai custom that says I cannot merely *breathe* . . ."

Though he wasn't quite as strong as Saber or Wolfer, he had spent most of the last ten years running around in shapeshifted form almost daily, leading an active, muscle-developing life. Holding her with her back draped over his left arm, he used his right one to scoop under her left leg, lifting it high and forcing her to balance on the toes of her other foot. This time, he blew firmly on her left nipple, circling the stream of his breath around the turgid peak beneath her garment.

"Oh, Gods!" Somehow, the new position tied everything together. It wasn't just his breath teasing her other nipple or her previously stimulated skin, but the way he had lifted her knee put pressure on her femininity. Especially as he shifted his grip a little, causing her upraised thigh to cross over the other one in rhythmic little nudges. That was when he blew directly upon her nipple again.

Shuddering, she cried out again, abdomen clenching, limbs tensing. As she drifted down, she opened her eyes, blinking at the snowstorm-painted ceiling, unable to believe it—he had just given her an orgasm, and he hadn't actually *touched* her . . . Slowly, he lowered her leg until her feet had good purchase on the floor, then righted her until she was standing on her own. But he didn't let go of her. Amara decided that was a good thing; she wasn't sure if her legs could be relied on just yet.

"You . . . that . . . *How?*" she finally managed to demand, still not yet composed. "I didn't know that was possible that you could . . . that I . . ."

"You challenged me," he stated, displaying some of the arrogance Dominor was usually known for . . . though not for this. "In *my* best area of expertise, no less. You will note, of course, that everything I did to you was perfectly allowable by *your* rules," Trevan pointed out mock-condescendingly. He dropped the condescension and smirked again. "Now, just imagine what I could do with you if we used *mine.*"

Amara blinked up at him, dazed by the possibilities. True, it hadn't been the largest climax of her life, but she hadn't known it was possible for a man to give a woman even a modest one without breaking the rules for courting a maiden. Rules which he *hadn't* broken . . . technically.

Trevan swatted her on her pert backside. That made her gasp and glare at him, but at least it broke her stunned reverie. "Time to go to the kitchens, woman. *We* have a table to set."

As soon as she passed through the door ahead of him, Trevan paused a moment to discreetly readjust himself in his trousers. *She* may have had her release, but he would have to wait for a moment of privacy for his. Somehow, he didn't think his proper, Destined bride would try to arouse and satisfy him in quite the same way.

A disappointment, to be sure, but at least now he had a good hope of attaining the ultimate prize.

FIFTEEN

❧❧❧

Her sister *was* alright, just as Trevan had said. More than that, Arora surprised her by whispering to her that some of *these* people knew *what* she was, some sort of living container for a Fountain, a wellspring of magical power that normally was found only in a place, not a person. There was hope that they could find more information on the matter, but not just yet. Both Shifterai women might have protested at the delay, but Kelly had obtained sketches of building designs at some point in the day, and everyone suddenly found themselves busy preparing to actually build a house.

There was some debate over what "style" the house should be, and how to fit it best to the local climate, which ranged from warm to hot for three-quarters of the year. Kelly's proposed solution for cooling the houses they would build seemed absurd on the surface, until she explained it to everyone.

"Look, in one of the cities back where I come from, one of my friends lived in an *apartment* complex—it's a series of tenant buildings. You know, with suites of rooms rented to different family groups. It's different from castles, in that none of the families are servants of the others, because they just live next to each other," she amended at the puzzled looks from most of the others.

"Ah! An 'apart-mint' is the same thing as a tenement building," Morganen explained, clearing some of the confusion from the others' faces.

"Anyway," Kelly continued, "the city was in a very hot desert, and the building my friend lived in was cooled by a series of water-pipes that ran up one side of the walls, over the ceiling, and down the other side. The water circulating through the pipes leached away the heat of the desert and left the interior of each apartment-suite pleasantly cool."

"Circulation Artifacts are time-consuming to construct, and we cannot spare that kind of time for this project," Dominor dismissed. "Nor the materials. Or do we need to repeat the other night's argument about lack of sellable Artifacts?"

"I'm working on that," Rydan interjected, drawing attention. He didn't speak up often, so it stood out when he did. "I've been purifying a vein of marble for Truth Stone material."

"Well, that's good to know—thank you for *finally* sharing that with us," Saber stated sarcastically, "but unless you can deliver a hundred of them for sale by the next trade ship, we're still short on ready funds. Dominor's right. If we make circulation Artifacts, that's one more drain on our expenses. We do have a reserve cushion, but it is dwindling, and we are going to run out of money in a turn or two of Sister Moon."

"But we don't *want* to circulate the water," Kelly pointed out, earning puzzled looks from everyone, even her husband. "Or rather, we don't want to *re*-circulate the water. Our chief exports are the salt and algae blocks extracted from the local water. The more water we run, the more blocks we produce. Of course, when the city grows large enough, we'll run the risk of diluting the bay with too much freshwater, but by the time *that* becomes a concern, we'll have a strong enough economy to be able to retrofit each house's cooling system with recirculation devices."

"I can understand the cooling properties of water," Mariel agreed. "It's always cooler near a large body of water on a hot day, whether it's a lake or a river, or the ocean. But this is winter, and it's cold enough that fires have been needed each night, and sometimes each day. If you run cold water through those pipes in winter, won't that just make everything colder?"

"Not if they have a heating lever on them, like the sink taps do," Alys offered. The curly-haired woman rarely spoke up at the dinner table, but this time, her words caught the others' attention as much as Rydan's had. More, given their practicality. "If you run hot water through a pipe, the pipe radiates heat . . . and it's still running water, so we're still contributing to the local economy."

"But if it's running up over the ceiling, heat rises, and it won't be very efficient at heating down by the floor, where your feet will get cold," Koranen pointed out.

"Then run more of these pipes under the floor," Amara snorted. The others eyed her askance, save for Kelly, who grinned.

"Exactly—and it's a technique my old world uses. As Kor so aptly pointed out, heat rises. Of course, the *main* drawback to this design is our limited supply of metal for piping," the redheaded woman admitted ruefully.

"Use stone." Rydan explained as the others glanced his way again. "All of the original street pipes were crafted from stone. It won't take much effort to regrow them. Just a lot of power."

"Exactly—and you're just the man for that job," his twin agreed. Trevan snagged one of the outworld blueprints. "If we use stone posts and arches for the structural supports instead of wooden beams, we can pierce each one with a channel. Stone is resistant to the rise of heat, so adding water to the equation would increase the efficacy of the cooling system, at least spring through autumn. As for running hot water through the floor, stone retains heat, once you get it up to temperature, so things should be pleasant when it comes time to switch the system over."

"Leaving out the question of hot water running under the floors, that would require a lot of stone to have enough of a cooling effect in this climate through the worst of summer," Koranen pointed out. "And we'd still have to use wood to cover up the exterior."

Amara snagged a sheet of paper and one of the silverpoint-like pencils Kelly had brought to the dinner table. They drew darker lines than silverpoint, though not quite as dark as charcoal. She spoke as she sketched. "Why cover it up with wood? Here, these are what some of the houses in some of the eastern kingdoms of Aiar look like. The lines sections are timbers, the white is a clay-and-plaster mix smoothed onto a weaving of wood layered in between the beams. Instead of dark wood, we'd have gray granite, but the striping effect can be quite attractive."

Trevan took the paper from her and an outworlder pencil of his own. The end had a pink spongy thing that could be used to erase the marks the implement made. He rubbed and scribbled on her paper, speaking as he sketched quickly.

"If we arch the stone 'beams' in the walls up and over the windows and doorways, plus have the vertical pieces and a few horizontal cross-pieces beneath the sills . . . and maybe have rounded tops to the windows to echo the water pipe arches, like so . . . with rectangular windowpane sections below the arches that can be opened or closed . . . and round out the tops of the doors themselves—it's harder to build in carpentry, but arches are more structurally sound when it comes to stone than squared-off lintels—then we just put the same sort of curved ceramic tiles on the roof that we have here at the palace . . . and . . . there! How does that look?"

Lifting the paper, he turned it toward the majority of the table. Serina cocked her head, Saber arched his brow, and Rydan tapped on his shoulder, getting Trevan to show him the design he had sketched for a few moments.

"I like it," Wolfer said, while the others considered the design. "It's not like Katani architecture, but it is nice."

"It's not like Guchere or Natallian buildings," Mariel agreed.

"And it's not quite like Aian buildings, either, even the eastern styles," Arora agreed.

Dominor smirked. "Well, Brother, it seems you have a talent for more than just sex and sneaking around."

Amara was looking at Trevan when the dark-haired mage made his quip. She noticed how the redhead flushed a little, his mouth tightening slightly. A glance around the table found most of the others looking amused at Dom's comment. Remembering Trevan's earlier comment about what she saw in him, versus what the others saw, Amara pushed to her feet.

"*Stop* it."

Her stern demand made the other adults blink. Even the boy, Mikor, looked over at her, pausing in his doodling on one of the scrap sheets Kelly had brought. "Stop what?"

"Stop belittling him. Stop making fun of him. Stop closing your eyes to what he really is, and stop *limiting* what you see in him!" Even her twin stared at her, but Amara couldn't let it rest there. She frowned at Dominor. "Saying that he's worth nothing more than 'sex and sneaking around' is like saying your wife is worth nothing more than being skinny and having pale hair! Or that you're nothing but arrogance and disdain—or that Aikelly is nothing but attitude and bossiness, or . . . or that Alys' only abilities are keeping her mouth shut and feeding the chickens!

"There is more to each and every one of us—*far* more—than just a few recurring traits," she reproved the others, frowning at each of the adults at the table. "I may be paranoid and prickly, but there is far more to me than that—and there is far more to Trevan than just 'sex and sneaking around'!" Dropping back onto her chair, she toyed with her mug of fruit juice. "I appreciate your willingness to forgive my earlier mistakes, but I will *not* stand by and watch you make them yourselves with one of your own."

Silence followed her words. Finally, Mariel spoke, leaning back so she could look past Evanor and Amara to Arora. "Is she *always* this fierce?"

"Yes," Arora agreed. "Especially when protecting someone."

"But only when they're worth my time and effort," Amara stated in a quelling tone. She received a slow, warm smile from Trevan at that.

"I think that I shall want to be on your good side, then," Dominor murmured, reaching for his mug. "My apologies, Trevan; my comment was thoughtless and tasteless. Please forgive me."

Trevan dipped his head, accepting it, and lifted the paper again, dragging the topic back to house building. "So, what do you think of our design?"

"It looks like it should be easily adaptable to the floor plans the architect drew up," Kelly admitted. "Anyone opposed to this style? No? Good. We need to get started as soon as possible. Rydan, can you fix the lay of the pipes tonight?"

Cat showed up at her doorway, when she retired for the night. He twined around her ankles, then scampered into the suite ahead of her, running to her bed and leaping onto the mattress. There, he sprawled and purred, begging for a petting. Grateful the fickle feline had returned, Amara joined him, seating herself on the edge of the mattress and twisting a little so she could stroke her fingers over his soft coppery fur. Green eyes blinked lazily up at her, and his purring increased.

Dominor's comment from the supper table lingered in her thoughts. Sex *and* sneaking around . . . Glancing down at the ginger tom on her bed, Amara threaded her fingers through the long fur at the nape of his neck . . . and tightened them into a firm grip. His eyes widened in alarm, and he shifted his muscles to escape, but she had him by the loose skin of his shoulder blades and kept him pinned to the bed.

"The 'talented at sex' part, I think I can agree with . . . but would you like to explain the part about 'sneaking around,' Trevan?" she inquired coolly. "Or should I just throw you out?"

The feline stopped struggling against her grip, slumping into the bedding. A ripple under her fingers, and Cat expanded, until she had a fistful of Trevan's tunic collar. Giving her a sheepish look, he braced himself on his side, his cheek on his palm. "Is there anything I can say that will get me in the least amount of trouble? Beyond an apology, of course."

"You can start by telling me why," Amara ordered, removing her hand from his clothes.

"At first, because you were an unknown quantity. You had also lied to me about your sister not being at the north end of the Isle, and you weren't exactly the friendliest person I've ever met," Trevan admitted candidly. "So it seemed wisest to spy on you, at first."

"And afterward?" she prompted him.

Squirming around, Trevan curled himself so that his head landed in her lap, allowing him to smirk up at her. "You have a divine touch when it comes to petting and scratching me."

Irritation undone by his boldness, Amara tipped her head back and laughed. His smile deepened, until he looked like a well-petted cat, despite his current human shape. The touch of his hand on hers bemused her, as did the way Trevan dragged her fingers to his scalp. A nuzzle of his head, and she got the idea.

Stroking his soft, long hair back from his face, she scritched delicately behind one of his ears. He rewarded her with a sensual, realistic purr. Not a tongue-trill just when he exhaled, but the vibrant, in-and-out, soft palate rumble of a contented cat.

It felt a little strange to have him in her bedchamber after dark. Courtship rules among the Shifterai demanded that a man stay out of the maiden's *geome* between sunset and sunrise, though he could speak to whichever maiden he was courting through the felted wall of the tent. But she wasn't on the Plains, and it wasn't fair to demand he stick to the rules of a land so far away from here that it wasn't even the same season, never mind the same continent.

"You can't stay here, of course," she murmured. His purring stopped, replaced with a pout. Amara sighed. "I'm doing the best I can, Trevan, but all my life, I was told over and over how men and maidens weren't supposed to be in the same enclosed space together after dark. I can't just let go of that in the span of a single day."

"Not even in my cat form?" Trev bartered. To sweeten the deal, he stretched himself languidly, arching arms and spine over her lap. "I also owe you for standing up and defending me at supper, tonight. Especially if you think I'm worth your while . . ."

Amara hesitated. He had spied on her as a cat, had taken advantage of her good nature, ensured that she rub her hands all over his shapeshifted body in a way that, were he in his human form, would have been quite shameful, and done so without any sign of remorse . . . until getting caught. But on the other hand, he looked unbearably appealing, sprawled like that. And his offer—given how he had made her shudder earlier, she could only imagine how he'd want to show his appreciation. But he had spied, and she was a maiden, and . . . and . . .

It was the second languid arch of his body that ruined her resolve, for his belly just begged to be rubbed. His outer tunic was pale cream wool, today, a little coarser than the one he had loaned her. Splaying her palm over his stomach, she rubbed it gently in circles, feeling the dip and rise of the contours that defined his muscles. Trevan relaxed into her touch, smiling lazily. Smugly.

Smugness, she wasn't going to support. Removing her hand, Amara gave him her final answer. "Not even in your cat form . . . however cute it may be. Not tonight."

Curling up off her lap, Trevan braced himself on his palms, craning his neck to look at her. A smile curved his lips. "Well, if not tonight, then there's at least some hope for tomorrow night!"

"You are incorrigible," she chuckled, shaking her head.

In reply, he leaned close enough to rub his cheek against hers; his skin felt a little raspy, thanks to the slow growth of his beard. "Of course I am. And you *like* it . . ."

Arching his back and craning his neck again, he blew a stream of cool breath from just below her chin down to the valley between her wool-covered breasts, detouring toward one tightening tip. No sooner had Amara shivered in memory than he stopped, however. Uncurling himself from the bed, he stood, swept her a bow, and left her bedchamber . . . leaving Amara with the feeling she should have invited him to stay, instead of stupidly sending him away.

Under the same impulse as before, Amara shoved off her bed and gave chase. She caught up with him in the hallway, in the act of opening the door to his own quarters. "Trevan?"

Twisting to face her, he gave her an inquiring look. For a moment, she hesitated, held back by too many years of being a good daughter of the Plains—then bounced up on her toes and pressed her lips briefly to his, their bodies brushing together. "Good night!"

He caught her around the waist with one arm, pulling her back against him the moment she started to retreat. His other hand delved through her hair, holding her head in place for a second, more thorough kiss . . . and a third, much longer one . . . and a fourth that was so much more. Amara returned each suckle and nip, proving she could learn quickly at other things, not just shifting her shape. Each kiss left her breathless, and each led to another one, leaving her clinging to him.

Trevan couldn't get enough of her. *She* had kissed *him*, and that meant anything went—*almost* anything, kissing-wise—but he had forgotten just how much he enjoyed drowning sensually in a woman's arms. How potent the mating of two mouths could be. He wanted more; he wanted to touch her everywhere, to pull off the clothes separating them, and . . . his conscience prickled sharply at that impulse, even as his hands shifted from her face to her throat, sliding slowly toward her breasts.

. . . *Touching genitalia is forbidden—and you said you'd wait for* her *to go first!* . . . *Oh, Kata,* he groaned mentally, thinking of her *touching* him . . . and the part he wanted her to touch most stiffened painfully with wanton desire. He wanted nothing more than to en-spell their clothes out of the way and bury himself in her body, drown his lust in her sweet, willing . . . innocent flesh.

Detouring his hands to her arms, he pushed her away. She clung for a moment, almost weakening his resolve, but Trevan firmed his thrust, forcing her back a few steps. Amber gold eyes blinked, dazed and disoriented. Fumbling behind his back, Trevan caught the door handle, opened the panel, and retreated. He thrust out his other palm as she followed.

"*No!* Good night," he added more gently.

"But . . ."

"*Good night.*" Closing the door firmly in her face, Trevan spun and braced his back against it. His body ached, bereft of the suste-nance provided by their kisses. Gritting his teeth, he tried to resist, but it was no use. Hands sliding down his stomach to his thighs, Trevan pulled up the hem of his tunic, then delved his fingers beneath the waistline of his trousers. The first feathering touch of his fingertips inside his undergarments made him groan loudly, he was that painfully aroused. Yanking his belt apart and tugging at the lacings holding his clothing in place, he loosened everything enough to shove the fabric down to his thighs.

Her voice floated through the door as he groaned a second time, cupping himself again. "Trevan? Are you all right?"

Thumping the back of his head against the age-worn panel, Trevan fought for breath. His left hand closed around his shaft, while the right one dove lower, cupping his sack. Fingers rippling, he massaged gently, too close to the edge now to stop himself. But she wouldn't stop until she received a reply, he knew that about her. Tersely, he projected his voice to her, though it wobbled from the way he panted in time with his exertions. "Amara, if you want me to be a *gentleman* tonight . . . go to bed! *Alone.*"

"What? *Oh!*"

Her exclamation, full of wonder and realization, tipped him over the edge. Three firm strokes, and his gut clenched. Struggling to stay silent, to spare her any further embarrassment, Trevan panted, exhaling sharply with each mind-numbing pulse, left hand tightening rhythmically, milking each spasm. His right hand stroked that spot beneath his sack that sent shivers through his blood whenever it was touched lightly.

"Good night, Trevan," he heard her say through the wood separating them. "Um . . . sweet dreams . . ."

Desire shot through his sensitized flesh at *that* suggestion. Sucking in a sharp breath, Trevan forced his hands to let go, to think of unappealing things. Such as casting a chilling charm on his undertrousers to cool his ardor.

It's like a damned itch, indeed. It just feels so good, you want to keep scratching, he thought in rueful, amused disgust, eyeing the stains on the floor. A snap of his fingers and a muttered, *"Dormundic,"* cleaned up the mess. Along with stray bits of dust accumulated since the last time he had spell-scoured his quarters. Carefully *not* thinking about what sort of dreams would be sweetest, Trevan headed for his bed.

It happened too quickly. One moment, they were getting ready to depart the breakfast table, and the next, Morganen and Arora bumped into each other accidentally as they both headed for the door. The pair locked into a strange, light-pulsing grip—literally, as their hands caught and held for a moment. Light that traveled away from her twin and into Morg, as if it was being drained from her. Then the youngest mage tore himself away, staggering back with a cry, leaving Arora swaying on her feet. Amara shoved Wolfer out of her way, catching up to her sibling.

"What did you just do to my sister?" she demanded, hands lifting to steady Rora's body. A black-clad body got there first, insinuating itself in her way. Rydan cupped her twin by the arms, steadying her. It was disconcerting to see Arora *accepting* his touch, after more than a year's worth of shying away from even the most casual touch.

"I'm alright, just a little disoriented," Arora reassured her, or tried to. Amara didn't like the *disoriented* part.

"What did he do? What was that light—you, stop touching her!" she added, whapping Rydan on the arm. He released her twin.

Arora, displaying a lack of good judgment, moved toward Morganen, who was pressed against the far wall of the northern hallway. The mage, his light brown braid looking frizzy with escaping strands, scrambled away from her. "Stay away! Don't touch me!"

"I didn't . . . I didn't hurt you," Arora offered, her tone more quizzical than assertive. "I mean, what did I do?"

"Just don't touch me!" the normally affable Morg snapped, backing up toward the donjon, putting more distance between them. "Don't you *ever* touch me!"

Spinning on his heel, he hurried away. Koranen called after him. "Morg? Are you alright?"

"I have work to do!" With that non sequitur, Morganen fled.

With the mage gone, Amara returned her attention to her twin. "What did he do to you?"

"I don't know . . . but I'm *fine*," she told Amara. "I was a little dizzy for a moment, but I'm already feeling better. In fact . . . I'm more concerned about what I may have done to *him*."

Amara moved a few steps away, in the direction Morganen had retreated. He had taken the direction of the donjon, and it wouldn't take long for him to lose himself in the sprawling wings of the palace. She debated going after him and demanding a better explanation than that, until something her sister was saying caught at her ears.

"According to your Arithmancer, here . . . I'm a living Fountain."

Whirling, Amara glared at her twin. "Arora!"

"They have a right to know!" Arora retorted. Her green gaze reminded her sister that these people were sheltering and protecting both of them. Amara subsided as her sister went on. "I *am* a living Fountain. I *think* he drew energy from me, but . . . I'm not sure. I've spent most of my life containing my power, instead of using it, so I'm not sure what actually happened just now.

"But then, that's why Mara and I fled the Plains," she admitted, making Amara wince slightly at the casual use of her name. Not as much as she would have, were she not trying to set aside her old life, but she still winced a little. Arora continued grimly. "There are mages out there who *aren't* as ethical as the lot of you are."

Amara looked at the others, gauging their reactions to her sister's news. She saw concern on their faces . . . but none of the power-lust she had seen in the eyes of the mages who had previously chased them. Closing her eyes for a moment, she opened them only to find Rydan deftly moving between her and her twin a second time, this time to escort Arora back to her quarters.

The sight of him touching her, knowing he was a mage, made her nerves prickle . . . but she backed herself down. *Arora wouldn't let him touch her if she didn't trust him . . . and she does have good instincts for who is or isn't trustworthy. And I keep forgetting he has his own Prophecy part to play, too. All of these brothers do.*

Slipping her gaze over the others, she noted the brothers with wives, and the two still present who had none. Or rather, the one. Trevan had her, if Fate and the Seers were to be believed. Rydan . . . had her sister. *Who knows what sort of woman awaits Koranen, or his twin.*

Trevan touched her elbow, capturing her attention. "Did you sleep well?"

"Yes, though this . . . oddness may ruin tonight's good sleep," she admitted, gesturing at the hallway to indicate what had just passed.

"You know, Evanor *did* court his wife with offers of massage," Trevan murmured in her ear, standing close enough, she could smell the faint but spicy scent of softsoap clinging to him.

"Considering what you can do just by *breathing*," she dared to tease dryly, "I'm not sure if that would be a wise idea."

"But it would be a *fun* one," he countered, grinning.

"Break it up, you two. We still have a house to build," Kelly directed them. "You can flirt all you want later."

Picking up Amara's hand, Trevan pressed his lips to her knuckles. Under the guise of the courtly kiss, he threw in a quick, subtle lick of the seam between two of her fingers before releasing them. "Draw well, Amara. I'll be back in the afternoon to flirt with you when my work is through."

Amara admitted to herself that she was already looking forward to it, as he nodded politely to both women and walked away.

SIXTEEN

❧

"And this one?" Amara asked, pointing at a box with a lever and a sort of compass-like contraption attached to it. Trevan was giving her a tour of one of his workrooms, showing off all of his inventions. She had already admired the contents of his woodwright shop earlier, which was a building attached to the base of his tower, just inside the guard wall encircling the castle compound, but most of that was nonmagical in nature. This was a room at the top of his tower, where he did most of his construction work.

"That would be an experimental temperature-control Artifact. This lever here sets the desired temperature for the water flow," he explained, pointing at the parts of the device, "with hot and cold water flowing in through these pipes here and here, where they're mixed by the lever. The lever in turn is influenced by this gauge here, which detects whether the air is hotter or colder than the water flowing through the pipes. The combination of lever and gauge widens or narrows the shunts for the two pipes, mixing the water until it comes out through this bigger pipe here. From there, it can be routed up through the rest of the piping in a house."

Amara quirked her eyebrow, puzzled for a moment. But only a moment. Both of her brows lifted in sudden comprehension. "I see! You run water that's cooler than the air during the day to absorb and carry away the day's heat, but if it gets cold at night—colder than the water used during the day—then the water is made warmer, and it *radiates* its heat. This is very clever! You won't have to remember to adjust the temperature, because this thing will ensure it remains the same, whatever time of day or night! It balances the interactions of water and air automatically, doesn't it?"

"Exactly," Trevan agreed. "Of course, based on some water usage projections that Dominor ran, the spells will have to be renewed roughly once every six months, but it won't cost the house owner that much to have them renewed, since the actual spell is based on the contraction and expansion rates of the gauge's mechanism, and the spell is only required to nudge the shunts wider or narrower in response to that. Which in turn depends on where the lever is set."

"What about this thing?" Amara asked next, pointing at an awkward box with tiered rows of letter-marked levers at the front. "Are the letters some sort of mnemonic code? And what do they do when you touch a lever?"

"You know how books are printed?" he asked, and received a nod. "Well, this thing is like that, only it's an idea I found in a book from Kelly's world. Instead of setting up a whole page of type all at once, then imprinting several sheets of paper, this is supposed to print each letter as you go, as soon as you press its lever. You see, you insert the rods of a scroll here and here, and when you hit the keys, the scroll moves horizontally, allowing you to print the type across the sheet. *This* mechanism automatically rolls the parchment up a little and sends when you get to the end of the line, while this lever is for magically erasing any mistakes you make, if you accidentally hit the wrong lever."

"Show me," Amara urged.

Trevan grimaced. "Actually . . . I'm having a problem with the printing spell. If you hit the levers too enthusiastically, they print too many letters in a row. And if you hit too many levers too quickly, it squirts ink all over the place, making a mess. But I'll get it right. I just have to find the right combination of runes and sigils to enchant the levers."

Frowning thoughtfully, Amara eyed the lever-printer. "I'm confused about something. If that cryslet thing you showed me can capture a message and play it back, why not use a verbal spell to print each word?"

"I tried it and ran into too many problems. First came the homonyms, words that sound similar in a particular language, but are spelled different. Some people have terrible diction, too, which makes it difficult for the spell to understand what they're saying. Another problem is the fact that I've drunk Ultra Tongue. The letters being used are Katani characters, but what if I try speaking in Aian? There are certain consonant sounds in foreign tongues that Katani letters don't exactly cover," he reminded her. "The spoken word isn't nearly as interchangeable with the written word as one might think . . . though I am thinking of ways to include a toggle to change the lettering between languages. It's just easier to stick with one language at a time, for the time being, especially when there are so many other problems I still have to consider."

"I see. So what is this thing?" Amara inquired, pointing at a filigree-edged wand, tipped at either end with a crystal. One of the clear gems had a flat, chisel-like end, and the other a sharp, triangular point.

"A tool for etching metal. I like my Artifacts to be attractive as well as functional, especially the things I intend to sell. Sort of like my preference in women," Trevan dared to tease, smiling at her when she looked up at him. "I like the women who are intelligent most of all, but paying a little attention to one's appearance—like you clearly do—doesn't hurt."

That arched her brow again, but not with confusion. He was clearly referring to her subconscious choice of hair and eye color. Amara smirked, more comfortable with this flirting business now that they had been doing it for a few days. "Careful, Trevan. Flirting with me might get you into trouble."

"I'll risk it . . . if it also gets me a kiss," he teased back, shifting close enough to brush his body against hers. Finding a woman who was intelligent enough to follow along with the intent of his experiments was heady. They hadn't yet progressed beyond kissing and embracing, but he held hope of enticing her into more each time they were alone together; maybe this would be one of those times. "Care to lend me your lips for a little while?"

"What would you do with my lips," she asked, licking them, "*if* I lent them to you?"

"Kiss them, of course."

"Just my lips?"

"Well, I'd *also* like to borrow your arms," Trevan drawled, leaning closer, deliberately brushing his chest against her breasts. "If you'd care to lend them."

"I see. And what would you do with my arms?" Amara inquired, twisting away and putting her back to the workbench holding his latest Artifacts.

Trevan shifted to stand in front of her, his green eyes gleaming from the lightglobes he had rapped to life around the room. Once again, he stepped close enough for their torsos to brush, which meant this time she was trapped against the counter. "Why, I'd beg them to hold me close, of course."

"Arms don't hold very well without . . . hands," Amara managed, though she stumbled over the last word. Her position had made her lean back a little, so that she could look him more easily in the eye, but that had thrust her pelvis forward, into his. Specifically, into his flesh, which was undeniably aroused. Her gaze flicked down, then back. "You . . . ah . . ."

"Sorry." Some of the mood was spoiled. Trevan shifted back from her, putting space between their bodies.

For a moment, Amara hesitated, torn between her upbringing and her need to blend into the Nightfall way of life. Clearing her throat, she managed a smile and shifted her hand between them, brushing her palm over his hip. "I, ah, see you're always prepared for your work."

Distracted by the touch of her fingers on his body, so close to where he wanted her to go, Trevan had to regather his scattered wits. "My . . . work? What do you mean?"

"Well . . . you always seem to be carrying around"—Amara swallowed and shifted her right hand a few inches to the left—"this . . . *Gods* . . . really big . . . tool . . ."

Her hand had landed on his cloth-covered manhood, scorching him with sensation. Stunned, he blinked at her blushing face. All the breath in his lungs shuddered out in the next moment, when her fingers rippled, exploring the shape of him.

"I've, um . . . been wondering what you use it for. Since you carry it everywhere," Amara added, feeling rather bold at the sight of the effect she was having on him. "But I haven't seen you using it, yet."

His legs were going to give out. Bracing his palms on the edge of the workbench to either side of her, Trevan struggled to control the sensations she was invoking. He *was* a gentleman, had been raised to be a gentleman, but if she kept touching him, he honestly didn't know if—

"May I . . . see it?"

"Please!"

He didn't know whether it was a plea for her to go ahead, or a plea for her to have mercy. Or maybe a plea for both. She removed her fingers, only to fumble at the thigh-length edge of his tunic. Instinct made him grab for the buckle of his belt; within seconds, it was on the floor, followed a moment later by both of his shirts. He didn't care that it was a cold, rainy night; her slightest touch had him feeling as hot as Koranen.

Bracing his hands on the edge of the counter again, he locked gazes with her and found the strength to speak his mind. "If you go through with this, I *will* return every . . . single . . . touch."

Amara hesitated, thinking about that. The intensity of his gaze, the tension in his body, they warned her he was quite serious. And yet, this *was* what local couples did when they courted. It still felt a little wrong to seek this level of intimacy with a man . . . but it also felt strangely, deliciously naughty to stare at him, knowing she was going to touch him, and touch him inappropriately. He was lean but muscular, with a handful of smaller scars scattered here and there, and a larger one on his upper chest near his right shoulder—she wanted to ask him about that big one, since it was rare for a man of the Plains to carry a scar, but didn't know if it was acceptable to ask about such things in his culture.

They had already made several culture-based mistakes, assuming certain things about how they should act around each other. The two of them might have addressed those problems, but more could crop up . . . and she didn't want to spoil the seductive mood between them. As it was, she was still fighting her own upbringing, at least a little. It was after sunset, she was alone with a half-naked man in a fairly remote location, far enough away that no one would be likely to interrupt them—all scandalous enough on their own—and yet there was something within her that found this all very exciting, very naughty to even contemplate allowing.

She had never really rebelled before now, but she suspected that was as much because no other man before this one had been interesting enough to make her think about rebelling. It was kind of exciting, even thrilling, to do something this forbidden for its own sake . . . but it was more for Trevan's sake. He was unlike any other man who had courted her, and she liked it. More than that, she liked *him*.

So far, he had aroused her with his kisses, teased her with what were supposed to be socially acceptable touches, and even brought her to a stunning climax simply by breathing on her. But not once had he done anything to her that *she* hadn't instigated first. Which meant if she wanted to find out anything else about Nightfall courtships, she needed to show him *she* was serious about learning. *And with him for my teacher, I finally believe it'll be worth learning something about lovemaking.*

With Trevan, I finally see what all the fuss is about, between men and women.

Smiling, she lifted her fingers to the laces at the front of his fitted, Nightfall-style *breikas* and picked at the bow holding them together. He shuddered for a moment, then stiffened his body, holding himself still, save for the shallow breaths he took. Amara kept herself to her task, gently loosening the overlapping front of his trousers. Grasping the fabric on either hip, she tugged down until his pants were at his knees, exposing his plain beige undertrousers.

Heart pounding in his chest, Trevan twisted away from her. Not far, just enough so that he could turn and put his back to the workbench. He needed it to support his unsteady legs. At her puzzled look, he swallowed and found his voice. "Please . . . continue."

Now that was a suggestion she could definitely follow. Stepping in front of him, Amara tugged on the laces of his undertrousers. Since they were a simple drawstring, the fabric dropped as soon as the ties were loosened, though the fabric caught on his erection before it could completely fall, keeping him somewhat covered. She had to actually touch him, making his shaft twitch and bounce, in order to peel away the soft, undyed cotton. Her fingers encountered flesh that was warm, velvety-soft, and firm.

Shifterai maidens weren't ignorant of male anatomy. With most of their men being shapechangers, naked male anatomy was a fact of daily life, though most often that male anatomy came in the mostly ignorable form of animal anatomy. Human anatomy was usually already covered up by a layer of fur or feathers by the time a man had to drop his clothes and shift his shape in public, but she had seen such things before.

She hadn't, however, seen strawberry-copper curls nestled around the base of a fully erect shaft, before. Redheads were rare on the Plains, after all. The crinkly texture intrigued her; it looked very different from the smooth, silky strands growing from his head. She also had never seen a manhood that didn't have a cowl of flesh half-covering its tip. At some point, someone had apparently removed his foreskin. It intrigued her enough that she touched him again, rubbing the pads of her fingers over his smooth, hot skin, stroking up and down a few times.

He panted heavily at the pleasure stirred by her explorations, When she raked her fingertips lightly through his nether-hairs, however, Trevan nearly bit through his bottom lip. Firm touches were quite enjoyable, and for that reason preferable most of the time, but feather-light ones were unbearably sweet, when applied down there. Pure torment, in fact. Her fingers drifted down below his shaft, trailing through the hairs on his sack.

"Mercy!" Trev gasped, startling her into jerking her hand away. Panting heavily, he stared at her with wide, wary eyes.

Amara flushed, uncertainty creeping through her curiosity. "Did I do something . . . wrong?"

"No." Gods, that was the last thing he wanted her to think.

"It's just . . . you have a natural touch for what I find most . . . stimulating. *Too* stimulating, considering how much I want you."

"Oh." Eyeing his shaft, Amara noticed the liquid seeping from his tip and repeated herself. "Oh. Um . . . right. What should I . . . ?"

"Anything you want. Just . . . do it firmly, not lightly."

"Firmly. Right. But won't I hurt you?" she asked.

Trevan shook his head. This wasn't the first untried woman he had instructed on how to please a man, but this set of lessons might well kill him. Or at least embarrass him prematurely; Amara wasn't some village girl, after all. She was his Destiny. "You can grip the shaft somewhat firmly, like you would clasp a hand, but leave the sack alone, for now."

Eyeing his jutting manhood, Amara angled her hand and clasped it exactly as if it were another hand. "Like this?"

If it hadn't felt so good, he would have laughed. She had literally grabbed him like his masculinity was an out-thrust hand waiting to be shaken. Freeing his hand from the workbench, he touched hers, guiding it around so that her fingers, not her thumb, wrapped around the top. That lifted his flesh near vertically. "Like *this* . . . and then you stroke . . . like that . . . ohhh, yes. Like that."

He almost made the mistake of teasingly asking if she had done this before. With any other woman, he might have, but this wasn't any other woman. With the strict, formal upbringing she had apparently followed for most of her life, Trevan realized that asking such a question would probably ruin whatever progress he had made with Amara, and he didn't want that. Especially not when she passed her thumb over the tip of him on an upstroke, spreading some of the moisture there. His hand quickly went back to the counter behind him, helping to hold him in place.

"Do you like this?" Amara asked him, now that she was on her own, working his flesh without his hand to guide hers.

"I think that would be obvious even to the—oh, Goddess—smallest of minds!" Trevan managed to gasp. "Gods! You have a real aptitude for this."

Amara blushed, though she was more pleased than embarrassed at his compliment. Twisting her hand slightly so that her palm and fingers spiraled down and up with each stroke, she asked, "Do you want to, you know . . . climax?"

It took him maybe a quarter of a heartbeat—a rapid heartbeat—to make up his mind. Then again, his mind wasn't exactly in control anymore. "*Yes*, please. What you . . . what you do is . . ."

"I know," Amara said when his train of thought seemed to stall. Mariel had told her about this part. Easing down to her knees, she leaned in close, pressing her lips to the head of his shaft.

Trevan choked, doubling partway over. *That* was unexpected! His left hand flew to his sack, trying to stave off his ejaculation, but her hand got in the way; no doubt she thought it was his way of instructing her what to do, for she cupped the soft globes of flesh lightly, rather than tugging on them firmly, as had been his intent. With a gut-wrenching, drawn-out groan of her name, it was all over. Over her hair, over her cheeks, over her forehead, over her tunic-dress, and over the fingers that still clasped him, though surprise had loosened her grip after the first moment.

When it was indeed over, struggling for breath, for calm, Trevan cleared his throat and carefully inquired, "Are you all right?"

"I think so." She hadn't expected a faceful of . . . liquid . . . but she wasn't harmed by the warm, fragrant stuff. A little embarrassed, but not harmed. The flesh cupped in her palm was softening a little; releasing him, Amara dug into her gathered sleeve, fishing out a scrap of cloth she had found that morning to use as a handkerchief. Mopping the musky residue from her face, she hesitated, then brushed at his partially deflated shaft, cleaning it, too. When she was done, she looked up at him, still on her knees. "How are you?"

"Oh, just fine. Perfect. *Wonderful*, even," Trevan admitted, his voice still a little breathless. His flesh twitched with renewing desire at the thought of what she had just done. Pushing that desire to the back of his mind, he helped her to her feet, then pulled up his garments, lacing them back into place around his waist. She blinked at him, glancing between his trousers and his face, making him feel a touch defensive. "What?"

"Aren't you going to . . . aren't we . . . ? Um, can't men go a second time?" she asked, turning a little pink.

It was his turn to blush. Knotting the outer laces firmly, Trevan said, "I *could* . . . but that isn't the point."

"It isn't?"

He couldn't resist her confusion. Cupping her jaw, Trevan kissed her softly, thoroughly. Her lips parted under his, and he could taste a hint of himself at the corner of her mouth, but the rest of her was deliciously feminine. Humming in pleasure, he devoured more and more of her mouth, pulling her against his temporarily sated body. It pleased him to no end when she wrapped her arms around him, too, and that she snuggled close when he ended the kiss, shifting to rest his jaw against her temple.

"So . . ." she murmured after a few moments. "Are you going to do the same to me?"

Trevan stilled for a moment, then shifted, scooping her up into his arms. This wasn't the right place for that particular discussion, however pleasant their previous interlude had been. Heading for the door that lay across from the one they had entered through, he stopped in front of it and lifted his chin at the panel. "Can you get the door open? Unfortunately, I don't have my twin's innate ability to open and shut doors without a touch."

Amara, reaching for the knob, looked up at him. "Your twin does that, too?"

"*Yours* does it?" he asked, surprised.

"We've tried not to let anyone see it, since it sort of gives away her secret, but yes. She has this way of opening doors, whether they're locked or not, and she does it just by looking at them. I think it's an extension of what she carries inside of her," Amara offered, opening the door to the next room. Then double-blinked, because she *had* offered it to him freely, without hesitation. *Father Sky . . . I think I do trust him that much.* Staring up at him, she thought, *But then, everything I've seen about these people . . . I think my twin was right. Completely right.*

Ugh. I'm going to have to eat grass for her, too . . . Is that a bed? *Why does he have a bed in his workshop?* She blinked at the brocade-padded furniture and focused on the rest of the room they had entered. There were a couple of tables with strange, crystal-studded Artifacts, a pair of mirrors flanked on either side by a lightglobe stand, and in the middle of the room, a sort of cross between a couch and a bed. Trevan settled her on the couch, then went to some of the globes, rapping gently on them to fill the room with light. But rather than coming back to her, he gathered up the Artifacts and carried them out into the other chamber.

"Trevan?"

"Just getting rid of some unnecessary equipment. I'll be right back," he reassured her, making a second trip. With the third, the objects were gone, but there were still the mirrors to deal with . . . or not. Trevan eyed them speculatively. Without the recording devices activated and in the same room, the mirrors would do nothing but reflect . . . and that gave him ideas. Dragging one next to the fainting couch, he positioned it just so, then found some chains in the other room. It didn't take long to enchant the chains into rings secured on the ceiling, nor to lift the second mirror with those chains, hanging it over the divan.

"Um . . . Trevan? Why did you put that up there?" Amara asked, peering up at her reflection. It was an odd angle for viewing herself, one that wouldn't be comfortable unless she was lying on her back.

"You'll see . . ."

There wasn't a fireplace in this part of the tower, but he did have a brazier box, which he brought in next. They could have retreated to either his or her quarters, true, but Trevan figured this was slightly more neutral ground, even if this room had been outfitted previously for analyzing his failures with the illusion-women Koranen and he had initially thought might be the solution to their celibacy problems.

It was just as well the attempt to create a functional illusionary lover had failed; Amara herself had reminded him a few days ago of certain potions one could take in order to temporarily switch genders. Unfortunately, if he or Kor had taken one of those potions, the only other person they would have had to interact with carnally would have been the other of the two of them, and they would have had to interact carnally, in order to record the appropriate responses. True, same-gender pairings were sanctioned by the Gods, but incest definitely was not.

Koranen would just have to remain celibate, while Trevan would have to be more careful about not rubbing his and Rydan's good fortunes in their seventhborn brother's face.

As it was, he found it difficult to not demand more out of Amara than she was willing to concede. Doing this in a bedroom would probably be too intimate for both of them; it might make her feel pressured by the thought that he wanted even more from her, things that she might not be ready to give. Not that he didn't want such intimacy. He simply wanted her to trust him fully before either of them explored each other that far.

Of course, over the next several minutes, his pants would have to stay firmly in place while he helped her explore. It was just as well she had taken some of the edge off his desire; not all of it, but enough to help his self-control. Adjusting the brazier box to keep the room warm, he returned to her side and knelt across from the mirror still standing on the floor. Steeling himself for what he was about to do, Trevan began.

"Here, lie down," he urged her, adjusting one of the two brocaded pillows at the padded arm end of the fainting couch. "Make yourself comfortable."

"What are you going to do?" Amara asked.

He smiled. "Return the favor, of course. Now, you may watch me directly, or you may watch the two of us in either of the mirrors—don't worry, they're warded against scrying—or you can just close your eyes and *feel* whatever I do to you."

That made Amara a little nervous. The last time she had *felt* what he was doing . . . Well, she did trust him, but she was also warily curious about what he had in mind. Relaxing against the pillow he had positioned under her head, Amara nodded permission.

He started by gently skimming his hands over her trousers and the front panel of her *chamsa*. The lightness of his touch was ticklish, yet not unpleasant. He stroked upward from her ankles in short passes, adding an inch or two each time; the higher he rose, the more she anticipated him moving even higher, until her thigh muscles spasmed under his palms. As if that was his cue, he trailed his fingertips down the outside of her legs, returning to her ankles.

"May I remove your footwear?" Trev asked. At her nod, he murmured, "*Sartorlagen*," transferring both her boots and her socks three feet to his right, where they promptly fell to the floor. She jumped at the unexpected *pop* of displaced air, but he rubbed his palms up her legs in a second set of short strokes, this time touching her more firmly than before. It was soothing, distracting, and stimulating all at once.

This time, when he reached the tops of her thighs, he skirted the edge of her mound and drew his fingertips down the insides of her legs. Amara felt her breath catch when his hands moved inward, and discovered she was rather disappointed when he merely returned to her ankles, of which one now bore a thong-strung amulet to prevent accidental conception. As she wondered what he would do now, Trev slid his palms under her heels and began massaging the soles of her feet with mirrored swirls of his thumbs. With the imprint of his fingertips still tingling her inner legs, Amara felt each rubbing caress shooting straight up her legs.

Her soft moan of pleasure seemed to inspire him, for he shifted his hands to just one foot, kneading it expertly enough to make her moan again. When he shifted to massage her other foot, Amara had to swallow a protest at the abandonment of the first, but only because the second one had grown jealous, and was finally getting its turn. After a while, he resumed touching both of her feet. Amara moaned again, for he mixed in feather-light touches with those soothing rubs, stimulating her nerves from heels to toes until her whole legs tingled.

"May I remove your trousers?"

It took her a few moments to process the request, mainly because Trevan didn't stop massaging her feet; he was doing this thing with his fingertips, sliding a finger from each hand gently, stimulatingly between her toes, from the littlest to the largest, over and over. "Uhhh . . . yes?"

His fingers stilled mid-toes. "Do you *really* want me to remove your trousers?"

She had to give him credit for making sure she actually thought about her answer. Of course it wasn't easy to think, given how the redhead had made her whole body ache with something so innocuous as a foot rub. *I did wonder what he could do, if he tried more than just breathing . . . and Mother Earth, give me strength, because I do want to find out!*

Nodding slowly—blushing—Amara met Trevan's gaze. She was

as ready as she was probably ever going to get. "Take them off. Take it all off."

His fingers spasmed, clenching her feet for a moment. Amara watched his throat bob from a swallow, noted how he closed his green eyes for a moment, then opened them, fixing her with a determined look. Focusing his power carefully on what he wanted it to do, he said, "Thank you. *Sartorlagen.*"

Her *breikas* and undertrousers *popped* to the side, dropping to the floor with a soft *flumpf* of fallen linen and wool. But that left her in her *chamsa* and undershirt. A glance up at the mirror showed the front panel covering one leg more than the other, but she was still reasonably decent. Lifting her head, she studied Trevan quizzically. If he had a spell to remove her lower garments, surely he had one for the upper half, too. "Not the rest?"

A shake of his head dismissed the idea. "We're in no hurry. Just lean back, look up, and enjoy."

With that, he began massaging his way up her legs, starting once more with the soles of her feet. Before he even reached her ankles, Amara was moaning. He did everything from ticklish caresses to firm kneading and back again. Only when he started on her knees did she realize he had shifted the front panel of her *chamsa* out of his way.

Looking up at her reflection in the mirror suspended overhead, she could see a hint of shadow at the top of her thighs. She could also see how the flesh of her muscles dimpled under each progressively closer rub of his fingers. It contrasted with the lightest strokes that threatened to raise goose prickles. The moment Trevan ventured onto the territory above her knees, Amara surprised even herself by parting them. That dropped the rest of her dress panel off to the side, fully baring her thighs all the way to the top.

She might have felt embarrassment at her wantonness, but the intensity in his emerald stare, the tension in his muscles, made

Amara feel powerful instead. *She* was enticing this man, luring him into touching her indecently, and *he* wasn't going to think less of her for doing it. Then again, she wouldn't have parted her thighs for anyone else. It wasn't about being in a strange land and having to adapt to the local customs; it was about this man, who saw so many things within her that didn't always show, but which *were* there.

Whether his faith was blind or not, she didn't know, and she didn't care. Amara lifted and parted her knees farther, giving him faith of her own. A strangled sound escaped him, sort of a short grunt, and it looked like his teeth were tightly clenched behind his closed lips, but his hands continued their slow, mixed torment until—finally—his fingertips brushed the inner creases and folds of her pelvis.

Switching position, Trevan hooked his arms under her knees. He pulled her down the couch, startling her, until her bottom was near the foot of it. That allowed him to kneel in front of it, chest level with the divan, and drape her legs over his shoulders. Amara craned her neck so she could stare at him, then dropped it back, looking up at their reflections overhead. Golden red hair spilled over her thighs as he leaned forward, caressing her skin, but it was the steady, cool stream of air he blew around her mound that did her in. Eyes crossing, then closing, she bit her bottom lip, only to release it with a startled moan.

His breath felt good, titillatingly good . . . but his tongue felt even better.

Arching her head back, she lost sight of their reflections in the mirror. Not being able to anticipate where he would trace that tongue, what he would lick, what he would flick, made things more intense. Amara clutched at the edges of the cushion underneath her straining body. The sensations and their intensity were vastly different from when she had touched herself in the past; they made her moan loudly, squirm restlessly.

Catching sight of herself in the side mirror, she stared for a moment, watching his head bob quickly down and slowly up, down and up . . . much like a grooming cat. But that thought didn't disgust her. Lovemaking with a Shifterai was different than it was with a non-shifter, freer and far less restrained than the ways of outlying lands. Between two consenting, married adults, anything that brought pleasure was permitted, even encouraged.

For all that he was a spell-shifter, Trevan *was* a fellow shapeshifter, and creative enough, she didn't think he would be offended by a suggestion—proffered much later—to try nonhuman loving. For now, she shifted her hands merely from clutching at the padded bench to clutching at his scalp, encouraging him with breathless moans and tugging fingers. He pulled back long enough to mutter something, then gently prodded her depths with something warm and wet, soft and yet textured.

Amara vaguely realized that he was now only using one of his hands to keep her folds open to his mouth, that he had done something to his tongue to make it shapeshifter-like, turning it long and agile. That he was rocking into her rhythmically from more than just the soft thrusts of that tongue . . . but it didn't really matter. Trevan of Nightfall had lifted her up into a realm where she floated on each trembling sensation. Tongue pushing and pulsing inside of her, he brought her to the edge of her desire, on a cliff higher than she had previously known, and pushed her over with the baritone-deep vibrations of his drawn-out groan.

She didn't know if she cried out, didn't care if she thrashed or not. When she drifted back down from her plummet, Amara was so relaxed, she had to pry open her eyes and look up to make sure she hadn't shifted herself into a limp puddle of sated flesh. That gave her a clear view of his head, still centered over her groin, and the way his right arm rhythmically moved. A curious glance to the side showed why, in that mirror's reflection; he had bared his man-

hood again, clothes shifted out of his way. As she watched, Trev
stroked himself rapidly, a swift counterpoint of fingers over flesh
compared to the languid, thorough swirls of his tongue against her
slick, sensitive flesh.

His muscles tensed with a grunt as she watched. Liquid spilled
over his fingers. Watching him climax excited her; it sent another
ripple of pleasure through her body. Struggling to calm her breathing, Amara relaxed into the bench. At least until he shifted his
shoulders out from under her legs and pulled the front panel of her
dress back over her lower body, covering her exposed flesh. Her golden
gaze darted to the front of his trousers as he stood and tugged on
them, confused and still expecting him to remove his lower garments, but he tucked the fabric together and fastened the ties back
in place.

Licking her lips, she asked, "Trevan? Aren't you going to . . . ?"

"Not tonight. *Manumundic,*" he added. When he glanced at his
hand, checking it, she realized he had cleaned it with magic. Offering her his spell-scrubbed hand, he pulled her all the way to her feet
then steadied her as her legs wobbled a bit. "*Sartorlagen.*"

Amara gasped, startled by the sudden sensation of fabric wrapped
once more around her legs. She blinked, wrinkled her nose, and
reached awkwardly behind herself, tugging at an uncomfortably
placed fold. Trevan grinned.

"Sorry about that. Sometimes the spell bunches things up in
back," he apologized. "But it's a quick way to deal with clothes."
Wrapping his arms around her, he lifted her up in a brief hug, whispered the charm again, then set her back down on neatly shod feet.
Then nuzzled his face next to her ear and pressed kisses along the
side of her throat. "Mm, you smell good . . . Like you enjoyed yourself thoroughly."

When he nibbled his way down her jaw, then claimed her mouth in
a deep kiss, Amara could smell herself on him. His cleaning spell had

apparently taken care of the mess on his hand, but not anything else. It wasn't an unpleasant smell; in fact, it reminded her firmly of just how wonderful he had made her feel. The moment he released her lips, she sighed and tightened the arms that had snuck around his back.

"Are you sure we're done for the night?" she managed to ask without blushing too much. "I liked all of that. Or . . . I've heard men have a limited number of times . . ."

"Oh, I could go again," Trevan admitted, scooping her into his arms. "But there are more reasons to take our time than there are to rush."

"Then why did you pick me up?" she asked.

"To carry you back to your suite. Your legs didn't look very steady . . . and if I've done my job properly, they *shouldn't* be," he quipped, smirking at her.

She gave him a dirty look. Lifting her chin at the lightglobe stands, Amara asked, "Aren't you going to rap those off, to conserve their power?"

"With Koranen in the family, why bother?" Trevan scoffed. "Though if you could get the door . . ."

Amara sighed and shifted her shape. His arms fumbled, hands scrambling to catch her rapidly shrinking figure. Cloth vanished, replaced by sleek black fur, until he had an armful of house cat. Purring house cat. Chuckling, Trevan adjusted her new form so that he could cradle her against his chest with one arm, and used the other hand to open the door.

"So much for my impressing you with my muscles," he muttered, carrying her toward the stairs.

"Mm . . . bhut you cann phet mmme dis way," Amara offered—and nearly found herself dropped. She hissed and dug in her claws, making Trev yelp. He hurried awkwardly to get her properly supported again.

"You . . . you can *talk* in an animal form?" he asked her, astonished. "I can't do that with *my* spells—that's not fair!"

She purred and narrowed her golden eyes. "Hi amm Shiffderaiy . . . pardon my dicshunn," she added. "De mout isn't shaped hrrright, khayninz in de wrong plaze, lips nod rrright . . . but how do hyu tink Shiffderai coorrdinnate our attacks, if we cannod talk?"

"I thought you said Shifterai focus on pure forms. The pure form of most animals doesn't exactly permit human speech—as you've demonstrated," Trev said.

"Inn de warbandz, der are nno vrulz. And hyu are nod pettink me," Amara reminded him, lifting her furry head a little in silent, regal admonishment, as only a cat could. "Ped mmme. Pleaz."

Closing the door to his tower behind them, Trev obligingly scratched behind her ears as he headed for the drawbridge into their wing of the castle. "I see I'm going to have to consult with Wolfer and Alys on this, since they're the other two spell-shifters on the Isle. I mean, if *you* can manage to talk, I don't see why we can't come up with a modified spell that would allow *us* to talk. It gets rather exhausting if we have to switch back and forth between forms when reporting whatever we've seen . . . Actually, I should put that aside for the moment. I have far too many tasks immediately ahead of me as it is."

They entered the palace proper, dimly lit by the lightglobes resting in their wrought iron sconces.

"Mmm . . . so you take mmme to hyur bet, dis timme?" she asked, arching her back into the strokes from his palm.

"No."

Narrowing her eyes at that, Amara jumped down, transforming even before she hit the ground. Trevan stopped himself before he ran into her, only to be poked in the chest by her finger.

"And why not? Didn't I throw myself at you, just now? I *never* throw myself at a man!" she sharply reminded him.

Catching her hand before she could poke him again, Trevan lifted her finger to his lips for a brief, quelling kiss. "My dear lady, aside from the fact that both of us have to get up early to help fix breakfast, then work all day on raising the walls of that house out there—which would not leave us nearly enough time for a *proper* tumble—I *will not* compromise you with intercourse while you are still a maiden."

That confused her. "Trevan, that makes no sense. The only way I'd *not* be a maiden is *if* we have intercourse, and—"

Touching his finger to her lips, Trev silenced her. "According to *your* traditions, an unmarried woman is called a maiden, whether she is a virgin or a widow with three children . . . and maidens are *not* allowed intercourse."

She blinked at him, astonished by that piece of reasoning. "I was right the first time—this *is* an island of madmen! Or at least, you're trying to drive *me* mad. Aren't we supposed to be courting your way?"

"We will court *your* way as well as mine," Trevan said, drawing her close by her shoulders so that he could give her forehead a kiss. Turning her around, he pushed her toward the stairwell. "Unfortunately, we honestly don't have enough time for a proper romp in the bedding. I like to pay as much attention to the details of lovemaking as I do the details of Artificing, you see. As far as the two of us are concerned . . . I've only just begun to set out the first of my many, many tools."

Only the first . . . ? Amara thought dazedly. *Gods above—what* else *could he show me?*

SEVENTEEN

❖⟨∙⟩❖

The house looked magnificent. Crafted from gray white granite arches filled in with pale blue–painted wood, smooth-paned windows, blue-painted shutters, and blue roof tiles, it was a beautiful two-story structure. They had no true clay on the island to make the roof tiles, but they did have plenty of quartz, lime, and salt to make faience, plus other powdered minerals to tint it almost the same shade of blue as the tiles roofing the palace. It might have been faster to make wooden shingles, but they were less practical for the hot summers of the island than tile.

Koranen admitted to the others that he liked working with faience, even if it did take both himself and Rydan three nights and days to go from grinding the quartz to firing and cooling the finished product in sufficient quantities to tile an entire roof. Faience held a double advantage over clay, in that it could be rapidly spell-dried without the same risks of cracking that clay held, and that the drying process actually created its own watertight, colorful glaze. It was also a lot prettier than wooden shingles would have been.

When the last roof tile was fixed in place, the entire population of Nightfall came down to the cove to admire the first new house on the Isle. The building was a lovely, artistic, sturdy structure decorated in the colors of the partly cloudy sky and capable of weathering the coming years with grace and dignity.

The land the house stood on was not so magnificent. True, Wolfer, Alys, Mariel, and Trevan were all still working on transplanting bushes from the jungle, forming a garden inside the low stone wall that had been erected as a sort of property marker. That wall was only waist-high at the moment, but more could be added later, and the garden would hopefully survive the transplanting and bloom vigorously once spring arrived. But that was still a part of the house they had built. Outside the walls, the view contained a flattish maze of granite gray cobblestone streets connecting to granite gray foundation blocks, with brown mud everywhere in between.

At least the streets and foundations along the north shore of the cove had been aligned to match the pattern Amara had drafted. Morg had managed it. Amara hadn't seen it happening, since she had started work on the plans for the eastern hills of the city, but even Trevan, working around the cove, crafting boards for future construction, hadn't noticed the shifting of the streets underfoot until it was time to go to lunch.

The most he had seen was his youngest sibling scribbling marks on the uneven cobblestones and cracked foundations. Occasionally, Morg would check on the map Amara had drawn and look at a bright-glowing crystal not much bigger than the glass marbles used for illusion-courtiers, caged elaborately in silver and gold. What that was for, Trevan didn't know, but by the time the rest of them came back from lunch, both the roads and the foundations had been realigned to match the map, the crystal was no longer in sight . . . and Morg refused to tell anyone how he had done it, let alone the amount of magic it had taken.

The last of his brothers could be rather annoying, sometimes.

But now, though the streets were bare and in desperate need of grass to tame the soil churned by their efforts and sodden with the previous day's rain, they led down to the water's edge in an orderly fashion, where a brand-new stone-and-wood quay poked out into the cove. Trevan had already toured the interior of the house with Amara, admiring the smoothed stone arches, the polished wooden accents, the gleaming glass, and the pale blue paint they had used, and now waited for Kelly and Saber to finish the final inspection.

Saber had thought about using more of the image-shifting paint in the interior, echoing the walls of the castle, but Evanor had pointed out that it was distracting, expensive, and no longer a necessity to guard against scryings and their associated, mirror-Gated attacks from their enemies.

Kelly had suggested a compromise, having Trevan come up with mock-frames to outline rectangular sections of the special paint, so that the house—bare of all but a few minimal pieces of furniture— still had a couple of fanciful decorations inside, as a sort of house-warming gift for the new occupants. It wasn't much, but it compensated for the fact there had only been enough time to haul down a table, a couple of chairs, and a pair of beds from the castle. Everything else, their first official settlers would have to provide.

And he was coming, too; the boat just now reaching the shelter of the cove was barely big enough to boast three sails, two medium and trapezoidal, the third one triangular and bowed out at the front to catch extra wind. Amara, shading her eyes with her hand, shifted them to the keen vision of a hawk for a moment. "I see . . . two? No, three figures on board. Two working the sails, and the third holding that wheel thing."

"It's called the tiller, and it's used to control the rudder, which steers the ship," Trevan said. "Some use ropes, some use gears, and some use spells to connect the two, but the best is to use a combination of the three, to survive rough waters. I studied a book on the construction techniques for ships when I was a boy. I've forgotten at least half of it, but I remember that much."

Amara shrugged. She didn't know much about sailing other than that her first two days on board that Amazai ship had left her distinctly queasy, until she grew accustomed to the constant rocking motion, and that crashing into a reef was a really bad idea. As far as she was concerned, if she ever had to travel elsewhere, even for the shortest visit, she would just swim with her own fins, or fly with her own wings, or find some swift, smooth, magically safe way to travel rather than bob around on a fragile boat. The most she was interested in, ship-wise, was planning proper moorage for the incipient port city around them.

It took her a few moments to consciously realize what she had just decided. Amara blinked her eyes back to normal and glanced at Trevan. He had shaded his own eyes, though if he was using his magic to peer at the ship, she couldn't tell. *I just thought about not leaving this island, of staying here of my own free will. That means I'm finally growing accustomed to the thought of staying here* . . .

Glancing her way, he caught her stare and smiled. "They'll be at the dock in less than half an hour, at their current rate. Think we should warn Kelly there's at least one more coming than expected?"

Kelly's voice drifted down from overhead. A glance upward showed she had stepped onto the balcony over the front entrance, though it was doubtful if the view was all that enjoyable just yet. "Don't bother, Trev; I already know there's a third person coming."

"Who would that be?" Trevan asked, curious. "Did you invite someone?"

"You'll see." Her tone wasn't exactly happy, which confused the two down on the ground. Closing the balcony door, Kelly disappeared from view. She and her tall, golden-haired spouse reappeared at the front door a minute or so later, both in their aquamarine clothes.

Amara wasn't sure about the cut of Kelly's outfit; there was a skirt-like thing over tapered, fitted trousers, a bodice-thing cinched around her chest—on the outside of her clothes—and a blouse with gathered sleeves that were a lot fuller in their cut than the pants. If they were going to the trouble of coming up with unique architecture and so forth, Nightfall probably needed its own distinct style of clothing, too.

Not that Amara wanted to give up her *chamsa* and *breikas* immediately, but she privately acknowledged that clothing often promoted a sense of local pride and unity. Shifterai clothes differed from Mornai clothes, which differed from Verenai, and Amazai, and Tokrenai, and that was just on the Aian continent alone. But for that, Evanor would be the one to speak to, as well as Kelly. Both of them did the most sewing in the family, and thus had the most experience at designing clothes.

But that was a task for later. With that small ship in the distance tacking toward the new docks—golden from fresh-cut lumber and readily visible, compared to the weathered, blended silver of the old, surviving quay—it was time to go down to the actual harbor. Or what passed for the harbor. Two docks and a scattering of old, rotting pilings weren't very impressive, in her opinion. She slipped her hand into Trevan's so that their fingers laced together, intending to walk down the gray stones of the gently sloping streets with him.

The startled look he gave her was quickly followed by a smile so warm, it made Amara stumble with surprise. Steadying her, Trevan squeezed her fingers gently, then swung their hands a little as they walked, still grinning. She didn't know what she had done to delight him so much, but Trevan was clearly pleased by whatever it was.

Trevan could barely contain himself. *She just clasped hands with me! Her sister said this would be a definite sign that a suitor's interest was acceptable. And now it's acceptable! Gods . . . it's also something I've missed doing with a woman since . . . since I don't know when, but she's touching me* in public*!*

He wanted to kiss her, to scoop her up, twirl her around, and kiss her in front of everyone. Self-restraint had to be practiced, however; what was acceptable in private, where no one could see her discarding her upbringing, might not be so acceptable in public. Even if she was trying to court him by non-Shifterai rules.

It wasn't easy, waiting for her to instigate each move in their courtship dance, but it was slowly becoming worth it. His Destined woman was holding his hand in a public show of her acceptance and affection. Maybe it was silly, but Trev felt more like he was floating than merely walking at Amara's side.

By the time they reached the dock, the figures on the ship were visible even without enhanced vision, though it still took several minutes more before the dark-skinned fellow standing at the side of the hull could toss a couple ropes out to the waiting welcoming committee, along with bundles of reeds to cushion the ship against the wharf. Koranen caught one of the ropes, Wolfer the other, and by looping the ropes against the cleats salvaged from among the junk stored in the old boathouse on the other dock, they had the slowly coasting ship halted and secured.

Between the height of the tide and the size of the sailboat, the deck and the dock were almost the same height. Saber stepped forward, extending his hand to the light brown-skinned woman waiting at the railing while the two Katani men finished securing their ship. She accepted his assistance, hiking up her skirts a little in order to step over the low ridge of wood bordering the edge of the broad quay, and grinned at Koranen, who was staring openly at the calf she had bared.

"Welcome to Nightfall," Kelly stated, drawing the other woman's attention. "I am Queen Kelly, this is my husband, Saber, and we're very glad you could come."

The woman dipped a somewhat formal curtsy, though she smirked as she did so. "I don't think I've ever been *thanked* by a wife for coming, before." She started to say something more, glancing at the others, then refocused her attention on Wolfer's wife, who was blushing. "Well, well . . . Analia. Or should I say, Alys? That was very clever of you, giving a fake name when we first met. So, which one of these men is your childhood friend, hmm?"

"That would be me," Wolfer stated, moving to stand by Alys, whose face was now even redder than before. "You know my wife?"

"Wife? You've married him? Congratulations!" Moving forward, she wrapped her arms around Alys in a big embrace, then pulled back and winked. "I trust he's one of the *good* ones?" the woman asked Alys, the tone of her voice suggesting some sort of innuendo. "Or at least that you've tried to make him into one?"

Trevan, unsure what was going on, wondered if Alys was going to faint, but the young woman managed a hoarse, "Oh, *yes*. Um, thank you. Your advice *really* helped me a lot."

"It certainly did, if you married him," the woman chuckled.

Wolfer's brown brows rose. "*This* is that woman you told me about? The one named . . . ah . . . what was it?"

"Cari, of the Trenching Wench," the woman supplied, holding out her hand. Wolfer bowed over it, and she dipped her knees. "I was very surprised to be formally invited here—and by a queen, no less! But that reminds me, which one of you is Trevan?"

"Yes, well, about that . . ." Kelly started to say, even as Trevan lifted his hand, capturing the newcomer's attention.

"That would be me." Releasing Amara's fingers, Trevan stepped up and bowed over the Katani woman's hand, addressing her courteously out of habit. "I am delighted to be singled out by such a lovely lady, if puzzled as to how I could have caught your attention."

"Oh, look, the others are on the dock! Which one of you would be Marcas?" Kelly asked brightly, interrupting Cari before she could reply.

"That would be me," the lighter-skinned of the two men stated. He gave her a bow, then gestured at his companion. "This is Augur, my friend. He, ah, tends to household things on the land while I'm out at sea."

Where Marcas had light brown skin about the same shade as Cari's, and longish brown hair parted into two braids, the fellow Augur was nut-brown with a bald-shaved head. Freshly shaved, too, for when he doffed his knit cap and bowed, a small scab from the razor he had used could be seen. "A pleasure. Uh. Your Majesty. Um . . . forgive us if we give insult by accident. We're not used to, you know . . . royalty."

"Relax," Kelly ordered him. "We're too new a kingdom to demand formality, just yet. I'm really glad *someone* is willing to take a chance on settling here, and I'd definitely like both of you to feel comfortable about doing so. Since your ship is secure for the moment, why don't we walk on up to the house so you can see the first of the enticements for moving here?"

Amara, wanting to clasp hands with Trevan again, realized he was still holding Cari's hand. His attention was on Kelly, true, but he was still holding that other woman's hand in his. Heat flushed through her cheeks, skin prickling with disbelief and outrage. *He holds hands with me on the way down here, he says he wants to court me . . . but he holds hands with the first new woman he meets?*

It didn't help that she was exotically pretty, with curly dark brown hair and long, dark lashes around her rich brown eyes. She had more curves than Amara did, and was probably dressed in the height of local fashion, with that low-cut bodice and blouse; in fact, the only differences between her and Kelly's outfits were that she wore a pair of layered skirts instead of skirted pants, the fabrics were made from linen and wool instead of silk, and the hues were warm shades of pink accented with red and brown ribbon trim stitched in fanciful, swirling patterns.

Her own shades-of-cream outfit, barely ornamented by a bit of simple embroidery, looked plain by comparison . . . and for the first time since being introduced to Queen Kelly, Amara felt distinctly naked without her pectoral. The intricately pieced collar, fashioned from animal figures carved from semiprecious stones and linked together by golden links and beads, had been lost overboard along with most of her and her sister's other belongings. Shapeshifters wore their pectorals proudly, because the carvings displayed which pure forms they could turn themselves into—and the more pure forms a shapeshifter could take, the more rows a pectoral had.

But she had lost hers. She had lost her clothing, she had lost her homeland . . . and she was losing her man. Amara had never felt like this before; she had always been the one men turned to, not the one they turned from. Uncertainty plagued her, mixing in with her jealousy . . . until she realized she *was* jealous. *That's it—I'll make him jealous of me! I could have had any man I wanted, back home! I've seen any number of maidens recapture a man's attention when she showed favor to another in his presence.*

Let's see how he *likes it, if* I *flirt with someone else.* Knowing she would have to do so by the local standards, Amara strode forward and did what she had seen Mariel doing to Evanor a time or two: She looped her hand around the elbow of the sailor with hair and smiled at him.

"Hello, there! My name is Amara, and I am *pleased* to meet you," she offered brightly.

Trevan stared. *That* was unexpected. *What in Kata's Name has gotten into her? She's acting like . . . like she's* flirting *with him! In front of me! She's putting her hands all over another man, when she* knows *I'm the . . .* Oh.

Awareness filled him of where *his* hand was. Snatching his fingers away from Cari's, he flushed with embarrassment. Old habits were hard to break, even after more than three and a half years of exile-enforced celibacy. Whenever Trevan had been introduced to a single woman—even a professional wench—he had always flirted with that woman, even if it was nothing more than a lighthearted, courtly flirtation. He had done so purely out of habit, as he had always done . . . and upset Amara in doing so.

In fact, he would have smacked himself in the forehead, if the woman at his side hadn't interrupted his self-castigation, glancing between Amara and him. "Excuse me, but is there something going on here that I should know about?"

"Um, things may have changed a little bit since I issued that invitation," Kelly said quickly.

"Is there something *I* should know about?" Marcas asked, eyeing Amara askance.

"Just that I'd *really* like to get to know you better," Amara managed to make herself say flirtatiously, sneaking a peek at Trevan to gauge his reaction.

Trevan was *not* pleased by her attempt at flirtation. Before he could say anything, however, the third arrival, Augur, caught Amara by her elbow, giving her a little shake. "Get your hands off him!"

"Augur, this isn't exactly how we *discussed* this," Marcas warned the other man through gritted teeth.

"I am *tired* of hiding!" Augur retorted, scowling at his companion. "I agreed to leave Katan because *this* place doesn't have a God and a Goddess, and I *hoped* we could be *ourselves* for once! I *said*, get your hands off of him," the bald-headed man ordered Amara. "He's *mine*."

Comprehension dawned. Eyes wide, humiliated by her mistake, Amara jerked her hands free, snapped them into wings, and fled in sparrow form.

"Gods above—*dinurma*!" Trevan hastily cast the spell after her fleeing form. The tracking spell snagged her tail feathers, allowing him to relax. As much as he wanted to give immediate chase, he had just figured out why a professional wench had been invited to the Isle. Turning to Kelly, he planted his fists on his hips. "You brought Cari here for *me*, didn't you? Why didn't you rescind the invitation as soon as you knew Amara was on the Isle? Did you really think I'd go through with a plan to set me up with a wench, once my own woman showed up?

"Or did you think in your dislike of her that even a professional wench would be a better match for me? No offense to you is meant," he added quickly to Cari, who dismissed it with a shrug.

Kelly defended herself quickly. "I *didn't know* she was on the is-land, when I sent that invitation. I thought you could have some fun with a professional, record what you needed for those illusions you wanted to create, and there'd be no harm done. But once it was sent, it was sent," she told him. "And there're more reasons to bring her here than just *your* pleasure, even if that particular reason no longer counts."

"Oh, Gods," Koranen groaned, burying his face in his hands. He dragged them up over his auburn hair after a moment, heat ra-diating palpably from him as he grimaced. "You were bringing her here for *him*, to record the necessary input for the illusionary women for *my* sake . . . but if *they're* courting each other, and *he* won't do it anymore—Gods in Hell! Does anyone mind if I just drown myself, right here, right now? Because I would be a *lot* less frustrated if I were *dead*!"

Morganen slapped the back of his twin's head. "Knock it off, Brother! And watch your language. Your woman *is* coming, I promise you that. You've been patient this far, so you can just be patient a little longer. *You're* not the one who has to wait the longest of us all. Now, stop threatening to scorch the brand-new dock. She's not the only person to make a major mistake in judgment, recently—for what it's worth, Kelly, you have my sympathies. I believe you said your people call it a case of been there, done that?"

"That one would apply, yes," the freckled woman agreed wryly.

Cari put her hands on her own hips, eyeing Kelly skeptically. "If I'm not here to service any lonely males, then *why* am I still here? 'Cause even I would like to know that much. I think I deserve to know it, too."

"You're still here because Alys spoke glowingly of your vast knowledge, your courtesy, and your professionalism," Kelly told her bluntly. Her cheeks were a little pink, but her tone was serious. "When I sent that letter to you through the mirror-Gate, I wanted to meet you in person, because I wanted to see if you would consider moving to Nightfall Isle to open up an official, royally sanctioned Wenches Guild."

Trevan's wasn't the only jaw to drop. Even Cari gaped at her.

"What?" Kelly asked defensively, eyeing the others. "I've actually given this a lot of thought in the last few days. By formally organizing a guild, such activities can be regulated and monitored for the safety and health of both the workers and their clients. Wenches—and the male equivalent—would have certain rights and protections under the law, if they're duly registered as Guildmembers.

"And while such activities would be taxed—the same as any

other business—Guildmembers could receive tax breaks for complying with such safety measures as frequent mandatory health checks. That alone would help discourage the spread of sexually transmitted diseases as the population of Nightfall grows," Kelly said. "Plus, it would ensure that the professionals—male or female—will keep themselves in good health, as well as giving them reliable access to contraceptive methods and so forth. By legalizing professional sexual services, it regulates the working conditions, enforces minimum age limits, and will allow more time to be spent on tracking down and stopping serious crimes by our eventual law enforcement agents, rather than wasting their efforts on petty vice."

"As fascinating as this is," Trevan interjected when she paused for breath, "I have a woman to go catch and explain things to. The *only* woman for me—sorry, Kor."

Koranen folded his arms across his chest and sulked silently. Snapping his fingers to activate the tracking spell, Trevan shifted shape and launched himself into the air, winging away from the dock. Once again, he had to go chasing after his Destined bride. That thought alone kept him from being too irritated by the whole mess. Once he caught her quick, he *would* hold her fast.

Back on the ground, Augur elbowed Marcas, giving the other man a pointed look. Sighing, Marcas folded his arms across his chest and faced Kelly. "I—*we*—want it made very clear, here and now, that we *are* two male lovers, and that we will *not* put up with—"

"—Yes, yes, whatever," Kelly interrupted, holding up her hand. "Frankly, gentlemen, so long as you are both above the legal age for such things—which admittedly I haven't fixed officially, yet, but which will probably be either sixteen or eighteen or something—and that you both freely consent to being together in whatever ways the two of you find most enjoyable, but that you *don't* go doing it in a public square, once we actually *have* a public square . . . with all of those basic caveats of legality and public decency acknowledged and set aside, *I don't care.*"

Both men blinked at her. Augur recovered first. "You don't *care* that we're . . . ?"

"Nope," she confirmed, shaking her head. "Why should I? It's not that a big deal."

"That's not exactly the attitude in Katan," Saber told his wife, explaining their incredulity. "At least, not openly, because the Gods decreed it was acceptable. Most people prefer not to talk about it, because the Empire has a married God and Goddess for their Patrons, and thus almost everyone believes relationships *should* be male-female among the populace."

"Which means, if they don't talk about it, and if they find out about it regarding *you*, they might refuse to talk to *you*," Marcas agreed, eyeing Kelly. "Which can make it difficult to own a business, shop in a marketplace, or even just walk down a street, sometimes."

"Well, I see no reason why the discrimination should exist here," Kelly said, shrugging. "So long as both parties are adults, that the relationship is mutually consensual, and that people keep their public displays of affection to the mild stuff—like hugging and kissing and holding hands, but nothing more—I honestly don't care who sleeps with whom, in my kingdom. I'd *prefer* it if people made a formal, legal commitment to share their lives with their beloved, rather than hop from bed to bed indiscriminately," she added candidly, "but that has nothing to do with gender and everything to do with promiscuity.

"As far as I'm concerned, the two of you can get married to each other, own a business, even raise a few kids to be good future citizens of Nightfall. The *commitment* between you is what will make those things work, not the orientation," Kelly finished. "So why should anyone here object?"

"No one truly objects?" the sailor asked cautiously, glancing at the others. Several heads shook.

Morganen spoke up for his brothers. "We don't have any reason to object. *We're* still working on fulfilling Seer Draganna's Prophecy, which is the reason why we were sent into exile. My brothers and I don't have to worry about you being competition for our women because of it, so there's no worry in that direction. You also don't have to worry about any of us flirting with either of *you*, thanks to the same Prophecy."

"It's a situation in which everyone wins," Alys agreed, glancing at the others. "You get to lead a happy, safe life in a place where you'll be appreciated for what you do, not who you love . . . and *we* get happy, productive citizens. So why should we object?"

The two Katani men eyed the Nightfallers, then each other. Whatever passed in their silent exchange, they evidently came to an agreement. Marcas caught the other man's hand and smiled down at their interlaced fingers. "To be able to hold your hand, just to be able to *hold* it in public . . . and *no* one will care . . ."

"Well, *I'm* now eager and willing to stay," Augur agreed dryly. "Um . . . Your Majesty . . . would it be all right if we told some others, ones who are, you know . . . like us? About your policy, I mean. For potential new settlers to know."

"So long as they're willing to work hard and understand there aren't a lot of amenities on the island for incoming settlers just yet, I don't see why not—but *also* make it clear that opposing-gender couples will be just as warmly welcomed," she warned him. "Not just same-gender couples. I'll not have any discrimination on *either* side of the who-to-love argument. Now, come on up to the house. You two can walk with Saber, who knows a lot more about the exports and imports than I do, and I'll walk with Cari and chat about Guild ideas," Kelly offered, "and we can send the others off to relax, now that you've been officially greeted and welcomed to the Isle."

"That would be nice, since I don't trust my wife to be sensible about getting enough rest in her increasingly delicate condition," Dominor agreed, shading his eyes with a hand, "except there's another ship approaching the island. Someone seems to be making an unscheduled visit, Your Majesty . . . and it *doesn't* look like one of the freelance traders."

EIGHTEEN

❧❦❧

Fluttering down onto a chunk of half-buried rock, Trevan transformed into a sitting position and leaned back on his hands, peering up into the canopy of limbs and leaves. There weren't quite as many of the latter as could be found in the summer, but Nightfall was too warm a location even in winter to be completely deciduous. Still, despite the screening of greenery between them, he could see the golden glitter clinging to his avian quarry.

"You know, while I do appreciate the verses of the Prophecies all but guaranteeing the two of us a 'happy ending,' I *do* grow weary of chasing you every time you feel the urge to run off," Trevan chided, "instead of *talking* to me."

"*Chirrup!*"

"Bird forms aren't nearly as well suited for human speech as cat forms," he demurred, giving the sparrow a wry look. "I realize that's

not saying much, but I must insist that you get your sweet little self
down here and back into your normal body. Now."

The bird hopped sideways on the branch, chirruped quietly for a
moment, then fluttered down out of the trees. Landing a body
length away, Amara folded her arms defensively over her chest. She
didn't look at him, just glared at the jungle floor off to one side.

"Well?" Trev prodded her. "Are you going to just stand there all
day, or are you going to talk to me?"

She tightened her arms over her breasts and set her jaw, but said
nothing, clearly in a sulk.

"Amara, *talk* to me," Trevan said, leaning back on his palms.
"Staying silent is foolish, when we could be discussing the problem."

"*Foolish?*" she demanded, glaring at him. "You *flirted* with her! In
front of me!"

And now we get to the crux of the matter, he thought, sighing. *I
suspect this is another cultural quirk.* Leaning forward, he braced his
hands on his knees and gave her a quelling look. "Amara, I was
raised to be *polite* to women. As a youth, I translated that to mean
charming. For me to take a woman's hand and to compliment her
is . . . is like *you* being fiercely protective of those you love. You
don't even think about it, because it has become part and parcel of
who and what you are. I don't think about being charming, because
that's just who I am. But being charming and polite to someone isn't
the same thing as wanting to court them."

"Well, you could have fooled me—and you *did* fool me. I made a
fool of myself with those men, trying to show *you* how it felt to
be . . . to be *spurned* like that." Amara scowled at the trees off to the
side instead.

"Do you want to know why that woman was invited here?"
Trevan asked her. She glanced at him, then looked away. Trev took
that as permission to explain. "Before you came, my brother Kor

and I were . . . well, suffering from the lack of feminine companion-ship. Intimacy. Kor *cannot* be with a flesh-and-blood woman. At least, not a normal one, not until his Prophesied wife appears. But the illusionary women we were trying to create, they weren't capa-ble of responding adequately, let alone accurately. And we suffered for it, because of the illusions' inadequacies."

Amara blushed at the implication. "What has that to do with her being here?"

"She's a professional wench—she does for pay what your priest-esses do."

That made her snort. "Hardly! To instruct the men of a Family and attend to their needs is a higher calling than doing it for *pay*."

"Well, how do your priestesses gain adequate food, shelter, and clothing?" he challenged her.

"It is the Family's responsibility to provide those things, as a part of the priest-tithe," she said. "Which is given so that the priest-esses may concentrate on the important matter of worshipping our Gods and bending their magics and knowledges to the comforting, guidance, and healing of our people."

"And that's *not* a form of payment?" Trevan asked her. From her blush, he knew his point had struck home. "Kelly apparently thought that this woman Cari would be able to attend to my needs. And as a professional, she undoubtedly thought that Cari would not mind if we recorded her responses during her time with me for crafting an effective illusion-woman for Koranen to be with, in turn."

"I *knew* I didn't like her," Amara muttered. At Trevan's puzzled look, she clarified. "Kelly. She bought you a whore!"

"Kelly *thought like a priestess*," he argued in return. "When she learned how badly Koranen and I were suffering, she sought a means to alleviate that suffering—that sounds like a Shifterai priestess's sacred duty to *me*. Except that Kelly is happily married to Saber, so she did the next best thing she could think of, which was to find someone to bring here. She did so the morning before you and I met, so she didn't *know* you were coming into my life."

"Well, if she invited this . . . professional woman before she knew I had arrived, why didn't she tell her to go away *after* she knew I was here?" Amara demanded. "If it was not to insult me by throwing another woman at you, then what?"

"Kelly wants Cari to consider opening a Wenches Guild on the island," Trevan said. "She feels that if wenching is an official profession, it will be a lot more respectable. There will be laws on how such people should be treated by those in search of their services, like there are no doubt certain customs on how a priestess should be treated. Just because I no longer have a good enough reason for that woman to come here doesn't mean there isn't another, equally good idea for her presence.

"Kelly thinks like that, in strange, divergent layers. *You* think with the depth of your passion," Trevan said, pushing off the rock that had been his seat. Closing the distance between them, he cupped her shoulders. "You think with your heart. It's been wounded because of your experiences, but you think with it. Now, convince your heart that Kelly *isn't* going to hurt or humiliate you, and finish believing in *us*. Believe in *me*, too. I'm not going to hurt or humiliate you."

"But you kept holding her hand," Amara muttered. "You were holding *my* hand, and you went and held *hers*."

"Amara, in my culture, it's not the holding of hands that matters. It's *how* you hold someone's hand," Trevan said. Freeing her shoulders, he picked up her hand in one of his and bowed slightly over it. "Like this, your hand resting on mine, is a greeting between a man and a woman meeting in a social setting. Like this," he added, rearranging their grip so that their palms were clasped, "is a greeting between people about to do business together, regardless of gender. And if I were to take your hand the first way, but with one of yours in both of mine . . . it would mean I was flirting heavily with you.

"Sometimes, in very formal situations . . . or very flirtatious ones," he admitted, bowing over her fingers as he lifted them to his lips, "a man can bestow a kiss."

Feeling his lips, warm and soft, against her skin made Amara feel bad about her accusations. She had to admit that she *hadn't* seen him kissing that woman Cari on the hand, and . . . Her arm tingled and her cheeks heated as she felt his tongue touch her flesh, licking the seam between two of her fingers. Trevan lifted his head slightly, smirking at her.

"The longer a man lingers over a woman's hand—while paying attention to *her*, I should amend—the more he wishes to flirt with her. But I wasn't paying attention to Cari, when I held her hand for too long," Trevan stated, straightening. He kept hold of Amara's fingers, as he studied her blushing face. "I was distracted by the others and simply forgot to let go. It's considered rude to drop someone's hand as if it were on fire, after all . . . except for Koranen's hand."

That distracted her. "Why is Koranen an exception?"

Trev flashed her a grin. "Because sometimes his hand really *is* on fire."

Batting at him with her free hand, Amara tried to give Trevan a dark look, but failed. Lowering her arm, she covered his fingers, trapping them gently between her palms. "So . . . you don't want any other woman? Or man?"

"I most *definitely* do not want another man," Trevan assured her. He tugged her fingers close enough to press them to his chest. "My heart is yours. I'm not about to give it to anyone else."

"I've noticed that men are ruled as much by their bodies as by their hearts," Amara said skeptically.

Readjusting his hands, Trevan nudged hers down the length of his torso . . . and pressed her palms against his masculinity. "*That* is yours as well."

Again, she blushed. But it seemed that Trevan didn't mind her foolish, poorly planned attempt to make him jealous, and she conceded that his hand-holding with that . . . professional . . . woman did seem in retrospect to be merely politeness, at least by the standards of his people. The feel of his flesh beneath her palms was distracting, though. Tugging her hands free, she hesitated, then shifted them so that she could grip his own, entwining their fingers. She couldn't quite look him in the eye, but she had to know.

"And . . . if I want it? Right now?"

Note to self. Invent some sort of portable door, so that I'll always have one conveniently close to bang my head against, Trevan thought wryly. "You may interact with me in almost any way you wish . . . but not intercourse. That, you may *not* have until we are wed."

"But, why not?" Amara asked, finally lifting her gaze to his, seeking the truth in his eyes. "Mariel said your culture doesn't wait for such things."

He debated a moment . . . and gave her the truth with a small but confident smile. "So you'll have something to look forward to. Now, can we *finally* stop the chasing-through-the-forest part of our courtship?"

That amused a snort out of her. "You're not much of a hunter, if you don't feel the thrill of a really good chase."

"Ah, but that's the problem," Trev corrected her, tugging on her hands until their bodies were close enough to brush. "We haven't been doing any of the 'really good' chases. You've been running from me because you were afraid, or angry, or embarrassed. The *really* good chases are the fun ones, the kind that end in moments of delight and desire."

Tugging her fingers free of his, Amara stepped back. He gave her a puzzled look, so she gave him a reassuring smile in return. It was almost shy, since the idea that had sprung into her mind was a bit daring, but she smiled all the same. "Alright . . . we can chase each other around . . . but the rules are a little bit different."

"Rules?" Trevan inquired. "You have a game in mind?"

"Yes. Tag." Catching his face in her hands, Amara kissed him firmly on the mouth. "*That's* a 'tag'—and you're *it!*"

Spinning, she whirled away, darting between two trees. She was tempted to transform into a cat shape, which would make running through the undergrowth easier, but that would make it a lot harder for him to catch and kiss her. So she didn't, running fast and fleet-footed through the forest, dodging around the trunks of the trees, trying not to snag her garments on the bushes.

One of them caught her anyway, and she reached back to yank the panel of her *chamsa* free—only to have her hand caught by Trevan's. He tugged her into him, curling her to face his body. Unerringly, his mouth found hers, found it and devoured it. Ending the kiss only after a very satisfying amount of time, he whispered, "Tag . . . *you're* it."

Amara expected him to release her and run away. He didn't. She blinked at him, arching her brow in silent inquiry, and was met with a smirk for his reply. So she gave up, leaned in, and kissed him back. Until she had to pull back in order to breathe, of course. Panting, she smirked at him. "Tag."

Now he released her. At her startled look, Trev shrugged and spread his hands. "I'm supposed to be *chasing* you, remember? It's Destiny."

Rolling her eyes, Amara turned and started jogging deeper into the trees.

"Oh, come on!" he chivied her. "You can do better than that!"

"But what if I *want* to be caught?" Amara retorted over her shoulder.

Trevan had to concede her point. "Fine. If I catch you within a count of one hundred, I'll *tickle* you. Arora did say you were rather ticklish in certain spots, when I asked her about you."

Amara almost tripped at that. "She didn't!—She *wouldn't!*"

"She *did*," he drawled. "Of course, I had to tell her where *my* twin was ticklish, in exchange. Are you going to run? Or do I have to wriggle my fingers near your . . . *neck?*"

She did *tell him—I'm going to* kill *her!* Adrenaline spiked in her blood; her neck was ticklish, yes, but it was made even worse when she knew that the *other* person knew it was ticklish. A dozen times worse, if not more. Amara hiked up the front panel of her *chamsa* and ran as fast as she could, dashing through the trees.

Delighted by her response, Trevan loped after her. His legs were slightly longer, and his familiarity with the terrain was greater, but she was putting in a decent effort at staying out of his reach. He could reshape himself to something faster or slow her with a spell, but that wouldn't be sporting. Besides, he was enjoying the rush of chasing her, knowing what he could do to her when he caught her. Because he would catch her, eventually.

She was his Destiny. Grinning, he pushed himself faster, ducking under branches, dodging around tree trunks. If he remembered this bit of the forest right, there was a curving rise off to the left with a fairly steep slope gouged out of it, where a mudslide had taken out part of the low hill years before his arrival on the Isle.

All he had to do was . . . there, dodge to the right to cut her off . . . and *that* herded her to the left. Catching the bole of a half-grown tree, he swung around it to change his direction without losing momentum and raced after her. Ahead of him by two body lengths, she burst through a thicket of berry bushes, arms raised to shield her face—and skidded to a stop, presented with a weatherworn slice of earth.

The brush-covered top of the miniature cliff was merely half a body length above her head, but it was sufficient to check her progress. She looked quickly to either side, realizing only now that she was trapped in a C-shaped alcove, and that delayed her just long enough for him to catch up. Spinning her around, Trevan used some of his momentum to force her back into that wall. Crowding in close, he pressed her into it with his body, glad the cliff was made of compacted earth. He wanted to pin her in place, but not hurt her.

Breathless from his presence as well as their little chase, panting with nervous excitement, Amara waited to see if he would tickle her or kiss her. The earth at her back was a little uneven to be pressed against, but not too uncomfortable. It was the lump digging into her lower abdomen that made her feel uncomfortable. In an aching-with-desire sort of way. Shifting her hands to his waist, she rested them there for a moment then slid them to his back when he just stared at her with those intense, green eyes of his.

He wasn't kissing her. He wasn't touching her intimately, either, if one didn't count the pressure of his frame pinning her in place. Excited by their chase, aroused by his presence, Amara shifted her stance, widening her knees, and daringly slid her hands down to the curve of his backside. That got a reaction out of him; he blinked twice rapidly, then licked his lips.

She couldn't wait any longer. Pulling his hips firmly into hers, Amara kissed him. A muffled sound escaped him, somewhere between surprise and pleasure, or at least she hoped it bordered on pleasure. When she felt his masculinity twitch against her lower belly, hardening further, she knew which way the sound had leaned. Biting gently on his lower lip, she opened his mouth to the sweep of her tongue, showing Trev how much of his earlier lessons she remembered.

Just when this exasperating, enticing, enchanting woman had learned to be so aggressive about indicating what she wanted, Trevan didn't know. It didn't really matter, either; the rules of their courtship were that when she demanded, he would supply. From the parting of her thighs and the way she squeezed his backside rhythmically, pressing his groin into her body, she definitely wanted certain things.

The ultimate expression, he would not give her. It was one of his long-standing and most successful rules regarding women: Make them want something more. He would not give in to the fullest sweet allure of her body until she was completely and indisputably his . . . but since it was up to her, by *her* people's rules, as to when that would be, he would give her an enticement. Something worth doing what her sister had said was the rather unique way the Shifterai chose to wed.

Shifting his stance, he slid his hands down her back to her own bottom, then nudged her legs farther apart with his knees. A lift from his palms, and he leaned in firmly, rolling his hips upward. Amara gasped as the ridge of his erection pressed up into the apex of her thighs. Her head fell back, freeing his mouth from her kiss.

Taking advantage of it, Trevan tipped his head and nibbled his way from her ear to her neck. This time, instead of using a modest pressure, he ghosted his lips over her skin, making her squirm and duck her chin in an attempt to avoid being tickled. Blowing on her neck was one thing—an erotic thing—but this was another! And yet . . . He pressed his groin up into hers, rubbing himself against her intimately through the layers of their clothes, and slowly flicked the tip of his tongue over the sensitive skin covering the pulse in her throat.

The two disparate places connected to each other and ignited in her belly. Arching her head back into the earth behind her, Amara let out a moan. Her hands, almost forgotten where they rested on his buttocks, clenched and pulled him harder into her, while her pelvis twitched upward in an instinctive reception. Rational thought vanished when he growled hot breath against her neck and scraped his teeth with unbearable gentleness along her flesh.

"Trevan!"

Trev growled again and rocked into her, quickly finding a plea-surable rhythm. He would *not* compromise her lingering cultural values with actual intercourse before she was his bride in truth. This was merely a simulation of intercourse, one in which they were both safely clothed. A delicious, warm, eager simulation, with excellent instincts on her part—particularly when she slid her palms up his back, then raked her fingertips down either side of his spine, emitting a growl of her own.

He bucked into her when she did that, hips spasming with pleasure. One of the corners of Amara's brain that was still functioning noted that and suggested that she remove his belt. It also suggested distracting him by turning her head and licking the curve of his ear. From the way he groaned and pressed into her again, she thought he rather liked that.

It wasn't until his belt buckle hit one of his boots that he realized she had wormed her hands up underneath both of his tunics. By then, it was too late. The moment he started to pull back, to try and calm them down . . . he felt her fingernails scraping down his bare back. "Mara!"

Unable to extract her arms from his clothes, Trevan gave in and grabbed her left thigh, hitching it up over his forearm, along with the front panel of her tunic-dress. A shift of his stance allowed him to thrust against her intimately, for all that both of their trousers were still safely in the way. It wasn't the same as thrusting *into* her, but rubbing himself against her felt too marvelous to stop. Mindlessly marvelous; it was all he could do to keep the nipping of his lips and teeth along her neck gentle enough to not bruise, just stimulate. He finally had a willing, passionate woman in his arms, and it was so very enjoyable.

This . . . whatever it was they were doing, it wasn't unclothed and it wasn't exactly lovemaking, but Amara admitted it was good.

Unbelievably good. It was difficult to think of just how much this man *knew* about lovemaking, if he could make her melt and claw and moan while still fully clothed. The thought of him stripping her bare, of his knowledgeable hands caressing her, of his talented flesh naked and hot as he moved it against hers . . . it sent another shudder of desire rippling through her muscles.

Somewhere in there, he shifted from her throat to her mouth, claiming it again. At first, he merely nipped at her mouth with his lips. But then his tongue invaded; it dove and thrust rhythmically, matching the nudge and grind of his erection . . . and when *that* pairing connected within her, Amara bucked in an explosive orgasm. He thrust faster, rubbed against her harder, prolonging her pleasure until it wrung a rough, shuddering groan from him as well.

His hips slowed and his tongue gentled, coaxing her panting mouth back into play. Eventually, he switched to scattering kisses over her face, from brow to chin and back. Lowering her trembling leg, he caressed her hip, then stroked her belly. Slipping his hand between her thighs, Trevan cupped her mound intimately. Amara shivered, enjoying the sensation the simple touch evoked.

His hand didn't linger there for long; he moved it back to her hip, then up along her ribs until he cupped her breast through the fabric of her *chamsa*. A sweep of his thumb over her nipple stimulated her a little, before he moved on to the next body part, keeping her arousal simmering that much longer. His other palm rubbed along her back, slowly calming her down from her pleasure.

Wanting to prolong the wonderful feelings herself, Amara returned his caresses as best she could, pressing increasingly sweet kisses to his face. By the time they were both just holding each other, feeling calm once again, her lips tingled from the slight beard stubble she had encountered along his jaw. Pressing a last kiss to the corner of his mouth, Amara tucked her head onto his shoulder, arms looped around his waist.

"I should go apologize to the others, shouldn't I?" she said. "I made a fool of myself, embarrassed Akelly in front of her guests . . ."

"Well, you did think you had a valid reason to be upset," Trevan said, content to hold her. His undertrousers were damp and in need of cleaning, but that could wait a few more moments. Wrapping his arms around her ribs, he asked, "Will you believe me when I say I'm not interested in anyone else? That I'm ready to settle down and be happy with you?"

"Happy? With me?" she quipped. "A prickly, pompous pain in the posterior?"

"You left out passionate, pretty, proficient, and perfect for me."

That lifted her head from his shoulder. Amara gave him a skeptical look. "I am hardly perfect."

"I said perfect *for me*," Trevan corrected. "You're right. You're not perfect, in a traditional sense. But you have a passion for life that matches my own, when you let it out—I have the scratches on my back to prove that."

Blushing, she ducked her head. "Sorry. I shouldn't have done that."

"On the contrary. I rather liked it," he drawled, nudging their loins together in pointed memory. "But you're right. We do need to get back to the shore and see how the others are faring, if nothing else."

"And an apology," Amara insisted, lifting her chin stubbornly. "I acted like a fool, embarrassed our Queen, and that requires that I correct any problem I may have made."

Trev smiled and pressed a kiss to her forehead. "That's something else I like about you. You're an honorable woman. Prickly, prideful . . . and principled. That makes you praiseworthy."

Amara eyed him askance, then chuckled ruefully. "If you keep this up, you'll run out of alliterative adjectives to apply."

"What, you don't think I'm smart enough to think of several more?" he challenged her.

"I *know* you are. That's one of the many reasons why I like you," she admitted. And found herself kissed thoroughly for it.

By the time they returned to the harbor, a second ship had appeared. Its crew were clad in the bluish green uniforms of the Katani government, when it finally reached the new dock and the sailors swarmed down on ropes to secure the frigate to the dock. But the man who appeared at the mid-deck railing was clad in the height of Katani fashion, his scarlet tunic and burgundy vest and trousers decorated with swirls of cloth-of-gold ribbon trim affixed with gems. Even his light blond hair, parted into two braids, was fastened at scalp and ends with jewel-studded clasps.

The man waited until a ramp was swung into place, then descended to the dock with the air of a man resigned to trodding his way onto a manure-strewn field. The group that had originally assembled to meet their unexpected visitors consisted of Kelly, Saber, Dominor, and Morganen. Trevan and Amara joined them, since the others seemed to have the transfer of their newest citizens' belongings to their new house under control.

Dominor recognized the man, but then Trevan knew his ambitious thirdborn brother had made a habit of memorizing important faces in the years before their exile. "I know you . . . Baron Sterr of Wulven, isn't it? Your barony is in the southeast corner of the Empire," Dom stated. "You seem to be a rather long way from home."

The baron gave the dark-haired mage an arch look. "I also happen to be the Councilor of Arrears and Reimbursements, Sub-Office for the Department of Taxation, and the personal adjunct to the Viscountess Thera, Councilor of Tax Collection. I am here to collect the back taxes that are due from the profits rendered from the arrears of the Count Broger case."

"Back taxes?" Kelly repeated, her expression incredulous. "There were no back taxes hidden in that payment! They were extracted prior to our receipt of the money."

Baron Sterr swept his gaze over her aqua-clad body dismissively. "You were misinformed as to the particulars of that financial transaction . . . as well as in your dubious taste in clothing."

Kelly's wasn't the only mouth to gape, though she managed to find her voice first. "My dubious taste in *clothing*?"

"I am a member of the Katani aristocracy. I was hoping to be met by dignitaries of this so-called incipient new kingdom, not some skirtless strumpet," the Councilor disdained.

"Skirtless *what*?" the redheaded woman demanded, hands clenching into fists. Amara's did, too, in sympathy. Kelly's choice of fitted trousers and a skirt-like shell with a hem that was high in front and low in back was a little different from what the Shifterai woman had seen so far in her travels, but it wasn't indecent and it didn't suggest a wenching sort of profession.

Saber touched his wife's arm, forestalling her. Standing as close as she was, Amara could just hear what he said, catching it over the creaking of the two ships and the lapping of the water against the pilings for the dock. "We do *not* need an international incident over this, Wife."

"He *insulted* me, Saber. If we let that go, anyone from Katan will think they can insult a Nightfaller any time they come here!" Kelly muttered back.

"Get to your point for being here, Baron," Dominor ordered, covering for his brother and sister-in-law's hissed debate.

"The taxes were to have been paid upon receipt. They were not. The total taxation due at the time the arrears were received was nine hundred fifty-three gilders, three silvaras, and thirteen copperas," Baron Sterr told them coldly. "Given the fact that the moneys were *not* handed back to the Department of Taxation at the time, the penalty for failure to pay taxes promptly, plus the penalty for back taxes due for the preceding three and a half years, and given the interim compounding of interest, you now owe the Katani government one thousand four hundred twenty-seven gilders, eight silvaras, and eighteen copperas. Provided, of course, you procure the back taxes in question promptly, as the interest on the fines and taxes *is* compounding each day of its delay."

Snapping open the lid on his cryslet, Dominor touched several buttons, then angled the creamy stone on the back of the lid at the hull of the ship. A moment later, a projection of Serina's head and shoulders streamed out of the glowing crystal, appearing larger than life on the planks.

"Yes, my love, you called?" her image asked.

"Lady Serina, a gentleman from the Katani Empire has come to the Isle claiming that we failed to pay taxes on the money that our unlamented ex-uncle held back from us while he managed County Corvis during our exile," Dominor stated. "This was the money the Council delivered to us during their visit about two months back. Did we, or did we not, pay taxes at that time?"

"We did not," Serina told him.

Baron Sterr curled his lip in a disdainful sneer. "Then you owe the Katani government one thousand four hundred twenty-seven gilders, eight silvaras—"

"We owe you *nothing*," Serina interrupted him. "The chests of coins from the estate payment contained a note penned by Councilor Thera of Tax Collection, stating that the taxes owed had already been extracted from the funds discovered in arrears, *before* they was brought to the island."

"Which only shows your gross ignorance of the matter," Baron Sterr retorted. Again, Saber had to catch Kelly's arm to keep her still. The Councilor continued. "*Those* taxes were the taxes due from the Corvis estate at the time the funds should have been tendered to the

Empire and were not. *These* taxes are the taxes due from the Corvis family, upon receipt of said money, as citizens of the Empire."

"Her letter clearly stated that *all* taxes had already been extracted prior to the coins in question being handed over," Serina countered. "This therefore included *all* the taxes due by the Corvis brothers at the time the arrears were delivered into our keeping. Nice try, whoever you are, but you will not be extorting any additional funds out of *this* family."

"There were no records made of any taxes being reserved from the funds delivered to the Corvis brothers," the Councilor for Arrears and Reimbursements stated. "You are therefore required to procure one thousand four hundred twenty-seven gilders, eight silvaras, and eighteen copperas before sunset . . . or the interest will compound, and you will owe more."

"According to Councilor Thera herself, that's not *our* problem," Kelly told him tartly, hands shifting into fists on her hips. "In fact, if there isn't any record of the taxes being reserved, that sounds like the work of an embezzler. I suggest you go back to your little Taxation Department and mount an investigation as to why those taxes were never recorded . . . and get off Our land."

"You have no authority to order me about, you lackwit! I am an official of the Katani Empire, a mage of great power and respectability— and if you will not be *silent* before your betters, I shall hex you into your proper place!" he snapped.

He lifted his hand, magic shimmering over his ring-studded fingers in visible warning. Amara had seen that same threatening shimmer before, when mages had openly attacked her Family, seeking to grab her twin. *Not again . . . Not ever again with my people!*

Swelling literally with rage, the Shifterai woman shot up over the others, barely remembering to cover herself from shoulders to soles in dark green scales for decency. The boards under her feet creaked ominously, while the others gaped at her, but Amara was fully in control of herself, despite her rage. Her mass only quadrupled despite how her size increased exponentially, until she towered half as tall as the masts of the bigger ship.

Snatching up the startled, over-jeweled bureaucrat, she caged him carefully but firmly in her fingers, trapping his arms at his sides. She knew that most mages had to make some sort of gesture to cast their spells, and this was the quickest way to immobilize the idiot. Hauling him up to her overgrown face, she snarled, "*You* have no authority, here!"

Inverting the mage with a twist of her wrist, she dangled his blond head in front of Kelly, who quickly snapped her gaping mouth shut, adopting a more dignified look under the wild-eyed gaze of the gaping mage.

"*This* is Kelly, *Queen* of Nightfall. You owe her a groveling apology for your shameful insults!" She gave him a little shake as the echoes of her enlarged voice died down, then dropped her volume to a more civilized level. "Would you like me to toss him into the bay, Your Majesty? Perhaps a good dunking would clean up his foul manners?"

"Ah . . . no. As *tempting* as it would be to see him treated with the same level of discourtesy," Kelly said, recovering from her shock with remarkable aplomb, "I feel it would not be polite and civilized. And *we* are polite and civilized, here on Nightfall. You may set him down again. I'm certain he has learned his lesson."

"If not, we can always cast him into the dungeon for a few days," Dominor offered dryly. "And fine the Katani government for the highly inconvenient and thus *expensive* cost of his stay."

Stooping, Amara lowered the mage until his hair brushed the planks. She then opened her fingers, letting him drop with an audible *thunk* of his head and a *thump* of his body. He grunted and snarled, twisting to face her, hand coming up in a casting motion . . . only to still himself quickly, faced with a snarl of her own as she stooped even lower, placing her enlarged head close to his own. The sight of exaggerated canines nearly the size of his own legs and the sound of a loud feminine growl sized to match them stopped him from doing something foolish. Wide-eyed, he slowly lowered his hand, letting the shimmering energies fade.

Satisfied, Amara shrank herself back down to her normal proportions, releasing her scales as soon as her clothing rematerialized. They were still intact, thanks to the glass-and-copper ring piercing her ear. Had Trevan not given her such a useful gift, she would have destroyed her garments, increasing her size so abruptly. She would have enlarged herself anyway, but it was good to know the earring worked so well.

". . . You didn't tell me you could increase your size like that," Trevan murmured into her ear.

"I will forgive you the insults you gave me, Baron," Kelly stated, folding her arms across her chest and glaring at the still-crouching mage. "But just this once. Nightfall is no longer a part of the Katani Empire. This means *you* have no authority on this island. *I* do."

". . . You didn't ask," Amara muttered back.

"We will be generous and allow you to see Councilor Thera's letter," Saber stated. "But if you try to destroy it, you will be arrested and charged with theft, destruction of property, and tax evasion."

"*Tax* evasion?" the shaken Councilor demanded, shoving to his feet. "I haven't evaded any taxes!"

"No, but if you tried to destroy the proof of our payment, you would become an accessory to the same crime you tried to pin on us," Kelly said. "We take tax evasion just as seriously as you do. But *we* don't try to frame people or falsely accuse them of wrongdoing."

"We of Nightfall also take insults to our sovereign seriously," Saber added darkly. "I believe you owe my wife an apology?"

"An apology?" Baron Sterr protested. "She's not even a real Queen!"

"Oh, please, let me chuck him into the bay?" Amara offered again, annoyed by the rude, red-clad idiot.

"*I* think there should be an insult tax," Morganen offered. "We'll let the first one slide for free with just a warning, of course, but second and third and fourth offenses get fined, with increasingly steep fees. Something on an exponential scale should be sufficiently painful."

"No, actually, I've changed my mind. If anyone from Katan wishes to press this matter further, they can just send Councilor Thera herself," Kelly said. She flicked a hand at the man "Amara, put him on his boat. Dominor, cast off the mooring ropes. Morganen, as soon as he's aboard, shove the ship out of the harbor and send them firmly on their way."

"What? *Shuotzon!*" the mage snapped as Amara swelled upward again. A glowing, translucent sphere wrapped protectively around him.

Amara enlarged her hand a bit more, picked him up by his ward-sphere as though it was nothing more than a giant glass marble, and lobbed him onto the deck of the frigate. Gently, of course, though the sphere-wrapped mage bounced off the center mast, yelling at her for the indignity. He righted himself with a twist and a roll and canceled the spell, no doubt readying some counterattack . . . but the other two had already done their work. With the ropes untied from the dock's pilings by a spell from Dominor, Morganen was free to slash his hand through the air, sending the ship *banging* away from them in a long line of scattered spray to the west.

"Well done," Kelly praised them as Amara shrank back down again. She eyed the other woman, the corner of her mouth quirking up. "So . . . you can make yourself fifty feet tall when you attack someone?"

"It's closer to thirty, actually. Even I have my limits," Amara admitted wryly. "But that's a few feet taller than most other Shifte-rai can manage."

Kelly eyed Amara. "If you don't mind my asking, why did you leap to my defense like that?"

"Because he was insulting you!" Amara snorted. At the bemused looks from Kelly and the brothers, she shrugged defensively. "If *I* have to be polite to you, *everyone* has to be polite."

Dominor literally choked on a laugh at that, forcing Saber to whack him between the shoulder blades so he could clear his throat. Morganen snickered audibly. Amara ignored them, folding her arms defensively across her chest.

"It also looked like you wanted to punch him, and I couldn't let you do that. Aitava told me that a Queen *never* engages in a com-mon brawl. Not personally, at any rate," she explained when Kelly and the others again gave her a bemused look. "It's one thing for a subordinate to step out of line and do something drastic; they can be 'punished' for it by their leader when in public, to maintain their leader's diplomatic dignity, and yet be praised later when in private. But a leader must lead by setting a good example at all times. Punching someone, however deserved, isn't a very good example of how one's subjects should themselves behave."

"So, you think you're my subordinate now?" Kelly asked her, amused. "Ready to faithfully obey my every command as a loyal subject?"

"I was *merely* keeping your hands clean, Your Majesty, protect-ing you from the consequences of a potential diplomatic incident," Amara retorted, irritated by the idea that the other woman could order her about on a whim.

"And *you* only protect those who are worthy," Trevan inter-jected, touching her elbow in silent reminder to behave. "Right?"

"Right," Amara grudgingly agreed. "Your family *is* worthy of my protection . . . though my *obedience* will take a lot more to win."

"I knew I'd eventually find a reason to like you, Amara," Dominor told her, smirking. "I might obey Kelly myself, but I, too, make her work to prove she's worthy of it."

"Yeah, by making you 'eat dirt,' Dominor. But I'll take whatever I can get from *you*," Kelly told Amara. She turned her attention next to her husband. "Saber, if the Katani Council of Mages is feeling particularly stubborn, they'll probably try to press this argument further. I'll admit that tax evasion has caught many a criminal back in my old world when other means have failed. But if they're not that stupid, it's probable that the Council will still try something else to bollux up our bid for independence. We'll need to be ready for it, whatever it is."

"The sooner we can pick out a Patron Deity or Deities, the safer we'll be," Saber told her. "Once we have manifested a God or Goddess to protect us, they won't be able to take Nightfall away from us. Which means you *have* to pick a God or Goddess for us to follow, and pick one soon, so we can work on raising enough faith to manifest Them."

"You *know* how I feel about the right to a freedom of worship. I *will* find a loophole!" Kelly argued.

"A loophole?" Amara asked Trevan in an aside, wanting clarification as the other two argued.

"Kelly comes from a universe where everyone has the right to worship whichever God they want, wherever they may go in their world. She defends that right very fiercely, even though that was there, and this is here," he explained. "She doesn't understand that Patron Deities just don't work that way. You only get one God per kingdom, or maybe two at most, such as when Kata and Jinga married to save both populations from starvation and war. That's the way it's always been, but she refuses to believe she can't change that."

"But, that's not entirely true," Amara said. "Before the Shattering of Aiar, any citizen of the Empire could worship any God or Goddess they knew, whether or not they were a local Patron."

Kelly broke off her conversation with Saber. "What did you say?"

"In the old Aian Empire, anyone could worship any God they wanted. The structure of the Empire allowed complete freedom of worship," Amara told her. "Of course, there was one caveat to that."

"Which was . . . ?" Saber asked.

"They had to be a Named God," Amara explained, grateful she had paid at least some attention to her sister's happy babblings about the past. "Once every four years, at the Convocation of the Gods, each of the formally acknowledged Patron Deities of all the known lands was Called through the Gate of Heaven by name.

"If a new kingdom arose in one of the intervening years, and they had successfully manifested a God or Goddess, the people of Aiar couldn't worship that particular God or Goddess among the others in the Grand Pantheon until They had been summoned by Name and had officially appeared at the next Convocation. Aiar was considered religiously neutral territory because it hosted the Convocation and could thus ask patronage and protection from any divinity that attended that Convocation."

Kelly blinked at her. "That's it . . . That's *it*! *That* is the solution I've been looking for! I could *kiss* you!"

"Hey, that's *my* job," Trevan interjected quickly as Amara flinched back. "Kiss your husband, if you have to kiss anyone!"

"Kelly, that whole idea is insane," Saber protested. "*Some* of your stranger ideas may work, but resurrecting the Convocation of the Gods? They may have managed it in old Aiar, but I can assure you, no record of *how* they did it ever escaped Aian hands!"

"He could be right about that," Amara agreed, grateful the redhead hadn't followed through on her threat. "The Convocation took place at the Palace of Heaven in the heart of the capital, but my sister never found any records of *how* the old Mage-Emperors managed it. Nor did any rumors about it survive the Shattering among our people's ancestors. They were the ones closest to the capital and thus most likely to have knowledge of the secret."

"I refuse to believe that this Convocation of the Gods cannot be duplicated," Kelly told the others, hands on her hips. "If it happened once, it can happen again. The answer *is* out there. We're just going to have to search for it . . . albeit as quickly as possible. Having *all* the Gods and Goddesses of this universe as our official Patrons would guarantee not only freedom of worship for everyone on the island, but it would *also* be a big enough threat to get the Katani to back down on trying to reclaim us, never mind their goal of punishing the brothers for merely existing.

"Dominor," she stated, turning to the thirdborn of the brothers, "*you* said that the Archives at Koral-tai were quite old and quite extensive, correct?"

"Serina and I are already scheduled to travel there on Arora's behalf, since my wife says there are texts describing the rarity of living hosts for Fountains," Dominor told her, catching on to her meaning immediately. "We can certainly stay a little longer and search the Archives for references to the Convocation, if you like."

"Please do. If the Gods of this realm arranged for *me*—an outworlder who believes completely in religious freedom—to wind up in charge of an incipient kingdom, as I clearly have," Kelly told the others, "then They also knew I'd be interested in reinvoking this Convocation thing the moment I heard of it. For which I have *you* to thank, Amara."

"You're welcome . . . though you might not thank me for it later," Amara cautioned Kelly. "You'll have to not only figure out *how* to open the Gate of Heaven, but you'll need to learn all the Names of all the kingdoms and their Patrons currently in existence. Some-

how, I don't think it would be prudent to forget even so much as one
of them."

"Good point. Morganen, get on it," Kelly ordered her youngest
brother-in-law.

"Me? Why me?" the youngest of the brothers protested, aquamarine eyes widening.

"Because she told you to," Saber said. "And because you probably
have more ways of finding out all the necessary information than
the rest of us do, even combined. Or would you rather stay and discuss how you managed to dismiss that Katani ship so quickly, *without* casting any obvious spells?"

Morg stared at his brother, then turned and bowed gracefully to
Kelly. "If you'll excuse me, Your Majesty, I have a lot of research to
do."

"We should make you tell us, anyway," Dominor stated, folding
his arms across his chest, shifting to block Morg's retreat from the
end of the dock. "Just how strong are you, and just how much do
you know?"

Morganen smirked. "As Hope once told me, a skillful mage
never explains his tricks."

"You *won't* get away with that forever, you know," Dom stated,
shaking a finger at Morg in warning. "We *will* figure it out!"

"Dominor, would you mind shutting the lid?" Serina's disem-
bodied voice demanded. "I'm still not completely over my morning
sickness, you know!"

Flushing at her scold, Dom snapped his cryslet shut, ending the
scrying link and sparing his wife from further dizzying views.

That reminded Trevan of something. Turning to Kelly, he asked,
"So, when will Amara and Arora get their own cryslets? And Marcas and Augur, for that matter?"

"I don't want to give them out immediately," Kelly hedged, flicking her gaze toward Amara. "Nothing personal, Amara, but until a

person *proves* they're committed to staying here, I'd rather people didn't receive them, since they might wander off with one, otherwise. And I'd rather they didn't fall into the hands of an Artificer mage skillful enough to figure out how they're made, without paying us for the privilege."

Amara folded her arms across her chest. "I am staying. Do you have a problem with that?"

"I don't know," Kelly returned, hands going to her hips. "Should I?"

"Are the two of you *always* going to fight like this?" Saber demanded, glancing between them.

Both women replied at the same time, eyeing each other. "Maybe . . ."

And broke up, laughing. Kelly waived off their argument with a flutter of her hand. "Alright, *alright* . . . after expressing a commitment, taking an oath to be a good, law-abiding citizen, and at least, oh . . . ten days of residency on the Isle, we'll consider the person ready to receive their cryslet."

"I've only been on Nightfall for eight days," Amara reminded her. "Do you expect me to leave in the next two days?"

"Well, we do need at least two days to come up with some sort of citizenship ceremony and plan a suitable party to welcome you and your sister into the family," Kelly pointed out. "And by then, your next set of clothes will be ready. Or would you rather not have something nicer to wear, now that I've had enough time to stitch up something fancy?"

"Actually, that reminds me of something," Amara told her. "We've been talking about city planning and building construction, designing a distinct 'Nightfall' style of architecture and arrangement, but clothing is just as important to the identity of a culture as buildings and so forth. Now, I'm not a seamstress, but I have seen a wide variety of clothing styles in our travels across Aiar, and I can sketch out what I saw. I was thinking we could design a style specific to Nightfall.

"I've noticed that Mariel and Serina like their *chamsa* style dresses, but they wear hose, you wear trousers, and my sister and I wear *breikas*. Alys wears those skirts that are like the Mornai fashions, and the clothing the men wear is too much like that red-clad idiot we just banished—you really should have let me toss him out into the bay," Amara added in an aside as she and Kelly started walking toward the shore. "It would have been *very* satisfying. But I was thinking about the weather, about how it's quite warm most of the time, and there should be fashions to suit the climate as well as the cooling pipes in the walls."

"I quite agree," Kelly returned. "I've been trying to convince Saber to let me wear a *bikini* when I'm on the beach, but *he* thinks it's scandalous, even if it's perfectly decent by *my* culture's standards . . ."

"Women," Saber muttered to his two remaining brothers, staring at the retreating, cooperating pair. At least, cooperating for the moment. "I'm not sure I'll ever understand them."

Trevan grinned. "I'm not sure I'd *want* to."

"You wouldn't?" Dominor asked, curious. "Why not?"

"Because where would be the fun in that?" Leaving his bemused brothers to stay or follow, Trevan strode after the two women, interested in hearing more about what that *bikini* thing might be. It sounded intriguing.

NINETEEN

⟨✦⟩

The party was going rather well, thanks in part to how quickly a canopied plaza had been created on the north shore. It had risen literally overnight, thanks to the strange, black-clad Rydan, and Amara's sister. Amara wasn't quite sure what to make of her twin's excited babblings about actually doing magic in some sort of roundabout way; Arora's talk of "empowering versus crafting" confused her sibling. She had to admit that her twin had been right all along, though; this *was* the right place for them to be, and not just for her twin's sake.

One glance at Trevan was enough to reassure Amara of that. He made her cheeks heat and her heart race. He challenged her mind to think and encouraged her heart to feel. Trev made her happy, something she wasn't sure any man before him would have been able to do. All she had to do was make him happy in return. Luckily, he seemed pleased by her, though she still wasn't completely sure why he had such faith in her.

Arora certainly seemed happy; strangely enough, so did the brooding, night-dwelling Rydan. Amara wasn't too sure about the hints of tension between her sister and him. His dark eyes would linger on Arora's laughing face, before drifting down her body. Arora would touch his hand and smile at him, or cuddle up to his side for a moment in a display of physical affection that—while publicly proper—was something normally reserved for married couples. Yet they didn't do more than hold hands, or stand side by side, or occasionally give each other prolonged looks.

Amara didn't think the two had become fully intimate yet, but she couldn't be sure. She reminded herself that this place *was* safe and that these people *were* trustworthy. Even the two newest citizens-to-be, Marcas and Augur—whom she had apologized to with as much dignity as her embarrassment could handle—weren't a threat to her sister. Of course, it helped that they were normal men, not mages. So Amara wasn't going to worry too much about Arora's safety for now.

As for the woman Cari, she was normal as well, if earthy. With all of the males safely interested in other women, or unable to *be* safely interested in a woman in the seventhborn's case, the professional wench had relaxed her flirtatious side, revealing a sensible nature and a good grasp of how to manage a business. The day after Cari's arrival, Amara had found herself talked into designing a Guild Hall and standardizing a floor plan for official brothels, replete with sections for male as well as female wenches, for those who served opposite or same-gender preferences, and private quarters separate from the areas frequented by their patrons.

Or as Cari had put it, "Even *we* like to be able to leave our work at the shop when it is time to go home and rest, the same as any other craftsman."

She had also pointed out to Kelly and Amara the need for plenty of public bathhouses and refreshing rooms scattered through the city, and discussed the needs of public washing troughs and professional laundries, since that was what she had done as a young girl, helping her aunt at a laundry shop in Orovalis City before discovering she had a natural talent for pleasing men. The edge of this plaza had a public bathhouse in fact, something that had been erected with swift enthusiasm by the others when they realized they wouldn't have to trek all the way to the edge of the forest for their needs.

But the plaza itself was quite lovely; it had a triple row of roof-topped, arch-connected columns around the perimeter, wide enough for tables as well as a broad walkway, a broad paved courtyard, and an octagonal stone platform in the center, flanked along three of its edges by tiers of fountains that trickled and splashed from a peak at the center to low pools on either side, before the water dipped back into the system of pipes that had been restored beneath the streets.

With lightglobes set in stone holders on the edges of the columns and a pair of bonfires on the courtyard floor to provide warmth as well as plenty of illumination, the post-sunset ceremony to induct everyone as citizens had looked wonderful. It hadn't gone completely smoothly, of course: Saber had kissed his wife's hands, causing Kelly to forget half of her scripted lines at the start of all the oath-taking; Alys had broken into a fit of the giggles mid-oath that just wouldn't stop; and the bald man, Augur, had shrieked and batted at one of his legs while in the middle of receiving instruction on how to use the cryslet thing.

He was merely the victim of what turned out to be a large but otherwise harmless spider investigating his trouser cuff, but which had caused a momentary panic among the others. Koranen had thought it looked like a baby version of a mekha-something-or-other, some kind of small but nasty magical beast. The ensuing scramble to contain it had led to the poor thing getting squashed and examined post mortem, before being declared harmless. That in turn had led to a brief explanation of the trials and troubles the eight brothers had endured during the years of their exile and many reassurances that there shouldn't be any more harmful creatures on the Isle.

It was during the feast after that little flap that the subject of marriage came up. Marcas was the one who broached it, glancing at the woman seated at the end of the bench-lined table Trevan had crafted earlier in the day. "Your Majesty . . . the other day, you said you wouldn't care if people of the same gender, well . . . if they wanted to be married to each other. Is that true?"

Swallowing her food, Kelly nodded. "Yes, that's true. Provided that you're both adults, you both consent of your own free wills, and that you're not related to each other within at least two degrees of blood relation. And provided you don't take it lightly. We do have a marriage ceremony that is legal and binding so long as Nightfall remains an independent kingdom. And it isn't too difficult to get legal permission to wed," she added, flashing them a smile, "since that basically means asking me to sanction it . . . but a divorce won't be easily obtained.

"You have to be seriously committed to making a marriage work," she warned the two men seated at the midpoint of the table, between Alys and Koranen. Kelly looked at Amara for a moment, then continued, lifting her chin a little. "In fact, I think I'll take a page out of someone else's book and suggest that wedding vows be taken on a Truth Stone."

"Does that mean we're not married?" Mariel asked Kelly. "Do we have to do it all over again?"

"Do you know how long it took us to settle on the perfect marriage ceremony?" Evanor added, exasperation coloring the blond mage's tone.

"No, no, you're married, and you're proving your commitment.

I'm just saying, all prospective spouses should have an opportunity to speak their Oaths on a Truth Stone—it doesn't *have* to be done on one of these Stone things," Kelly added quickly, "but given how Alys was almost sold into an unwanted marriage before coming here, I'd rather let people have a chance to prove it's of their own free will, or a chance to prove if they're being coerced for some reason. I'm just looking at the big picture."

"What about foreign marriages?" Morganen asked. "Serina married Dominor by the customs of her people. What if someone comes here and wants to get married in the Moonlands way?"

"I suppose those ways would still be valid," Kelly allowed, glancing at her husband. "If we're really going to seek a way to re-invoke the Convocation of the Gods, and gain the prot—"

Several of the others choked, cutting off Kelly's words. Amara waited until the worst of the coughing and throat-clearing had passed, then spoke up, answering for her.

"I think we forgot to tell you that. Aikelly, here, is going to attempt to re-invoke the Convocation of the Gods, ensuring the safety of Nightfall through the Patronage of all the Gods and Goddesses of the world. Just like the Aian Empire used to possess. Which would definitely make the, ah, wedding ceremonies of other lands perfectly valid in this one," she added, glancing at Trevan as an idea crept into her thoughts. "Beyond the shadow of a doubt."

"Marriage ceremonies are still legal from land to land," Arora dismissed. "That was set down in the Laws of God and Man at the third Convocation of Fortuna, if I remember the old records right— and no, I never read any information in the records at Shifting City about *how* the Convocation was created. Sorry."

"We heard that one, too, at the nunnery—about marriages being recognized in all lands, regardless of where they were performed," Mariel offered. She turned her attention back to Kelly. "Speaking of which, did you remember to ask Dom and Serina to look through the Archives at Koral-tai for any information on the Convocation ceremony, or should we use the mirror we gave the Mother Superior to ask her and the nuns to look into it?"

"They're looking into it," Saber reassured her. "We covered that before they left."

"Did they *have* to leave before tonight's ceremony?" Evanor asked, pouring more wine into his wife's cup. "It would have been nice to have my twin here to witness and take his own oaths of citizenship."

"We'll catch them when they get back," Kelly reassured him. "I'll repeat the ceremony either down here, or up in the donjon hall, that's not a problem. But finding out whether or not we *can* resurrect the Convocation takes precedence. If there is a way that we can, we'll need as much time as possible to dig up the names of all the kingdoms and their Patron Deities that currently exist. If they can't find anything at Koral-tai, we'll need to know it quickly so that we can try to find other sources for that information. But hopefully, it will be there. All we can do is wait and see."

The conversation drifted away from that topic. Amara snuck looks at Trevan, as he laughed and chatted with the others. He looked handsome in his green tunic, handsome and happy. Contented with his proximity, she looked around as she listened to him tease his twin about how much effort he and Arora had put into erecting the stone frames for so many buildings on the north shore.

Those frames rose like shadowed skeletons around the plaza, a good fifty or more, ranging from what looked like craft shops with living quarters above and behind, to the bones of a potential inn for visitors. There was more than enough work implied in those buildings to have kept her twin safely chaste in Rydan's company . . . but they weren't on the Plains, anymore. Maidenly restraint wasn't a concern for these people.

And therein lay her problem. Trevan was insisting on reserving that final step, intercourse, for marriage as a gesture of respect to her cultural upbringing. Yet it wasn't his upbringing. It touched her that he respected her background, but she wanted more between the two of them, a lot more. Amara silently pondered just how much more that might be, as the others continued to celebrate around her.

Evanor moved to the platform at the center of the plaza. There, he opened up the instrument cases he had brought, entertaining the others with music that would have delighted her at any other time. Mariel sang, too, including a song where her son played a simple pipe and Evanor strummed his gittern in accompaniment, then Mikor shifted to beating on a small hand drum, while Evanor sang and played. The boy looked happy to be included in the performance, grinning at everyone while he did a credible job of keeping time.

The boy made her think about more children eventually appearing on the island, and that led to thoughts of parents and of marriage. Amara's thoughts kept circling back to that last thought, marriage. For most of her life, she had been lectured to find a good man, to choose wisely, to not give herself to someone unworthy, to consider the power of her shapeshifter blood, and select a husband and thus a potential consort accordingly. But here in this land, having just given her oath to *stay* in this land, to support these people . . . she was free to choose whomever she wanted.

Not an unworthy man, of course. She wouldn't ever lower her standards by picking out a drunkard or a coward, or someone lazy or less intelligent than her. But while she would insist on a man who was clean and sober, brave and industrious, and definitely bright enough to be a good conversationalist, the only thing she *didn't* have to pick was a fellow shapeshifter, as would have been expected of her back on the Plains.

Though he wasn't a natural shapeshifter, Trevan met all of her other requirements. There was more to him than just a list of things she wanted in a mate. He had captured her interest with his wit, her attention with his charm, and her heart with his faith in her. Unlike any other man, she believed in *him*. He was more than worthy of her . . . and despite her rocky beginning in this place, Amara believed she just might be worthy of him in turn, if he gave her a chance.

But then, that's something I think he's already willing to give me, she thought as Wolfer pulled Alys to her feet, coaxing her into dancing to the lively music Evanor now played. She jumped a little when Trevan leaned over and murmured in her ear.

"Would you like to dance? I can teach you, since they're doing fairly simple rounds at the moment," he offered.

Nodding, she rose from the table, placing her hand in his. Leading her to the uncovered part of the plaza, Trevan showed her the repetitive steps, stomps, and spins. It was fun, and it took her mind off the problem of marriage for a little while. After a couple of dances, one of their spins ended up with them next to one of the small bonfires crackling and snapping on the stones, warding off the winter chill in the night air. The flames weren't very high, though; Koranen was busy chatting with Cari about something and had neglected to add more wood, leaving the glowing embers and their crackling logs knee-high at most.

The music ended at that moment, Evanor protesting that he needed to rest his fingers for a few minutes. Amara stepped back from Trevan. He followed, catching her hands. Tugging them free, she stepped back again, then sideways a little, edging around the bonfire. He frowned at her, and she did her best to smile reassuringly . . . but the redhead followed her, frustrating her.

"Amara?" Trevan asked, touching her cheek, then smoothing back a wisp of hair that had escaped from the braid she had coiled around her head. "Is something wrong?"

"No, everything's fine," she placated him, shifting back again. He closed the distance between them, reaching for her. Annoyed, Amara tried to move to the far side of the fire again, this time actually turning her back to him, but he followed, catching her shoulder.

"Did I offend you?" Trevan asked when she sighed, irritated.

Given their history, it was not an unreasonable question. But it annoyed her. "No! Just . . . stay there."

Pulling free of his touch, she skirted the fire, trying to get to the far side. Only to be thwarted as he rolled his eyes and pursued her anyway. "Amara, stop it. If something's wrong, *tell* me. Don't walk away!"

"*Yes*, something's wrong!" she finally snapped. "*Stay put!*"

Her demand caused the conversations of the others to falter and die. Aware of everyone staring at her, Amara felt her courage falter, embarrassed at having caused yet another scene. She opened her mouth to apologize, not sure if she could go through with her idea after all. Arora rescued her, hurrying up to Trevan's side.

"Why don't you go stand over here, hmm?" Arora coaxed him, catching his elbow and tugging him away from her twin. Trevan wasn't the only one who frowned; Rydan did as well, narrowing his eyes and abandoning the conversation he was having with his eldest sibling.

Rubbing at his arm as soon as she released him—for her touch thrummed with the vibrations of a very powerful level of magic, making Trevan wonder how his brother could tolerate the idea of physical intimacy with the woman—Trevan let himself be positioned across the fire from Amara. In the next moment, the significance of it struck him. Eyes widening, he stared at Amara, who looked more flushed than the heat of the flames and embers could have caused. A sideways glance at Arora showed her smiling and backing away from him. Giving him room.

Rydan, however, was still frowning at Arora. "Why did you touch him?"

"Because he was being rather dense about it, though I suspect he finally has a clue, now," Arora stated, slipping her arm around the black-clad mage.

"A clue about what?" Kelly asked, drawing near.

Again, Amara's twin came to her rescue. Amara was grateful, even if Arora smirked while she addressed the curiosity of the others, raising her voice so that all could hear her.

"When the kingdom of the Shifterai was formed, it was agreed that though the men could take the form of anything that walked on the earth, swam through the water, or flew in the sky, it was the women who controlled the fourth element, that of fire. We are the guardians of the hearth and the flame . . . and it was decided that any man who wanted the honor of claiming a woman as his wife would have to brave those flames in order to do so. But *only* if the woman herself asked.

"Thus every maiden raised or adopted onto the Shifting Plains is trained to *not* hold out her hand to a man when she stands across a fire from him. Not unless she wishes to offer herself as his wife. She may hold out her hand to the side, or walk around to face him directly, but if she offers her hand to him through the flames of a fire, it is her way of accepting him as judged worthy of her. He need not *accept* the invitation, of course," Arora added, daring to tease her sister, "but that is the custom, where we come from.

"And if he does, if he leaps, or steps, or even crawls across the dangers of the fire to her, grasping her offered hand in front of many witnesses . . . they are wed!"

Face burning, aware of every eye upon her and Trevan, Amara squared her shoulders and lifted her arm. Offering Trevan her hand from the far side of the bonfire. She kept it there, holding his gaze.

Dropping his gaze, Trevan eyed the base of the fire. He backed up almost a body length, then raised his eyes back to hers. Her hand was still there, palm up and waiting. Nodding to himself, confident he could make it, he sprinted forward and thrust hard, leaping over the burning logs.

Their fingers caught. Skidding from his momentum as he landed, Trevan swung around to face her, pulling her against him.

"Witnessed!" Arora shouted gleefully.

Amara wrapped her arms around him, burying her face in his neck and hugging him hard. He was surprised to feel her trembling as she did so. Holding her close, he whispered sweet, soothing nothings into her hair, her ear, nuzzling her gently, until she lifted her face to his, allowing their mouths to meet.

Amara met his lips willingly, grateful beyond words that he had leaped. By Shifterai custom, only a husband and wife could kiss in public. Though he had kissed her in private, something quite permissible under local custom, he hadn't done so in front of anyone else before now. This, however, was about as public as a kingdom of so few citizens could get. She kissed him back willingly, grateful that he hadn't rejected her outkingdom offer.

"And I thought *I* could produce a hot flame in a heartbeat . . ."

"Do you think we should get a bucket of water?"

"I am *not* leaping across a fire to marry you, Marcas—and don't *you* think of trying it, either!"

"Take it elsewhere, Brother," Saber ordered Trevan as the pair parted for breath. "Congratulations, but take it elsewhere."

"And don't sleep too late in the morning," Kelly added. "You'll need to sign a license and marry the Nightfall way. Evanor went to a lot of trouble to come up with a nice, *local* ceremony, so you might as well use that one, too!"

Trevan, arms looped around Amara's back, eyed his sister-in-law. "Kelly, do you really think I'll be done making love to my wife by *tomorrow* morning? *Please*," he snorted, mock-offended. "I have a reputation to uphold. Try at least three days hence!"

Mariel clapped her hands over her son's ears, but it was too late; Mikor was already making a face.

Trevan quickly whispered in Amara's ear. "Let's fly out of here before they tease us any more."

Together, they shifted shape and launched from the ground as a hawk and an owl.

Morganen smiled as he watched the pair go. He might have messed up the start of the other two's relationship, but this one had progressed quite well, despite Amara's prickly nature. Not that he blamed her; he, too, could be quite defensive when it came to his family. He just preferred to be subtle rather than blatant.

"And another couple gets paired off," Kelly observed, moving up to join him. "Tell me, Morg, did you have anything to do with that storm that wrecked their ship, sending Amara and Arora our way?"

"Not a single thing," he promised his sister-in-law, sipping from his cup of wine. "I just made sure they reached the Isle without Rydan noticing and going into hiding."

Kelly eyed the pair of shadows at the edge of the covered walkway and smiled wryly. "Looks like he's noticing her now. About that apology you made, the other day . . ."

"I made a mistake," Morg told her. "Not a big one, as it turned out, but that's all you need to know, and all I will say. Change is coming to Rydan's life, and she's very much a part of it. Let them come to terms with it on their own . . . lest he dig in his heels over it."

"Not a word," Kelly promised her brother-in-law. Lifting the cup in her hand, she added, "A toast, then, to yet another happy couple match-made . . . and one more couple closer to your own joy in life."

"Hear, hear," he agreed, thinking of her best friend. "The sooner all of this ends, the happier *I'll* get to be."

His quarters were very colorful. Cushions in dozens of hues lined the furniture, while strips of cloth hung on the walls, hiding most of the image-changing paint. Thickly spread carpets covered the floor, competing for attention with a variety of distracting, if age-worn, patterns. And the tops of the tables she could see were cluttered with stacks of papers and baskets of sketching tools, not too dissimilar from the ones she had used for drafting out the city plans. It was obvious he had a habit of scribbling out an idea whenever one came to him, and that intrigued Amara. She knew a lot about what kind of a man he was from what he had shown her and the way he had treated her, but there was still so much more to learn.

A lifetime's worth, with any luck. Crossing to one of the three tables in the room, she peered at the top sheet of the nearest stack. She didn't know what the symbols meant—they were magical, and thus untranslatable by Ultra Tongue—but she was fairly sure the rest of it was for a system of pipes, and some sort of odd, inverted funnel thing. Trevan, moving up behind her, wrapped his arms around her waist and peered over her shoulder.

"Those are plans for a rainshower system. The Natallians don't take baths, you see. They have these pierced pipes that cross the ceiling and dribble water in a line. I overheard Dominor complaining about how the small amount of water falling on a particular body part took forever to rinse it—one thing we don't have to worry about is saving water. So I thought if the holes were instead concentrated into a broad, flat surface, it would be more efficient. But I haven't had time to craft a prototype, yet."

Leaning back against his chest, Amara peered up at him. "Is there anything you don't do well?"

"Gardening, definitely. I have no affinity for coaxing green things to grow. Which is a bit ironic," he admitted wryly, "since most mages have no problems tending plants. I also never learned the knack of crafting poetry that rhymes, I'm hopeless when it comes to playing any instrument other than a woman's body, and I . . . What?"

Amara had laughed at his choice of words. "A woman's body is an *instrument?*"

"Of course," he replied, mock-indignant. "All those gasps and moans and cries that can be coaxed forth under the deft touch of hand and mouth, don't you think that's music?"

"Well, what about a man's body?" she asked, turning in his arms to face him. "Couldn't yours be played the same way?" She blushed as she said it, but Amara was married, now. She was finally free to explore her sensual side. Lacing her arms around his waist, she looked at him. "That is, would you mind if I tried?"

If he let her do that, he'd not last the night. Not this first time, when he needed everything to be perfect for her. "You may practice on my body all you like . . . but I want to play with yours, first."

Shifting his arms, Trevan picked her up. He carried her to the bedroom door, pausing to let her open it. The room beyond was dark, but years of familiarity allowed him to carry her straight to his bed. Seating her on the edge, he rapped the lightglobe to life, then crossed back to the door, shutting it. He wasn't his twin, able to manipulate doors with just a look and a thought.

It did give him the chance to survey her on his bed. With the light behind her, most of her features were silhouetted. Reaching up, he rapped the lightglobe hung next to the door, hard enough to brighten the room and light up her figure. "I hope you don't mind . . . but I want to see you."

"You've already seen me," Amara pointed out, remembering the interlude in his tower.

"Not all of you. Nor you, all of me." Staying by the door, Trevan unbuckled his belt and cast it aside. Pulling both of his shirts over his head, he sucked in a sharp breath. The layers of wool and linen had kept him insulated from the chilly air in his room, but without a source of heat, they would both be too cold to enjoy what came next.

Giving her a wry smile, he crossed to the fireplace, made sure there were plenty of logs laid in place, and muttered a fire-starting charm. It caught quickly. A judicious fire-speeding spell that Koranen had taught him reduced the first of the logs to hot embers within moments, billowing heat into the room. Sweating because of his proximity to the fire, Trevan piled more wood onto the coals, then wiped his hands on his trousers and stood, facing her again. Nothing would be allowed to interfere in their pleasure, tonight.

Amara let her gaze drift over his muscles as he worked on the fire, then on the lean length of him as he stood and turned back to her. He looked very much like he had that night in his tower, save these clothes were a little fancier. This time, he would be removing all of them. Aware that she should be doing the same, Amara stood up from the bed and began peeling off the layers of her own clothes. The heat now radiating from the hearth made her layers of wool superfluous, anyway.

Pleased by her participation, Trevan took the time to remove his boots and socks. The sight of her bared breasts distracted him when he was about to loosen his trousers, though; they were somewhat small compared to some he had seen, not really needing any support from an undergarment, but that was fine with him. Trev had learned long ago that while larger breasts were more visually appealing for most men, they were actually less sensitive to being caressed. For him, giving his partner pleasure was the most enticing thing about lovemaking.

Unlacing her boots, Amara pulled them off and tucked them under his bed, then freed the laces on her *breikas*. She supposed she could have simply enlarged her size to remove her clothes, and not donned any feathers or fur for an alternate covering, but the moment she let go of her shape, her clothing would come instantly back. The crux of passion was said to be too distracting for most shifters to hold a shape, but she wasn't sure how Trevan would feel about experimenting to see if it was true or not. Perhaps he would be interested later. Right now, she didn't think so.

Certainly, he was ready for more conventional lovemaking; when she straightened from pulling off her lower garments, leaving herself clad only in her contraceptive amulet and the pins holding up her hair, she found him equally naked, and blatantly interested in her. He was lean, but as muscular as any man of the Plains. A large, pale scar marred the flesh below his right shoulder, and he had several small scars on his torso, but otherwise his skin was smooth. Curiosity overrode modesty, prompting her to cross over to him. Trevan cupped her hips, glancing at her hand as she touched the old wound.

"What happened?" Amara asked cautiously, hoping she wasn't treading on socially forbidden ground. She had wanted to ask earlier, but had refrained. Now they were married; as his wife, she had more of a right to know.

"An attack from some enemies. It went right through." He dipped his shoulder, twisting to show her the greater scarring on the back. "It was before Mariel came to us. Morganen did what he could to reduce most of the damage, but the wound was deep. He ran out of the right herbs before it finished healing, since we have to import them from the mainland. The scarring is just on the surface, though," he dismissed, flexing his arm in a small circle. "It only looks bad. I have full use of my shoulder, see?"

"You couldn't shift the wound to heal it?" Amara asked him. At his confusion, she explained. "Natural shapechangers can shift a wound out of their flesh. It can take several shapeshifts to do so, and it's proportionately exhausting, but we tend to heal without scarring."

"Spell-shapers can't do that. Does it bother you?" Trev asked quietly, worried about that. His previous partners back on the mainland had openly admired his appearance, flattering him by drawing attention to it, but he hadn't allowed it to turn his head. Those had been transitory encounters, moments of youthful fun. Amara's opinion was far more than that, to him.

She shook her head. "No—not unless you count the wish that I could have been there to defend you, at the time."

"Considering how impressive you were on the docks the other day, I think I shall take great comfort in that," he mused, smiling at the memory of her literally picking up that officious idiot from the mainland. "But that is a thought for another day. Right now, all I want to think about is you and me, and how impressive we can be, together."

Her gaze dropped to the space between their bodies, and the jut of his masculinity. Blushing, she cleared her throat. "I'm already impressed . . ." Trevan laughed at the innuendo, and she pinched him for it, making him squirm to defend himself. "I *also* meant by your skill!

"But I haven't shown you *everything*, yet." Catching her wrists, he pinned her arms behind her back. The maneuver pressed her naked torso deliciously into his. Hearing her breath catch, seeing the interest gleaming in her amber eyes, Trevan couldn't resist her. Closing the remaining distance between them, he claimed his wife's mouth.

TWENTY

※

From a soft press of lips, it soon became open-mouthed, hungry kisses. Amara wanted to free her hands and touch him, but the way he held her was kind of exciting on its own, masterful. She could have increased her muscles, shifted herself free, yet there was no need; she trusted the man holding her.

The moment she relaxed into his kiss, pressing her curves against his muscles, warm and willing, Trevan knew he had passed some final test. Her capitulation went to his head—mostly the lower one, making him twitch against her stomach—but somehow, the upper one managed to stay in control. The important thing to remember was that she *was* a maiden, and that meant taking as much time and care as possible to get her ready.

Keeping hold of her wrists, Trevan ended the kiss and drew her over to his bed. Once there, he pulled her down beside him and brought her hands up to his mouth, licking and suckling her fingers, her palms, the delicate skin of her inner arms from wrists to shoulders. Immersing himself in his task, Trevan laved her arms until her skin was damp and her chest heaved in the quest for enough air.

A tug on her waist got her to stand, and a twist of her hips put her back to him. Amara craned her neck, trying to see why he wanted her this way. A moment later, she felt his tongue at the base of her spine, between the curves of her nether-cheeks. Disconcerted, she made a sound, a squeak; it shifted to a moan as he dragged the damp appendage slowly up the length of her back. Goose prickles erupted across her skin, interrupted by shudders whenever he paused to swirl his tongue, remoistening it with the maneuver.

With her hair braided and pinned up on her head, he had an unimpeded path. When Trev reached the top, he circled the tip of his tongue, half-standing off the bed, and placed the first two fingers of each hand on the creases between her pelvis and thighs. Amara squirmed at the ticklish touch, but it was nothing compared to what he did next. His fingertips trailed slowly up her skin, scissoring open and shut as they rose up her belly, along her ribs, and over the curves of her breasts. Those fingers lingered briefly on her nipples, tightening them with pleasure, before continuing their path up to the tops of her shoulders.

Once there, he rested all of his fingers lightly on her skin and began licking his way back down her spine. A moment later, as she moaned sensually, he dragged his fingers back down to her breasts, where they parted to circle around her curves twice, before rejoining on the underside and continuing down to her thighs. By that point, he had reached her bottom, and began licking outward and upward from the centerline of her spine in damp streaks.

It wasn't easy, making sure he had enough saliva for the task. His tongue scraped on the drier spots, but that was alright; when the bottom point of the chevrons he was tracing was at her waist, he paused to suck on her skin as best he could while repeating the two-fingered sweep from earlier. This time, he paused those fingers just below her breasts, planted his remoistened tongue on her spine, and dragged it up to the middle of her shoulder blades. Shifting his hands, fingertips still brushing her ribs, he rubbed the pads of his thumbs back and forth over her nipples.

Amara cried out, aroused unbearably by his touch. She wasn't ignorant of the ways of husbands and wives, but this—! No one had ever mentioned anything like this! Instinct arched her back, buttocks seeking and pressing into his groin, rubbing his hardness into the small of her back. She felt like an animal in heat, with her hide being stroked in all the right ways.

Trevan dipped down to the base of her ribs and licked straight up her spine, dragging his tongue firmly up her flesh. The move enflamed her rising desire. Needing even more, Amara cupped her hands over his, pressing them to her aching body. In silent demand, she drew his palms up to her breasts.

He didn't keep them there for more than a few circling rubs. Sliding his hands under her arms, he pushed her limbs up over her head, then guided them behind, until she got the idea and laced her fingers behind his neck. Murmuring a wordless approval into the side of her throat, Trevan trailed all of his fingertips in scissor-sweeps down her arms and over her breasts, pausing to spiral around her soft curves. Amara gasped when he plucked gently at their peaks, head arching back against his shoulder.

Panting, she wondered vaguely how much more he had to show her, how much more she could endure. She whimpered when he tickled his fingers back down to her abdomen, brushing them back and forth across the dark hairs shielding her mound. But when she started to lower her hands from behind his neck, he lifted his own quickly and hushed her, silently ordering her to keep them there. Complying, Amara endured his tickling caress as he repeated his previous downward path: to her breasts and a circling touch, a couple of feather-light tweaks that teased at her nerves, and then a sliding touch down to her pelvis.

This time, he swerved his palms to the outside of her hips, and crouched behind her. The ticklish caress of his hands on the backs of her thighs made her gasp, made her legs twitch and part. Amara wasn't sure what he was up to, but held on to him, too invested now in his lovemaking to quit. Stooping a little more, Trevan startled her by scooping his hands under her thighs. A heave lifted her up off her feet even as it parted her legs. A second, higher hitch had her clutching at the back of his head for balance, but he leaned back a little, legs braced wide for stability.

"Trevan?" she gasped, unsure of his intent. She felt so exposed like this. He grunted and lifted her a little higher, and Amara quickly lightened her mass in response. This time, his second grunt was a mixture of surprise and gratitude. Lifting her more easily allowed his manhood to slip free from her back, jutting out underneath her loins.

That was when he lowered her, just a little. Enough to deliberately glide his flesh along the length of her moist, intimate folds. Not into her, not yet, but along her femininity. Shuddering, Amara clung to the back of his neck, her only point of leverage and stability in this unbelievable pose. He didn't stop there; thrusting his hips back and forth, Trevan teased her body, nudging the sensitive peak hidden in her folds with each heated rub until she shook and cried out with each stroke.

Overwhelmed, desperate now for more, much more, Amara squirmed free. Trevan tried to catch her, to stop her, but she increased her mass abruptly back to normal. That slipped her out of his grasp. Stumbling around to face him, legs wobbly from sheer desire, she firmly pushed him back. With the bed directly behind him, he toppled to the mattress with a grunt. She didn't really see his stunned expression, though; the part of him that thrust straight up, visibly damp from her pleasure, was her sole focus and goal.

Climbing onto the bed, Amara swung her thigh over his hip, mounting him as she would have a horse of the Plains. For a moment, she wasn't quite sure how to make things work, but he managed to get a hand down there, gripping his base to aim the rounded, reddened tip.

"Lower yourself . . . there," he directed her, his free hand moving to her hip. The position allowed him to rub the head of his shaft against her folds, keeping her aroused while coating his flesh in more of the slickness that seeped from her depths.

If he had roused her to the point where she just had to join with him, he wasn't going to argue. Everything else he would have done to her before this point, he could and would still do to her afterward. When she reached down, hand cupping his, repositioning him at her opening, Trevan knew it was time. Letting her guide him, he held his breath, waiting for her to ease herself into place.

Breathing deeply, wanting him inside of her and knowing she had to relax, Amara sank slowly onto him. It was a tight fit, of course; she had to rock gently, gradually impaling herself on more and more of him. But as expected, there wasn't much pain, just a stretching sting. By the time her groin was snugged against his, she was biting her lip from bliss, not discomfort. *This* was what had been missing, this sensation of fullness, of pressure and heat and delicious connection between their bodies.

Rising with a flex of her thighs, whimpering from the necessary loss, she dropped herself back down firmly. Trevan shouted and caught her hips, slowing her. "Gently! You'll hurt yourself!"

Not so innocent as to not know what he was talking about, Amara opened her eyes and smirked at him. She was now fully his wife, and felt a rush of confidence from that delicious fact. "I was riding horses by the age of three, Atrevan. Every maiden on the Plains knows that usually helps ease the way."

"Atrevan?" he queried, distracted by that.

"The man who marries a Shifterai princess is given the title of 'prince' appended to his name," she explained. Then gave him a not quite shy smile. "I can't think of anyone more deserving to be my prince than you."

Trevan pulled her down to him, lifting his head to meet her descending lips. Her words pleased him deeply, gave him hope that she did love him, though she hadn't actually said it, yet. So he kissed her, slanting his mouth across hers, claiming his very own princess.

The change in her position put pressure on their bodies in a new way. Amara moaned into his mouth, flexing her back to grind her hips into him. It stung, but not too badly, not enough to distract her from her need. Hands slipping to her hips, Trevan showed her how to move on him, how to rock her body in slow, deliberate movements that made her ache in a good way.

Soon, her pace increased, enthusiasm rising within her flesh with each intimate stroke. But it wasn't enough. "P-please," she panted. "More! How do I . . . ?"

Curving his arms behind her back, his fingers over her shoulders, Trevan lifted his feet so that his heels were braced on the edge of the bed. That gave him the leverage to pound up into her. Amara gasped, hands fisting in the covers. A sweet force built up within her, blow by blow; each jolt made her cry out and strain into him.

But like the storm waves that had crashed that ship on the reefs, she finally broke over him, yelling his name. "Atrev!"

For a moment, it was all he could do to hold on to her thrashing body. Her ecstasy thrilled him beyond bearing, though, and with a choked cry of his own, Trevan came as well, body spasming beneath her. "Mara!"

Muscles quaking, she slowed her rocking as he slowed his thrusting. Unable to support herself for much longer, Amara finally collapsed on him, face buried in the curve of his throat, the wonderful maleness of his hair and his skin filling her lungs with each deep-labored breath. A corner of her mind worried vaguely that she might be too heavy for him, but she was too limp and replete to really think right now.

Trevan stroked his trembling hands over her sweat-slicked back. She had drained him, yet his loins still twitched in delicious little pulses. Heart pounding underneath her lax weight, he let his feet slip one at a time back to the floor—he quite understood why she couldn't support her own weight anymore. It seemed like he should have been disappointed with his performance; before being exiled, he had developed a certain level of stamina for such things. He couldn't quite berate himself, though; one sideways glance at her head showed him just how thoroughly he had melted his strong-willed wife with marital pleasure.

Smirking, he dredged through his temporarily tired brain until he remembered the charm he wanted. "*Trezenus.*"

Pins flew away from her scalp, arrowing onto the nightstand with faint clatters. Her braid unwound itself from her head, then unraveled, shaking waist-length locks across his shoulders and face, until he had to swipe at the strands to clear them from his mouth and eyes. Roused by his efforts, Amara lifted her head with a groan, then gasped, green eyes widening at the sight of her own hair. He smirked again, brushing the light brown strands back on one side, tucking it behind her ear even as he made her aware of her change in shape.

"Beautiful . . ."

About to chastise him for changing her preferred shape, Amara felt her irritation melt away. There was no denying that his smugness was well earned; her muscles threatened to shake, and she wanted nothing more than to relax back against his chest and rest for a while. Shaking her head, she summoned up just enough of a sense of self to change back. With a curtain of black hanging down around them, she matched her mouth to his, thanking him with her tongue and her lips.

Trevan let her distract him with a kiss for a little bit, but when she snuggled her cheek onto his shoulder, sighing, he dared to tease her. "I hope you realize you're merely challenging me to relax you so deeply, you lose your shape a second time?"

The thought of what else he could teach her about lovemaking roused her interest, in spite of her pleasant, limp exhaustion. "Atrev?"

"Yes? And you can still call me Trevan, you know," he added. "If I may call you Mara once in a while . . . ?"

Given that the two times he had done so had been during moments of passion between them, Amara couldn't exactly complain. "Alright . . . Trev. Um . . . were you joking about that 'couple of days' thing? For making love?"

Trevan hugged her, smiling. He shifted one of his hands to the back of her head, gently smoothing her soft hair. "If you'd like to rest for a little while, I'm sure that can be managed. I wouldn't want to make you feel too sore on your first night of married life."

"Trevan," she chided, "just answer the question."

"No, I was not joking. Aside from breaks to use the refreshing room, maybe a playful bath or two, and stealing food from the kitchen," he warned her, unable and unwilling to stop himself from smirking a little, "I fully intend to keep you all to myself, so that I can thoroughly demonstrate my love for you. And make up for lost time."

"Lost time?" she asked, lifting her head.

"It's been more than three and a half years since I last made love to a woman," he admitted with a mock-sigh. "I am *sadly* out of practice."

The dazed look in her golden eyes made him grin openly. Snapping out of it, Amara gave him a dirty look. She relented within moments, though, focusing on what he had said. "You love me."

"Of course I do. I would never have accepted your offer of marriage, if I hadn't grown to love you," Trevan pointed out reasonably. "I *do* know the difference between love and sex, despite my skill for the latter. I don't want just sex; I've had my fill of that. I want *love*. Your love," he added pointedly. He gave her an almost shy look, one filled with hope and uncertainty. "I *do* have your love, don't I?"

"Of course," she scoffed. "I offered to marry you, didn't I? That's proof enough in itself."

"Well, *we* actually *say* 'I love you' in this corner of the world," Trevan retorted wryly. "I love you. There, see? Easy to say, and deeply appreciated when it's reciprocated."

"Well, *we don't* say it, on the Plains. At least, not often," Amara conceded. "We *show* it. Deeds speak louder than vows, you know. And by keeping it rare and thus valuable when given, we keep it from being tossed about casually."

Sitting up with a grunt, Trevan righted both of them so that he could look at her more easily. That caused his flesh to slip out of hers, but that was something that could be remedied easily enough. Cupping her face, he looked into her eyes. "As I've told you before, you're not on the Plains anymore. And I would like to hear you say you love me at least once a day."

Despite the soreness that lingered from riding him, Amara decided she wanted more of his expertise. "Show me how much you love me, and I'll tell you how much I love you."

Trevan grinned, already planning his next few moves.

"But not just this," she added with a brief gesture between their bodies, making her words clear. "I like it . . . I *love* it when you share your work with me," Amara amended her choice of words, wanting to show him she would and could meet him halfway. "I love it when you listen to me when I share mine. And I love it when we exchange ideas, and make each other's work better. I love flying with you as a fellow bird, and I loved it when you held me in your arms, as a cat . . . and I also love holding *you*, as Cat."

"That can be arranged," Trevan promised her, leaning in to give her a gentle kiss. It wasn't erotic, but it was right. Perfect, in fact. Pulling back, he smiled softly at her. "It seems Seer Draganna was right yet again."

"About what?" Amara asked, distracted by his kiss.

"She predicted I'd chase down the right woman one day and find in her my sense of home. You." Lifting her fingers to his mouth, he kissed them, then cradled her hand against his chest. "I won't deny that I've been with a lot of women in the past, sought out and enjoyed their company . . . but none of them made me want to stay with them. None of them were complex enough to hold my attention for more than a few days. But you are."

"I am?" Shaking off her surprise, Amara corrected herself. When she had first arrived, she was too serious and wary of everything and everyone, but now she felt safe enough to tease, even if it was on herself. "Of course I am! I'm the most complicated woman in existence. Even if it gets me into trouble day after day . . . If you're not careful, I'll get you into trouble, too."

"But we cats *love* getting into trouble," he teased back, nibbling on her jaw. "*And* getting back out of it again. Life wouldn't be fun without at least a *little* trouble to keep things interesting."

"Well, troublesome or not, you'd better not stray. I may have chosen to be a Nightfaller, but I was born and raised a Shifterai, and they're very strict about adultery on the Plains," she warned him.

"You haven't *seen* trouble, until you've seen a wronged and wrathful Shifterai woman."

"Believe me, now that I have *you* in my life," Trevan promised his fierce, infuriating, utterly fascinating wife, "this is one Cat who will *never* stray from his Home."

Song of the Sons of Destiny

The Eldest Son shall bear this
    weight:
If ever true love he should feel
Disaster shall come at her heel
And Katan will fail to aid
When Sword in sheath is claimed by
    Maid

The Second Son shall know this
    fate:
He who hunts is not alone
When claw would strike and cut to
    bone
A chain of Silk shall bind his hand
So Wolf is caught in marriage-band

The Third of Sons shall meet his
    match:
Strong of will and strong of mind
You seek she who is your kind
Set your trap and be your fate
When Lady is the Master's mate

The Fourth of Sons shall find his
    catch:
The purest note shall turn to sour
And weep in silence for the hour
But listen to the lonely Heart
And Song shall bind the two apart

The Fifth Son shall seek the sign:
Prowl the woods and through the
    trees
Before you in the woods she flees
Catch her quick and hold her fast
The Cat will find his Home at last

The Sixth Son shall draw the line:
Shun the day and rule the night
Your reign's end shall come at light
When Dawn steals into your hall
Bride of Storm shall be your fall

The Seventh Son shall he decree:
Burning bright and searing hot
You shall seek that which is not
Mastered by desire's name
Water shall control the Flame

The Eighth Son shall set them free:
Act in Hope and act in love
Draw down your powers from above
Set your Brothers to their call
When Mage has wed, you will be all.

—THE SEER DRAGANNA